Lover in Darkness

A Darkest Kynd Novel

S. C. Dane

Published by
Melange Books, LLC
White Bear Lake, MN 55110
www.satinromance.com

Cover Design by Caroline Andrus

Acknowledgements

Because books don't write themselves, I'd like to thank my small pack of women warriors—You three have always had my back.

No book would be polished and produced so finely either without the help of my editors at Melange-Books—Sherri Good and Nancy Schumacher. You are strong women, too. Lucky for me that I'm surrounded by gals I can use as inspiration for my kick-ass heroines.

Lastly, I'd like to thank my teachers, whether from the classroom or from life. You've taught me the only thing that matters is what you find on the inside of a person. Thanks to you all, I've got my Kynd heroes and their Chosen Ones. This series wouldn't have been created without your wise voices guiding me.

Once the Kynd existed under God's grace, bearing witness to all things passing. Until the Schism when God and Lucifer clashed and the archangel was flung from the heavens. Refusing to choose sides, the Kynd were damned, too, forced to bear witness without the touch and comfort of another, their honorable name disintegrating into the dust of history. Now they are remembered merely as gargoyles and chimeras, and in their deaths, they become monsters of stone—Grotesques. Their Chosen Ones can save them. But after enduring centuries of solitary madness, who could love something so doomed.

Chapter One

Perching on the building's ledge was pathetic. Darken knew that. It was so damned typical of what the rest of the world expected of him and his Kynd, he wanted to fling himself off the granite wall fifteen stories to the concrete below.

The landing wouldn't kill him, but this was about the symbolism.

Craning his neck farther out to get a peek at the parking lot beneath his roost, he watched a light snow fall. While the humans in their cars chased the moments of their lives hither and thither, the wet tarmac below became a square, black pool framed by fresh white.

So not symbolizing what his world was about now. Nothing black and white about it, not since he'd severed ties with Death and snubbed his nose at God to save his brotherkynd, Merrick, skidding his world into a one-eighty.

He was no longer a burr stuck to Death's cloak, severing souls with the scythe he'd carried. Now his weapon leaned in the corner of a spacious bedroom suite, gathering dust.

Just the way he preferred it. He was through with killing, especially since doing it called in the very reapers he wanted to avoid.

Severing souls from their dead or dying bodies bit ass, but so did sitting on this snow-covered ledge, some two hundred feet above the rest of the world. The only thing keeping his clothed ass in this cliché was the man sitting beside him.

His fellow Kynd, and in this particular case, a chimera made up of three creatures—gargoyle, vampire, and grizzly bear.

"Hey, Urick, maybe she's not coming. Maybe she had other things to do, or the roads are too slippery." Even as he spoke, he scanned the area below them, watching headlights glide through the night as cars navigated the little city of the Maine Medical Center's campus.

"She'll come." The answer billowed on a puff of frosty breath, ringing with more determination than actual belief.

Darken pulled his attention off the ground below to his brotherkynd, who perched beside him. The bear chimera stood over six and a half feet tall with shoulders wide as a bank vault. Since joining Darken and the others, he'd shaved his long hair, hardening his edges so he looked like what he was—one tough son of a bitch. Though he didn't have to, the giant of a man wore human clothes on this frigid night, when he could have shifted into his heavy pelt to protect himself.

Except this vigil wasn't about the comfort. It was about appearances, and though the woman Urick watched for night after night would probably never glance out the window to see him, the bear chimera wanted to make sure she didn't see him as…a frigging *bear*.

Human beings did not fall in love with animals. At least, not in the sense Uri wished for.

"Christ, just go in and introduce yourself the next time you see her. Quit hovering like a ghoul." Despite the insult, Darken kept the barb out of it. He knew damned well why Uri didn't just go inside. Like the rest of the Kynd who had decided to sever themselves from God's eternal punishments, the chimera wasn't wrapped tight enough for human company.

Entering a busy hospital was tantamount to a species' suicide. The scent of blood alone would likely send the bear of Urick's chimera into a frenzy. Never mind the vampire portion.

Jesus, Uri was so doomed. Especially if that was his Chosen One who came almost every night to visit the sick kids in the Oncology ward. Darken rested a rough hand on his brother's massive shoulder and gave a tender squeeze.

Roosted in their shared silence, their breaths puffed around them as they gazed through the glass, watching the purposeful business of the staff.

"I am a ghoul." Growled so low, Darken almost missed the curse; yet, he knew it came from the most ragged part of Urick's heart.

He didn't answer. Instead, he kept his eyes on the elevator, hoping like hell this woman would show to ease the chimera's mood.

No such luck. And once tapped, the bear's volatility was hard to cap. Just like the rest of them—the five Kynd who'd dared God's wrath. None of them were wrapped too tight after thousands of years of torture.

"I'm a fucking loss, man. I can't even stand in the same room with a human without sizing them up for a meal." Uri couldn't, but now wasn't the time to agree with him. Too bad the gargoyle third of the chimera wasn't strong enough to make him vegetarian like the rest of the Kynd.

"You do just fine with Angelia." Merrick's life-mate, who had remained with them even while the angel chimera had been getting his ass kicked in Hell. She had needed to be with the Kynd as much they had needed her. She'd been their tie to Merrick. Along with having some kind of mojo with that eerie—chunk-of-tome-penned-by-God-Himself—Scriptum, it made her one necessary human to have around.

Besides, she stilled their battered hearts when little else could.

"Angelia doesn't count."

No. Darken guessed she didn't. She was Chosen. A special woman in extraordinary circumstances, yet so down to earth she warmed and rooted every one of them, no matter how fucked up they were.

"Then feed before you come here. *Jesus*." As he cussed, Darken stiffened, readying himself for a swift cuff from the bear chimera. He wouldn't be jumping the fifteen stories to a painful near-death, he'd be thrown instead.

A menacing growl eddied around them, but no bulldozer of an arm struck out to fling him off the ledge. Maybe Urick was getting better after all. Discretion kept him from pointing that out. It wasn't exactly accolades. The bear was right, he *was* fucked.

Darken sat tight on the ledge beside his comrade, both immersing themselves in the silence they'd kept a few moments before. The snow continued to fall, capping their shoulders and heads, turning them into white dusted mounds. Still, Uri's woman didn't show.

And they were running out of night. "Bear, man. I'm sorry." He was, too. He liked hearing the rapid beat of the chimera's heart whenever they happened to see his suspected Chosen One.

Once, they'd positioned themselves so Uri could watch her interacting with the children, and Darken would never forget the smile on his brother's face.

It was why he endured night after freezing night of perching on this hospital's window ledge. He wanted to bask in the peace that radiated from the chimera whenever they watched the human woman.

But it wasn't happening tonight.

"Come on, bear. I don't know about you, but I do not want to get caught up here when the sun comes up." Neither did the chimera, he suspected. Not only would he turn to stone like the other Kynd, Uri was part vampire. The sun wasn't his friend on a couple of levels.

Darken clapped his hand onto the wide shoulder, spraying snow like it was powdered sugar.

"I thought tonight…" Uri let his protest trail off into a snarl.

Yeah, they both were hoping to see her, for their own reasons. God, he was such a shit, sometimes. He should be out searching for his own Chosen One, not siphoning the magic from his brother like a voyeur.

He could leave Merrick and Angelia, trusting they were both safe now that they'd mated and Merrick was free of the Kynd's curse. But leaving the bear on his own wasn't safe for anyone.

Especially if it turned out the human woman wasn't Uri's Chosen One.

What a mess that would be.

"I know, Uri. Come on." Sympathetic to his brother's plight, he tugged on his shoulder to get his ass in gear, and offered him a sharp-toothed grin. "If we're lucky, maybe I'll run over a deer on the way home."

The bear chimera frowned, but an accident like that wasn't such a bad idea. Vehicles could be replaced, and his brother could use the bloody nourishment.

Not that it was meant to be. There had been no Bambi to flatten with the truck, so they'd made it home in typical fashion. To spend the day with empty stomachs, their bodies immobilized in stone.

Chapter Two

Darken felt the first tingle of his stirring blood before the winter sun disappeared from the western sky. The snow had just quit falling, so the horizon spread out in front of him like an inverted canyon. Muted reds, pinks, grays, and blues stretched as far as his solidified line of vision could see, the landscape's sharp edges softened by a foot of fresh powder.

Solidified. Yeah, all he could see all fucking day long was what sat in front of his frozen eyes. On the lucky days, a bird flew across. Or a deer poked its wary way along the edge of the field. Hoo-fucking-rah. Since he couldn't move his eyes, the visitors disappeared like they'd exited stage right, the heavy curtain of his skull blocking the rest of the show.

Because he, a cursed Kynd gargoyle, was solid stone in the daylight hours. He was a crouching, pissed off statue, immovable. *Vulnerable.* He'd be dead if someone took a sledgehammer to him.

Fear pumped his blood faster, and Darken uncurled his fists in slow motion, anxious to move even though the sun hadn't yielded its power yet. Christ on the cross, would he ever get used to the helplessness? It made him fretful as an old lady, his anxiety escalating the nearer his freedom came.

Like it could be snatched away at the last second.

Every night it was like this, and he hated that he couldn't get a handle on it. That no matter how hard he tried to convince himself he was okay, he still couldn't stop the roaring panic.

Appropriately, he hated the Others for it. Chickens, every pathetic one of them. Not a single fae, shape-shifter, or ghoul came fucking near to offer help. None of them could muster the balls to get involved, not even to swirl a little protection magic over their safe house. As if the past two thousand years had been the Kynds' fault. As if they'd signed up for twenty centuries of torture, doing things that had gone against their natures.

Violent things, despicable things.

Deep breath, gargoyle. Yeah, he needed to calm his ass down. He and his brethren were all right. The safe house, generously provided by the ballsy three-man-team of the ruling Triumvirate, was built like a fortress and nestled in a very secluded spot.

As added protection, they'd bolted every door, inside and out.

So, they were safe. He just had to remind himself every night.

Besides, they had Merrick guarding them during the daylight hours. Merrick wouldn't hesitate to annihilate trespassers. As the previous guardian of Hell's archway, he'd done just that for more than two thousand years.

Unwillingly.

Let someone threaten his brothers? The chimera would kick Other ass for funsies.

Darken filled his lungs with his first breath of the night, feeling it spill through him, the expanding of his lungs settling him down. Moving again was a hard fist to the face of his panic.

Now what he felt was the anger he always felt at dawn when he turned to stone. The mood livened his blood, got his body moving faster. So, maybe he'd nurse the pissed tit for a little longer. Hit the shower.

Nothing like playing furniture to make a body feel dirty.

He needed to slough shit off, to clear his head after so many hours of hanging out with his frigging thoughts. Jesus, he needed free of this curse. So what if he'd been enduring it for a mere four months. He hated it as much as he'd hated having to follow Death, carrying that damned scythe like a knight's fucking page.

Two thousand years of severing souls…

The water jetted out hot and caustic, just the way he liked it. A little sandblasting went a long way to making him feel halfway normal. When his skin started to burn, he ended the shower, wrapping a towel around his hips as he stepped out of the tub. He swiped the steam off the mirror with his clawed hand to stare at his puss.

Marvelous. Pass for human and integrate? He leaned forward to sneer at his reflection, his lifted lip not quite exposing his fangs. *Sure*, he shrugged, why the hell not? It wasn't as if the Others were welcoming them with open arms. At least the humans didn't know what they were. If he and his brothers kept their mouths shut and their hands to themselves, they could pull it off.

Riiiiight.

Because they weren't wound tighter than a hair trigger, ready to demolish whatever was in reach. Comforting thought, that. Too bad it wasn't true. No matter if he twisted his useless nut sac in a knot to keep himself reined in, the urge to lash out remained.

Darken fought it like an addiction.

He was Kynd, God damn it. Thrashing that scythe to sever souls had not taken away his gentleness.

It. Had. Not.

His fists closed over the edge of the bathroom sink. A soft pop and he loosened his grip on the cracked granite, his hope unraveling like a sweater with a thread caught.

He wasn't better than the rest of them living in this house. Only better at pretending he had his shit together.

The proof? His fucking room would like to take the stand against him, your Honor.

Darken walked to his closet, past the evidence that he did not control his seething anger. His bed, never slept in, tilted off one leg like a wounded tortoise. The fist-sized starburst in the wall above it glaring like an accuser's eye.

Esteemed members of the jury, here stands testament to this Kynd's lack of control. His physical strength too great to allow him to walk free among innocents. His anger too volatile to trust...

Shut. The. Fuck. Up.

With long strides, he walked to his closet, ignoring the other glaring verifications of his volatility. As he slipped his jeans over his bare ass, the door to his room buckled under the weight of a pounding fist.

A much welcomed—and needed—distraction.

"Rapunzel, quit fussing with your hair and get your butt downstairs!" *Kallen, the rotter.* Another gargoyle with some assembly required. Like the rest of them, Kallen had some serious shit brewing in his head.

7

Damaged from two thousand years of solitude? Nah. The guy just got off on thrashing the hell out of shit, swore it calmed him down.

Another series of door bending hits then Darken heard the retreat of booted footsteps heading toward the stairs. He shrugged into a black t-shirt that quipped *Kitten thinks of nothing but Murder all day* and followed the other Kynd to the first floor.

The wide staircase clung to the western wall, unwinding down to the foyer, like a dead dog's draping tongue. As if it had died of sheer exhaustion.

Head. Out. Of. Ass. Because comparing his new home to Death wasn't fair. For anyone. Anton Delacroix of the Triumvirate, Angelia's father, had gone beyond the beyond in providing this safe house for them.

The place was huge. High ceilinged. And sturdier than a draft horse stallion.

It had to be. The current residents were beasts who couldn't keep their shit…

Head. Out. Of. Ass.

He hadn't shed his residual fury, so he knew to lash himself with a tight rein. Knew not to let his guard down until the hours blessedly carried him farther from having played statue. Yet, inexorably dragged him closer…

With a growl, he trucked a right angle, heading east down a huge channel of a hallway where he found everyone in the library. Twitching, toe-tapping, claw-biting—like they awaited the birth of Rosemary's baby in the walnut paneled room. Anticipation spiked with dread.

All eyes turned to him when he sauntered in.

"What?"

"Nice shirt." Drakus unfolded his massive self from the windowsill like origami in reverse. At over six and a half feet tall with auburn hair, the bastard was beautiful, even with the tattoo staining every inch of skin from his forehead to the tops of his feet.

The artwork was just one more reason to hate the fae. They'd marred the dragon chimera's skin with a tattoo of…you guessed it: a fucking dragon. Warning anyone who wanted to befriend him that the guy was a flying, scaly, fire-breathing, village-burning son-of-a-bitch.

Faery bastards. Drakus had once been a decent being before…*shit*, he needed to lift the needle from this frigging broken record.

To do it, he peered down his front, stretching the t-shirt at the bottom so he could read it. "Yeah? You like it?" He did too, which was why he had it. Along with a slew of others with caustic sayings. Kept things fun as far as he was concerned.

Parking on the arm of the vintage sofa, the heavy leather creaked under his ass. The two other gargoyles, Kallen and Kronos, filled the seat cushions, making them the three monkeys who spoke, saw, and heard no evil.

Darken almost got up, but with an unconscious gesture, Kronos curled his fingers around his wrist. Needing the touch. As all Kynd did. To them, the contact was mother's milk.

A glance down proved it. Kallen's boot abutted Uri's. Like oil tankers lashed together at the pier. The bear chimera had inevitably sidled over for a subtle dose of cozy.

The sole exception to the Kynd's craving to touch was Drakus, who stayed by the window by himself. Behind him, a sheet of plywood filled the casement where glass used to be. A clawed wing had busted the window during one of Drakus' unsettled moments, and like most of the repairs needing done, the window would get fixed when they got around to it.

The Kynd weren't exactly carpenters like Jesus was, but no one would come near them. Not even Other repairmen, though they'd been offered exorbitant sums. It seemed no amount of money could get them anywhere near God's cursed creatures.

It might rub off. Cowardly sons of bitches.

At least the dragon chimera sat close to Merrick and Angelia, so he picked up some comforting connection without having to touch.

Darken plucked a button on the pleated leather.

Six Kynd in one room.

It was a fucking miracle.

"All right, boys, here's what I found." Angelia rose with the Scriptum's front and back covers nesting on her forearms, her fingers curled around the top edges holding the pages open. She was beautiful, too, the classic blonde haired, blue eyed siren with girl-next-door charm.

But that wasn't the only thing holding them in thrall.

She was Merrick's Chosen One.

Her hip fell against the chimera's shoulder, like the woman needed to constantly touch, too. Captivated by her, they all watched her do it, hunger deepening every slate colored eye in the room.

To have that? *Jesus, Mary, and Joseph.*

Desperate, the five unmated Kynd hovered like anxious fools. Had Angelia, with her uncanny connection to the Scriptum, found a Chosen One, a potential life-mate for one of them?

A life-changing reward if they found her. Yet searching wouldn't come without its costs. Failure would etch their scars deeper, and none of them could afford it. Drakus might have been the worst off, but it didn't mean the rest of them were doing so hot.

Christ, one look at Uri's pale, grizzled face made that obvious. Seriously, the guy needed nourishment. But who the hell would donate? Sure, vampires had their sources, but with the bear snarling behind Urick's rabid eyes, no one wanted to chance that he wouldn't take a good hunk of flesh along with the sip of blood.

And the other full gargoyles like Darken?

They had their own demons to contend with. Kronos had been punished by God to witness nightmares. Every time a human or an Other had had a bad dream, there was Kronos. Forced to experience the horror twenty-four seven. Because in some part of the world, someone was always sleeping.

Twisted? The guy hadn't felt anything but sheet-wringing terror for more than two thousand years. To say he no longer had much in the way of coping skills was grossly understated. *His* screams were enough to wish for soundproof walls in the safe house.

Kallen? He needed these forays to find a Chosen One like a plant needed water. But only if things went south and they could resort to violence.

Oh yeah. They were just a fantastic group some woman would be lucky to become a part of. Chosen his ass. Who in their right mind would find them anywhere near tolerable?

"Hey, brother, you with us?" Merrick eyed him like Darken *was* Kitten thinking about Murder. Angelia's hip was still clinging to the brotherkynd's thick shoulder.

Okay. So maybe these unique women did exist. Angelia was proof of that, right? Merrick might have been freed from turning to stone, but he still waged war with his demons. He wasn't a walk in the park.

"All right, so I think I found a lead." From the Scriptum. That book might have been about the Kynd, but it was Angelia's, in a creepy sense. Every word written belonged to her somehow, all she had to do was figure out how to decode whatever it was singing in her head at the time.

Her triumph was a contagion, and Darken looked beside him to see Kallen grinning expectantly as a low hum vibrated across his skin.

Then got cut off like someone flicked a switch. *Merrick.* "Don't be so happy, Kallen. It takes us back into Hell. The Second Circle to be exact. The one guarded by Minos."

Well, shit.

To get by Minos, they would need someone with wings, and Merrick's were currently laying in the belly of hell, shorn from the chimera's back by Lucifer's angels.

Drakus was the only other one who had a set, and the last time the dragon chimera faced off with the Great Judge hadn't been pretty. For anyone.

"Shit." Darken sat back as he looked at his brotherkynd. No way was he going to put the dragon through that again. He was only just getting his shit back together, and what little there was hadn't been easy to harvest. Darken saw the man's reluctance, even as he nodded his stained head.

Like Jiminy Cricket, all conscientious, he said, "No. Forget it. We can't ask Drakus to go back in there." He pegged his gaze on Merrick who, he figured, would fully understand.

Instead, determination and simmering rage stewed in those slate eyes.

As if there wasn't a staring contest going on in front of him, Drakus hopped to the floor, landing nimbly in spite of his size thirteens. "You're not asking. I'm volunteering." Like Uri, he practically towered over Darken, and that was saying something, considering he easily stood at six four and had shoulders a linebacker would covet.

"Like hell."

"Exactly," Drakus retorted. The man didn't even flinch, his gray eyes hard as cement. Darken read nothing of what was behind them.

"If a Chosen One is there, she doesn't belong in that Circle, Darken,"

Angelia piped up, placing herself between the two of them, her book still cradled in her arms.

Merrick stiffened but didn't budge, though he was poised to spring like the lion he was if either he or Drakus couldn't keep their fury leashed.

"We know what it is to not belong," Drakus growled, his lip pulling back to reveal one thick-ass canine. He might have been clothed, but those would shred like tissues if the dragon spilled forth.

Darken shook his head, stepping back to give Drakus breathing space. Ordinarily, he'd do the opposite and reach out to touch his brotherkynd. But not Drakus. The man was too seriously effed up.

"Brother, no life-mate is that important." Did those words just come out of his mouth? A Chosen One not important? She would be worth the world to the Kynd she was destined for.

"Not that imp—?" The rest of Drakus' protest got lost in the beastly snarl scraping up his throat, as the round pupils in those gray eyes turned to slits. The chimera swallowed repeatedly as he flexed his fists, obviously trying to control himself. Shiny, thin scales erupted along his lower arms.

Space be damned. Darken stepped forward and lowered himself to his knees, caressing his fingers along the chimera's calf, the tension roiling too fast and thick for anything good to come out of this confrontation. If Darken didn't cut it off, they were both going to get hurt. He'd be sporting new holes and gashes, and the dragon would slide back from any positive ground he'd gained.

Because regret could unmoor any poor bastard. And that's what Drakus would feel if he unintentionally hurt any of them.

The warm sliding of fingers around his wrist made him look down. Angelia's small hand curled along his own, anchoring the three of them together. She started to hum something wordless while Drakus leaned into their hands like a neglected stray, his head tilted as if tuning his ear to the woman's song.

Not her song alone, though. She was humming something from the Scriptum, he was sure of it. He could feel it, just like the dragon could. The song was buttery light, something warm and soothing.

This is what Angelia did when she visited Drakus in the daytime?

Explained why the chimera was making a little progress.

Darken closed his eyes to the bliss radiating from the three of them.

"Better?"

His body still suffused with that golden glow, it took a second for him to realize Angelia had spoken, not hummed. "Darken, you can let go now."

"Hmmm?" He lifted his gaze to the woman kneeling beside him. God, she was beautiful. No wonder Merrick had fallen for her.

Shit. Merrick. He'd growled something.

"Ah, sorry, man. Got a little distracted. You were saying?" He turned to Merrick, hoping the brotherkynd wasn't pissed he'd been emotionally fondling the other man's life-mate.

The guy looked almost as soothed as Darken felt, his lids a little heavy. If it wasn't for the death grip his claws were digging into the desk in front of him, he'd have thought the chimera was as entranced as he and Drakus were.

Apparently not.

"Meeting's over," he announced, his slate eyes riveting onto his woman as he stood up. "Angel?"

She took the hand he extended to her and let him pull her close. Drakus didn't seem to mind, though, like maybe this happened all the time—Merrick interrupting the groove-on when he couldn't stand the sharing any more.

Exhaling as he shook his head, he turned in time to see the others filing out of the room. Like they'd witnessed enough and were beating a hasty retreat for the fire exit. Fine by him. He wanted to leave, too.

"Darken?" This time when Angelia spoke, he wasn't transported. He lifted an impatient eyebrow instead. "Kristov wanted to see you. He asked that you drop by tonight."

Of course, he had. Ever since the Kynds' return from Hell four months ago, the Triumvirate had been keeping tabs on Darken. He'd murdered a vampire by chopping off his head with a scythe, so the leaders of the vampire realm were keeping the peace by making sure the gargoyle's blade-swinging was a freak occurrence.

That he'd played guillotine to save lives was the only thing that had kept the Triumvirate from imprisoning his stony ass the second they'd learned about it.

Darken nodded, acknowledging he heard the message, then left the other three standing in the library to sort out whatever it was they did.

13

He headed for the garage, eager to put as much distance as he could between himself and the mated pair. Which only infuriated him more. He was Kynd, damn it. He wasn't supposed to seek distance. But seeing the unique connection between Merrick and Angelia made him envious, which wasn't something he should be feeling, either.

It pissed him off. Meeting with Kristov was the kick in the balls he didn't really need just then. But, along with the rest of the Kynd, he'd sworn an oath to abide by the Triumvirate's laws if they wanted to remain in this realm.

So, he'd answer the summons like the dog on a leash he was.

Chapter Three

Heading for the five-car garage, Darken halted at the door connecting it to the main house and flipped the main light switch. Only two vehicles flashed their chrome. The other bays sat vacant as craters—scars to remind him of why the other brothers weren't up to driving.

Road rage would take on a whole new dimension with Drakus behind the wheel.

Swallowing a curse, Darken aimed the nose of his Dodge Ram for the road, the headlights swiping across the heavy woods surrounding the safe house as he headed north. Behind him, the stone megalith he now called home disappeared into the wild landscape.

In front of the truck, the ice covered track nearly blended with the snowbanks, and darkened spruce trees stretched their black points to a pincushion sky.

By the time he reached the Vampyre's private home, his mood was almost as black as the tar he'd been driving on for the last fifteen miles. In the wash of the truck's headlights, he could see the house's outline.

Not nearly as sprawling as his own, but big for one guy. What did Kristov have, bowling lanes where he and his blood-sucking friends partied like it was 1999.

Or maybe the guy thought he'd fill it with 1,999 concubines and the unavoidable litters of kids.

Did it really frigging matter? He and his brothers wouldn't be invited to sample the wares, no matter how professional the Vampyre's women were. Kynd might as well be lepers for all the acceptance they'd received from the Others.

Trolls would be welcomed before they were, and didn't that nasty tidbit of truth leave a shitty taste in his mouth.

Whatever.

He knocked once as a warning and shouldered his way through the front door.

Kristov materialized in the grand vestibule instantly, his lean body doing a little wobbly, like the Tasmanian Devil coming to a full stop. Minus the slobbering, of course. The Vampyre was a bit too refined for that, what with the culture dripping off his sun-deprived skin and all. "You came."

"You beckoned."

Ignoring the insult, Kristov ushered him to an honest-to-God sitting room, like he should await a visit from the Queen or some shit. Darken wedged his huge frame into one of the brocade chairs, the skinny legs bitching about the load.

Made him feel so much rosier. Really.

Drumming his fingers on his knee as he glanced around, his anger bubbled to a froth. Which wasn't good, all things considered. Like how things got broken when he slipped his leash.

The Vampyre left him to pour two glasses of red wine at a solid looking oak bar, the kind of heavy structure that gave Irish pubs their cheer. It was the only masculine thing in the mausoleum of a sitting room.

In fact, it looked so out of place, Darken took a closer look at his surroundings while his host divvied the wine.

There was a feminine touch to the room, along with the rest of the house, he realized. Like whoever decorated had a delicate sense of style. Which didn't jibe with the muscular Vampyre.

But the oak bar did.

So, Kristov had a mate, after all. Except Darken couldn't smell anyone else. The man lived alone.

What the hell? "You know, if I had a woman," he taunted, oozing disdain as he pretended to pick at a thread sticking from the arm of his chair. "I sure as hell would have her living in my house, especially if she was the one who decorated it with this foo-foo." He left off plucking at the thread, and limp wristed, twirled his hand to indicate the four walls festooned with silk wallpaper and flowing drapes.

Half a second later, he was on the parquet floor looking into a fang-

16

bared puss, long teeth bared to strike. A swift punch to the Vampyre's head was the only thing keeping his neck whole, and Darken flipped to his feet to reverse positions, his own canines unsheathed.

The Vampyre teleported them, yet it was a slow drag across the room. The gargoyle's ferocity was too great for the bloodsucker to pull him any farther. But it didn't mean Darken had the upper hand. He was still a little disoriented, and Kristov was fast even without teleporting, a fact he revealed with a punch, slicing his knuckles wide open on Darken's sharp teeth.

The tang of blood filled his mouth. On a roar, he retaliated, shackling the Vampyre's wrists in his hands, the crush of bone exhilarating. No wonder Kallen got off on the violence. Unleashing it helped him to breathe. To think straight.

His mind was clearer than it had been in months, helping him to see right into the empty eyes of the ancient Vampyre. Empty because there was no heart behind them. Not even for this fight.

Easing his grip, Darken managed to back off a tad. Enough so Kristov would know he was relenting without releasing. In case the heartless one decided fighting was a better option than standing down.

Straddled, with one arm raised to hold Kristov against the wall, he basked in the calm the fight bathed him in. *Maybe I should give in to it...*

His resistance to that siren's call crawled up his back and across his shoulders, the constriction familiar. *Controlled.*

Feeling Kristov's muscles relax beneath his palm, he let him go, shoving himself back a few feet.

The two stared each other down like a pair of bulls. Each one sizing the other up, like maybe they might have to go another round.

As the Vampyre tensed, Darken struck his palm up. "Wait." They didn't have to do this. The gargoyle would win this fight. Then where would he be? As much as he hated being tied to the rules of the Triumvirate, he needed the leaders. Without them, hard telling where his brethren would be right now.

Besides, his curiosity was piqued. A ruling Vampyre with a dead heart. Did wonders never cease?

Mining deep, he dredged up his affability. "You ripped my favorite t-shirt." He offered a grin as he dabbed his fingertips to his bleeding lip.

"Truce?"

The Vampyre cradled his broken wrist against his stomach, his eyes flaring before sputtering flat.

But Darken had seen what he wanted and flopped his heavy ass onto the girly chair he'd been sitting in before Kristov had relocated him to the floor.

"I'm sorry, man. I had no right." He'd been a self-loathing schmuck when he'd insulted the Vampyre. Given the man's reaction, obviously his woman wasn't elsewhere out of choice. The house was a frigging shrine. If his head hadn't been so far up his own ass, he would have seen that. Kristov had lost his life-mate.

"It has been a long time since…" Kristov said no more, like his throat strangled his words. Instead, he returned to the bar, offering Darken the glass of wine he'd poured before knocking him to the carpet.

He didn't let the glass go when the gargoyle reached for it. "You are Kynd. I should have known you would see. It is I who am sorry. I should not have invited you here."

Darken's lips curled in a genuine smile. "But you did. I don't want you to regret it." Surprising the crap out of him. Since when did Kynd cozy up all friendly with other species?

Ever since the Scriptum, that ancient text about the Kynd, had made its appearance, would be his guess. Thank God, literally, the thing was in their possession. Or, in truth, Angelia's.

Inwardly, Darken shrugged. *Same thing.* Merrick's Chosen One fitted well with them. When their group energy hummed, strands of Angelia's wove through it. Perfectly. Seamlessly. Strengthening their power base.

Which made her as much a part of the Kynd as the rest of them.

"I had hoped to ask a few more questions about Aro. The incident doesn't sit well with us."

Ah, yes. The reason for the summons, and bringing Darken's thoughts full circle. Aro, the leader of the Literati and the one who had inadvertently—and mistakenly—brought Angelia and the Scriptum together.

Aro had also made the mistake of slicing his head off on the blade of Darken's scythe. Putting Darken under the scrutiny—and the tight leash— of the Triumvirate.

Even though Aro had had it coming.

Though Kristov was right to have questions. Darken and the other Kynd did, too. Like, what the fuck had motivated the head of the Literati, an esteemed curator of Other lore, to not only undermine the governorship of the Triumvirate, but also to upend the structure of Hell itself by eliminating the Guardian, Merrick.

Who just happened to be Kynd.

Aro's plot reeked of collusion. Yet they hadn't discovered who he'd been colluding with. Aside from the obvious: Lucifer and his Dark Angels.

Who just happened to be the ones who'd torn Merrick's wings off his back.

In trade for the Scriptum.

So much…collusion. With no concrete answers.

"It bothers you, too, I see."

"What? I'm sorry." He'd lost himself in the tangle of his thoughts, forgetting Kristov. "You were saying…"

"Nothing that can't wait another day. Besides, I'd rather talk to you about Urick. He worries us."

Us. As in Godrick, Anton, and Kristov. The three Vampyres of the nosy Triumvirate.

"He's doing fine." Meaning, he struggled as hard as the rest of his brothers. Besides, Kynd took care of themselves. Urick had enough problems without the Triumvirate getting involved.

The arched brow bespoke the Vampyre's disbelief. "Yes, well. Surely, you know that as vampire, he must feed. Like you all, he fights hard. But he will not win this battle." Kristov took a sip of wine, collapsing into the corner of the sofa like a man who'd just shucked a heavy load.

Maybe he had. His concern for Uri aside, it couldn't be easy keeping his own secrets. A leader of thousands without a heart?

Right ballsy, really. Darken took another sip of wine, feeling its warmth slip down through his chest, into his stomach. Ignoring his host's warning, he tipped his glass. "It's been a long time since I've tasted anything this good."

"It was a fine year." Kristov rolled the crystal goblet in his fingers as he peered closely at the swirling contents, clearly playing along with the evasion.

Darken used the silence to study the room they were in, to open his senses to what he'd missed before.

The Vampyre had doted on his life-mate, had indulged her. As any honorable male would do for the one who held his heart in her keeping.

Brows lifting, Kristov took a breath as he leaned back, relaxing a bit. "I hope you will return for another glass sometime." On the surface, it wasn't much of an invitation, but then Darken had been the one to tear off the veneer of this visit, hadn't he.

Kristov was offering more than a truce. He was offering him friendship in the only way a broken man could. Showing true concern for his brothers when he didn't actually feel it.

"You know, I would like that. I could bring cheese doodles." *And find out why you're so interested in the bear.*

"Don't get carried away." The Vampyre grinned, his emerald eyes sparking briefly before dead-lining again. But Darken figured he was glimpsing something rare. A man without his mask. Which was a gift the Kynd in him wasn't too far gone to recognize.

"I'd be glad for the call." He reached for Kristov's hand as he stood to leave, the wine in his empty stomach warming him as much as the Vampyre's offer. Maybe it wouldn't be a bad idea to bring Uri along the next time.

Holding up his bruised arm, Kristov shook his head. "I think I've taken all the hand-holding I can stand." But he smiled. A forlorn reaction given the lack of shine in the eyes, but already Darken was growing accustomed to it.

The look wasn't so bad, once he realized the Vamp's heart had been blown apart like it had stepped on a land mine. Humpty Dumpty had nothing on that. Too many splattered bits, and no cracked shell to contain the seepage.

Lose your life-mate, lose yourself.

God, the thought made his own chest hurt.

As soon as he was back in his truck, he headed for the city, anxious to share the rest of the night with his brothers. Grateful he had them, no matter how messed up they were.

Tucking his hand behind the zipper of his coat, Darken rubbed his palm across his aching heart.

Tonight, he was glad he had a date with a certain hospital's window ledge. He was already late for it, but he didn't think Uri would care. Kallen or Kronos would be with him, so the bear wouldn't be alone.

Darken squeezed his pec again, a sigh escaping his throat, easing the ache in his chest.

The Kynd were finally together after an eon of forced separation. Even if none of them ever found their life-mates, at least they had each other.

Chapter Four

Sitting in a plastic and metal chair in a private hospital room, Daniela barely registered the hard edge cutting into the back of her abundant thighs. How could she, when her own discomfort seemed paltry compared to what lay in front of her?

The patient's facial injuries looked nauseatingly sore, like a whisper across the cheek would hurt. Which she guessed it would, given how stretched and bruised the woman's skin was.

Daniela's stomach executed a slow roll as she gazed across the bed at the battered face, swollen from surgery on the broken jaw, both eyes blackened puffs. Bruising drained down into swollen cheeks.

The victim was a mess. Worse, the smell of antiseptic ripened the nauseating image. Daniela might have been able to stomach the view if the pungent odor wasn't wafting so ripe, like pain exuded from the woman's pores.

Fuck. She didn't often swear, but this was one of the worst cases she'd had to document. And as the liaison for battered women between the hospital and the Portland police department, she'd seen a lot of brutal cases.

She fought her revulsion for this one. It wouldn't be very professional of her to vomit in the little kidney shaped tray on the metal dresser next to the woman's bed. But, God, the smell was awful, reminding her of violence, of searing pain. And let's not forget defeat and loss.

So much loss it left her clients numb, oftentimes mute.

It was her job to coax them back to the land of the living, to the one place they were doing their best to avoid. Because returning brought back the terror. When tears flowed like salty rivers down damaged cheeks, cascading toward cracked and blood-scabbed lips.

Daniela squirmed herself upright, stiffening her spine against the carnage in front of her.

One man had done this. A husband who'd given this woman three children.

All of whom were currently huddled in the counselor's office several floors down from where their mother now lay broken.

God, the awfulness of this. Daniela felt her own tears well, and she got up to drag the beige hospital drape around them. Sometimes the women preferred the feeling of being cocooned, as if the heavy curtains kept the demons at bay.

She supposed they did, in a sense. Because sometimes those cloth walls created the illusion of being closed in, snuggled and safe.

The woman on the bed shifted, her eyes following Daniela's path along the rim of the bed.

"Better?"

A slow blink was her answer. Because it hurt too much to nod or speak.

Jesus, she shouldn't be here now. She should put away her recorder and give the woman time to heal before she resurrected the monster who'd done this to her. Except this was the time to do just that. Get the facts before the trauma was dulled and the women started blaming themselves, started dredging up excuses for why their spouses or boyfriends had been forced to beat them.

Dinner was cold, or the woman took too long at the store, flirting with the cashier like the lazy cunt she was. At this point in an abusive relationship, any reason became viable. The men were like nitroglycerin with no bump in the road for their victims to see coming, the violence striking with the swift fury of a winter squall.

But never ended in the hospital room, no matter how much professional intervention and support the women got. Because the pieces still had to be picked up. The first tenuous and terrifying steps away from the safety of the hospital still had to be taken.

Daniela eased back down in her chair, moving slow so she wouldn't startle the battered wreck on the bed. Sad, but the woman would be wired for abrupt violence, no matter how sedated she was.

"The children are okay. He's in jail," she said when the bruised eyes rolled toward the slit in the drapes. The corner of a swollen lip pulled upward as heavy lids did a slow blink.

Daniela reached her hand to a bandaged wrist. Not to hold. Never that. Because sometimes the grip was too stark a reminder. Or the arm was broken. Or slashed with defensive wounds. As was the case this time.

Shit. She'd been doing this too long; she needed a break.

"I hope he rotsh there." *Or not.* Courage like this kept her going.

She offered a reassuring smile. "We'll do everything we can to make sure that's exactly what happens." She pressed her finger to the *on* button of her recorder. "Ready?" *To nail some ass?* She wanted to ask, but couldn't. Even with the evidence in front of her, she wasn't allowed to influence the testimony. She was there to record, nothing more.

Broken jaw and lying on a hospital bed, the woman managed to set her shoulders, determination glistening from her watering eyes. "You besher ash."

Oh yeah. It was times like these when Daniela got fueled for the fight, pulled her hat back out of the ring, and readied herself to go for one more round. The hollowness in her guts never left, but that was just part of the job. A part she never wanted to lose. Because if she ever lost this feeling of horror, it would be time to put up her recorder.

Two hours later, and the day long over, Daniela slipped out of the hospital room, leaving the patient to her exhausted slumber. It had been an ugly and long battle, beginning in a kitchen with worn linoleum and ending in a hospital bed, the ordeal forever recorded on the device in her canvas bag, and in the haunted eyes of three innocent kids.

Tomorrow she would relive this. Tomorrow she would transcribe every horrible word the victim had spoken, the violence resurrected with the press of a button as she typed out every word. Then she'd hand one affidavit over to the hospital for their records, and another over to the police.

So they could nail the son of a bitch who'd done this.

For now, though, she needed air. The bite of a winter's night to scrape her nostrils and lungs like a pipe-cleaner, ridding her head of the stink of antiseptic. Bundling into her calf-length, quilted coat, she headed outside to wait for her ride to pick her up.

Girls' Night Out. The once a month gaggle she had with her old college roommates.

God, she needed it. After what she'd just gone through, unwinding with friends would go a long way in restoring her faith in humanity.

An icy wall of air slapped her the moment she stepped out into the frigid Maine winter. Automatically, she sucked in a cold breath, as if she'd plunged into a frozen pond, the horror of the hospital room instantly forgotten when the moisture in her lungs turned to ice crystals.

Trying to trap what body heat she could, she found the closest park bench, stuffed her mittened hands into her deep pockets, and huddled around her ample midriff.

But, she didn't pull her hood up. Instead, she craned her head back to view the skyline, her breath now puffing out in steamy tendrils above her face. This was the real reason she'd opted to wait for her ride outside. Daniela loved the night sky, especially in winter, when the stars took on a sharper, colder glint, like real diamonds.

Around her shoulders and below, the yellow-white glow from the Maine Medical Center marked a fuzzy underline beneath the nightscape. She twisted on the bench to gaze at the star-spangled sky above her and to get the full effect of vertigo from peering up beyond the high walls of the hospital.

She loved the rush of that, too. It felt as though she was falling, when really she wasn't. Winter clutched a freezing hand around her exposed neck, convulsing her body into a quick shiver that rippled away as swiftly as it had come.

Cramming her hands deeper and pressing her elbows tighter, she kept looking skyward, the cold making her eyeballs freeze and then water. She stood up to increase the dizziness.

A redneck carnival ride, her friends called it.

Daniela gave in to the giddiness of her cheap thrill and sidled closer to the brick walls stretching ever higher, intensifying the sensation of falling, and making the walls appear as if they leaned inward, stretching thinner toward their peaks.

Her body slowly twirling, she was well into the dark recesses outlining the separate buildings when she finally staggered like a drunk, her wool mittened hands stabbing out to catch herself when her big ass tipped toward the crushed rocks beneath her boots.

Her back fell hard against a stone wall that oomphed as it wrapped strong arms around her.

For a couple of heartbeats, she succumbed to the strength of those arms, basking in the sensation of a rough cheek caressing the top of her head, the arms snuggling her closer.

For those two seconds of weird surrender, she felt utterly cherished by the huge guy holding her. And there was no mistaking that whoever held her was large and masculine. And very muscular. She could feel the width of him through both of their thick winter coats.

Nice. *But very wrong*, her brain told her. Daniela spun, pushing herself away from the person she'd fallen into.

Person? Surely, she'd hit a brick wall, not the gorgeous guy standing two feet away from her, his arms empty but still open, like he hadn't realized he'd let her go. He looked a little glazed, like he'd been wonked in the cranium with a baseball bat. Or was smelling Grandma's apple pie.

"Sorry! I was staring up and lost my balance, got a little dizzy from the…" Daniela's excuse fluttered away as shiny gray eyes leveled on her like a pair of new nickels. "…height," she muttered, ending it. She had never seen eyes like that before.

The man tilted his head, like she was singing Oh, Hosanna! or something; and he closed those eerie gray eyes, like he was harking to her every word, or smelling really hard.

She thought her redneck carnival ride strange? This guy cornered the market.

Hoo-kay. She ought to take a big step back. As in, return to the lighted area where there were more people. *Witnesses.*

But she didn't. Instead she stood there, rooted as if her steaming breath anchored her to the strange guy, her wooziness gone and no sign of alarm to quicken her heart. She ought to be scared, standing in the dark so close to a man this size. She could make a thousand guesses what he could do to her.

For all her girth, she wasn't ruggedly built. Her defense against an attacker? Sit down. Because there was no way in hell someone could drag her heavy butt away to do terrible things to her.

Yet, she guessed this guy could. He was enormous. And as she'd already discovered, built like a brick shit house with so much muscle he probably bench-pressed cars to while away his idle hours.

"Hey, are you all right? I didn't hurt you, did I?" She didn't have a clue how she could have, but he was still looking as if he'd been struck.

* * * *

His eyes still closed, Darken leaned closer to the voice purring across every nerve ending in his body. Was he all right?

Never better. Truly.

Then he lifted his lids to gaze at the source of that beautiful voice.

Speaking of beautiful. Darken's eyes widened to absorb every detail of the woman who stood before him, even though she was wrapped from shoulder to shins in a black, puffy coat. The skin of her face was flawless, with a hint of blush, like rose marble, setting off dark, almond shaped eyes with thick lashes so long they fanned her eyebrows.

Her lustrous dark hair, pooling around her face because of the stiff collar of her winter jacket, would make a mink jealous. So inviting were her locks, he was reaching to touch them before he realized he'd stretched his arm toward her.

And fisted his offending hand. If he hadn't followed the path her eyes took as she watched him tremulously reach for her, he wouldn't have stopped himself from bunching that luxurious hair into his rough palms and rubbing his face all through it.

Holy God. She was magnificent.

And getting scared. The woman was stepping back, straining the strings his soul was already lashing to her.

To see her falter away? *Hurt.*

"Chosen One," he hissed from his leaking lungs.

The woman took another step backward, stealing a quick glance over her shoulder toward the safety of the pooling light, like she was gauging the distance and length of time it would take for help to reach her.

"Ch-chosen?" His gaze followed the drop and lift of her throat as she swallowed.

He was nodding, but not sure if it was because he agreed she was his Chosen One, or because he really liked watching her body move, no matter how minutely.

Music jingled in his sensitive ears, a crazy techno beat. It came from her.

The woman's almond eyes widened just before she yanked off one of her fuzzy mittens, snagging the musical interruption from her coat pocket, and sticking it to her ear. "Yeah!" she said, those pretty eyes still latched onto his face. "I'm out front. Where are you?"

She turned her upper body to look behind her, and the loss of her gaze left him stripped. He felt like he stood naked, and suddenly unsure, before her. "Oh, I see you now. I'll be right there."

The woman stared back up at him and the world re-bloomed inside his chest.

"My friend's here to pick me up." The woman jacked her thumb over her shoulder, the cell phone still in her fist. "I gotta go." She took a cautious step back, and he took an unconscious step toward her, then another, not stopping until her palms were pressed to his chest.

God Almighty. He almost curled himself around those hands, his eyes closing in supplication they felt that good.

It took a few slogging heartbeats for him to realize she hadn't lowered them. That her hands were still pressed against his chest even though he was no longer forcing himself on her.

She wanted to keep them there?

Unable to believe his own senses, he flicked his startled gaze from her hands to her face. Why would a human woman continue to touch him?

She is my Chosen. The thought settled home in his heart.

Her lashes fluttered before she trained a steadier look on him, as though she was mustering her courage to do it.

She probably was. He knew what he looked like. He wasn't human like her. Sure, he could pass for it if he disguised the details, but she was staring straight up at him, their faces closer than any human's had ever been. Except for Angelia's.

Which meant she was getting a real good view of the unhuman color of his eyes. She would see his sharp teeth if he released the smile growing like a fucking flame inside him.

If he touched her hair like he wanted? She'd get a load of his claws, too.

Shit.

28

Darken stepped back, stifling his curse. What the hell was he supposed to do now?

Let her go.

Yeah, he wanted to do that like he wanted to kiss the hem of Death's cloak. Wasn't gonna happen. Instead, he wanted to play Quasimodo and snatch her to him so he could steal her away for his very own. Stuff her in his truck and drive like a raped ape to the safe house.

As he handled her as gently as rose petals.

Fantasize much, gargoyle?

He did. But his thoughts were a little like cats right then. He was having a hard time herding them. His emotions were ricocheting all over the Christless place, helping him as much as a tidal wave helped to water a house plant.

Darken had to get a grip, or he was going to lose this woman before he even had her.

"Listen. I, ah…" He scrubbed his hand along the top of his head, mussing his hair. "I was wondering…" *Where the hell my brain is.* "I was thinking maybe I could see you again? If you wanted. I could meet you here tomorrow night? Treat you to dinner?"

The whole time he blathered, he fought the urge to touch her, to run the pads of his thumbs across her pink cheeks, to drag her against him like he had a few moments before, her soft body smooshed in his embrace.

Naked.

God, he was drowning in the scent of her!

Then he felt *it*. A rousing between his legs that electrified his lower guts. Once again, Darken had to struggle to keep his hands under control. But, holy Christ, he needed to shift the swelling behind his zipper before the crushing sensation killed him.

But the woman watched him very closely, her deep brown eyes shimmering from the cold shine of the winter moon. She bit her lip, and his breath caught as he imagined those little teeth on his bare skin.

"Ah, yeah. Sure. Why not?" She shrugged, the gesture nearly lost in the deep quilt of her coat. "Seven o'clock?"

Darken stifled the watermelon smile that nearly exploded onto his face. He couldn't let her see his teeth. Not yet. "I'll be waiting. Right here." Hell, he figured he could wait right there through the next day so he wouldn't miss her. Who would notice an ugly statue?

She gave him a shy grin and a hesitant wave. Both nearly buckled his knees. "Bye, then. See you tomorrow night." Ducking backward toward the lights at the entrance tarmac, she got into the car idling at the curb.

Darken watched, immobilized, rooted like a tree, as she and the car disappeared in a puff of steam and red taillights.

* * * *

Saying anything past the initial *hi, have you been good?* was a little beyond her for the moment, so Daniela just stared out of the windshield, the splash of oncoming headlights flickering into her eyes.

She barely noticed.

Her hands at ten and two on the steering wheel, Amber left her alone with her thoughts. Pretty considerate, considering they hadn't seen each other for a month. But her friends had always done that, left her to herself after she'd done her redneck carnival ride thing.

At least, that was the excuse she'd given Amber to explain her silence. She didn't want to admit she'd been talking to a complete, and very large stranger she'd just met. Alone. *In the dark.*

Her excuse for being inwardly distracted wasn't a total lie. She had been gawking up at the night sky and had nearly fallen on her butt. *But,* thanks to said stranger, she hadn't. He'd wrapped her up in his muscular arms, pulling her so close to his warm body she was grinning now just thinking about it.

Surely, there was something wrong with that? They had never left the shadows during the whole of their encounter. He hadn't followed her to the car or stepped out into the flood of lights at the hospital's entrance.

Like he was hiding.

Smiling was not a healthy reaction. The guy was probably a serial killer, or he could be one of her client's abusive boyfriends or something. Why else would it seem like he was hiding?

Because he was most likely sneaking a cigarette on hospital grounds. *In the dark. Without a whiff of tobacco for a hundred miles.*

Her frustrated, circling thoughts getting the better of her, Daniela almost blurted out what she'd done. Just in time, she caught herself. She did not need anyone worrying over her because there was nothing to worry about.

No, she didn't ever have good luck when it came to men, but she was going to trust her instincts on this one. There was nothing wrong with the man she'd just met. She had *liked* how petite she'd felt in his arms, how precious he'd made her feel in those few seconds, as though she was a loaf of fresh bread from the oven that he would savor.

"Ericka's already got a table for us," Amber announced, derailing Daniela's carnal musings. Just as well. They were getting her nowhere. Wouldn't until tomorrow night when she could touch...*gah*!

"And drinks ordered, I hope," Daniela muttered. She could use one. Between her visit with the woman with the broken jaw, and the weird encounter with the stranger, her nerves could use some ironing out.

Dear God, what if she became one of her own clients?

Pulling into the Olive Garden, Amber squeezed the Hyundai into the nearest available space. At the back end of the parking lot. "Sorry. The place is full." She had the keys out of the ignition and into her purse before Daniela could undo her seatbelt. "Come on. Let's get inside before Ericka loses our place in line."

She had to hand it to Amber. As a friend, the woman knew when to keep her peace and when to lay it out. By the time Daniela shut the car door, her friend was already half way across the lot, her long legs eating turf like a thoroughbred.

It was times like these when she wished she had the nerve to join a gym. Hurrying to play catch-up reminded her of the ass she carried behind her. Which she forgot as soon as she and her two dearest friends were seated at their table, drinks in front of them, the aroma of hot food promising their order would be arriving soon.

Ericka swirled her red wine around her glass and leaned back on a sigh, her short, spiky hair not moving an inch. "Okay. Spill it. What aren't you telling us?"

Daniela glanced up. "You're freaky, you know that?"

"I do. The kids tell me that all the time. I'm not Mrs. Batface for nothing, you know."

"Ugh."

"I know. But I tell myself it's said with love, admiration, and a touch of fear." She set her wine glass down and leaned in with a mascaraed wink.

"All part of my super powers as a guidance counselor to fifteen hundred teenagers."

The three women shared a loud laugh, inviting curious looks from neighboring diners.

"But true. So what's up?"

"She was on a redneck carnival ride when I picked her up."

"Uh-huh. And?"

"She's been mum ever since."

"As usual." The two women nodded, co-conspirators in unwrapping the mystery of Daniela's silence. "Come on, fess up. This isn't your typical space-gazing gone mute, and I know it wasn't your visit to the hospital. Not with that Mona Lisa smile pasted to your lips."

"You should have been a detective, not a guidance counselor."

Ericka waved her off. "Same thing. Without the homicides. Spill."

"All right already. Sheeze, you're worse than a dog with a bone." While Daniela decided how much to reveal, Amber signaled for another round.

After the waiter left, she and Ericka both nodded as they sat up straight and expectant. "Okay. Ready. Go ahead."

One deep inhale for courage, and Daniela loosed her secret. "I met a guy."

A squealing pig couldn't have done better. "Oooh, do tell!" Her friends, God bless them, never seemed to notice she was a size eighteen. Or that most men were nice but never flirty. Not like they were with long-legs Amber. At least beautiful Ericka was off the market, with a loving husband and a two-year-old waiting for her at home.

"Where? Is he cute? When's your first date?" The questions came in stereo, and she felt the tension ease, to be replaced by blushing heat and the gushing of her earlier excitement.

"At the hospital. Very. And tomorrow night." It felt good to share. She'd been agonizing over nothing, surely. She'd met a handsome guy at the hospital, and she was going to have dinner with him the next night. Harmless. Fun. Intriguing. Said her second glass of wine.

It was surprisingly effortless to leave out the weird details, like his eyes, that he wouldn't step into the light. Or that she didn't get his name.

She hadn't offered hers, either. Simple oversights they would both correct tomorrow night. And with any luck, Mr. Mysterious would be sharing more than his name.

By the time she and her friends had fantasized every possible scenario of the coming date, dinner had been enjoyed with more wine, and they'd shared a cab to their different houses, leaving cars to be picked up the next day, when they'd sobered up.

* * * *

The hard clap on his shoulder was what had broken Darken from his stupor. He had sensed and sniffed Urick, who had come up behind him, the bear chimera's hand clutched to his shoulder as he drew up close beside him. Kallen had pressed to his other side, basically sandwiching him.

It had felt good to have his brothers touching him. During the two thousand years they'd been exiled from each other, he'd missed their unique connection as much as they all had.

Now, though, they were stuffed into the extended cab of his truck, waiting for his woman to come out of the restaurant she'd gone into with her friend.

The Olive Garden. Could a place be any more public?

They were waiting because Darken hadn't been able to stand the pressure squeezing his chest as the distance between him and the woman increased. The three of them had followed the flashy, little sedan through the city.

Yet, once the chase ended, none of them had dared to go into the popular place after her.

"Good thing we're Kynd, or this waiting would suck," Uri growled from the back seat where he was stretched out, looking comfortable enough considering his boots touched the opposite side of the cab. And he was still in his gargoyle form. Two months before that wouldn't have been the case. There were deep gashes in the seats where the chimera had lost it and had slipped into his bear. Uri seemed to be getting better. So, why Kristov's interest?

"True enough."

"You're kidding, right?" Kallen scoffed from the passenger seat, resetting his wide shoulders to get a better look at Darken. "Your knuckles

33

are so white they make my eyes hurt."

Darken released his grip on the steering wheel, self-consciously tucking his fists under his armpits. "Piss off."

The other gargoyle shrugged, unfazed.

Because he was right, which did nothing for Darken's dilemma. He was minding the wait like an expectant father who hears his wife screaming in childbirth. Helpless to do anything but wait. And pace.

He reached for the door handle, ready to burst outside to give his boots some exercise.

Kallen grabbed his elbow. "What are you doing, idiot?"

Darken glared. "I'm getting out."

"To do what? Hover and fret until you scare the bejesus out of your Chosen? Think man. Look at yourself."

"She's not my Chosen One." As he bit out the words, he felt the wrongness of them, the ache of his denial in the pinching of his heart. *Christ, I'm in trouble.*

He was, because Kallen was right about that, too. Pacing and locking himself to the window to stare would do nothing to endear himself to the human woman. As it was, he was stunned she'd agreed to see him again.

"Sure. And you asked her to dinner because you eat out all the time. I bet you can't even tell us the last thing you ate."

Darken bristled to the challenge. "It was a…" He couldn't remember, it had been so long ago. "*Fuck.*"

"You ate a fuck. Good for you. How'd it taste?"

Shoving himself back against the seat with a two-ton sigh, Darken released his hold on the door handle. "Shit."

Kallen's hand found his and gave it a squeeze. "No problem, brother. We'll get you close to your woman." Uri rustled behind them to push his huge arm through the bucket seats, closing the circle of their Kynd touch. Immediately, a blanket of calm snuggled over his itchy skin, suffusing Darken with renewed hope that things would be okay. If he kept his shit together.

He had, after all, asked the human woman to dinner. What the hell had he been thinking when he'd blabbered that invitation?

Well, he hadn't been thinking. It was desperation, pure and simple. Because that's what humans did when they courted; men took women to dinner or a movie. Bought them flowers.

Acted sane and mannerly. Like those humans sitting down to a nice dinner in the restaurant neither one of the Kynd in the truck wanted to go into. And certainly, regular humans didn't act like damned hand grenades poised to blow, either.

Darken sat up straight, his heart flipping fast like Thumper's excited foot. "There she is." His hand was on the ignition in a blink, the truck engine humming expectantly.

The women were getting into a cab. They were laughing, huddled together against the cold, a chill breeze whisking their hair and scarves as their merriment swirled around the night air.

Twirling tight around his guts, stirring the slumbering beast nestled on his balls.

His woman was a dark-haired beauty. Breathtaking. Even from across the parking lot, Darken could catch the shine of those heavy lashed eyes. In that instant, he was very glad to be gargoyle, able to see at great distances, to hear the nearly inaudible.

All three Kynd fell silent as they tailed the taxi, lagging far enough back not to be noticed. It wasn't hard. All Darken had to do was follow the tug of the strings branching out from his paper-thin soul toward the woman.

Toward *his* woman.

How she was his Chosen, he didn't know. She hadn't been discovered in the Scriptum, or on some mission in their search for the word of God. She'd just literally bumped into him and fallen into his arms.

Maybe he was wrong, then. Maybe this woman wasn't who he thought she was. And he could harm her. One moment when his control slipped…

His foot eased off the gas pedal.

"Dude, what're you doing?" Kallen's puss from the passenger seat a poster for disbelief.

"Slowing down."

"Duh, whack job. But, why?"

Why? Because he was a whack job. He had nothing to offer this woman, even if he was wrong and she was his Chosen. What would he do, adapt to human society?

35

Not unless he lost his fangs and claws and didn't turn to stone every sunrise.

Okay, so if he found his Chosen One he would no longer turn to stone, but to change into something else? Something not so…grotesque? Would take a miracle, and Darken figured he'd used up his favors from God.

He was gargoyle, and that was that. *She* would have to be the one to adapt, to learn there were Others living in a world parallel to her own—without losing her damned mind.

"He's scared." Urick's pronouncement smacked the proverbial nail on the head. Which didn't mean it didn't hurt like a bitch. He *was* afraid. Just like Urick was. And like his brother, he didn't yet dare enter the human world on such a personal level. Shit could go very wrong, very fast.

"Okay," Kallen conceded, a bit. "But keep your boot on the pedal, man, while I talk sense into you." Darken glanced at the gargoyle beside him, who was smiling softly, understanding warming his gray eyes.

Reassured, he pressed his foot to the floor.

"Good, man. All right, so you're scared. We all are." The bear nodded in the rearview. "But that doesn't mean we give up. Right?"

Kallen answered himself, revving up like a cheerleader. "Right. So, we take the plunge. We *try*. Look how it turned out for Merrick. Even without his wings, the bastard's living Heaven on earth, for Christ's sake. That's gotta be worth the risk."

He was really warming up, his breath coming fast. "And if you've found your Chosen, then you're already one lucky son of a bitch. The two of you will figure it out, God will make sure of it. Shit, the Man *wrote* about it."

"Then why didn't Angelia see this coming?" He wasn't quite ready to concede to the other Kynd's rationale. Not when an innocent's life was at stake.

"She just hasn't gotten around to it, that's all. The damned book is code. It takes time."

"You should be a lawyer."

Kallen grinned, his sharp teeth striking in their full reveal. "Yeah, I should. But you don't get to beat shit up."

Darken gave him a sideways glance. True enough. He'd felt loads better after he and Kristov had gone a round. He answered Kallen's rationale by speeding up.

"That's the brotherkynd I know and love," he laughed, and Darken felt the lift of his heart in his thick chest.

"Yeah, but no kissing." He grinned, relieved that the truck homed in on the cab once again. As the taxi slowed and pulled to the curb, he kept the Dodge Ram gliding along, passing the salt coated car like he was just another vehicle sharing the road.

"She's getting out." Urick was turned, looking out the tinted back window. Darken cut a right at the next street, killing the headlights as he shoved the truck into park.

He resisted the sudden urge to pray, figuring God might have put this woman in his lap, but the rest was up to him.

"Wish me luck," he said as he rolled his wide bulk out the driver's side door. With Kallen's cheerleader routine pushing his back, and the absence of a crowd, Darken felt brave enough to show himself again. "I'll call before the sun comes up."

His cell phone had other ideas.

Merrick. Standing in the open door of his truck, Darken flipped the Blackberry to his ear. "Yeah?"

"Angelia thinks she's found a way around Minos but wants to run it by everyone else. Can you get back before dawn?"

Shit. That trip back into Hell to rescue Shades from the Second Circle. At least it sounded like Drakus wouldn't be needed. If Angelia had found another route...

"We'll be right there. Twenty minutes." Darken slipped his phone into an inner pocket as he climbed back in behind the wheel. He didn't need to repeat the conversation, not with the hearing his two passengers possessed.

"Well, shit." The cheerleader sounded...disappointed.

"My sentiments exactly." He'd been primed for action, now his intentions were being redirected. Just when his balls were coming into play. He felt Kallen's disappointment, along with a whole lot of *what the fuck?* Like he'd arrived for the Super Bowl, but got the wrong day.

His body hollow as an empty stadium, Darken scraped his hands across the top of his head and took a deep breath. Along with a mental step back.

To scope out the field.

His brethren came first. Always. He'd been the one to call them away from their God-given punishments, so they were his responsibility.

Their needs? Head of the line.

He'd just have to wait until the following night to see his female, as first planned.

And yes, damn it, he would take the human woman out to dinner, just as he'd asked her. His fears could mope at the frigging curb. He could handle being in public if he stayed calm.

He'd just make sure they were seated next to a door in case he had to bolt at the last second.

Game. Plan. Things were playing out just fine. He could relax his metal-bending grip on the gearshift and gently...slide...his truck...into Drive.

His nerves running a little roughshod, he put the truck in gear and returned with his brothers to the relative safety of rural Maine.

Chapter Five

After the third outfit she'd tried on and discarded, Daniela wasn't feeling as positive about her date as she had been the night before with a few glasses of wine in her not so slender belly.

Now she just stared at herself in the full-length mirror and sneered with an overly critical eye. "You're fat," she sighed. "Plain and simple." None of the dresses were flattering. So what if she'd thought they were when she'd worn them before.

Now, they looked like moo-moos, draping her blobby form and accentuating every bulge.

She was going to be the beast standing beside the beauty.

Because the next day hadn't brought clarity to sodden her image of the man she'd met the night before. Almost twenty-four hours later, and she still thought him gorgeous, recalled those eerie, shining nickel eyes, the span of his thick shoulders.

He was beautiful in a very masculine way, and she was going to disappoint him.

It had been dark when they'd met, after all.

"Crap." Resigned to her night ending before it even began, Daniela ditched the dresses for a pair of black pants disguised as a long skirt and hauled on a black, long-sleeved t-shirt. Over that, she donned a short-sleeved t-shirt, one that said: *"What doesn't kill you makes you stronger. Except for bears. Bears will kill you."*

She had a drawer full of zany t-shirts like that. She chose this one for the courage it half-inspired. She wasn't going to come face to face with a bear, but the first part of the logo made her feel a little braver.

Wrapping a silk scarf around her neck like a six foot boa constrictor, she was ready.

Twenty minutes later, she cruised through the hospital's main parking lot, creeping past the spot she'd agreed to meet her mysterious stranger.

He wasn't there. And she pretended her disappointment didn't exist.

She'd expected he wouldn't show, really. After she'd left him, he would've come to his senses and realized what he'd done.

Still, a part of her hoped it wasn't true, and that little kernel was what got her chicken ass out of the car. While she walked toward the flood of lights marking the hospital entrance, she kept telling herself he was just late, she was probably early, and that the whole encounter had been a figment of her imagination.

Three solid arguments. But the best one was the last one.

There was no one to stand her up because she hadn't met any tall, dark, and handsome stranger.

Insecurity blew away like a zephyr wind when Mr. Mysterious stepped out of the shadows, the lights of the hospital behind him outlining his huge body.

Oh. My. Gawd. He was just as gorgeous as she remembered. More so now that she could see him in better lighting. Her heart did the crazy-dance, making her breathless.

Her hand pressed to her middle, she pushed back against the growing pressure expanding inside her. Crazy expectation, titillation…

Then he started walking toward her, and her keen heart dropped into her stomach, though she'd been preparing herself for his brush off.

Because he strode toward her like he was on a mission, his whole body tense.

Even gutted, she couldn't drag her eyes off him. He moved with a roll only a very strong man could pull off. Long, thick legs ate up the sidewalk as fast as his heavy boots could clomp down, his fists balled at his hips.

As he steamrolled closer, Daniela saw the clench of his jaw and wondered if his teeth were cracking under the pressure. His silvery gaze pinned to her like a set of headlights.

Like a pedestrian who'd stepped off the curb into the path of a bus, she fell back, her feet tangling with themselves. As if they stepped on each other to get out of the way.

Her retreat stopped him cold, the man's back ratcheting so straight it was like he hit an invisible wall. Shining gray eyes still pinned on her, he took a deep breath, giving his head a hard shake, and readjusting his broad shoulders.

As though he reassessed his approach.

Daniela gave him all the time he needed. She'd worked with enough battered women to know she didn't want to be one of them. Not that she felt any ill intent on his part. He battled himself, not her.

Still, it didn't hurt to be cautious. The guy was big, and moving her from point A to point B would take nothing more than a flick of his thick wrist.

But then he lowered his head and peered down through shaggy, blonde bangs, and her body responded just as it had when she'd found herself in his arms.

Just like that, his look of shy chagrin calmed her.

Running a palm over his mouth, he said, "I'm sorry. I'm a little nervous."

You think? His voice ground out like sandpaper, but it was the hungry look in his eyes that finally released her breath, making her blush.

He watched her like a man who'd just got his sight back after being blind for a few years. That cherished feeling she'd felt the night before had been no illusion—it flooded her now. "Me, too. I mean, I didn't expect you to be here. Not really."

"Not be here? You're crazy, right?" But she saw the flash of guilt before that hungry shine came crushing down.

Damn. Why couldn't she have been looking the other way and not seen the guilt?

He'd lied. The man had come, but he'd had second thoughts about it.

Removing herself a bit to put some distance between them, Daniela looked over her shoulder to where her car was parked. The warm flush of feeling cherished cracking in the frigid cold of a Maine winter. "Look. Let's not pretend here, all right. Last night was…I don't know…a fluke, I guess. Moon sickness, or something. So, I'm going to go."

She was half turned when he grabbed her elbow. Then dropped it like it scalded him. He even ran his palms up and down his thighs, like he was erasing the feel of her.

Which was the last crumb in the sad, empty cookie jar of her self-respect.

Daniela bolted.

"No!" The word erupted like a shotgun blast behind her as he leapt to grab her again. This time, though, he clasped her to him like a treasure nearly slipping his grasp.

"No," he breathed into the crown of her head, his cheek caressing her hair, his hands gripped tight to her upper arms. He held her to him as close as their bulky coats would let him. "I'm sorry. You're right. I wasn't sure about meeting you here. But not for the reasons you think. Please," the warmth of his breath curled along the edge of her scalp. "Don't go."

Now what, pray tell, was she going to do with that heartfelt confession? She couldn't very well deny him. She'd feel like she was kicking a puppy. As handsome as he was, he apparently had insecurities larger than her own.

As soon as she relaxed, he wrapped his bulk around her back. He sniffed her hair, too. Odd, but the gesture livened her in a place that shouldn't be tingling on a first date. Never mind there were no warning bells pinging between her ears.

His strange possessiveness should be blipping like a war ship on her radar.

But then he spoke again, his voice like roughened whiskey. "We got off on the wrong foot. It's me. I'm not used to interacting with hu— *people*."

So, Mr. Mysterious was a hermit? Explained the whole standing in the shadows thing, she supposed.

The urge to flee evaporated. "Okay. Fair enough. I won't run." He relaxed his grip so she could turn around to face him, his hands sliding down her forearms then encircling her wrists to keep her close. "But I'm not contagious. You don't have to wipe your hands clean."

She was forgiving him, but she wasn't a door mat, either.

He shook his head, looking at her from under his unruly bangs. "Wasn't."

Yipes, this guy might be built like a mountain, but he was vulnerable. An incongruity she found endearing, her own fears settling themselves on the back burner.

"Clean slate," she said, taking a fortifying breath. "Dinner?"

His jaw clenched tight again like the idea was riding up his ass.

"Not dinner out? Can you cook, then?"

"I make a mean toast," he said with all seriousness.

"Ah, that bad, huh?" He was a bachelor, what did she expect? Most of his meals probably involved pouring hot water over a cup of noodles.

"I practiced." He seemed proud of the fact, his lip curling ever so slightly.

"You practiced making toast?"

"In case I could convince you to eat in. Then I could make you toast." He wasn't kidding in the least, and it made her laugh. Forgetting where they were standing, she fell against him, savoring the absurdity of him. Admitting his lack of skills in the kitchen made him very human. Not like a superhero at all.

Instantly, his arms banded around her. "You're strange, you know that?" she said against his chest.

"Yes." A short answer that scraped wondrously the whole way up the front of her, the sound of it reverberating under her skin everywhere else.

* * * *

She had no idea how strange he was, compared to her. But, it was highly probable she was going to find out. When she'd turned to run, his world had gone instantly bleak.

How could he let her waltz out of his life when she'd become important to it in a matter of hours?

The problem lay in finding the least traumatic way to introduce her to the world of the Others. But for now, it could wait. Just because he was in it up to his stony crack, didn't mean she was. The woman could walk away from him without a glance backward.

Just thinking of that sent chills scurrying across his rough skin, and his fingers curled unconsciously tighter on her arms. He'd have wrapped a leg around her, too, just to feel more of her, to siphon off a little comfort through more touching if he didn't think it would wig her out.

Curse the needs of his Kynd; because if he caved to those urges, she was sure to bolt, and there would be nothing he could say then to make her stay.

I'm a gargoyle who needs to touch a lot sounded like a bad line in a B-movie. No matter how much truth there was to it.

"So," she said, interrupting his pathetically needy train of thought. "Dinner. Your place?" When he peered down at her upturned face, he almost agreed, stuffed her in his truck, and absconded with her to the safe house.

His place? Oh, yes, Quasimodo would like that very much.

But.

"Not a good idea. I live with my brothers. No privacy." He didn't lie to her, at any rate. There were seven of them living in the safe house. It was a huge place, but his brothers would be curious. And so would this woman. Talk about a train wreck you could see coming from a mile down the tracks.

"All righty." She stretched the words out like she was thinking of an alternative that didn't involve her home, either. He couldn't say as he blamed her. A woman should be cautious.

He felt the tingling of pride that she was.

Meanwhile, they were still standing in a parking lot, on a freeze-your-ass-off February night.

Darken sucked it up for the sake of his woman, and before he caved to his Kynd yearnings to pour his entire body over hers to keep her warm. "Out it is. You name the place, and I'll take us. No toast."

Her laughter put helium in his boots, so he felt as though he drifted upward off the concrete. "Good. I know some really great spots. I'm guessing its bacon burgers for you and a pitcher of ale?"

Ah, no. Kynd, when they did eat, were vegetarian. But she seemed so pleased, he didn't have the heart to disappoint her. Hell, if she suggested they eat rubber tires, he would do it.

The woman started shaking her head as though contemplating an afterthought. "No," she mumbled. Then said, "No…that place is always packed. Great food, but everyone knows it. Let's see…" Her fingers, blanched from the cold, teased a button on her coat.

"We'll decide in the truck," he said, cupping her hand within his. "You're freezing your butt off."

"I've got enough to spare," she grumbled low, obviously to herself; but his hearing wouldn't have missed it. An image of her bountiful ass bloomed front and center in his mind's eye, and damned if his hands didn't itch to grip the real thing.

Darken suppressed a ravenous growl. "Your ass is wonderful."

She replaced the surprised look on her face with one of cynicism. "Says you, who has never seen it. It's been hiding under my coat like a giant tortoise."

The image almost had him showing off his fangs in a wide smile. She had sass, and that was like an aphrodisiac. On impulse, he swept her off her feet and up into his arms, the little squeal she emitted rolling his guts like sweet taffy.

His appetite returned with a vengeance, only it wasn't food he craved. To hell with dinner. He wanted *her*. So badly, base desires swamped him. He wanted to ravage her right there on the pavement, the public be damned.

When her dark chocolate eyes searched his face, he offered her an apologetic smirk. The last thing he needed was to scare her.

Yet, he couldn't put her down, not when she felt so right cradled in his arms.

Besides, he was inadvertently groping her, that ass she'd insulted resting wonderfully in the crook of his elbow, her thighs on his forearms a luxuriant bounty.

Screw his truck. He wanted to carry her wherever it was they were going.

Except they'd already arrived at his parking space. Unwilling to release her, he grappled with how to open the door without letting the woman go.

"Ah, Mr. Mysterious, you can put me down now." The front of his coat was pinched in her fingers, and she was tugging on it to get his attention.

Blood rushed to his cheeks, flaming them. "Sorry." Gently, he lowered her to the ground, making sure there was no ice she could slip on. "Here." Opening the truck's passenger side door, he helped her in, lifting her hand to guide her up into the high cab.

Feeling the strain of releasing her deep in his core, he shivered to ease the discordant tug.

She is human. He had to keep reminding himself of that so he wouldn't smother her. Humans did not constantly touch. In fact, most hardly touched at all, and he'd do well to remember that.

Still, he was behind the wheel with the heater blasting in a matter of seconds, as though being outside while she was in, was too much to bear. "Okay," he puffed on his hands as he rubbed them together. "Where to?"

"Alfio's. We could walk from here." She grinned at him, like getting into the truck had been a comic routine. And he guessed it had if the restaurant was close enough to walk to.

Except it was cold out. He didn't want his female catching a chill.

Then again…he'd have to hold her close to keep her warm as they navigated the streets and sidewalks. Personal warnings about keeping his distance could suck it. "Walking it is."

Before he could get his door open, feminine laughter rippled through the cab of the truck, tickling across his skin, under it. "We're loaded already, so let's go."

Damn. But a grin threatened in spite of his disappointment. He liked how his body rode his woman's giggles.

He pulled the Dodge out into traffic as she directed. "Go straight a bit, and hook a left onto West. Good. Left onto Carleton. Okay, now! Turn right onto Congress."

Focused on their route, she seemed unaware how she livened, her body revving and a little jerky like the truck, just like the directions she gave.

Starved for her, Darken drank in every nuance.

"That's it on the right," she said, sitting back as if suddenly aware she'd been leaning forward. A little excited. A rosy bloom brushed her cheeks, and watching it, he almost drove his truck onto the sidewalk.

He couldn't tell if her embarrassed grin was for him or herself. "We're here," she said, tucking a lock of abundant dark hair behind her ear.

So they were. The destination sobered him.

Ignoring the screaming of his senses to abort this trying-to-function-in-public charade, Darken helped his woman out of the truck.

As her feet touched down on the cobblestones, he did not let go of her hand.

Chapter Six

So, the initial greet of the date had been full of more ups and downs than a trapeze act. Which was okay by Daniela, especially since she and the gorgeous one were now going into a restaurant to share dinner.

Even though they hadn't yet shared names.

Details. They'd deal with in a bit, after getting comfy in the cozy bistro.

She liked Alfio's. They whipped up some very delicious pizza, and she never felt self-conscious about savoring it. The wait staff seemed to appreciate her discerning palate, when most everyone else assumed, based on her girth, she bellied up like a pig to a trough and munched indiscriminately.

Adding to her usual insecurities that niggled every time she entered any dining establishment, she realized she was dragging her date in through the door. All six and a half feet of him.

Daniela's feet stopped just as his did, her cheeks flaring like she'd stuck her face up to one of the pizza ovens. Drawing courage with a deep breath, she turned to face her embarrassment head on.

But she didn't see what she expected. She'd been dragging a human mountain, not because she was eager to dive into her plate, but because he didn't want to go inside. The man was digging in his heels, lowering his center of gravity like a dog going to the vet's or the bathtub.

Daniela forgot her own anxieties when she peered up that mountain to catch her date's expression.

Like earlier, his jaw was clamped shut, his nostrils flared. And his eyes were as far from new nickels as she could imagine. This time, she was looking into the gray storms of the Bering Sea. As though there was some cataclysmic clash going on behind those slate eyes.

Her first instinct, despite her years of helping battered women? She put her arms around the man's waist to comfort him. "Hey, you all right?"

It took a couple of seconds for him to peel his eyes off the front door, like he'd been gaping at the jaws of hell instead of the entrance to a pizzeria.

A quick roll of his shoulders to settle the mercurial storming of his eyes, and he gazed down at her with less animosity and apprehension, and more resolve.

Daniela found herself searching her memory for names of phobias.

"Sorry." His voice scraped hard and deep across her eardrums like it took a monumental effort just to speak.

The large hand she held felt like stone and had grown just as cold. "We don't have to do this." Not if it made him this uncomfortable. Obviously, he hadn't been kidding about being a hermit.

He shook his head, refusing her offer. "No, it's all right." His lip quirked into that shy grin she was already growing fond of. "Mind, though, if we sit close to the door?"

He moved them toward the entrance. Though the closer they got, the more she could see where he'd be uncomfortable. He was going to have to shoe-horn himself in at one of the tables, a bull at the proverbial china shop.

Or Godzilla razing a path through Tokyo.

God, the guy was huge. And hey, those chicks in the corner had better peel their eyes off her candy…

As though he hadn't noticed he was getting sized up like the flavor of the month, he moved in behind her, helping her out of her coat. Hanging it on one of the little hooks by the door, he shucked his.

And Daniela dined before the food arrived. *Screw you, anorexia girls, for once…this one is mine.*

Her date's backside was…spectacular. She knew about his wide shoulders. But his narrower hips? An indulgence, like chocolate truffles. Beneath his shirt wasn't bought-in-the-gym bulk. Uh-uh. This guy was built like a jungle cat. Lithesome. His muscles etched, lean, and corded. Not cumbersome.

They shrieked quick-in-a-blink devastating power.

Daniela's knees went quaky.

Then he turned around to face her, and all her carnal thoughts blew away on a burst of laughter.

His long-sleeved t-shirt read—*If you say "gullible" slowly, it sounds like "oranges."*

Still giggling, she presented hers like one of Barker's Beauties, her hands showcasing the goods with a downward sweep.

The appreciation glowing upon his handsome face made her think of sunrises. "Nice." He reached out for her, like he wanted to press their irreverent shirts together, but stopped himself.

Instead, true to his suggestion, he wedged himself behind a table near the exit, leaving her little choice but to sit with her back to the room.

So he could get a good gander at those women?

A second later, he dragged her chair next to his, legs screeching on the wooden floor. An embarrassed smile shined out from beneath gray eyes. Eyes that hadn't strayed from her. "There."

Well, he certainly made it clear his personal space was about the size of a teacup.

Eyeballing the cramped space as she grew hyper aware of everyone in the room, she solved a physics equation. *My ass...the distance between the table and the back of the chair...equals...*

Screw it. Here goes what's left of my pride.

As she sidled in, Darken did the unexpected, pushing the table away from the wall, his glare daring anyone to challenge it. "This place is too fucking small," he said, stretching his massive self, making the little checkered table look like the saucer to his teacup.

It took her a second to sift through her feelings about that. Being with this guy was unlike anything she'd ever experienced before. So far, she'd been insulted, concerned, entertained, and cosseted. And that was just within the first half hour of their date.

Now he was looking at her expectantly, his eyes shining like newly minted nickels, his hand gripping the back of her chair.

Making it seem as if he opened himself up to embrace her.

Insides turning to cream...

Despite the fact the color of his irises was so startlingly unusual.

In the darkness the night before, she hadn't realized how gray they truly were. Granted, the lighting in Alfio's was intimately dim; but this close, she could tell she'd never seen eyes like his before.

Dropping his lids, he reached to fiddle with the globed peppershaker, then fisted his hand before stuffing it back under the table. Behind her back, she heard the creak of wood protest under his other fist.

With his warmth engulfing her, she couldn't mistake the heady, masculine smell of him. Not cologne or aftershave, but something strong enough to override the scents of garlic and oregano. A little something that made her scoot closer.

Darken tensed around her, his body drawing ever closer, even without seeming to move.

* * * *

He felt her body relax the second it happened, and Darken struggled against every instinct not to curl his arm around the woman to press her even closer.

Lord, he wanted to, especially when she'd obviously noticed one of his Kynd traits and didn't shiver with revulsion or bolt.

He'd caught her staring at his eyes. His fangs or his hands were going to be next, and he dug his claws into his palms as a wave of alarm washed over him, making his heart clunk in his chest.

With a deep breath, he rubbed his palms on his thighs as he eyed the door.

Even if he had to make a mad dash for it, he was going to knock everything in his path sideways. He was too crammed into the small space of the restaurant.

The thought made him edgier. He was supposed to be fitting in.

Damn, this was a bad idea.

It wasn't that he was claustrophobic. God knew how many times he'd been in tight places to extract the souls Death had come to reap. But at least when he was Death's assistant, it didn't matter what he was. A soul didn't give two shits about the hands holding that awful scythe.

This woman would. So far, she seemed really into him and claiming more space for the both of them had been...a stroke of genius. The moment she'd shimmied her plump rear towards him, he'd instantly thought Heaven was overrated.

God, what a divine creature!

He didn't want to screw this up. With any luck, when she did notice his hands—and she would—she'd think something terrible had happened to him like maybe he'd been burned in a fire, or some other ghastly accident that could turn regular human fingernails into claws.

As if it was lucky to be maimed instead of admitting he was a gargoyle.

Jesus aching Christ. He needed to get beyond the first date jitters so she'd learn to like him no matter who, or *what*, he was. He also needed to figure out how to shift his erection so his zipper wasn't biting into the fucking thing.

Clearing the logjam in his throat, he said, "So, I know you have great taste in t-shirts, but I don't know your name." Shifting slightly to gaze down at her, he got a close-up of her flawless skin, the rosy blush of her cheeks a pretty accent to her sable hair.

She tucked a tress behind her ear, flashing the soft, pearlescent pink of her fingernails.

Darken felt a fluttering thrill in his stomach.

"It's Daniela. And I have an embarrassing collection of shirts just like this one at home. Compliments of *The Onion*."

Her little grin? Rocketed him into the stratosphere. Never had he needed to grip onto something so tight to keep his cool.

"Darken. As do I." His tight grin came off shy. He hoped it did, anyway, as he stuck his hand out for a common, human greeting. A risky gesture given the claws, but he needed the excuse to touch her skin. Otherwise, he was going to implode.

Automatically her hand reached out, her fingers slipping like tulip petals along his calloused palm. He folded his around them, his heart flapping like a duck bathing in a pond.

Anxiously, he watched for her reaction. He felt the skip of her pulse before it steadied, and she squeezed his hand in return. Reassuring him beyond measure, so that his muscles trembled briefly. "Bears, huh?" he managed to wheeze, hoping to sound half-way normal.

She grinned and nodded, her brown eyes crinkling warmly. "They can kill you," she agreed. "And take your pic-a-nic basket."

His bursting laughter caught them both by surprise. "That's a good imitation of Yogi Bear."

"I've had a lot of practice." Color blossomed upon her creamy cheeks. "You should hear my imitation of Porky Pig."

"The Loony Toons. Best cartoons on television, hands down."

"So true!" Her laughter mingled with his as she leaned closer, their shoulders bumping. Darken thought maybe his heart would blow right out of his frigging chest.

"The first time I heard classical music was when Bugs Bunny and Elmer Fudd were doing a spoof of Wagner's *Ride of the Valkyries.* You know," Daniela batted her long lashes as she tucked her hands under her chin and lisped, "you're so wuv-wee."

Drowning in her smile, he sang, "Don't I know iiit." Quoting Bugs, but he meant the woman beside him as he relaxed into her, growing more comfortable by the second.

Daniela was captivating. Funny, gorgeous, guileless.

Perfect.

Preoccupied, he might have missed the waiter approaching, but his body tensed the closer the kid got to them, instincts warning him of impending danger.

Darken slipped his hands back under the table.

"George, good to see you." Beside him, Daniela sat up straighter, wiggling to adjust that plump ass.

"Hi, Daniela." The young man stopped at their table, rocking forward on his toes. "Would you and your guest like menus?" The kid wore a smirk like he and Daniela shared a joke.

Darken repressed the urge to bite him. With sarcasm, of course.

Or slice his head off with Death's scythe.

"No, thanks. We're going to have the butternut squash pizza with ricotta and cranberries. My friend hasn't tried your pizzas yet." A saucy wink followed the confession.

The waiter was all over it, nodding as if they shared some secret code. "And drinks?"

"White wine for me. Your choice." She turned to him, her eyes narrowing as she puckered her lush lips. "Hmm…a Smitty's and a water with lemon. Hold the Smitty's."

The kid smiled, showing off a row of perfect teeth, compliments of a talented orthodontist and parents with deep pockets. "A glass of water and a white wine coming up."

"You've been here a few times," he growled low into her ear, his jealous ire turning to amusement, softening the scrape of his voice. He liked her confidence that she would take the initiative and order for him, knowing he didn't frequent places like this.

"It's not far from the hospital. It's a good place for me to knit my thoughts after meeting with a patient."

"Then you work at the hospital."

"Only as a liaison between them and the police department. I interview their domestic abuse cases."

The skin at his nape grew taut, like he was getting lifted by the scruff of his neck. "You what?" Not that he needed her to repeat what she'd said. He needed a second to rein in his impulses.

His gut reaction was to fold himself around her and keep her as far from violence as possible. It didn't matter that the physical abuse was over by the time she arrived, it was enough for her to be skirting the residuals. To have to "knit her thoughts" after coming in contact with one of its victims? Unnerved him on too many levels.

Mainly? He'd been hoping to graft her to his life—a life inherently violent. How was that for a cruel joke?

"Yeah, not the most glamorous job in the world, I know," she said, either misreading his unease or ignoring it. "But being an advocate means something. I make a small difference, even if it's temporary and the woman goes back to her abuser. I know I'll wind up seeing her again, but that's not the point."

He honestly didn't know what to say, so he just leaned his head toward hers while struggling with the impossibility of...*them.*

"The point is..." Daniela's voice dropped to a scratch as the space between them disappeared. "...I'm there at all. An ear, mostly, to hear their stories. Let them spill whatever poison they need to leak out."

"And do what with it?" His traitorous fingers inched toward her thigh.

"Type it up. Hand it over to the officer on the case. Sometimes I get information they wouldn't have, so it helps with a conviction." She shrugged, making light of the role she played.

Darken felt the full hit of that dismissive shrug low in his gut. What she did was important, even if he was waging an internal battle with the knowledge of it. The Kynd, before they were expelled from Heaven, had been God's eyes and ears. So he knew all about the importance of bearing witness.

That his woman shouldered the duty alone troubled him. He was angry she should have to. Proud she could.

The Kynd had always had each other to share their burdens.

Well, they had until God scattered them to the far reaches of every damned plane conceivable.

Too many were still out there suffering, unaware of the work he and their brethren were doing at the safe house, of their quest to undo God's judgment, of their searching for the Chosen Ones meant to free them from their Grotesque fates.

How Daniela fit the Scriptum's puzzle, he didn't have a clue. But he could calm himself down, rather than reacting like a damned Neanderthal.

She helped people cope with the staggering aftermath of violence. Surely, her skills would help her assimilate with the realities of his world. Maybe even help his brethren. Tough shit if he didn't like it. For the sake of his loved ones, he would endure.

Things will be fine with my Chosen.

He forced his body to relax, to indulge once again in the soft contours of the woman beside him. Savoring the ways the curves of her soft body seemed to meld with the hardness of his.

"You get a lot of convictions?" he asked, his body vibrating like a tuning fork. Unwilling to distance himself, he knew how they appeared to the other diners.

Like lovers.

Apparently, Daniela didn't give two figs either. She didn't draw back or scooch her chair away from him. Instead, she tilted her chin up so she could gaze straight into his un-human eyes.

As she did so, her hair slid along his with an intimacy that rushed through his blood. "A surprising number of them considering."

"Considering?" he squelched, his question riding his exhalation. Which she breathed in.

I am. Struck. Stupid.

Unaware he'd blanked, his Chosen continued, Darken hanging on every pucker and lift of her lips. "Considering most victims rarely make a clean break. They have to deal with the fallout."

"Ah." Checking back in despite the fact he'd been walloped with a baseball bat, he got what she meant without her having to go into detail.

The victims got the shaft, no matter what.

He could come up with a hundred clichés to joke about that, pun the shit out the words, but his heart wasn't in it. Most likely because he knew the nature of brutality.

All too fucking well. All too fucking well enough to shove him back into the scathing glare of reality.

He might have been exonerated for the savage crime he'd committed against Aro, but he'd been quite capable—and willing—to sever the vampire's head from his shoulders. He'd reveled in the slash of his blade across that leech's flesh, had exulted in the briefest bump of bone as spine met steel....

So, yeah, fallout came in many forms, and the shaft...

The kid arriving with their drinks saved him from plunging into that looming chasm.

"Thanks, George." Daniela drew back to sip her wine. "Delicious."

Her pleasured smile sprung an urge in him to taste it for himself. Straight from her lips.

"Good, huh?" he rasped, instincts alone registering the retreat of the other male. Since his main focus was stuck elsewhere.

"I haven't had a bad one, yet. George has a knack for picking the right wines." She took another sip before placing her stemmed glass on the little table, the tip of her tongue dabbing her lip. "How's your water?" she asked, her dark eyes shining with teasing merriment.

Words fell out of his mouth without thought. "I'll wager a guess and say George serves a mean water, too."

* * * *

With his humor being as quick and light as hers, Daniela forgot all about how too gorgeous her date was.

Well, almost. It was hard to ignore those eyes...

Unnerving. In the best sense of the word. They pierced her. Wormed under her skin with a buzz she likened to…humming. Under. Her skin…

With a delicious shiver, she thought it easier to overlook his fingertips, which were disfigured. Though she saw little of them.

He kept his hands out of sight. An intentional concealment not lost on her.

How many times had she herself tried camouflaging her own flaws?

Besides, she was encouraged by his wanting to touch her anyway, despite both of their imperfections.

His little caresses made her feel desirable, über feminine, and sexy— something she didn't have a lot of experience with. Yet, she felt herself wielding it like…a woman well aware of her effect.

With his rapt attention, the man was winning her over in spades, despite their unconventional start.

She took a breath to tell him how glad she was he hadn't let her run back to her car when he stiffened beside her, those strange eyes dragging his gaze from her to a man standing by the kitchen doors. Across the length of the room.

Daniela felt suddenly cold, like she experienced a drop in barometric pressure. Or watched a lethal predator size up its prey.

She *did not* just feel Darken's body rumble beside hers.

In a blink of her mascaraed eyelashes, he stood, hands fisted like battering rams at his outer thighs. Like a foggy image at the back of her mind, she found herself surprised that he didn't upend their table.

But he hadn't moved forward yet, either. He just stood there like a stone monolith, his muscles tightening, bulging. The Bering Sea returning to his eyes with the ferocity of a hurricane.

"Darken?"

The tilting of his chin was the only acknowledgement that he'd heard her.

"Who is that man, Darken?" Daniela's fingers lit upon his elbow, in spite of the fear rising in her.

As fear gave weight to her touch, he flinched, blinking down at her, the storm of his gray eyes quelling the instant they met hers. He offered the twitch of a smile. "Sorry. I didn't mean…*hell*. I'm sorry."

Sitting back down, Darken covered her hand with his, holding her touch to him as if he needed it there. And indeed he might; she felt him stiffen anew when the stranger approached their table.

The man, who was quite lean and tall, was blonde like Darken, except his eyes were the exact opposite on the element scale. The stranger's were a clean gold; warm yet hard eyes, with none of the emotion swirling like Darken's mercurial gray.

Daniela's grip on her date's elbow tightened.

Maintaining a healthy distance despite the crowded tables, their uninvited guest said, "Darken, so good to see you out."

"Godrick." The deep baritone of Darken's voice was like a physical thing crawling across her skin, leaving in its wake a rash of goose bumps. "Checking up on your pet?"

For the briefest moment, the man scowled. "Just making sure. There is much at stake here." Like it needed saying. Even Daniela, who didn't know the guy, felt the truth of his words.

No idea how—or why. She just did.

Darken's acknowledgement was a subtle nod.

Goldy's response in turn was a twisting of his lips. A friendly smile? "Aren't you going to introduce me?"

There was a pregnant hesitation before her date said anything. "Daniela, this is Godrick. Godrick, Daniela."

The man leaned forward as if to approach, then seemed to think better of it. "*Daniela.* A lovely name. It means *the judgment of God* in Italian, does it not?" He slid a gold eye toward Darken, who appeared to have placed himself between her and the stranger without even moving.

"Yes," she said. "So few people know that. Your family's Italian?"

"You could say that, I suppose. And yours?"

She was losing her initial fear of the stranger. Odd, given how wary she usually was of new men. Maybe since meeting Darken she was losing some of her paranoia?

"Salvai," Her name slipped from her mouth as she leaned into the big body next to hers, gaining no small amount of comfort from it. "My grandparents were immigrants."

The gold eyes narrowed as if noting her subtle shift. "*To save,*" he translated. "Interesting."

"Leave her be, Godrick." Darken's words vibrated across her skin again, only this time there was no mistaking their rumbling. He *was* growling.

Like some kind of beast.

Their visitor placed one Cole Hahn shoe behind the other, the back of his thighs hitting a table behind him before he stopped.

Daniela blinked, unsure if she'd seen that right. "Well, Daniela Salvai, it was most enlightening to meet you. Enjoy your meal."

Godrick dipped his chin with an old world salutation, then left, leaving Daniela feeling like she'd just witnessed a scene from *The Godfather*—all subtle innuendo with a piquant of violent undertones.

She suddenly had no more appetite. Not even for Alfio's wintery squash pizza.

It took a few seconds for her to realize Darken was speaking to her. "Hmm?"

"Would you like me to take you back to your car?" His beautiful nickel eyes like slate, showing none of their mercurial quality, revealing nothing of his thoughts.

Or of his emotions. It was as if he'd shut down, the visit from the strange man obliterating his earlier ease as if it had never existed.

She sat beside a six foot-four inch, muscled giant who wanted out of a very public place. Yesterday.

"Y-yes, please." She got up to go, a little nervous and very disappointed with herself. Darken had flat out told her he didn't like being in the public eye. Now she understood why.

He had secrets.

Agoraphobia, my ass.

He was hiding something crucial about himself. And judging by the interaction she'd just witnessed, it was something she most likely wanted no part of. She took her coat, pulling it on as she stepped out into a frigid February night, her breath fogging.

Before the door latched behind them, Darken moved in close to her, draping his bulk across her back as he kept his face angled, like he cocked an ear for hints of danger.

Did this Godrick guy wait in the shadows like a sniper?

Faster than she could breathe the words *red flag,* Darken pulled his truck away from the curb, the Dodge aimed for the hospital like an ambulance carrying the top triage patient.

The only thing missing were the flashing lights and sirens.

Oh, we're here. Relief nearly swamped her as they turned into the lot where she'd left her car. So, he wasn't taking her hostage, or speeding out of the city in a furious fit, selfishly uncaring if anyone else was in his vehicle, if they got hurt when he crashed.

Shit. Shit, shit, shit. He didn't need to look at her for her to be the object of his attention—using his body as a shield, driving fast through the city streets, yet careful.

And for the one time, for the one frigging time when she'd been feeling beautiful and coveted, her date turned out to be...

Well, hell, she didn't know. Some kind of thug on the wrong side of the law, she knew that much.

All she had to do was recall that gold-eyed man and Darken's menacing reaction to him.

The potential for violence had sat between the two of them like a bomb ticking. Loud. And. Clear. She was kind of surprised guns hadn't been drawn. Bullets flying like in a Quentin Tarantino film.

Yeah. Go figure. The only man who'd been interested in her in one hell of a long dry spell probably had more contact with the cops than she did.

As if the gearshift was made of eggshells, Darken put the truck in park, deliberately turning back the ignition to kill the engine, his held breath making his chest look even bigger.

In the cold blanket of a silent winter night, the engine ticked out the last of its heat. With a large fist, Darken clutched the steering wheel, as if the truck would take off like a spooked horse.

"I'm sorry," he grated out. "You weren't supposed...I didn't want you...*fuck.*" He let go of the wheel to rake his blonde hair. "Sorry. I shouldn't swear in front of a lady. I didn't mean I didn't want you. Because *you are* a lady. What I meant was I didn't mean to...what I'm saying is..."

If she let her guard down in the face of all his babbling, she'd tell him it was all right. She'd tell him what she saw didn't matter, that the incident back at the restaurant wasn't his fault. He'd shown her nothing but gentleness, his shy wit...

But she couldn't. She wasn't an idiot and hadn't spent so much time with battered women not to see the signs in spite of his kind attentions.

There was something about her date he wasn't telling her. Something big, and most definitely brutal.

She would not be one of her own clients.

Stammering, she said, "I'm sorry, Darken. I can't." Like a chicken grateful she'd been spared the ax, but confused as to why, she got out of the truck, her emotions in tumult. She wanted to stay, but needed to go. She wanted to get back in that truck and tell the man it was okay, that she understood sometimes things were beyond one's control.

But she wouldn't.

Instead, she heeded her years of watching women lay in hospital beds, their eyes lifeless or flicking with fear.

She would not be one of those women.

As she walked away, invisible strings tugged on her like hundreds of bungee cords. She pressed the fob to release the locks on her car and folded herself into the refrigerated interior, where the cold she felt wasn't in a battered body or broken bones, but in her heart.

Darken waited for her to start her engine and back out.

So considerate…

Before she caved, she pressed her foot to the accelerator. Stretching those tugging ties until they snapped.

Chapter Seven

Not even the sight of the setting sun eased Darken's fury. He'd spent the day frozen in place, his emotions torturing him because he couldn't do a damned thing about them. Not then, when he couldn't move, and not now, while the blood began to sluice through his veins, enlivening him.

He was fucking doomed like the rest of his brethren, even if he would feel better by beating the living snot out of Godrick.

Merrick's salvation had been a fluke, a weak moment in the Almighty's master plan to royally screw the Kynd.

The proof in his logic? Godrick, the blood-leeching son-of-a-bitch, shoving his nose where it didn't belong.

Oh, Darken knew why the Vampyre had shown up at the restaurant. He'd been worried that the gargoyle, one of the royally fucked Kynd, was going to blow the Others' cover in a public place and hurt a human.

He was worried the nearly Grotesque gargoyle was going to come unwrapped.

I could punch a third eye hole into his skull...

Yes, his going out with the human woman had been a gamble. Hell, they'd all known it. The night before, like the Brady Bunch, his brothers had gathered in the frigging kitchen to shower him with their support, to offer their help.

Angelia had shown them how to make toast, for fuck's sake.

Toast.

A comforting worm of humor wriggling into his thoughts, Darken recalled how they'd gathered in the kitchen. A cavernous room lined with black granite countertops and warm-wooded cabinets, the vaulted and crowned molded ceiling above them.

Six huge, bungling men had perched expectantly around one very considerate woman. A ring of nervous and protective muscle surrounding a bright flame.

Like stray puppies at the pound they'd hung on Angelia's every word, fed off her calming energy as they'd teased each other. Empty, plastic sleeves around them, they'd burnt too many slices of bread, slathering on sticky peanut butter and slimy jam.

All of them proud of their accomplishments in their own grumbling, begrudging way. Even Drakus.

They were looking out for each other, as the Kynd had always done before they were divinely rent apart. Godrick had no right to interfere with that.

The Triumvirate and what they had at stake be damned. Like they all were.

They were so pathetic, hoping to assimilate themselves into normal society, as if neither of them had endured two thousand years worth of torture in their own private hells.

A knock on his door wrenched his thoughts out of his ass. He sniffed. *Angelia.*

"Just a second." Darken snagged a clean shirt before letting his brotherkynd's life-mate into his suite. He opened the door to a girl-next-door-beautiful woman, who wore faded jeans and a green silk top with so many wraps and ties Ernő Rubick wouldn't figure out how to put in on.

"Hi," she said, walking into the room with the ease of a dear friend. "Thought I'd come up to see how you're doing, since Godrick can really be a turd."

Well, he had to say this for Angelia, she didn't beat around the bush.

"Trust me, I know." And she knew what to say to make a guy feel better. He meant that without the slightest hint of sarcasm. She walked into his room without fear because she was utterly, and undoubtedly, a woman he loved like his brotherkynd. A...sister. Hopefully, the first of many.

"Yeah, I guess you would." She was also a human who'd grown up in the realm of the vampire. Her adopted father was one of the three ancient Vampyres who made up the ruling Triumvirate. The woman knew what she was talking about.

"Between him, Kristov, and my father? Godrick's definitely the one with his panties in a knot."

"Great image. Thanks."

"Anything to help." She smirked as she reached for his hand, pulling him down onto the edge of his bed to sit with her. Which was one of the things that was so great about Merrick's Chosen One. She got the whole touching thing; that the Kynd needed it like they needed air to breathe. And she wasn't skeeved out by that.

"You want to tell me how it went?"

"No."

So they sat there on the bed, his large knuckled hand clasped in her slender one, while the stars blinked on, proclaiming the end of another day.

"I like your t-shirt today."

"What?" He hadn't looked when he'd pulled it on. *Never make eye contact when you're eating a banana.* "Aw, shit. Sorry." He had his fingers rolled around the neck to drag it off over his head when she stopped him.

"Don't. It's funny. The guys will love it, like they do all your shirts."

"Yeah?"

"Mm-huh." They went back to just sitting on the bed, but Darken shifted a little closer now that they weren't holding hands.

"Daniela, that's her name. She collects funny t-shirts, too." It was out before he could stop it, then realized he didn't want to. He wanted to talk about the woman, even though doing it made his cheeky t-shirt feel too small on his body.

"Of all the women in the universe, this one has a sick humor just like you. Go figure."

Yeah, go figure. Freaking Angelia. "You think she's my Chosen One?"

"Don't you?"

"Shit. Yeah, I do."

"Then why are you sitting on your bed with me when you should be out with her?" she teased, bumping her shoulder to his.

"Because Godrick showed up and tried to glamour her."

A knowing nod and the teasing laid to rest. "And you got pissed. As you should have."

"Damn straight."

"Damn straight, cowboy. So, why are you still sitting here and letting Godrick win?" Her shining smile reminded him of why Merrick had fallen for his Angel.

"You're a piece of work, you know that."

"That's what Merrick says. But, when you're right…" She shrugged, bumping shoulders with him once again.

"You think I should try to approach her? After she got scared?"

"I do. I think if she's your Chosen, what happened last night can be got over. Just go and be yourself. Heck, if she's half as crazy with the cynicism as you are, the two of you should do just fine."

"A prediction?"

Her smile was warm. "From the heart, not the Scriptum. I still haven't found anything, but the name helps. Did you get her last name?"

"Salvai."

Angelia tucked in her chin, her eyes widening. "You're kidding right? *To save.* Her name means God's judgment to save? My God, Darken, what're the chances? Go get her, stupid!" She shoved him, lifting his heavy ass off the bed. "Go on! Go fight for your woman."

He gave her a withering stare.

"All right. Wrong choice of words, but you know what I mean."

Darken didn't wait for more of this sister's advice. She was right. Daniela probably was his Chosen, and he'd be damned if he'd let Godrick interfere with his fate. Grabbing his keys and coat, he bolted from the room, then hightailed it back to give Angelia a quick hug, lifting her off her feet.

Her laughter was a song on his heart. "Go on, fool. And change your t-shirt," she shouted after him.

But he was already halfway down the stairs.

* * * *

Daniela had spent the better part of the day at the hospital, now she just wanted to soak in her tub with a glass of wine, and forget the past twenty-four hours.

The latest victim she'd talked with had related her story in a voice too wet with tears, squeezing Daniela's heart until she thought the damned thing would suffocate.

In spite of the sobbing and the bruises, the woman would go back to the man who'd done such damage to her. She knew that as sure as she knew her hot water heater carried only enough in its tank to fill her tub three-quarters full.

Didn't matter, though. With displacement, her naked body would be submerged in the hot fluid, and that's all she needed.

Aside from the sweaty bottle of Chardonnay within arm's reach of the tub, of course.

Daniela intended to drown both her aches.

With her knees protruding from the steamy water like twin volcanic islands in the South Pacific, she let more thoughts nibble on the tails of the ones before them, until she wound around to her failed date the night before with Darken.

Darken. What kind of name was that, anyway? What mother named her infant after something you'd see in a *Star Wars* movie? The poor bastard. She imagined what it was like for him growing up, getting teased by the other kids.

But she couldn't picture it. Not him as a little kid, and certainly not him getting teased. There was something primordial about the man, something that warned the average person not to fuck with him.

He'd *growled,* for ever-loving sake.

What normal person could even do that?

More importantly, why didn't it bother her as much as she knew it should?

Because she'd let her guard down and he'd nestled right in, like it was the most natural thing in the world for him to have his bulk curved protectively around her.

She'd *liked* it. He'd made her feel delicate, feminine. *Sexy.*

And that was something, considering the size of her. On good days, she liked to think of herself as Rubenesque.

Darken had coaxed that out of her without even trying.

All he'd had to do was feast on her with those strange gray eyes of his, and she'd morphed into a vamp, complete with batting eyelashes and a coy smile.

Buoyant in the tub, she looked down the length of herself.

Well, no rose-colored glasses for her tonight. She was back to being Shamu.

A getting drunk Shamu that is.

The bottle of wine beside her sweated out the last two inches left in its bottom.

She was reaching for the slippery neck when her doorbell rang, followed by an insistent pounding, like whoever was on her doorstep had little faith in pressing a fingerprint-sized button stuck to the doorframe.

With her arm halted mid-stretch and dripping, she thought of who it could be.

Her doorbell chimed again, followed by the rapping. Whoever it was had a fist like a battering ram.

Daniela sat up on her knees, the bathwater sloshing, threatening to escape the rim of the tub.

Darken.

He had fists like battering rams, and in a rush, the memories of him standing so tall and immovable in the restaurant flooded into her head. As if her brain was a basin and someone had opened the gates of the dam above it.

Her heart thumped madly, skyrocketing her blood pressure, along with the wine in her bloodstream.

She wasn't scared that he'd found her house. More like…excited.

Which was wrong. *Wrong, wrong, wrong.*

Like a PTA mom at a carwash fundraiser, she buffed her body dry, hurrying to get to the front door before the man gave up and left.

In the span of thirty seconds, she called herself an idiot half a million times.

She should not answer the door.

It probably wasn't even him.

Breathless and wrapped in a fluffy towel, her hand poised on the door handle, she came to her senses. What in tarnation was she doing? Standing on her front porch was danger, with a capital D.

D for Darken, her rebellious thoughts chimed in, yanking the rug from under the feet of her good judgment.

"Who is it?" Like she didn't know. Daniela leaned ear-first toward the door.

"It's Darken, Daniela." Despite her anticipation, she still sucked in her breath, her spine going straight as the deep gravel of his voice scraped through her. "I know. I'm at your front door when I shouldn't be. But, I had to see you, apologize for last night. Explain things."

There was a pause on the other side of her door, and in the silence she felt her heart thumping steady and realized her lips were curled in a happy grin.

Shame on me. She was going to be one of her own clients if she kept this up. Because the man was right. He shouldn't be at her house.

As though he knew she was hovering on the other side of the door, her unexpected visitor lowered his voice, which did nothing to ease the delicious drag of it through her belly.

"I followed you home from the hospital—I know, that's not good. You'd be smart not to let me in. Hell, I wouldn't let me in. I've been sitting in my truck arguing with myself about that. I should have driven away. I shouldn't have followed you. So, really, I can't blame you for not letting me in. But, could you meet me somewhere else? In public, if you want. If you'd feel safer?"

God, the man could ramble. Which made her think of last night, when his tongue had tripped all over itself as he'd tried explaining himself in the truck.

Riding on the heels of that thought, she realized without the heavy plank of wood between them, their faces would be inches apart. She'd be looking into those mercurial gray eyes, and damned if she wasn't transported north, back to the Bering Sea.

Only this time she imagined the steel gray of the rolling swells, a quiet day with seagulls cartwheeling like brilliant white kites in the somber sky above.

God, she'd had too much to drink. The wine was turning her into a sappy poet.

One without a lick of common sense. Because her fingertips were now pressed against the door, as though it was his face, the wood becoming his cheek they were touching with reverence.

She was drawn to this guy like metal flakes to a magnet.

"Yeah," she said, her voice a scratchy whisper, like they were lovers in a darkened room. She felt his silence, his expectancy. "I'd like that. To see you again."

Her insides grew tight, filling her, and her grin stretched farther into her warming cheeks.

"Christ, yes," was the response breathed on the other side of the door. "Tell me where. When."

So thick was his relief, she felt it through the wooden barrier. "Lunch. At Alfio's?"

Silence. She waited a heartbeat. Two. Three.

"I can't."

Was it normal to be so disappointed? If not for the fact he'd plastered himself—just like her—to the opposite side of the door, Daniela wouldn't have been able to ignore the rushing back of her insecurities.

Mentally, she pfft a raspberry at them. "Dinner, then?"

"Absolutely." He didn't even hesitate, so double pfft to her insecurities.

God, I'm drunk.

"Tomorrow night. I'll pick you up?"

Daniela nodded, then realized he couldn't see it. "Okay. That'd be good." He couldn't see her sloppy grin either.

"Seven o'clock." He didn't ask, but she heard the excitement in his deep voice. He wasn't being bossy, just eager, and that made her happy, like hearing the silly slap of ducks' feet.

Because it wasn't often a man got anxious for her. Hell, it was pretty much never. Never like this, anyway. "I won't be late."

No, she didn't think he would be. She heard his heavy boots clunk down her porch steps, but they sounded light despite his heft. Maybe he was dancing like Fred Astaire?

Maybe she should put the cork back in the wine bottle.

But before she did, Daniela peered out from behind the drapes of her living room window as that gorgeous man, who'd just asked her out again, slid into the cab of his truck and pulled away, the exhaust pipe trailing steam in the red glow of its taillights.

Chapter Eight

An hour after sunset, Darken was lacing on his boots while Urick sat on his sofa watching him like a starving man steaming up the glass of a café window. The bear wanted a taste of the tantalizing pie—but couldn't get in through the door.

Which sucked the anticipation right out of Darken's upcoming date. How could he look forward to his second chance when Uri couldn't even have the first?

Cupping the ends of the armrests so he sat like the monument of Abraham Lincoln, Darken leaned back in his chair, the weight of the world sitting on his lap. *Shit.* How could he go out tonight, maybe really enjoy himself, when Uri would be perched on a frozen window ledge, helplessly peering in on the life, and the woman, he couldn't have.

Rousting himself from his chair, he resettled himself on the sofa next to the chimera, their outer thighs touching. Their size difference obvious in the way Urick's knee stuck out farther and higher than Darken's.

Leaning back on a sigh, he pulled the larger Kynd into his embrace, one elbow jutting toward the ceiling as he tugged Uri closer.

His lids sliding closed, he thought of the many centuries he'd gone without this contact. Now he savored the warm, heavy bulk of the larger man on his chest, those thick shoulders shoved up under his chin. Even though they pushed his face toward the ceiling.

"You know, we've got this backward. You should be holding me. I'd fit better in your arms than you do mine." His grin faded, and with it came the swell of sadness he'd tried to stave off.

Squeezing the man he held, he sat quietly, sharing the burden of the bear's sorrow, of his frustrated rage. Somewhere in a normal world, people

69

were sharing laughter, or sitting down to dinners with their families.

As they'd done for millennia. While the Kynd had festered and succumbed to their loneliness.

Darken knew it was his own fault Uri suffered not only from his rage but from bloodlust. After all, he had been the one to call them together, had asked the others to abandon their God decreed punishments in the name of the Kynd.

He owed the man a moment of peace.

No matter if God had forgiven them. *Somewhat.*

They weren't exactly rocking it back in Heaven, now were they? And to kick a stray dog, Uri suffered with his earthly needs. The man needed blood, something he'd never required before being ousted from the sanctity of God's elite realm, or before choosing to rejoin his brethren.

Fuck. Darken couldn't imagine it. But as attached as he was to his brotherkynd, he could feel it. And right now, it was eating a hole through the bear the size of Switzerland.

Scampering off to his date like a happy ending to a fairy tale tasted like rot in his mouth.

And weighed heavy on his torn heart.

His gaze drifted to his bare wrist, to the veins running like a map of thin blue rivers just under his skin. He didn't have to press his fingertips to the steady throb to know it thumped perfectly to the pulse of the chimera he held in his arms.

With a steadying breath, he peered down over his cheekbones to gaze at his boots, which he'd propped up onto the coffee table in front of him.

Big. Sturdy. Just like the rest of him.

Surely, he could hold his own against the bear if shit careened downhill.

"Uri."

"No." The bear's voice vibrated against his chest, the warmth of the man seeping through his shirt and deep into his skin.

"Christ, you don't even know what I'm going to say."

"Yeah, I do. And I told you *no.*" The chimera pulled out of the embrace to stand up, towering to his full height like a bear, his gray eyes underlined with the crescent moons of twin bruises. Even haggard as he was, the guy was a frigging tank.

"Why not? You don't think I'd taste good?" Darken cajoled, but hell, realistically he didn't have much in his arsenal to convince the guy to use him.

Except determination. He'd meant what he offered.

Two long, thick fangs descended passed the chimera's top lip as his pupils blew wide open, swallowing the gray with a fathomless black.

Vampire.

Darken shrugged. "Ooh, you're a scary S.O.B., I'll give you that," he challenged, pulling his top lip off his set of ever-present fangs. Not anywhere near as long as the bear's, but they'd do the job.

Bending his elbow, he sank his shorter choppers into his inner wrist, the puncture of his skin popping as though he bit into an apple. His blood, freed from its track, bubbled against his lips, the blue rivers now a red rivulet coursing thick down the skin of his inner forearm.

Holding both his arms out from his sitting body, he all but dared the other Kynd to bring it on.

"You son of a bitch." Urick growled, trembling. His eyes flashing from black to gray to black again.

Darken braced himself. "Take it, Uri. *Please.*" He could see the vampire's need in his taut features, the flaring of his nostrils as he inhaled the scent of life. Traces of fur thickened at the man's jawline.

The bear wanted out, too. "You *lousy* son of a bitch." The insult was more snarl than actual voice, but Darken didn't need cue cards to get the message. Uri glared murder as he shivered with starvation.

"Do it. We'll be fine." He sounded every bit as confident as he'd hoped he would, but bluffing against the bear chimera taxed his bullshit skills.

Small price, given the sacrifice he'd asked of his brotherkynd. Uri had left his God-decreed punishment the moment he'd heard Darken's call. The least he could offer him was a pint of blood.

Like a friendly neighborhood blood drive with the Red Cross.

Who was he kidding? He was going to get mauled if Uri couldn't cage the beast.

Meh. So he'd give a pound of flesh, too.

As if he were covered in his pelt, Uri shook his entire bulk. Then, he tilted his head from one side to the other, like a boxer getting ready to bounce into the center of the ring.

Clear as the starting bell, he warned, "Do that again, and I swear I'll rip your arm from your shoulder." The face glaring at him housed gray eyes and a relatively fangless mouth.

Damn, but the chimera had more inner strength in his left nut than Darken would ever possess.

Still, he goaded. "Not hungry, huh?"

The brutal look he got made him feel every bit the asshole.

"I'm sorry, bear. *Christ*, I just wanted—"

"I know what you meant to do." Gripping the front of his button down, Urick tore it off his thickly muscled torso. "Clean yourself up. You've got a date in an hour."

The tossed rag hit the center of Darken's chest before dropping into his lap.

Uri pointed a clawed finger. "I want details when you get back. Just like a girly sleepover."

Darken just stared up, too damned sad to laugh. Only half his smile made it to his face as he watched the other Kynd pivot, lumber out of the room, then shut the door with a soft click.

Truly, that man possessed a strength he couldn't even touch.

To be saddled with the horror of a hunger so strong you might not control it? To know if you couldn't you'd kill someone, most likely someone you cared about?

Damn him. He never should have offered his blood to the bear. He only wound up torturing the guy. And awakening both beasts.

But those beasts needed nourishment, before Uri lost control of both. Maybe Kristov hadn't been blowing smoke up his ass. Maybe the Vampyre understood and had asked after Uri, not out of worry for the general public, but with concern for his brother.

With his dead heart, sucker?

Maybe. The Vampyre did lead thousands, had brought the lesser vampires to a peace none had known before.

Worth a try. Darken gripped his fist around the puncture wounds on his forearm to staunch the bleeding. By the next night, the bite marks would be gone, leaving no trace of a scar.

On the outside, anyway.

Meanwhile, he had to act stable as hell for Daniela in less than an hour.

And the clock kept ticking.

* * * *

Urick walked back to his room like his surroundings were made of glass—easily demolished. And for him, they would be. His bear itched like gangbusters to leave his incensed trace for all to see. Which translated into slashing his six-inch claws through walls or throwing furniture across the room.

Something he'd not done for almost two months.

He had Darken to thank for this tantrum. And a tantrum it was. The bear wanted the bloody flesh denied him. The vampire wanted the blood.

Badly.

The scent of it still clung to the insides of his nostrils, so every breath became a torture.

His thick chest squeezed, his breaths coming in short gasps. Urick halted in the corridor to grip onto something—he didn't care what, so long as it was heavy enough to keep him grounded.

Because lately when the hunger for blood hit him like a body blow, he was teleporting, winding up in places too fucked up to deal with. No thanks to God, but he was glad none of his brothers had yet to witness it.

Walking out of the frigging hall closet wasn't funny. Teleporting left him disoriented and scared as hell. He never knew where he was going to wind up.

So far, his brief disappearances kept him within the walls of the safe house, which wasn't reassuring. It kept him too close to those he really cared about when he needed to have a locked and sturdy door between them.

Because he only relocated when he couldn't get his fucking hunger under control.

Like now.

A tingling at the base of his skull struck fear that clutched his guts, and his breath came in hard pants. His glances around the wide hallway grew frantic. There wasn't much for him to latch onto here, nothing heavy to keep his ass right where it was.

What if he teleported to the vulnerable Angelia?

Fuck, fuck, fuck. As if his fear melted the bones in his legs, he dropped to his hands and knees, bellowing his terror like the bear he was. He was almost crying, his dread for hurting those he cared about overwhelming him.

He was still bellowing when he suddenly found himself in his own room, and he clapped his jaws shut the instant he recognized the familiar surroundings.

Thank Jesus.

He was still on all fours, his chest heaving, and his heart pounding so hard against his breastbone it hurt. Sweat dripped off him like he'd stepped into the shower then abruptly changed his mind.

Collapsing onto his back, he clasped his hands to his face. How much more of this could he handle? Denying his hunger was killing him. More to the point, since he was damned near immortal, rejecting his natural urges was going to get someone else killed.

He should beg God for forgiveness; ask to be returned to his other living hell. At least there, he hadn't needed to surrender to his baser selves, the hunger hadn't clawed at him like a living thing.

The Kynd in him refused to partake of flesh, in blood form or not.

Yet, since rejoining the Kynd, his hunger chewed at his guts, twisting them so he had to curl around himself like an abandoned fetus.

Mewling. He hated himself in these moments, when his helpless tears dribbled down his cheeks. He didn't even get relief during the day. Instead, he suffered all the agony of his hungers, but did it silently and precisely frozen.

Was he Grotesque? Absolutely. But he wasn't lucky enough to remain that way. Every sunset brought mobility, and that translated into his continued nightmare. At least as stone, he stayed put and couldn't harm anyone.

Returned to flesh? He was death waiting for the one drop of blood that would prove too much, that would unleash the starved beasts he barely strangled.

God help me. Maybe he should have taken Darken up on his offer. At least the gargoyle might stand a fighting chance against the bear. Hell, he'd proven he could take the thrashing when they'd been reunited after their millennia-long separation.

But the bear along with the vampire? He didn't have the stomach to find out. Instead, he got his big-ass feet under his wobbly knees long enough to stumble to his bed.

Pathetic, that's what he was. Cowardly, too, because he didn't want to succumb to his lust for blood. He was too afraid it would render him unfit to claim his Chosen One if they were ever to meet.

And that would be most devastating of all. He had gambled his life for his brotherkynd and had been rewarded with hope.

To be unburdened by his fate of becoming permanently grotesque? He kept his claws pierced into that precious emotion lest he lose it. Hope was all he had, the only thing allowing him the strength to fight his hungers.

Every night he sat on that freezing window ledge, hoping to catch a glimpse of the one being who filled him with something akin to peace. She was his salvation. For her he fought his urges to become un-Kynd.

He just had to figure out how to get near her without a wall of glass between them.

Please, God, let it be soon. Because he didn't think he could keep up the charade of getting better much longer, not when he was now teleporting. He was growing more dangerous by the day.

Pathetic. He was begging like the coward he was, waiting for the night he'd be strong enough to grasp what could be rightfully his. But if this woman he watched wasn't his Chosen One and he mauled an Innocent?

"Fuck me," he growled, heaving his heavy frame off the frigging edge of his bed. He needed action, not to be sitting alone in his room twiddling with his pitiful thoughts. Grabbing another shirt, he slipped it on as he left his room.

He'd talk with Merrick and Angelia again about the trip back into Hell. The Scriptum had hinted at a way they could sneak in and out of the Second Circle to rescue a Shade, but if they wound up having to fight Minos during this mission, so much the better. A lot of fighting would feel good, and if he was lucky, maybe he'd actually get killed doing it.

Chapter Nine

At exactly seven o'clock, Darken pulled up to the curb at Daniela's house. The dirty spray from passing cars had frozen in the head of the pathway, making the walk treacherous for someone not geared up for it.

Someone like his Daniela, who could slip and hurt herself.

At the thought, his breath lodged under his sternum. His Chosen One injured? Not on his watch, if he could help it.

And help it he would. He had himself reined in so tight he was hurting himself.

Which was fine by him, just so long as he wasn't hurting anyone else.

His finger poised to push the doorbell, he lost himself to staring at his claw. Christ on the cross, he better not loosen a single stitch of his control. Sure, Daniela had seen his claws already, had even seemed to accept them.

But not because she knew what they really were.

Exactly the problem. Somehow, he had to explain things without revealing too much, without scaring the living bejesus out of her.

He poked the damned bell, his heart thudding hard and fast in his chest.

Inside, he could hear Daniela rushing from one room to the next. "Be there in a sec!" Her voice washed like a caress over him, and he shut his eyes to savor it—and to will the twitching of his cock to cease.

The sensation ungrounded him. It was too foreign, too electric. It robbed him of his determination to talk, to explain things with words. Instead, it demanded attention, so he wanted to rub himself all over the woman, coating himself with her scent.

Yeah, as a Kynd he communicated a lot through touch, but this…?

Darken worked his hips, pushing the heel of his hand against the pressure behind his zipper. He didn't need this distraction. He had enough to deal with, and grappling with his newly aroused dick wasn't a burden he needed.

Nor were the other alien but persistent urges it bombarded him with.

How in hell did his goddamned cock know to covet the feel of the woman's hot sheathe gripped around it? He was a bloody virgin, he knew less than nothing about pleasuring a woman—

The door swung inward and there she stood.

His jaw dropped open.

Daniela's arched eyebrow clapped his mouth shut. "Ah, sorry." A sheepish grin erupted on his lips, burning his cheeks like a blowtorch.

She was standing before him like a gratified goddess, her dark eyes shining with pleasure. For reasons he scrambled to understand, she liked how flustered he was. As though she could read and appreciate where his thoughts had led him.

He'd have to trust his Kynd instincts on that one. Virgin he might be, but he was adept at gleaning information and piecing it together in a flash.

This woman standing in the doorway could be pleasured by his touch.

He crammed the lid on his exultation.

Casual. He couldn't be acting like a horny moron, not with so much at stake. "Hi." He reached to cup her hand in his, to pull her closer. To touch her.

She came willingly enough, but then pulled her hand away to turn back toward the door.

Panic erupted in his breast. *She shuns me? Retreats into the safety of her home?*

Again, his jaw fell open.

She pulled the front door shut then turned back around, her keys jingling as she slipped them into her purse. Eyebrows waggling, she said, "Locked door. Keeps out the burglars."

His knees made a crazy wobble.

Too stunned, he offered his arm, and she slid hers through the inside of his elbow, accepting his escort down the slippery walkway to his truck.

"So, where are we going this time? Alfio's again?"

"I don't know. I was going to leave that up to you," he admitted without looking at her. He knew if he did, he'd have her swept off her feet and crushed to him for all he was worth.

"Want to make me toast?" She halted a few feet from the truck, forcing him to turn and face her. Her brown eyes still glittered with satisfaction.

"Yeah," he gushed as his lungs lost their air. "I'd like that." She'd know just how much when he started explaining who and what he was. And why Godrick had seen fit to materialize at the restaurant.

"All righty, then." She swung their hands. "Let's head back up those steps and get inside where it's warm."

He couldn't believe his luck, but he followed her like a stray dog wanting a home.

* * * *

Daniela was going against everything she'd learned about playing it safe.

Inviting a strange man into her house was a cardinal *don't*. Except the moment she'd swung her front door open and saw the man standing on the other side of the threshold, he'd felt like no stranger.

Her heart did a rat-a-tat-thump and then swelled to fill her to bursting. No way on God's green earth she could have mistaken his thoughts, which made her feel so dang pretty her heart did the happy dance. Toe-tapping her caution to the proverbial curb.

He really did think she was beautiful. Which, of course, shouldn't have rendered her dumb. *Which I'm not,* she quickly reminded herself. It's just that he felt right, and she couldn't explain it to herself any better than that at the moment.

Besides, right then he was standing inside her front door as though he was afraid to step away from it. He still wore his coat, for goodness sake. "Make yourself at home," she invited, shedding her own heavy jacket.

Halfway to the kitchen, she noticed he hadn't moved.

"Darken?"

"Yeah?" His gaze lifting from the floor to hers, his voice scraped a tender spot inside of her.

"You going to take off your coat and stay awhile?"

That sheepish grin returned, erasing his fixation with his boots.

"Good." She gave him two thumbs up instead of wrapping her arms around him like she wanted to. Gads, but he was handsome.

It wasn't so much that either, as the look in those gray eyes whenever he beheld her. He looked at her so covetously, as though he couldn't believe his incredible good fortune. It made a lady feel right beautiful, and she didn't think a woman could ever tire of that.

Then he took off his coat, and Daniela scrapped her noble thinking. The man was eye candy, no matter what she wanted to believe about his gaze on her. Having a man with that much chiseled muscle take her in his arms? Well, she'd feel freaking *dainty.*

This time he was wearing a short-sleeved t-shirt. Black, like his jeans that rode low on his hips. His boots were black, too, and the whole dark ensemble enhanced the lean cut of his big body, of his sea-colored eyes.

Daniela was going to be sporting her own sheepish grin if she didn't watch it. "So, white wine or red to go with your toast?" She headed for her kitchen, hoping the bar with the hefty stools would be a strong enough barrier to keep her body to herself.

"Red. Please." He followed her, the bulk of him filling what she'd always thought to be a good sized kitchen. The closeness augmented the width of his shoulders, the smooth humps of his biceps.

Stuffing a stray lock of hair behind her ear, she preoccupied herself with getting them stemware. "Here," she handed him the bottle and corkscrew. "Make yourself useful." She winked so he wouldn't think her bossy, but watched his big hands wrap around the bottle.

Frowning, her gaze flicked upward.

Darken fell utterly still, his attention riveted to a spot on her floor near the sink. Like he was poised for the lash of her criticism.

Because now that she was seeing his hands up close and with better lighting, she could see they weren't mutilated by some injury or birth defect. Those were claws at his fingertips. Sharp, slightly curled, and a little pearlescent.

Daniela took a step back before she could stop herself.

When he sighed, his entire body softened, as though caving in on itself.

Darken met her confused stare with...resignation. Then expectation shrouded in silence.

Giving her a minute to sort this out.

People didn't have claws. Wolves and tigers did, but not human beings.

"Unless you're not—" Daniela slammed her mouth shut before she voiced such an outlandish thought.

"A person?" he finished for her.

Breathless, she said, "That wasn't what I was going to say."

She was going to say *human.* Saying he wasn't a person was, well, just not true. Of course, he was a person. He was standing in her kitchen, talking. He drove a truck. The man wasn't a circus bear performing tricks.

He didn't answer her. But he watched her very closely now, no longer pretending not to focus on her reaction.

"Truth?" She gave him a weak grin. "I was going to say you're not human."

His voice came out a strained whisper. "You would be right." His odd gray eyes searched hers.

Daniela shook her head. "That can't be."

Very slowly he placed the wine bottle and corkscrew on the counter, then turned, holding his hands toward her, palms down. "You can look closer if you like." He was as cautious as a deer entering a field during hunting season, giving her courage to inspect what he offered.

As their hands came together, she felt the roughness of his palms, his calluses catching on her fingertips. When his warmth enveloped her skin like a mitten, a light tremor ran through him.

Without looking up at him, she drew her fingers around one of his, tracing the curve of a claw, running the pad of her thumb across the razor sharp point.

She glanced up at him, still delicately pinching the claw between her fingertips. "These are strong."

He nodded, his eyes holding hers.

Daniela's heart quickened as she lifted his finger to her lips, pressing a kiss to his knuckle.

Darken shuddered at the contact. Lashes dropped to conceal the surrender in his gray eyes. As she caressed her cheek to his fingers, his claws curled inward so he wouldn't cut her.

"Daniela." His fingers squeezed hers.

"Shhh. What else?"

"Holy Christ."

At his plea, she stepped into him, his scent filling her. She was no bloodhound, but she recognized something masculine when she smelled it.

Darken exuded something rich and spicy.

Tenderly he removed his hand from hers to draw her closer, his strong arms pulling her to the wall of his chest, where his sheer size encapsulated her.

Feeling a little disoriented, she repeated, "What else?"

Giving her another squeeze, he stepped back, stiff arming her so there would be a little distance between them. He did not let her go, but held her gently by her upper arms.

After a deep breath, he lowered his head as if to kiss her.

Surprising herself, she leaned into him, tilting her chin.

But he didn't claim her lips in a kiss. Instead, he inhaled as he nuzzled her neck, his tongue sliding a wet path, sending ripples to her core.

She stilled as she registered first the tenuous pricking of teeth to her skin, then the more assured pressing of the sharp ridges as his tongue laved away the startling ache of his bite.

Her body responded by arching toward the wall of this man whose warm breath inflamed her pulse. "Vampire?" The word rode on the hitch of her breath as her head tilted farther back, inviting him to touch more of her with that sensual mouth of his.

He responded with a growl as his hands cupped her ass to pull her tighter against him. "Not vampire. *Kynd.*"

"Oh, you're being kind, all right." Daniela was about ready to show him some kindness herself by relieving that bulge behind his zipper.

His chuckle rumbled in her ear, sizzling straight through her to wet her panties. "Not *nice*," he moaned. "*Gargoyle.*"

"Monosyllabic sentences. Mama likes." She'd think about what he said later, when she wasn't trying to dry hump his thigh.

Tuned to her frequency, he cupped her ass harder, grinding his hips against her belly. There was a desperation to it, a hardness in his muscles as he strained to touch every part of himself to her without being overbearing.

She pressed her palm to his fly, her stomach fluttering at the size of the bulge.

Darken gasped. Just before his sharp teeth found her nape, his fist coiled in her hair.

"Easy," he murmured against her skin, but whether it was to remind himself or her, she couldn't tell. His tongue flicked out, eradicating clear thinking from her cranium.

She'd analyze all this later. When her feet were back on the floor.

Darken had lifted her like she weighed nothing, one arm supporting her ample rear, the other still pressed to her back with his fist tangled in her hair. He never moved from the center of the kitchen, but stood with his booted feet braced apart, panting against her cheek.

Daniela arched into him, pushing her full breasts toward his face, begging him to pant his hot breath on her nipples.

With a growl, he buried his face into her cleavage, and for the first time since never, Daniela rejoiced in her big breasts.

So did he. They were heading for the floor, and not because he could no longer hold her weight. Darken was growing wild, his knees giving out to the rocking of his hips against her inner thighs, so they ended up on the floor.

His thrusting begged for freedom, and Daniela was nothing if not generous. With her hand searching between the heat of her mons, she found the tip of him protruding from the waistband of his jeans.

Holy shit. He's big everywhere. Daniela closed her fist over the cap of his weeping penis.

* * * *

When Daniela's fingers brushed the head of his cock, Darken thought he might go mad with the impossible pleasure of it.

Then she closed her hand over him and his thoughts exploded along with the spasms of his hips as he pushed into her grasp.

"Dearest Christ!" he yelped, his balls constricting tight. He'd never experienced anything like this. He had no mind. He was supposed to be explaining something, convincing the human he wasn't like her, to not be afraid of his claws or his fangs.

Somehow, she'd bypassed the predicted course of reaction and was exploring parts even he didn't know existed.

He couldn't stop. He had to stop. But still his mouth sought her warm skin, her ass a lovely cushion for him to hold onto while he came unmoored, while his tongue excavated the hot flesh between her bosoms.

He wanted to lick every inch of her, but was currently preoccupied with the heated scent wafting from her cleavage. It was utterly feminine. Some blending of a delicate perfume and heady, warm-blooded animal.

She smelled of the ancient earth mother, the bestower of life.

Darken wanted to bury himself in her. Every fucking inch, and never come out.

He was going to rut like a beast if he didn't calm himself.

The problem was that every time he tried to pull back, she took over, loosening the measly hold he had on himself all over again. She was as insatiable as he was. And he gloried in it.

The slide of his zipper rang like a chorus of angels in his head. He felt the release of pressure, the cool air wrapping the heat of his shaft, the cold shock of the kitchen floor tile against the head of his dick as it dropped away under its own weight.

Instantly it recoiled, bobbing against his stomach, and he readjusted his hips so he could lay himself along Daniela's thigh. Unable to stop, he glided the velvet tenderness of it along her leg while her fingers tangled in his hair, pulling his face to the nipple trapped beneath the silk of her bra.

He pinched the nub with his teeth, exulting in his woman's tight gasp. He might have never been intimate like this with another soul, but Daniela's body instructed him on a primal level.

Every nuance of pleasure she radiated, he intuitively homed in on it. He didn't need to be Kynd to capture the subtleties.

This woman knew what pleasure was and wasn't afraid to demand it.

Nor was she afraid of him.

But she doesn't really know. He didn't know where that voice came from, but he wanted to stifle it before it whispered any more sense.

Except the voice was too right, the words too true.

She didn't know.

Daniela accepted the fact of his claws and his fangs without understanding all they represented.

Kynd. Grotesques. Condemned beasts living nightmare lives of violence and terror. The very things she lived to eradicate. How could he let her give her beautiful body and spirit to him if she didn't fully comprehend?

He couldn't.

Real pain ripped at his heart as he withdrew, pulling his hypersensitive body from her grasp. Darken sat back on his heels as he pinned his raging dick behind its zipper. Wincing while he admired the beatific image lying on the floor before him.

Daniela's sable hair was spread out behind her head, her dark eyes glittering. Her neck...*dear God*. One side of her neck, blushing pink, sported two crescents of bright red pinpricks.

Where he'd bitten her.

An accusation, illustrating his very non-human teeth.

My fangs. "Oh, fuck." Rubbing his hands across his face wound up mashing her scent deeper into his skin. His stomach clenched with need, wanting him to do that over and over—slather her scent with his own.

Daniela sat up, her face flushed, her unasked questions ripe in her beautiful eyes.

He grasped her hand, pulling her around so he could drape across her back, drawing her tight against him. Selfish of him to steal the skin privilege, but... "I'm sorry. I got away from myself." At least he could apologize for the other part.

So much for his earlier plan to touch discriminately. *Carefully.* He'd shit-canned that the instant the woman put her plush lips to his very non-human fingers. Trashed it right along with his resolve to keep himself tightly wrapped.

What a naïve idiot he was.

He hadn't comprehended nor guessed the full power of a woman.

Until now.

Darken began to grasp the monumental concept of a Chosen One.

This woman would *own* him. Body and soul.

It scared him straight. Right back into keeping a firm grip on himself...*until she knows everything she's getting into.*

And then? Well...he couldn't fantasize about that yet. Because he didn't want her hurt, the reasons why filtering in like the rays of the sun—warming him, yet turning him into frightened stone at the same time.

She was a separate, living creature. He'd never be able to protect her all the time. What was he going to do, hover over her, dispose of every sharp object, demolish others who caused her any kind of harm?

Yessiree. That was *exactly* what he wished to do.

He pulled her with him as he got to his feet, but kept her back pressed to his stomach, loving the sensation of her plush buttocks fitted against his hips, his groin. Why in hell had he ever stopped them?

He could be physically attached to this woman right now if he hadn't.

Darken squeezed his arms tighter, drawing in Daniela's scent as he did so. He shut his eyes when he felt her fingers upon his, once again examining the razor tips.

Darken held his breath.

"What does it mean? To be kind?" Her feminine voice lilted up the length of his belly.

"Kynd," he strangled out. "Capital K." He spelled out the rest for her. "We are gargoyles and chimeras."

"Hmm. I thought gargoyles were grotesque statues perched on building ledges."

Here it comes...

"We're that, too." *But trying our damnedest not to be.*

Daniela turned in his arms, facing him. There was a glint of freshness in her dark eyes, her lush lips quirked into a teasing smile. "I'd say you're doing just fine. Because if you're grotesque, then I'm Twiggy."

A grin escaped him, finding a home on his face. "I'm not exaggerating. Come dawn, I'll be stone until twilight. And believe me that is not a pretty sight."

The humor left her eyes as she grew serious. "You're not pulling my leg here, are you?"

"I wish I was. But that's the hand we were dealt, until we find our Chosen One."

She turned Sherlock Holmes, narrowing her eyes. "Like what you'd said when we met. You think I'm this Chosen One?"

Reluctantly, he nodded. He wasn't sure how much he should tell her. So far, she seemed to be accepting his bizarre news with a strong spine, but how much could she take before she sent him packing?

He had to be careful. "You might be." It was enough of an admission without outright lying to her.

Daniela's dark brow lifted. "How will you know?"

Tread lightly, Kynd. "There are a couple of ways. But it will be a while before we're sure."

Chapter Ten

Daniela wasn't sure she could believe him. Okay, she could just go with this and swallow everything Darken was telling her. Seriously, now that he wasn't hiding anything, she could see his fangs clear as day.

They could be caps. Sure, they could be. But they looked utterly fundamental, not fake at all. Just like his eyes. He wasn't wearing contacts either. She'd peered close enough to check that out, too. The fluctuating gray was their true color.

Darken's large hand caressed a path down her back to cup her ass, and her cheeks warmed. She glanced downward, feeling suddenly shy. Yeah, they'd been heavily groping each other on her kitchen floor a few minutes ago, but this was different.

The face to face Q and A seemed more intimate somehow.

And the gorgeous man holding her was fondling her big butt like he couldn't get enough of it. She couldn't help but smile thinking about that. He really didn't seem to mind her extra padding, not if the way he kept squeezing her was any indication.

Besides, he might be looking wary as hell, but she couldn't miss the slow dropping of his lids every time his fingers gripped her flesh. Like he savored the squish.

"All right. Okay." She put her hands flat to his chest, internally fighting like a wildcat not to squeeze, too. Dang! But his pecs were meant for playing with....

"So, say it's true you're a gargoyle—"

"Which it is."

"*If* it's true you're a gargoyle, prove it. Show me something I can't explain away. Turn to stone, or something."

"I won't turn to stone for another..." Darken gazed up like she had a clock on her ceiling. "...about another ten hours. It's winter. We get extra time."

"Convenient." She didn't mean that the days were shorter.

"Lucky," he retorted, ignoring her accusation.

Daniela narrowed her eyes at him, but her grin itched to the surface. "You're too cute to argue with."

He looked utterly baffled.

"Come on," she playfully smacked his hard chest. "You know you're cute. I bet women have been tripping all over themselves to get to you since you hit puberty."

"No. We're shunned. We don't mix with the Others because they're afraid of what we might do. So, they ridicule us instead, which feeds the Grotesque curse and proves their point."

She didn't quite get all he said, but she caught the gist. "That's not right."

"Glad you think so." His eyes grew warm as he looked at her, the gray softening, reminding her of the pearl drops of a rainy day. *Falling...falling...*

"So," she sucked in a much needed breath. "Now that I know why you're a hermit, how about I make us dinner? We'll start with the wine that never got opened." She started to pull away, but for a brief moment, she felt the unyielding strength of his arms before he released her.

Darken took a deep breath, too, his chest stretching his t-shirt tight, then moved to get the wine bottle he'd laid on the counter before they'd done their bronc riding on her floor. Like she needed to feed the heat rising in her, she watched his backside.

Oh, hell yea. Mama liked. Thick, wide shoulders, narrowing waist, and high, tight ass. *Equals...delicious.* Who needed food from the refrigerator when she could feast on that?

"Darken, whatever you do, don't move."

His spine went straight, and she could just see a peek of his firm jaw as he tilted his head to listen behind him. Despite her grin, she kept her voice very serious, deepening the tone of it to make it sound authoritative.

"Move very slow, but I need you to put both of your hands on top of your head." Oh, this was fun. He was going to flex those muscles of his.

She leaned back against the counter to get a better view.

Darken's shoulders lifted, the muscles bunching as he raised his hands. Who needed shoulder pads? This man was a frigging brick shit-house.

"Okay." Daniela's smile sprung wide. "Very slowly now, reach down and touch your toes." He was just starting to bend at the waist when he caught on. Quicker than any cat, he turned and leapt across her kitchen to snag her up into his arms.

She yelped, her laughter ringing.

Darken's sharp grin was devilishly wolfish, and she had to admit she was turned on by that feral look.

"Minx," he growled, his gray eyes merry. She could see herself reflected in their shine.

"Just testing the waters."

"Did I sink, or swim?"

"Worried?"

"I am if you're the prize for winning." He lost a little of his smile, as though he were thinking of the possibility of losing. Daniela's humor dampened with his.

"Darken."

He focused on her.

"I like you. Strangeness and all. I'd like it if we kept seeing each other."

His wolfish grin returned. "So I swim."

"Yes," she laughed, burrowing closer to the warmth of his strong embrace. "You win."

* * * *

Darken wrapped himself around her like white on rice, because for once in more than two thousand years, he thought that might be true. That for once in an eon, he'd won. Surely, this human woman was his Chosen. Did it matter he hadn't found her on one of their missions to search for the word of God?

Yeah, she'd literally fallen into his arms, but her name must mean *something*. A name, when translated, that meant *God's Judgment to save*— couldn't be accidental. Nor could the fact how readily she accepted his explanations.

Not just those, either, but the reality of them. His Daniela didn't flinch from the touch of his clawed hands, she didn't shy away from his fanged smile.

He was so hopeful, he didn't want to think about the rest. He wanted to enjoy this time with a beautiful woman who made him feel...*peaceful.* Laughing, with her in his arms, he could almost forget the centuries of despair.

Yet he didn't quite dare.

She didn't yet know all of it. She didn't know about the violence, the wounds and the bloodshed as he and his brothers lost control. When their anguish grew too great and they couldn't contain it.

What would his little savior think then?

He pulled her tight before releasing her, then stepped back to finish pouring their wine.

What would this woman, who spent her life helping victims of violence, think when she witnessed Uri flip out in one of his rages? Yeah, his brother was doing better, but the man was starving to death. He was like a goddamned gas leak with a book of matches in his pocket.

And when he turned into a bear, or Drakus into a dragon? Or Merrick into a lion?

Jesus. Thinking of this shit made him realize he'd only crossed the first hurdle in a frigging marathon of them.

Hearing the suck of the refrigerator and the scrape of a plastic drawer, he turned, both wine glasses in his hands, to regard the finest ass he'd ever seen propped up in the air. Begging for his hands to grip it.

Involuntarily, his fists curled, shattering the crystal goblets, belching red wine to the tiled floor.

Daniela whirled around, her mouth a perfect O.

Worse, he'd seen her flinch like a gun had fired.

Despite her brave front, he suddenly realized, he scared her. Making him feel like the biggest jackass at the party.

An uninvited guest whose host was making the best of things.

Darken glanced down at the shards and splattered wine.

"It's nothing. Here." She hurried to grab a dishtowel off the counter, but he caught the faint quail in her voice.

He bent down with her to mop up his mess, their heads nearly bumping together.

"Damn, I'm sorry." In more ways than he could explain in one conversation. She'd been on edge *before* this crystal casualty, and that made him sorrier than all fuck.

"You shouldn't be." She held his gaze, her brown eyes reproving, like his apologizing was beyond ridiculous.

Christ Almighty, he was like King Kong in her delicate world. How easy it had been for him to splinter that glass. What if he'd been holding her hand? The bottom dropped out of his stomach, making him nauseous. Pricklings of sweat expanded between his shoulder blades.

"Are you all right? You didn't cut yourself, did you?" She reached for his hands, the softness of hers like flower petals. Her little gasp hitched itself to his heart, and he shut his eyes against the tumult of sensations.

"You're bleeding."

Was he? He didn't care. Losing a little blood paled in the face of the yawning gulf between him and this human woman.

"Darken?"

"Yeah?" Slowly he raised his lids, afraid of what he'd see.

"You're bleeding."

He shook his head, and rose. She followed him to the sink, their hands coming together on the faucets. The two of them were bumbling, like they should be sharing the same space. He didn't feel the rain of cold water, just her body pressed to his, her touch doing more for him than anything.

Desperately, he wanted to put his arms around her to pull her closer, to feel her reassuring weight against his chest. The need pushed on his throat, nearly suffocating him.

But he couldn't succumb to it. Not when he imagined tainting her beauty with smeared blood. It reminded him too much of her abhorrence for violence.

Of just how much he was *not* right for her. Whether she was his Chosen One or not.

She dabbed his cuts with a clean dishtowel, her hair falling forward, obscuring her face.

But fanning her scent.

Hitting him like a habit smacks a junkie.

His skin itched like a mother to give in to his urges.

"I should really go." Gently, he extricated his hands from her ministrations.

She didn't say anything, just watched him back up. But he saw the shadows of self-doubt cloud her expressive eyes before they turned hard. "Yes, of course. I'll get your coat."

The look stopped him cold. "Daniela?"

She halted, her back to him. "What."

Good frigging question. He knew what he should say, he just didn't know how, or even if he should. So, he stammered like a weak-ass idiot, as if choking out the words was going to make her accept them any better.

"The blood...to me...is nothing."

She didn't say anything. She didn't have to. He saw the expectant stiffening of her shoulders, like maybe she wasn't pleased with what she was hearing, but was glad he was being honest about it.

Yeah, he had a bridge he could sell himself, too.

"It's nothing because..." *Oh, God. Here it goes.* "It's nothing because bleeding...for me, for my brethren...is nothing new. We are unstable. We harm each other without meaning to." He waited for her to react, to scream at him to leave, or *something.* But she just stood there facing the door, letting him stammer on with his confession.

He had to take a breath to fill his deflating lungs. "You are amazing...accepting me for what I am. Not condemning me. But you don't know about the injuries, the *rages.*" His throat closed in on his confession. "If you did—"

"Don't presume to know me." She turned to face him then, her jaw set, her cheeks flushing. "*I* make up my mind about what is best for me and what isn't. Walk out, if that's what you want to do, Darken. But don't you dare presume to know what I can or cannot handle."

Well...*there.* He opened his mouth to protest, but shut it. He felt like one of those shiny, golden fish peering out from behind plastic bags of water. His future unknown, but still necessarily, and inescapably, connected to his environment.

"But I'm—"

"Scared shitless? Yeah, you look it."

* * * *

He did, too. For all his size and obvious strength, he looked like a stray puppy who'd pissed on her carpet. Like she was going to throw him back on the street because he'd done something very wrong.

Her heart melted, along with her anger.

Softening, she reached for him, taking his wrists in both hands. "Darken, I don't know if what you're telling me is true or not. Honestly. I mean, I *see* you standing here with…with your…with your fangs and claws, but it's still a tall story. You're talking gargoyles, creatures I know to be stone decorations on the sides of buildings. Not living, breathing…*men*."

She didn't dare delve too deep into this conversation, not when she stood so precariously on the lip of something she intuitively felt was altering her world. No matter what she wound up deciding.

He looked so damned sad. For once she saw what it meant for someone to carry the weight of the world. It was exactly how the man standing before her looked. She lifted his right hand and turned it palm up, tracing her fingers across his callouses, along his scarred wrist.

She swallowed against the fear tingling to life inside her. Those were *bite marks* puckering his skin. He trembled under her touch. "We'll take things very slow, okay? Show me what you're afraid of."

He shook his head without looking at her, his blonde bangs shielding his eyes. "Daniela," he sighed, yet it hitched in his throat, his body tensing, his muscles straining under his shirt. "You will run. You would be smart to run." His fingers curled around her wrist, his hand comforting and warm.

She fingered his hair away from his eyes and peered up into the anguished gray.

"I might. But we won't know unless we try. Right?"

He didn't answer her. Instead, he lowered his head, brushing his lips to hers, light as any feather. His breath came a little fast, his eyes searching, wary. Then determined, he tilted his chin for a truer angle to her mouth, where he nipped at her lower lip, his tongue slipping furtively to caress the little bite.

He leaned in for another nibble, and Daniela flicked her tongue to his.

Darken yanked back, his breath a surprised hiss; then pleasure bloomed as his gaze turned eager. His hands cupped her cheeks as he dipped in for another curious taste. She let him explore, inviting him to deepen his kiss.

Lifting her arms to grasp his shoulders, she gripped his muscles, pulling him closer.

He yielded with a low growl, pressing himself harder against her, his mouth a warm anchor as he played his tongue. His kiss intensified, his tongue triggering her imagination, where she pictured his mouth moving inevitably to other parts of her body.

The idea of his panting breath on her skin sent throbs of pleasure to her sensitive berry. She fought the urge to squirm as Darken slid his thumbs down the long tendons of her neck, tracing her collarbone. His claws left zinging lines of pleasure in their wake, and her nipples puckered, pulling her areolas tight.

Sensing her arousal, he deepened his kiss as his hands slid across her back, allowing him to yank her even closer, one leg wrapping around her calf.

"Daniela," he panted into her mouth, "I've never…" He resumed their kiss, his whole body growing taut. He released her lips, but hovered there, his eyes hooded. "I've never touched a woman like this."

Was he warning her? Didn't matter. She was a little gone at the moment, too absorbed in the burning ache he built in her.

"Glad," she said, then claimed his mouth, her hands clearing a path down his strong back to his firm ass. She gripped it hard, her fingernails piercing the denim. He moaned into her mouth as he ground his trapped erection against her soft belly. Like the feel of her inflamed him.

He trembled in her arms, the heat of his body flaring, so that she felt the air between them dampen, grow pungently spicy with his sweat. He smelled glorious. And very male.

His tongue slid a path down her chin and throat, teasing a moist circle before his sharp teeth clamped onto her flesh. Instantly, her arms fell away as if in surrender. Her bosom arched, beckoning.

Surely, she was going to collapse onto the floor again, with him right on top of her.

Except this time, he stood firm, despite the excited quiver of his body against hers.

He was a quick learner. A thought that was blown from her mind as her view went horizontal, her living room swirling past her line of vision, then her kitchen as he carried her down the hall.

Unerringly aiming for her bedroom, his face slightly lifted as though he followed a scent.

She had no time to be embarrassed as her comforter puffed up around her, Darken's hard body a lusting contrast on top of her.

But once upon the bed, he hesitated. His gaze hungry, it dragged the length of her, then returned to her face. She was trapped between the pillared strength of his arms braced on either side of her shoulders and his knees wedged between her thighs.

"This isn't slow." His voice scraped up his throat, as though he lacked air.

"No." It wasn't, but they could always backtrack after the deed. Right? She parted her lips to ask. Darken swept down, his mouth reclaiming hers.

Fuck the worries. Daniela clutched his hard biceps and pushed her butt into her mattress, the better to serve up her breasts. Pulling his lips from hers, he lowered one of his huge shoulders to clamp his mouth to one boob, his breath hot and moist against the satin of her bra.

She felt the point of his tongue as it circled her nipple, then the padded pinch of his teeth, which opened something inside of her. She felt herself cream like a river, wetting her panties, his name bursting from her throat in a raspy moan.

Darken lifted his head, his nostrils flaring, his eyes glittering silver with the light from the other room. "Stop me," he said.

"What? Why?" Her throaty giggle petered out when his expression shifted. It wasn't a dare. Even with his kissed-to-plumped lips, his mouth was set.

"Because this isn't fair." He sat back on his heels, her legs spread around either side of him, his palms hot on her knees.

"It isn't fair that we're stopping." Her retort coaxed a grin from him.

"True." Without a bit of embarrassment, he rearranged his hard-on. But the smile he had grew teasing.

Daniela's eyes remained on the bulge in his jeans. Man, it had to be killing him, big as it was. She had her own unrelieved throbbing to contend with. Bad enough, but to have to deal with an erection that size? The thing had to be painful. She lifted her gaze back to his handsome face.

"We could continue and deal with the consequences."

He seemed to seriously contemplate that, his eyes watching hers. Then, "No. I haven't a fucking clue what I'm doing here, Daniela. There's a lot you don't know. I'm not human. Our joining will have irreparable consequences."

Well, that might cool a girl off. "*Irreparable consequences*, huh?" But she laughed, she couldn't help it. "Sounds like a Hollywood blockbuster." Her voice went low as she tucked her chin to her chest to imitate a male announcer. "Coming soon to a theater near you."

Yeah, she liked his fangs when he smiled like that. Daniela propped herself up on her elbows. She liked that he didn't move from between her thighs, too. She enjoyed the feel of his hard body nestled against her.

He pulled her up so she sat on his lap, her legs and arms locked around him, one big hand cupped to each of her butt cheeks. Their faces were close, but she didn't mind if he didn't. "Fine," she sighed, all melodramatic as a bad actress. "The great sex waits. So, now what?"

Daniela copped a coy grin.

Darken's eyes narrowed. Underneath her, she felt him readjust himself, as though his muscles needed rearranging. "I don't know."

"You're not going to make this easy, are you?"

His grin returned. "Believe me, if there was an easy way to do this, I'd be all over it."

She believed him. Without looking too deep into why.

"Fine. If you're resolved..." Secretly, she guessed she was glad someone was applying the brakes to this date. They were traveling fast toward—well, she didn't know, either.

"Want to see my t-shirts?" She squirmed from his embrace and headed for her bureau. "Snap that light on by the bed, would you?"

She heard rustling behind her, then the room lit up with a soft, yellow glow. Holding up one of her shirts to her chest, she turned around.

My sense of humor earns me countless uneasy stares.

God, she loved that feral grin. "What else you got?"

A bit of rummaging, then, *I was addicted to the hokey-pokey, but then*

I turned myself around.

That one got a laugh, and Daniela got swept up in it, laughing, too. "Here's one you'll like."

With a shirt this awesome, who needs pants?

"Hey, I have that one!" When Darken stood up, he seemed to fill her bedroom. Closing the distance took him two strides. "Mine's blue, but I like the red."

His look was all suggestive. Daniela blushed. All the way to her toes. "Stop it." She cuffed him, turned to shut her drawer, then lingered when Darken laid his hand upon her back.

He removed it with a "Sorry."

Straightening, she said, "There you go again. Apologizing when you shouldn't."

"I just don't want to freak you out. Touching you too much…"

"As if that could happen."

"You're pretty when you snort."

"I don't snort!"

"Well, whatever you call that gurgling sound, you're pretty when you do it. But seriously, I'm probably going to mess up the whole touching, not touching, thing."

"Yeah? Why?"

"It's a Kynd thing. We touch. *A lot.* So, I'm not sure how much is good for hu—people, and how much is too much. We tend to err on the side of caution and not touch others at all. Which isn't hard, considering."

"Right. Nobody likes you." She laughed as she said it. Alone. "What?"

"I wasn't kidding about that. We're shunned. Not welcome in…"

"Go on. Don't chicken out now."

He paced, then realized he was doing it and sat on the foot of her bed. "Well?"

Shaking his head, he gazed up at her. "Not tonight. I think you've got enough to think about. Will you let me visit you tomorrow?"

"Are you bribing me?" She said this as she spread his legs with her knees and clasped her arms around his neck. "Because if you are, it's working. You've piqued my interest. I want to hear more."

"Same time tomorrow?"

"We can order in."

"I'd love that." He seemed to like where she'd placed herself, too. He'd put his arms around her without hesitating, that look of pure enjoyment glowing on his face again.

They gazed at each other for a bit, their smiles ranging from shy to not being there at all, then to bashful again.

"I should get going."

"Yeah."

Darken just kept gazing at her.

"Or you could stay and I could watch you turn to stone at dawn."

His smile disappeared for good as he stood up. Keeping one hand on her even as he moved away.

"Shit. It's my turn to say *I'm sorry.*"

"Shh. No." His knuckles lifted her chin. "Tonight's been great. More than I could have dreamed." Gray eyes became a rainy, Spring sky. Warm, full of...hope.

His kiss, when it came, filled her with his longing.

"Someday, *cor meum.* You'll be in my arms at dawn. I promise."

Well, what pray tell, could she say to that? Nothing witty, for sure. Not when her brain misfired with the image of this man sleep rumpled— in her bed.

He left with a soft brush to her lips, the front door snicking shut behind him. Daniela leaned her back against it, sighing. *Like a teenager with a crush.*

Which didn't dampen the glow.

Chapter Eleven

"I thought we had a way around this?" Darken watched Angelia pace in front of him, the rug beneath her shoes trampled in a worn circle. Her personal groove in front of the desk. The area in the library where she liked to think things through.

Merrick sat with his boots propped up on the gleaming wood behind her, gazing at his life-mate like a struck imbecile. His lopsided grin saying it all.

"I thought we did. But the more I'm figuring out, the bigger this rescue is getting." She circled the desk, perching her hip against Merrick's shoulder. Another favorite spot of hers.

Ignore their ease. Darken stood, leaving Uri and Kronos at the sofa, the sight of the other Kynd and his life-mate together swizzle-sticking his thought process.

He'd spent the entire day thinking of nothing but Daniela.

Unable to touch her because I was stone.

He'd thought before was bad? Being frozen all day now shredded his skull with the bat-shit crazies. Before, he'd just been furious about his fate.

Now? His Daniela was out there traipsing around in the world. In the dangerous world. Where she interacted with battered women, and cops, and therefore, the monsters who committed those violent crimes.

Holy Jesus, his skin crawled over his bones. Did all day, and was still doing it. Because he was here having this meeting when he should be with his woman.

"Darken."

His feet stilled, but his fingers wiggled at his sides. Like he was a twitchy gunfighter. "What?"

Angelia rounded the desk after severing herself from Merrick. Darken backed away from her. She halted, one eyebrow arching for a split second before she beamed a beauteous smile up at him. "Fine. I'll keep my distance. But know this—Merrick shares his life-mate with his brothers."

Now where the hell did that come from? Oh, right. *Angelia.* The Chosen One hardwired for the Kynd. The one woman in the Universe with the answers to their fates rattling around somewhere in her head. In her *blood*, for the love of Christ.

Merrick shares her? Of course, he did. He didn't have a bloody choice. Not that he looked as if he minded just then. He still wore that struck look on his puss. Like their day together had been…awe-inspiring.

Damn. He wasn't going to make it to seven o'clock.

Thinking of Merrick and Angelia frizzed his good intentions. Screw the set date, its set time. The sun had gone bye-bye, he needed to be with Daniela. To have her plump body squashed against his hard one.

That contrast easing him like nothing he'd ever known in his long existence. He craved it. *Needed it.*

Yeah, no exaggeration. And if he didn't get it soon, he was going to scream. Already the pressure was building, building, building.

"Yo, Kynd. Someone's talking to you."

Darken blinked, the snapping of fingers arresting his attention. Kronos. Six-plus feet of wiry muscle and grooves worn into his face where he'd done nothing but shriek in unholy terror for the past two thousand years as he witnessed nightmare after nightmare.

Kronos had shaved his head right after he'd joined Darken and the others. Because sweat had soaked his hair and the feel of it clinging to his skin drove him...babbling and rocking-body...nuts.

"Our girl is trying to make this quick so you can leave, but you've got to listen up."

"Right. All right." A few sharp nods and Darken refocused on Angelia. "Spill."

Her deep breath eats up precious time. But he waited. Knew he acted unreasonable. Just a hair's breadth away from rocking and babbling like Kronos.

"Once we get by Minos at the Second Circle and free the souls who don't belong there, we need a liaison to heaven."

A gruff laugh burst out from behind him, to his left. Kallen, parked close to Drakus, who sat on his usual sill.

"A liaison to heaven," he repeated, leaning toward the dragon chimera as he spoke to the rest of them. "Now that, my brotherkynd, is damned near the funniest thing I've heard since we got here."

He meant the more than four months ago, when they'd snubbed God and left their divine punishments to be together. Not like they'd been before they'd been relegated to every hellish realm in the universe, but at least they had each other again. Sharing, touching…

Kallen seemed to be heading toward needing another fix to keep his cool. A.k.a. a vicious pummeling. Someone else's. Not his.

Angelia frowned. "I know it's a tall order, but if we ask—"

"Who? God?" Kallen bit out.

Growling, Merrick rose from behind his desk. "Watch your tone with her." His black hair thickened around his neck, the lion part of his chimera seething to the fore. To protect his mate.

Tied as they all were to each other, every Kynd in the room stiffened. Hyper aware of the tension boiling deeper.

Drakus coiled his body to crouch on the windowsill, his skin shimmering with emerging scales.

Another growl answered Merrick's. Urick. Lumbering upright to his towering height, claws lengthening at his fingertips.

Shit. Palms up and facing outward, Darken made sure he made eye contact with each and every thinning soul crammed into the room. "Enough, guys. Just hold on a minute here. We don't want blood on the library books."

He attempted a smile at his joke.

The books, along with everything else in the safe house, displayed the hazards of sharing space with the fucked-up Kynd. Blood splattered the spines of half the leather bound collection. The other half teetered on broken shelves.

The library, the unlucky room to be designated their office, had seen its share of the unhinged.

But no room in the entire sprawling stone structure had escaped damage.

I'll bring my life-mate here? Daniela would see this ruin?

Suddenly, he saw their home through his Chosen's eyes. The stark and terrible evidence of their violent outbursts. Hand-crafted oak doors boasted splits their entire lengths. Some were canted, swinging on a single hinge, or were propped up beside gaping entrances. Elaborate archways now as vacant as gaps in a child's smile.

Floor to ceiling windows were cracked, fracturing the moonlight spilling across bloodstained rugs.

Polished wooden floors, once shiny as skating rinks, were now scarred where claws had scrabbled for purchase during countless fights.

The house had once been a stage for grandeur, its staircase spiraling dramatically, as if it was a velvet-draped arm ushering the way toward splendid settings above.

Aloft, the crystal chandelier hadn't escaped the carnage, either. Drakus and his wings had made sure the ceiling joined in the chaos of loosed rages. Great chunks were missing from the sculpted plaster, where talons had grappled for purchase.

The beasts had lain waste to the beauty.

And the chains. For the love of Christ, the chains. Coiled in a corner of every fucking room. Just in case.

They weren't unused.

It'd been by sheer luck Angelia hadn't been hurt during all of it.

Well, that and the fact Merrick protected her like a ravening she-bear with her precious cub.

But still. She was ass deep in the fray.

The life drained out of Darken, and he dropped to the floor, face in his hands. "Fuuuuck."

All eyes dropped with him, along with the tension, like he'd pulled the plug in the drain. "Darken, love." Paw-hands, tipped with six-inch claws, rubbed his shoulders, his upper arms.

"Bear, man..." Leaning back into that huge body, he reached up, placing his hands over his brother's. His heart thudded too hard, too slow. Like it did as he turned to stone every morning. "Can't...breathe."

Rolling to his knees, he let Uri hold him. "How can I..." He glanced up at Merrick, Angelia clutched tight to his body. "How can you stand...?" Shaking his head, he finished. "How do you let your Chosen live here?"

"It's not for him to decide." A sad smile gracing her lovely face,

Angelia unpeeled herself from the lion chimera to kneel before him. "That's not how love works. I stay because I want to. Because I love all of you."

"But—"

"Shut it, gargoyle." She pinched his lips together, grinning madly. Her navy blue eyes shimmering. "You'll discover that soon enough, I'm sure of it. Meanwhile, you're right about us. About this place. It's high time we repaired it."

Dearest God, but the woman understood. Without her, where would they be?

"If you're to bring your Chosen here, the home must be worthy. It must be ready."

All faces, his own included he was sure, turned petrified. And...expectant.

Every Kynd body tensed, muscles rigid. A hum vibrated, an electric current connecting them all. Angelia included.

"I'll talk with my father, see what can be done."

Her father, Anton. The third leg of the Triumvirate, and the Vampyre who risked everything for them, and still did. He'd do anything for the Kynd because they, along with Merrick, had saved his daughter from Hell.

They were careful not to take advantage of his generosity.

Which this might. Fixing the house was beyond their skill set. They'd need outside help, and who would volunteer? Darken suspected Anton would have to call in his debts. Force the Others to pay up on the Kynd's behalf.

No one, and he meant *no one,* wanted near them. The Kynd were cursed, and helping them might mean the curse could rub off.

"I'd grab onto one of those buffing machines if we got one." Kallen, his gray eyes eager to tackle something. The floor buffer a positive outlet? Stranger things were known to happen.

"Don't confuse it with your Chosen, gargoyle." Uri's jest kicked the hum up another notch, spreading smiles on faces that were usually grim.

Chapter Twelve

While the Kynd were enjoying a rare moment of peace across town, over the river, and through the woods, Daniela kept checking her watch as she made the glide down to the main floor of the hospital. In the slowest...elevator...known...to man.

She'd been called back in to take the same woman's statement as she had the night she'd met Darken.

Seems the woman's memory had kicked out another little factoid, and she'd wanted Daniela present while she'd talked to the cops.

Not only did the husband like to knock his little woman around, but he also had some friends in low places.

Like that was a surprise.

What caught the uniforms' attention was who his friends were. Turned out that when hubby's fists opened to slap at his wife, his mouth did, too. He'd bragged as he'd pulverized his beloved into the linoleum.

And she'd remembered. With a vengeance.

Hell hath no fury like a woman scorned. Or knocked around one too many times, and too hard.

The thought didn't make her smile. Inhaling a deep breath for patience, she checked her watch again as the elevator stopped at yet another floor.

Six forty-eight. No way was she going to make it back to her place before seven. And she didn't have Darken's cell phone number to let him know she was running late.

"Come on, come on." Punching the buttons wasn't going to get her to the ground floor any quicker, but at least she was doing something.

Two minutes later, or twenty-four hours, when she heard the ding for her floor, she pushed through the sliding doors like a filly at Churchill Downs, eating up track.

Anxious? A tad. Yeah, Darken would worry, but what if he gave up waiting and left. What if he thought she'd stood him up and gave her the heave-ho?

Pathetic? More than a tad. She had it bad for the guy, weird shit and all.

Hurrying around a corner, she almost ran face first into another woman. Her shoes sliding on the waxed tile as she dodged, she slipped and swung her arms out for balance, almost whacking the other person in the face as she did so.

"Daniela?" As though she hadn't lost her balance in the near collision, the woman snagged Daniela's flailing arm, keeping her from falling on her ample derriere.

"Violet!" Seeing who her savior was, Daniela latched on for stability. "I'm so glad it's you."

"Rather run down someone you know, huh?" Violet held on with both hands, turning her rescue into a hug before stepping back. "Where are you off to in such an all-fired hurry?"

"I'm late. For a date." Gads. Not only was she breathless, she sounded like the white rabbit from *Alice in Wonderland*. "Hey, you're late, too. Usually you're already up at Oncol with the kids."

Violet Aster was a regular volunteer in the oncology ward, spreading her natural cheer like a graffiti artist. Slathering beauty and color where things were usually grim.

Blonde, lithely muscular, and six feet tall, she could do it standing still as a model. Yet the woman got into the dirty, the tears, and blood, and the bald heads of the cancer patients, seemingly unfazed by the ugly.

"I know, but I had things to do. Better late than never, right?"

Daniela didn't miss the flash of white as the other woman straightened her shirt.

"Is that a bandage?" Senses ever on high alert for injuries to women, she blurted out her suspicions. "Did someone hurt you?"

Violet peered down her front, then beamed a thousand watt smile. Meant to dazzle and blind. "Pfft, that?" She dismissed, waving away Daniela's concern as she straightened.

Doing so set her apart, her height a barrier.

Instantly, Daniela backed off, aware she'd overstepped. "Sorry. You know me. But I hope it doesn't hurt." She glanced at her watch, steady on her feet and remembering why she'd been rushing. "Anyway, I've got to run. Have fun with your kids. And thanks for saving my butt. Literally."

"Better me than some hapless old lady with a walker." Violet winked and stooped for a hug. "Now, get going. Men won't wait forever."

She high-tailed it for the glass doors with a quick wave. Not looking back, she kept her thoughts on her friend.

They'd met in the hospital cafeteria. Instead of sitting alone at their own tables as they'd sucked down bad coffee, they'd shared one. One care-worn face recognizing another.

They'd talked. Swapped their tales of how they'd wound up at the hospital. While Daniela had been hired, Violet had volunteered. Parentless since a child, she'd wanted to help make other kids' lives a little more bearable.

Daniela hadn't pried further. Having been adopted as an infant, she totally got the whole stigma thing. If Violet wanted to share why she'd been orphaned, she would.

Meanwhile, they had become hospital friends, neither one trespassing into the other's personal life outside of what they did at the hospital.

Which seemed to suit them both just fine. They'd been meeting over those flavor crystals for more than a year, and Daniela counted on those wee hour coffee klatches.

Sometimes they talked about the kids with cancer or the women with broken bones, but mostly they just sat quietly, savoring the warmth of a coffee mug, and a kindred, caring soul.

A warmth she'd be sharing with someone else tonight.

If I can get home before he leaves.

Careful not to skid out on the ice, she obeyed red lights and yield signs until she crossed the bridge out of Portland into South Portland. Traffic spread out until homes replaced apartments, clipped lawns defeated dirty pavement. Sidewalks tidy.

Forever later, she turned left onto her narrow lane, the saltiness of Willard Beach air cutting streaks through the winter night.

Home. Relieved.

To see Darken's truck parked at the curb. Black, with its chrome shining in the moonlight. Ignition off. No one sitting in the driver's seat.

Where in hell is he?

Just seeing his truck her skin grew tight, her belly tingly. As she reached over to the passenger side to grab her leather bag and purse, her car door opened. A blast of cold preceded a voice that obliterated the bite of February. "Hey, beautiful, you're late."

A large hand with claws was held out, palm up, her dome light illuminating its otherworldliness.

Holy shit, it's real.

She'd forgotten. All day her clit had wrung with every thought of this man, but she'd forgotten…he wasn't a man. Well, not in the accountant-lawn-mowing-daddy with two kids kind of way.

Darken was all man, and then some. He was…

Crouching. To look into her car because she hadn't taken his hand as he'd offered. Now that hand was fisted at his stomach, and he grinned like when she'd first seen him. Tight lipped.

So as not to reveal his fangs.

But he couldn't hide his disappointment as he backed away, the car's shadow swallowing him.

The pang in her heart broadsided her. "Darken." With her arms loaded she scooched, stretching one leg to get out of her car. "Help me out here, would you."

Instantly he was there, his big hand on her elbow. Polite. His exuberance at seeing her subdued. But not his body. Oh God, nothing could diminish that. His height, the sheer breadth of him.

Her heart still stinging, she threw caution to the wind. She couldn't hug his big body because her arms were full, but she let him know she was glad to see him by pressing her body to his.

Instantly, she felt him flex as his arms came around her, his breath warm on the top of her head as he drew her in close. "I didn't think—"

"Shush. I was the one who didn't think." Rather than mold herself right there in the street and never leave the contours of that luscious body, Daniela pulled back, lifting her chin expectantly. Brazenly.

Man, but this guy brought out her chutzpah.

Their gazes locked. Nickel gray shimmering with apprehension. Need lashed by a tight rein. A strong jaw clenched, hollows casting shadows under strong cheekbones like smudges.

Such a handsome male. If the wanting in those eyes meant anything, *her* handsome male. He looked like he wanted to devour her, afraid he'd devour her.

Which amped up her female sensuality even more.

My man. Two words she never thought she'd utter. Not with such…sighing. If she was a cat, she'd slink and purr.

As she watched the shadows of his face, he tugged her even tighter against him. Yet, she couldn't peel her eyes off the hard line of his jaw, the patrician razor blade of his nose. "A kiss?"

Darken's nostrils flared as he sucked in a breath. "I'll be careful."

Because he might bite her? *God, yes.*

"Not here though." His idea, but it looked like it pained him. As though he didn't want to take the time to go elsewhere. As though she might change her mind in the time it took to get into her house. "It's not safe."

Whatever that meant. With Darken, she could be standing in the middle of a gang war and she didn't think any harm would come to her.

Huh. Guess she was done worrying about becoming one of her clients.

"Safe from what?"

"Me." *Or not.* His eyes squeezed shut as she stiffened. "I'm sorry. But, you had to know." Gone was the apprehension and need in those gray eyes when he opened them. Now they brimmed with regret.

"Know what?" The question perked him up, like he realized she still wanted to play.

"Hmm?"

"You've kissed me before."

The corner of his lip lifted in a reluctant smile. With a twist of devilry. "So I have."

Darken didn't have to squeeze her to him, she fell against him. As if the weight of her flirting tipped her center of gravity, so her body leaned into his. Beneath their heavy coats, she could feel the immovable strength of him. A mountain with…sensitive skin.

"You were very good at it." She nudged her chin upward. To greet the downward sweep of his.

"I probably need more practice, though."

"Yeah, maybe." She grinned as their lips brushed together, the cold tips of their noses touching.

"But we do need to get inside. Get you warm. There might be..." There was that rueful smile again.

There might be...what? "Fine. We'll go inside. Hold these." Automatically, he held his arms out for her bags while she readied her keys then punched the fob button to lock her car. They walked toward her front door, him just a little behind.

Like he did as they'd left the restaurant.

Making her edgy. Reminding her of why she'd run out on their first date. Darken held secrets, and if the blonde man who'd shown up at Alfio's proved anything, Darken had frenemies, too.

And because thoughts were snakes that ate their tails, she got led right back to the hand he'd offered to help her out of her car not five minutes ago.

A clawed hand. Big, calloused. Strong fingered. And clawed.

As she slid her house key into the lock, she felt his bulk rise up behind her. The smell of his leather coat and his warmth wrapped about her like an animal's pelt. A delicious twist in her lower belly, one that made her squeeze her clit and her ass cheeks as a tickling shiver shimmied through her.

God, Darken equaled carnality. Deep lusts she'd never felt before. A feminine surrendering she wanted to give in to. Lay herself wide open, naked, to take him.

All of him.

The warm muscle, his weight, she could well imagine his butt in her hands. Her squeezing as he thrusted...

Two grappling hooks gripped the doorjamb on either side of her as a low growl played along her neck. Darken nuzzling...

Keys forgotten, she tilted backward, into his embrace.

"Dilectum meum...electis meus." His big body tensed as he folded her closer, his face still buried in her hair, under her ear. "My Chosen. Open your door."

Huh? My door? Metaphorically, or really? Because she'd open her door all right, if that's what he wanted. Her heart pattered and fluttered, flushing her blood to her skin.

Another growl, more intense. "Daniela." One word, a caress.

Her knees went boneless.

His hand gripping over hers...sliding her keys...

Oh. "Oh!" Breathless, she straightened up, recalled that her body wasn't melting. "Open my door. Yes, I'll get it."

The chuckle behind her could melt chocolate. A sinful decadence. "Just get us inside, *amica mea*."

* * * *

He spouted Latin. Without a brain, his mouth poured out a dead language come to life on his tongue. Idiot. As if they weren't going to have a hard enough time talking about things they really needed to.

Such as...she smelled a trifle...off. He knew the scent. Just a trace of it on her coat, but it confused him. Why would there be the essence of vampire on her clothes?

Daniela's key chain jangled into the glass dish on the little table by the door. The woman herself shed her coat, and he lost track of his wits.

She wore a red dress. A long sleeved and short hemmed red sweater dress that hugged her curves so softly...

He bit his claws into his curled fists. To moor himself with a little pain.

A black belt circled high on her waist, accentuating the plump divinity of her ass. The calves of her ample legs...

Holy hell.

His dick roared to life at the sight of such a luscious female unwrapping herself.

Like a gift.

With his name written all over it.

Never mind the snowballs and hell correlation of their relationship. He'd figure out some way for his life to appear...okay, his dick was doing some heavy lying.

There was no way he could gloss what his life was like.

Stomach knotting with need, he narrowed the distance to that plump, red ass. His hands already reaching for that dip above his Chosen's welcoming hips.

She turned in his palms, the cashmere softness of her dress snagging on his callouses. Rather than let go, he dug his fingers in for a better hold.

The dress snagged more.

"Darken!" Daniela's breath washed over him in a surprised gush. The hips he held bowing as her back arched. Toward him.

Darken tugged harder, until his woman's bounty felt like a cushioned weight against his singing cock. Lowering his head, he dragged his tongue along the tendons of her neck.

Only to get a mouthful of cowl neck sweater.

Thwarted.

Daniela tensed as his frustrated growl rumbled forth.

"Darken?"

"What." He didn't lift his face from the warmth of her nape. Beneath his hands, she squirmed. A rippling ribbon of satin. Blasting sensation through his entire body, like his cock was a conduit.

"My dress."

"Is…" *In my way.* "Tantalizing."

Her feminine chuckle threaded through his whole body, easing the muscles off his bones. Relaxing, he drew himself upward and back, enough to see the woman he wouldn't let go of.

She gazed up at him, her brown eyes warm, but inside them he could see disquiet. Which matched the tight lines surrounding her smile.

He let her go, backing up several paces until he felt the cool air hovering by the front door.

A reminder. For himself to hover in the cold until she invited him closer.

Never, never take what isn't mine.

Darken dug his claws into his palms, feeling the twinge of pain as he lowered his gaze to the floor, head bowed before his Chosen One.

She had hesitated to take his hand when he'd offered to help her out of the car. She'd recovered from the shock of seeing it, but…

Slow, gargoyle. Lest he forget what he was. Where he came from. Who he belonged to, lived with.

They were all…beasts. Fanged. Winged. Muscles corded over bone. To withstand violence done unto their bodies. Skins of thick stone.

While the sun brought forth life to every living thing but them.

His *fuck me* garbled beneath the hand he dragged over his face.

As he drew air into his lungs, the need to lash out rose up inside him. The pressure from within too much. He needed to…demolish something to ease the smothering rage.

A detonation before the bomb went nuclear.

Her scent hit him like a cold water bath.

"Stop. Come no closer."

"No, you stop it. I don't take orders, understand?" Her tone was sharp, slapping his attention front and center. Yet, her touch. Fingertips to his locked jaw. Electric. Warm.

Without a thought, he tilted his head into her caress, his knees collapsing his bulk to the floor. So that he knelt before his queen.

"It's just a dress—"

"No. It's beautiful. On you, it's…" *Divinity itself.*

"…I wore to feel pretty, yes."

"It worked." Abashed, he looked up to her.

She shook her head, her grin indulgent. "You're something else, you know that."

Her words meant so much more than what she spoke. In their meaning resided the monster, forgiven for now. A temporary reprieve, because she did not understand. Didn't yet know everything.

He wanted to reach for her. So damned bad. But he curled his arms around his middle, stuffing his ugly hands under the panels of his coat. He gave her a smile. One he didn't feel within, one that didn't reveal fangs. The daggered ends of every tooth.

"I am such an idiot," she said, then cupped his face to place a kiss to his sealed lips.

Roses. As if he'd buried his face into the lush petals of a rose. A little dizzy, he softened his lips, opening himself to her. The moment he felt her plush little tongue sweep into his mouth, fear dropped over him, heavy and cold.

What if I accidentally bite her, make her bleed.

Tension kept his jaw still, while every muscle in his body begged to be released, to hold the deliverer of such bliss. Daniela's scent surrounded him, along with the heat of her voluptuous body. The power of it nearly undid him.

Knowing they'd kissed before didn't help.

Darken wanted to unwrap his arms from his body and coil them around the woman kissing him. He wanted to slant his mouth over hers, push his tongue deeper, hold the warmth of her nape in his rough hands.

As her mouth stilled over his, he felt her unspoken question. Hadn't needed to see the insecurity blooming in her dark eyes as she pulled away from her daring kiss.

Never had a beast hated himself more. "Give me a minute," he croaked, as he rose and gave her a wide berth, his boots pounding a desperate path for her bathroom.

Inside the crowded room, he found the privacy he needed to pop the cap off the self-loathing crawling around in his guts.

Gripping the edges of the bathroom sink, he glared at his reflection, the harsh foreground to the pretty landscape behind him. The flouncy shower curtain framed his chiseled and fang-laden face, illustrating his gothic self-portrait as if he'd been broad-stroked with a black paintbrush. Industrial-style.

"Abomination," he growled at himself.

Compared to his Chosen One, he was. A God damned gargoyle, in the literal sense.

The six Kynd who had dared God's wrath to escape His punishment were all damned.

"Unless we find our Chosen," he snarled at the drain. Head bowed, he wouldn't look at his mug again. No point. He knew what would stare back at him. Everything that wasn't human, not by a long shot.

Daniela was Darken's Chosen?

Then she's doomed. Just like they all were.

He ceased gripping the porcelain sink when a crack echoed in the small bathroom. "Fuck me." He'd grasped the sink so hard he'd fractured it. Damaging it just as he and his brothers did the safe house. As if he needed another reminder why Daniela would be better off—and safer—without him.

The idea of her not being with him hit his heart like a whip—sharp and stinging, robbing him of breath. With a clawed hand clutched to his chest, he stumbled back from the sink, away from the evidence of his destructive strength. The backs of his calves hit the toilet, forcing him to sit on the lid with a tongue-biting drop.

The pain brought burning tears and the metallic taste of blood.

He swallowed, shutting his eyes tight as he raised his face to the ceiling.

As if in prayer?

Hell, no. He leaned forward, elbows on knees, to stare at his big, black boots. The soles of which were lined with dried salt from outside. Tiny, accusing puddles dripped around the rugged rubber, his boot tracks staining Daniela's fluffy bathroom rugs like guilty fingerprints.

"Shit." He blazed a path of ruin everywhere he went.

"Darken?" A hesitant call, followed by an equally hesitant knock. "You okay in there?"

Never better, sweet.

He straightened up, filling his lungs as he did so. Now what? When he opened the door, she'd see…him. At his loveliest. "What the hell." He was going to have to reveal more about his life eventually. Nobody said it was going to be pretty.

Taking another deep breath, he stepped forward in his lug-soled boots, his big fist concealing the doorknob as he turned it.

* * * *

As big as he was, Daniela heard Darken moving around in her bathroom, so she wasn't surprised when he approached the door to come out. It wasn't that he stomped around in there, it was just that the size of him…moved air. Like even the elements got the hell out of his way.

Evidently, she wasn't as smart because she refused to step away from the door.

With her heart fluttering a little, her brain fabricated scenarios of how he'd emerge. Foremost was the one where he would yank the door back like it was nothing more than a graham cracker, and reveal himself as six and a half feet of angry.

And then? Oh, she'd documented the "What's Next." The hard hits to softer flesh, the battering rams of a man's fists, the cowering, the crying.

Imagination getting the better of her?

Nope. Darken had stalked off, his wide shoulders canted so he wouldn't bust down her hallway with them. *After* she'd kissed him.

Apparently, she'd read him wrong. She'd thought by the way he'd clung to her, he'd wanted more. Even after he'd retreated. As if…

As if he'd felt so bad for snagging her dress, he hadn't deserved her kiss.

Which was exactly what had gone down, she realized.

And ding, ding, ding. The man wasn't angry with her—he was upset with himself.

She'd kissed him, but maybe it was too much for superman in the bathroom to handle, his insecurities weakening him like kryptonite.

The door swung inward, slow-like, to reveal six and a half feet of…defeat.

Not violence, as she'd first feared.

Heart squeezing, she opened her arms. "Darken, come." As she spoke, she stepped forward, Darken's silver eyes closing as their bodies came together. His huge frame hard and muscular, yet yielding, as he pressed against her.

He squeezed her, his big palms spreading across her back.

As though he was eternally grateful she still accepted him?

"I'm sorry," he breathed, rubbing his cheek in her hair.

Yep. The poor bastard was sorry for coveting her. Yet, snagging her dress had meant nothing to her. Not when it was this man's strong hands gripping her hips.

She'd liked his intensity.

She wanted more. Craved it.

His insecurities outpaced hers by a country mile, so if there was manning up to do, well, screw it, she'd take the initiative. Again.

Force his hand.

She pulled back from his embrace to tilt her face up. "Kiss me."

Silver eyes gleamed down at her, searching, with a hint of surprise.

"I'm not kidding. Kiss me."

"What if I—"

She bit the nipple pebbled under his shirt, fanning her breath on the fabric as she pressed her lips around it.

"Shit!" Thick fingers raked through her hair, holding her head in place.

Nothing like the jolt of a lover to tell a girl she'd struck gold. She

115

gripped his ass and nipped again. As the areola around it tautened too, Darken rubbed himself against her stomach.

For a split second, she had the urge to suck in her gut, to pretend her belly was flat so it would be something desirous. But what would be the point. She could trap the rolls of her gut in a steel corset and the thing still wouldn't be tight.

Besides, Darken didn't seem to care. In fact, he seemed to take a heady amount of pleasure in the softness of her body, and that just tickled her pink.

Flushed her blood right to her swelling mons, it did.

So, she shut that scathing voice up in her head, and gave herself full rein.

Twisting her hips back and forth, she helped him rub harder and deeper against her, her breaths hitching as her desire skyrocketed.

"Woman."

Holy God, his growl. She thought herself unleashed before? Her need spiked, and suddenly her sweater dress felt too hot, like she was wrapped in a blanket.

Which sent her mind to her bed. Where she pictured Darken on top of her doing…nothing tender or gentle.

The idea had her hands rubbing up and down his back, like she was in heated overdrive. Her right leg went all come-hither, wrapping itself behind his knee to drag him ever closer.

Practically humping his thigh, she fisted the hair at the back of his neck and dragged his mouth to hers. "Kiss me," she said between panting breaths.

Darken growled again. In her mouth.

Such. A. Turn. On.

Their kissing turned feral, like they ate each other's faces, and she felt the slap of two big hands cup her ass. Next thing she knew, her back got plastered to the wall, the print of Edward Munch's *Scream* bouncing beside her as it threatened to crash to the floor.

She'd put it across from the bathroom door because it made her laugh. Like a warped *Oh my goodness! You're going out looking like that?* Twisted humor like her t-shirts—Ah, hell with it. She lost where she was going with that. Darken was grinding her up the wall.

116

Both her legs had managed to circle his hips so she sat on the gigantic bulge in his pants. Not one to let someone else do all the work, she rocked her hips, humping that protrusion until it pushed against that sweet bundle of nerves hiding behind her underwear.

When she pulled her head back for some air, Darken clamped onto her throat, working it like he had her mouth. It would leave a mark or three, but all she could worry about was crushing her breasts upward so he'd pay attention to those too.

Her fingers coiled into his blonde hair, gripping it tight as she held on. She felt the pull of his scalp but couldn't help herself. Darken's wanton aggression made her feel sexy.

Hotter than Hugh Hefner's *Playmate of the Year.*

With it came the rush of losing herself, of going…wild.

Held up by arms reminiscent of twin cranes, she felt positively petite.

The rest of Darken's bulk swamped her, not to mention the smell of his leather coat, the luxurious creak of it as his body worked itself against her crotch, as one of his hands left her ass to explore her thigh, her calf, then returned its gripping caress the way it'd come.

Another growl tickled her neck, sending her breasts into urgent nudging.

The scrape of sharp teeth on her tender skin blipped on her radar, but the heat pouring off her body shrouded it, so it was nothing more than a brief reminder.

That got washed away under the force of the man drilling her into the wall.

Which groaned under the assault. The paneling protesting the amount of pressure.

Holy…shit. It was as if her plump body had been designed for Darken's aggression, absorbing the crush of his wide and heavy form. Beneath her hands, she felt the length of thick bone, like his skeleton wasn't merely framework, but acted like scaffolding.

Inner pylons and anchors to stabilize the bulk of him.

Yet there was nothing cumbersome about him. As her hands groped across t-shirt, she felt the flexing of supple muscles. There wasn't an ounce of fat to soften the contours.

Only hers.

And the contrast had her pulling harder at the body already lunging against her.

The wall complained more as Darken's breath panted as hard as her own.

"Chosen...I'm...you're..."

"Don't stop." Daniela clung madly, her skin tight as she rode the crest of an orgasm.

Snarling, he spun them from the wall, holding her as he dropped to his knees, spreading her out onto the hallway floor.

His silver eyes shining bright as they dragged the length of her, she felt like a...feast. A banquet spread before a starving man. She let her abundant thighs drop open, revealing her cornucopia.

And Darken fed like a ravening beast.

Jacked up on his knees, he plowed his shoulders through her opened legs and latched his mouth onto her, his tongue lashing as he sucked deep. Through her feminine curls, his silver gaze pinned hers.

As though daring her to twist away as his big hands curled around her knees.

Possessive as a starving tiger.

Like she'd drag herself from riding orgasm number two?

She hadn't recovered from the first, her bones liquid as gasoline. Her blood, already smoldering, caught fire yet again, and of their own volition, her hips rocked against Darken's whip-like tongue.

"Oh...God...I'm going to come..." Breathless, she squirmed and shoved, her arms flailing as though she'd lost control of her body. Her brain registered that she'd cracked her paneling as she'd punched out her fist to ground herself, but she couldn't care.

Her world had narrowed to the juncture of her thighs, where sensation maddened her.

Where Darken gobbled and gulped, his sharp cheekbones flushed, demarcating the flash of his odd, yet brilliant, silver eyes.

Somehow, she ought to care that nothing human gazed over her jiggling belly. That the hands holding her legs apart had on the ends of them long, strong fingers tipped with claws.

Then orgasm number two crashed over her, lifting her away to parts unknown and uncaring.

* * * *

Her gasping screams frayed the ropes shackling him. So yeah, he heard the splintering of the wall's wood paneling, but he couldn't rouse himself to care.

Other things were aroused—or most importantly—one thing was spear-headed, hard-shafted, and throbbingly alive.

His cock.

It sang.

It pulsed.

It was fucking killing him.

Crushed down in his jeans, the thing needed out. Pronto.

Already it sought its own exit by unfurling and poking its mushroom capped head past the waist of his pants. Where it sat hot and sensitive against his lower stomach.

If his hands weren't occupied with cupping the precious flesh of his Chosen, he'd work himself to a state of relief.

Except he couldn't be bothered. Not when he gazed over the ample flesh of…ambrosia.

Smeared all over his chin and lips. The taste of Daniela pungent and delicious on the back of his throat. He'd stick his whole face inside her if he could. So, no, his thumping erection could wait while he lapped utter joy and abandon onto his female's visage.

It was like therapy watching her lose it. His anger dissipating with every panel-cracking thump of her fist on the wall. He felt a pang of regret that she was marring her home. But it wasn't like how he and his brethren trashed their place. Not at all.

For them, the destruction was rooted in angst and loathing.

For Daniela, it was abandon, pure and simple. The letting go of self to travel to a higher plane. Hers being one of true release.

Where four walls were just too small.

Knees and toes digging in for better purchase, Darken readied himself for thirds. Feasting and giving filled him with…a crushing sense of rightness.

He felt overwhelmingly full, as though this sensual connection to his female had begun as a seed. The more he fed it, the larger it grew, unfolding its good life inside him.

It wasn't hard to imagine that seed sprouting into a golden plant. One of light and warmth, as it spread its tendrils and leaves outward through his legs and arms, his chest.

Or maybe that was just his heart going spastic.

He had, after all, shoved her clear down the hall without realizing it.

But then, neither had she. Or if she had, she didn't seem too worried about it.

On her lips sat the faintest curl of a smile.

A woman well sated.

He imagined, as he pulled his face a few inches from her heat, that his lips wore a similar curve. Without wiping his mouth of the taste of her, he gently arranged the dress back down around her hips, careful not to snag the delicate softness with his claws or his callouses.

She sat up, lifting her butt to help him, a wondrous chuckle bubbling out of her. "Wow."

He noticed the shaking of her hand as she ran it over her hair. She smiled as she reached for him, her eyes lowering to his hips. "Your turn."

The muscles of his lower back flexed to shove his cock forward, yet he caught himself.

"No, amica mea." His hand covered hers as he shook his head. "I'm fine."

His defiant dick didn't think so, but this...moment...had been for her.

For thousands of years, the damned thing had lain dormant. It could go untouched a little longer.

Because this was about his Chosen One. Her pleasure came first, always.

He didn't have to take a moment to think about that. Not when it stroked every inch of his skin, smoothing the muscles along his very bones.

Her grin turned teasing. "You don't look fine." Quirking an eyebrow, she looked at the evidence poking out of his pants.

The flush he felt seared his cheeks. "Yeah, well," he coughed, pushing the thing back down where it'd come from. "I am," he said, ignoring the pain to press a chaste kiss to her plush lips.

She held his gaze for a few seconds before glancing around them.

"Huh," she giggled. "We turned my hallway into a runway."

So they had.

They were clear down by her bedroom, Daniela's feet still on either side of his thighs. Her legs still parted, her hair mussed. And her eyes...

For the love of all that's holy. They sparkled. In that moment, he could drag the moon and stars from the sky and give them to her.

Even with the hallway runner bunched up like an accordion. And the fissures along the baseboards of her paneling where she'd punched her fists for traction.

Without thinking, he took her hand and kissed her knuckles.

Tended to her tiny scrapes.

For a split second, he lost control of his tongue, the thing nearly darting out to lap her bruised skin.

But that would be...not human.

On that note... He licked anyway.

Better she learn early what she'd be in store for.

Her hand, circled within his fingers, tensed for the briefest of seconds.

As their eyes met, he caught the flare of comprehension, just before her fingers squeezed his.

"A gargoyle thing?"

"Something like that."

With her knees still bent at his hips, she quipped, "That's vague."

A shy grin burst onto his face before he could stop it. "You're right. It's more of a Kynd thing." *Aaand...* "It's also an Other thing. The shape-shifters lick their loved ones all the time." *...away we go.*

"Shape-shifters." Her disbelief showed itself in the tilting of her head and her lifting eyebrows.

Darken took a deep breath, his heartbeats growing heavy and slow, so they felt like punches to his sternum. "Yeah. Lions, bears—"

"And tigers, oh my!"

Feeling wobbly as shit with her joking, he added, "And dragons."

Cue the crickets.

"Dragons." Her gaze searched his face. Apparently, getting savvy to what he'd said, her eyes narrowed. "And those lions and bears, their real, too, aren't they."

What could he do except nod?

121

She burst out with a laugh, launching his nerve endings like a covey of startled doves. "Sure. Come on, Darken. I'm leaning toward believing you might be a gargoyle or something, but shape-shifters? Next you're going to tell me there are vampires and ghouls."

She didn't yet know the half of it.

When he didn't laugh with her or deny it, she fell quiet again.

"Prove it."

He thought his heartbeats had felt like punches to his chest? Well, lucky him. That fist just opened up to squeeze his windbag shut. Without air in his lungs, he couldn't answer her challenge.

"Judging by that look on your face, you can't." Daniela pulled her legs to herself to stand up. One hand on the wall while she adjusted her dress, she said, "I really am an idiot."

As she turned, Darken grabbed her elbow. He didn't remember getting to his feet, but then Kynd were lightning quick when they needed to be.

He needed to be.

He didn't like the vexation he saw in his Chosen One's eyes. Not when shadows of humiliation haunted those deep brown pools.

What was it about emotions that allowed them to get jumbled together, and yet still seem so clear.

"I'll show you," he said, as if the automatic pilot in his brain had kicked his good sense navigator out into the freezing atmosphere. "Tonight. Instead of dinner…" *I'll hang myself.* "…I'll take you to the safe house."

Hesitating, Daniela crossed her arms. "Where is it?"

"I'll drive you there."

"No. I'll take my own car."

Such steel.

She was going to need it.

With his legs feeling too loose, he said, "So be it."

Chapter Thirteen

Wedged into the corner of the leather sofa in the library, Urick thought the bunch of them looked like they were at an AA meeting. All shaky hands and furtive glances.

Not wanting a final decision to be made, none of them met each other's eye.

The stakes were too high.

A trip to Hell carried risks on too many levels. And yeah, they might reach the Second Circle and rescue those Shades who didn't belong there, but what about after. When those souls were free to find their way to Heaven, who was going to show them the way?

One of them?

Yeah, because they were oh so welcome in Heaven.

Besides, there wasn't any guarantee they'd be around for the After. Angelia thought she'd found a way around Minos, the Beast who guarded the Second Circle, but if Plan A didn't work?

When shit hit the fan, there was no telling how far their messy selves would splatter. As linked as the Kynd were to each other, that connection no longer worked solely to their advantage.

Sometimes the weight of one spinning off his axis would suck the rest of them into the vortex. Not hard to do, given they were already circling the drain.

They'd only made it into Hell as far as they had before because they'd had a united purpose—save Merrick.

One of their own.

This trip into Satan's theme park reeked of—

"Yo, bear, get your head out of your ass for a second. Angelia just asked you a question."

"I'm sorry. What?" He blinked like the bear he was. As if he'd stumbled out of his cave, fresh from hibernation.

Angelia's smile greeted him, warming the meat on his bones. She could do that. Like it was her super power, or something. Not necessarily uniting them, but centering them individually so they could, as Kallen aptly said, pull their heads out of their asses.

When she lit up like that, she grounded them. As if Merrick's Chosen One was the sun, and the Kynd were her orbiting planets.

Hell, one look at Merrick and you knew the bastard happily careened like a meteor straight for her.

Who wouldn't. She literally glowed, like her aura plugged in to a light socket. Didn't mean she was a lamp. Just that as Kynd, they saw more to her than the average…bear.

Instantly, he thought of Darken, who would have liked his joke. The guy lived for puns and irony and cartoons, so he'd totally get the Yogi alliteration.

Made him remember all the times Darken had teased him when his furred bulk filled the gargoyle's truck. Claws slashing his leather seats, he'd said "My Dodge might be a Ram, but it's not good eating."

Son of a bitch.

But it had calmed him down, helped him get a grip, so Darken wouldn't have to veer off into the woods away from witnesses. Man, how many times had the gargoyle plowed his Dodge through alders and ditches to do just that.

"Vehicles," he'd said, "are replaceable. You, brother, are not." A wink from those gray eyes and a sharp-toothed smile leveled Uri out like nothing else.

Well, except for the woman at the hospital. When he saw her, his muscles eased like butter on a bagel, his fur lying flat as a becalmed lake.

She could very well be his Chosen One, but he didn't yet have the balls to find out. Not when his hungers were getting worse. Flip that coin over, though, and if that female at the hospital turned out to be his, she could save him from himself.

Which was why they were even seriously considering this venture into Hell.

Maybe one of those Shades from the Second Circle would be a Chosen One.

According to Angelia, the Scriptum was guiding them in that direction. That ancient book about the Kynd hadn't been wrong so far. If he needed proof, it was written all over Merrick's love-struck puss. Oh, and looky there, his mouth was moving. Merrick was saying something.

"Urick, once we get those Shades out, would you be our liaison to Heaven?"

His laugh burst out of him. All hahahahaha.

Again, he thought of Darken. "Pardon the pun, but Hell no."

"Aw, come on!" Kallen shot up off the arm of the couch. "You're the perfect one to do it."

Urick rose for the face off. As he did so, the bear in him exulted, his laughter disappearing like it hadn't ever existed.

The gargoyle wanted a challenge? Uri's thick pelt erupted from his nape.

In the same instant, his eyes picked up the liquid hammering of Kallen's carotid artery. The male's heated blood beckoned as it sluiced through the twin channels running up his neck.

He shook his head, denying. The weight of his bear's pelt tugging the bare skin of his chest.

Stepping back, Kallen blinked. "What are you looking at."

Moments before, the gargoyle had been champing at the bit for a fight. It was how the guy managed. Blow off a little steam, and the brotherkynd could keep his worst impulses in check.

Uri couldn't stop his nostrils from flaring as he took a step closer, narrowing the divide between them.

Kallen stepped back again. "I'm no meal, Uri."

"You sure 'bout that." He might have recognized the growl of his own voice, but not the blistering intent. His empty stomach gripped like a fist, his veins burning they felt so hollow.

Feed.

He took another step closer, forcing Kallen to tip his head back. Exposing those thumping arteries.

"I'm no meal, brother." The male held his arms from his sides, his wide shoulders stiffening. "But if it's a fight you're looking for…"

125

"You…would…oblige." Damn. As a bear, he had a mouthful of daggers. But this time, only two fangs descended. Thinner, but curved. A quick flick of the tongue…

Yep. Vampire. The third part of the nightmare he called himself had trumped his bear.

Fuck.

Though, really, regardless of which had come for dinner, it was the gargoyle portion of the triad who sat out in the cold. No salads or apples on this menu. The carnivores were hungry.

"Uri." A woman's voice. Melodic. Like currents of music riding the air. His ear twitched just as the fist strangling his empty gut gripped tighter.

Around him, he sensed the rest of the brothers tensing and standing. On the windowsill, Drakus curled up onto his hands and knees, the dragon inside him getting ready to burst forth from tattooed, human skin.

Kronos, barely able to stand the touch of anyone, dabbed trembling fingertips to his furring back. "Brother," he warned with a raspy whisper.

Poor, poor effing bastard. Flip a coin as to who, Kronos or Drakus, was even more fucked up than himself.

Merrick stepped in front of Angelia, his shoulders set as if he still had his wings.

They were all poor, poor bastards.

But they. Were. Not. A. Meal.

Focusing on the gargoyle front and center, he watched Kallen snap his neck side to side. Like a heavy weight boxer limbering up before the bell rings. "So it's a fight then," Kallen said, just as he lunged forward.

Uri disintegrated into a trillion molecules and teleported from the library.

* * * *

Daniela could still chicken out.

Maybe.

Following a man she'd only just met deep into the woods of rural Maine was tantamount to…being the dumbest, most idiotic, and completely brainless thing she'd ever done. In her whole life. Bar none.

It could very well be the last.

"Stupid, stupid, stupid."

She drummed her fingers on the steering wheel, but kept her hands at ten and two. No point in being completely unsafe.

Riiight. Because skidding off the snow-covered road she was on wasn't a value-add to this disaster of a decision.

She could turn around.

But where?

The bright blue lights of the digital clock on her dash told her twenty minutes ago was the time to have done the one-eighty. Now she was too far down a remote road, where turning around could get her stuck.

More points for her mature decision making.

In front of her, Darken's taillights disappeared around a corner. As she crept along in his wake, she sat forward to peer around the trees blocking her view.

And nearly ran up his ass.

Daniela lifted her foot off the accelerator, remembering at the last second not to touch the brake. As thick as the snow pack was on the road, she'd skid out if her wheels locked up.

The Dodge Ram ahead of her continued on.

It took her a few seconds and some controlled breathing to realize he'd waited for her. Having lost sight of her car by going around the corner, he'd slowed to make sure she stayed with him.

That was either a little frightening, or...very charming. As if instead of controlling his prey, he was making sure she was all right. Perhaps worried that the second he couldn't see it, her car had plummeted into a ravine or some other horrible vehicle thing.

Vehicle thing? God, her head wasn't on straight. Clearly, she wasn't using the brain she'd been given. Otherwise, she and Darken would be sitting in a cozy restaurant, or curling up on her couch with glasses of wine.

Getting to know each other better on her turf.

But, oh no, she had to accuse him of lying. Had to challenge him to prove he wasn't.

Which meant what? That she believed he was one of these...Kynd, he'd called it? A gargoyle who turned to stone every sunrise?

Daniela drummed her fingers on the wheel again as she shook her head.

Dang it.

She was inclined to believe him. Mainly because she couldn't look at Darken and not see…someone who wasn't entirely human, even if he did have arms and legs and a head.

It was the eyes looking out from that head. Stormy, mercurial. Changing in ways human eyes just didn't.

But the rest of it?

People who were lions and dragons?

Baby steps, Dani. If she took this slow, she could get her head around the fact the world wasn't what she thought it was.

So, really, when she reached Darken's house, the logical tack would be to roll her window down without getting out of her safe car, tell him she'd like to see him again, perhaps closer to dawn, say good night, and drive away.

Rational.

She'd just begun to relax into her seat when in front of her, Darken's Dodge went sideways. In an instant, her headlights lit up the chrome of two thick lugged wheels, the glossy black paint job, and tinted windows.

With little time to react, she pressed her brakes while doing the quick math in her head. Her speed, and the distance, were adding up to a crash if she didn't…

Daniela cut her wheel, the nose of her car smacking into a snowbank then bouncing off, the angle of her tires kicking her ass end around so her driver's side door smashed into the bank.

Jarred, and with her breath knocked loose, her body slumped in the seat while her brain went into high gear.

Okay. She was okay. Nothing broken. No smell of spilled gasoline.

She shut the car off anyway.

Hands shaking, she reached for the door handle, shoving her shoulder against the molded interior. The door opened about three inches, the metal edge carving into the snowbank, then jamming.

Instantly, she felt trapped, her panic rising. She shoved again and again, like a scared animal ruled by instinct.

After the initial flurry, her brain took back the reins of control, and she stopped, her breaths coming fast.

Okay. If she just thought about this...

She'd notice she hadn't even released her seatbelt. "Idiot." She'd been trying to escape while still strapped in. Disgusted with herself, she flicked off the nylon strap, gathered up her long coat, and sprawled her huge assed self toward the passenger side.

The center console was a speed bump to her progress. "Frigging, fat, Goddamned son of a..." With a valiant lurch, she cleared the hump as she untangled her legs.

Butt harrumphing into the passenger seat, she felt a momentary flush of victory. She took a couple of seconds to get her breath, then shouldered the door, practically falling out as she stumbled to regain her composure.

For a silly instant, she thought of actresses stepping with the elegance of Arabian horses from their chauffeured limousines, fingers rested atop an outstretched palm as they unfolded their beautiful selves to step onto the red carpet.

Ha.

Daniela steadied her winter-booted feet and stood up straight, peering through the night as she zeroed in on Darken's headlights. The LED's reflecting off the snowbank cast long, creepy shadows across the road.

Illuminating...

Darken standing in the road, braced off like Wolverine facing Magnito.

Or.

A ginormous, naked man crouched upon the ice.

* * * *

Darken had only enough time to yank the truck to the left, hoping to give Daniela enough room to get her car by, before the grizzly got his bearings.

"Uri!" Holy loving hell, the bear had teleported. Into his fucking moving truck. "How the—"

A roar blasted his face, the sound as tangible as the heat of the bear's breath. Darken didn't have to see the inside of that maw to know how close those jaws were.

He bailed before his head became a walnut.

As his back hit the icy road, he lost his line of sight under Uri's bulk.

Pushing, his hands disappeared into thick hide, his own roar echoing into the starlit night.

At least outside he had room to maneuver. Even with Uri humped over him, the bear had the strength to sweep him closer to those mighty jaws.

"Uri! Fuck!"

He ducked his head as thick claws dug into his back. An adult grizzly's claws are slightly curled at the tips, it didn't mean they were dull.

"You're okay!" An odd thing to yell when he was the one getting mauled, but he'd gone enough rounds with his brotherkynd to understand why Uri attacked.

Fear. Plain and simple.

He didn't need his heightened senses to smell it either. He heard it in Uri's anguished roar.

Didn't prevent his skid across the road, propelled by a front leg that would shame a wrecking ball.

Scrabbling his own claws into the ice, Darken stopped his spin, the waist of his leather jacket keel-hauled up under his armpits. The ice beneath smelled of gravel, but cut at his clothes like razor blades.

He'd love to lay there and analyze the contrasts, but Uri was bearing down on him.

Bearing down. Funny. A grin on his face, he flipped to his feet, turning mid-air to face his friend.

Nothing like keeping your humor when things were hard to…bear.

Breaths steaming, he laughed; the sound string-halting the charging grizzly. "Hey, Uri, if I knock your teeth out, will you be a gummy bear?"

Spit slinging in strings, his brother swatted the road as he roared.

Bad hygiene aside, the power display was a beautiful sight. If Uri wanted to charge, he would without much warning. Which meant he was mustering some control.

Darken held both hands up, palms out. "You're okay, yeah? It's only me. Cool trick with the teleport, but you landed safely."

He took a tentative step forward. "All right? Easy, Uri. It's all right." Nonsense dribbling passed his lips, but nonsense like this was in every sleep-deprived parent's arsenal.

Shushing a screaming babe in the wee hours of the night, it didn't matter what rained from your mouth, just so long as it lulled the beastie.

Uri wasn't the exception to the rule. Swatting at the road again, his great head swayed as ice shards flew upward.

Darken inched closer. "That's right, let it go." Spoken with a calm he didn't feel. Because during this latest cockup, he'd had plenty of time to divide his attention.

Mentally, he exhaled a derisive snort.

He hadn't made any conscious decision.

He'd had a murderous grizzly in his grill, but the whole time he'd wrestled with the bear, his soul had been screaming at him to keep the violence of Uri's attack far from the woman in the car.

It was instinctive to protect her.

Imagining her getting mauled sent his stomach into a sick roll.

Too close. This whole shit storm was too close.

His fears had come to fruition. That he'd bring his beloved Chosen to the home of his brethren, and she would...see.

Well, brilliant.

She hadn't even made it to the house, and she was getting an eyeful of what his life was like. Any second now, she was going to back her car out of the snowbank and drive off in a terrified skid. Perhaps endangering herself more because...

Resisting the urge to squeeze his head until it popped while he screamed at Heaven, he swallowed his frustrated roar.

For Daniela's sake, and for Uri's.

Because a part of him feared he'd look like he did every God damned morning when the sun snuck up to snatch his mobility away—grotesque. And he didn't want Daniela to see that.

Vain? Fuck, he didn't know.

What he did know was that he wasn't going to lose it. The bear needed a steadying influence, and he would give it to him.

A win, win. Oh, and hey, another win.

In his peripheral, Daniela's car stayed still and dark. *Jesus, let her be all right.*

He couldn't think about that. He was barely keeping his shit together to deal with Urick. If he let his fears get the better of him, he'd picture his Chosen hurt, slumped over the wheel, blood oozing down her—

Like a failsafe, his hands fisted. The pain from his claws cutting into his palms grounding him.

The chainsaw of a growl dragged his attention back to the immediate problem.

If he didn't get Uri controlled, his Chosen could get good and really hurt. By a man who didn't want to harm the fleas in his pelt, let alone someone cherished.

If Uri hurt Daniela, this episode would turn into a catastrophe. A tragedy for everyone.

Standing between his salvation and his brother, he kept his fists up. Made him look like he wanted to go a few rounds in the ring, but he needed the bite of claws in his flesh to keep himself focused.

He lowered the needle back down onto his broken record. "Okay, Uri, you're okay. You landed good. No harm done to anybody." He hoped like a mother fucker.

Daniela wasn't showing signs of life, but…

"Listen, yeah? There's a woman in the car behind me. My Chosen, you remember? She's come to meet you guys." The grin was heartfelt, but felt strained. His cold face stiff.

"I know, right? Why in hell would she want to. But the thing is, she does. Needs to. So, for her, let's please show her were not all fucked. Please, Uri."

The grizzly plopped his furry ass onto the icy road, his muzzle lifting to catch a scent.

"Aye, in the car behind me." *God, don't let me hurt Uri to keep my Chosen safe.*

He prayed.

After two thousand years of refusing to lift his soulful yearnings to Heaven above, he prayed.

Worth it.

His Chosen was. Darken didn't care if he humiliated himself. If God was listening and decided to keep Daniela safe, then he would happily grovel.

As he took steps toward his brother, and away from his Chosen, he learned a new kind of torture. With a desperation that felt like the flaying of his skin, he needed to turn back around and check on his woman in the immobilized car.

He stopped halfway, some ironic point between the two things who mattered most, and held his hands out, palms up toward Uri, as if in supplication.

"Shit." Not exactly words of finesse for a delicate problem. Glancing over his shoulder, he didn't know whether to laugh with joy or growl with warning.

Daniela, bundled in her long, quilted black coat, stepped out of her car. She kept the opened door between herself and...

A naked man sitting on an icy road with nothing but the blue of the moon to cloak him.

"Uri, you're gonna freeze your balls off." He stepped toward the man sitting in the road at the same time he reached out for his Chosen One.

Divided.

With her hands clutched to the top of the car door, Daniela flicked her mittened fingers at him, the universal sign language to *go, go on, git.*

Long seconds passed before he could obey the order, proof, indeed, of where his loyalties were tipping.

* * * *

Daniela didn't have a clue why there was a naked man sitting in the middle of the frozen road. All she could tell was that Darken knew him.

And cared a great deal about him.

One of his brothers?

They were both breathing heavy, like she'd missed some serious action while trying to un-beach her Shamu ass from the car.

Even though it was dark, she could see slash marks in Darken's jacket. Which kept her orca ass right where it was, thank you very much. If she had to, she could duck into her car real quick.

Like it was Goal in a game of freeze tag.

Only neither man seemed to be wanting to make a go for her, even though they kept glancing her way.

Instead, the huge, naked man on the ground rolled to his hands and knees and curled in on himself as he bellowed at the earth. In the moonlight, his muscles looked blue and shadowed. And very thick.

Darken just looked plain stricken, as if he didn't know which he should do first.

Not waiting for him to make up his mind, and throwing caution to the wind—*like an idiot*—Daniela bee-lined it for the yelling naked guy.

Yeah, she'd been all shoo, shoo to Darken, telling him to go help his brother while she stayed safe by her car, but this man's keening struck her in the gut. The place the battered women in her life kept well honed.

Because pulling the stories of abuse from those women wasn't a job. It was a calling. One she felt right down deep in her pudgy belly, at her very core.

Just because this was a man, and a ginormous one at that, didn't mean she could ignore that aching twist in her gut.

There was nothing feigned about this man's pain. No ulterior motive.

Darken reached him first, as though her rushing forward unstuck his feet.

He was kneeling, and pulling his arms out of his shredded coat when she got to them.

"Is he all right?" Her hand went to Darken's shoulder as she leaned in, the warmth of the man filling her cold palm and stealing up her arm. "What happened?"

Darken went still under her hand.

"What? He's okay, right?"

"You didn't see, then."

"See what? You two fighting?" She'd missed it, sure, but she'd live. Dealing with the aftermath of violence was one thing. Seeing bodies clashing was quite another.

She'd be just fine without the visual, thank you very much. This was as close to the front lines as she wanted to get.

Even if there weren't broken bones and bruises.

Which she could tell there weren't just fine. A naked body in the moonlight had a way of revealing those kinds of details.

"Here." Daniela began to shrug out of her coat.

From between the arms he'd folded over his head, the stranger on the ground growled. *Growled.* As in sound rumbled out of him that should have come from…

Heck. Nothing human. What if Darken hadn't been lying.

"No. I'm good." The words, at least, were human.

134

"Brother." Darken spread himself over the man's gigantic back. His gaze however, lasered straight to her. "Keep your coat, *amica mea*. It's freezing out here."

Did she have to say, *duh?* It was why she was offering her coat to the naked guy. As thoughts were wont to do, another ran parallel with the first. *Brother.* As in, closely related.

Made her focus more intently, suss out the details.

Like the claws on the ends of those fingers.

They were the twins of Darken's.

"And he's sitting on the ice." Another fact. In her mind, one which took precedence over physical anomalies. Her skin still felt tight from the man's keening wail, so first things first.

Take care of those in need.

As she removed her coat, the cold hit her like an immovable force, so how was Darken's brother feeling compared to her. She draped her coat over the man's back, and over Darken's shredded jacket.

Then used her wide ass to make room for herself, bumping her hip into the man who'd led her here. To this Godforsaken woods in the middle of nowhere.

Like the cold, the man was immovable. An arm like a tree trunk braced her bulk. "No."

It was instinct to resist, one eyebrow lifting. "No? As in you're telling me what to do? I don't think so."

"You shouldn't get near him. He's…we're…" Head bowing, Darken eased his hold but didn't relinquish.

"He's in pain." Like that explained enough.

Apparently, it did. Sighing, Darken moved forward with her. "Brother, let's get you into the truck."

Feet shuffling, Daniela fell back as the man got his legs under him. As he unfolded, she turned Pez dispenser, her head tipping back as her mouth opened.

Darken inserted himself between them, and for the first time in her life, she felt…

Like a flower standing amongst the redwoods. Darken's brother was a giant. Not that the man made him look small, just that the two of them together made her feel dainty.

For reassurance, she put her hand in Darken's as she reached to adjust her sliding coat. The man was huge, but he'd still feel the cold. She dug that tidbit of knowledge out of her own personal landscape.

Just because her body wasn't toned, didn't mean it wasn't acutely tuned. Just as this man's bulk made him look invulnerable, obviously, he wasn't.

The instant her knuckles touched his skin she felt the current sizzle through her.

What in hell.

Connected through touch, the men felt it too, if the *holy shit* looks on their faces were anything to go by. They didn't recoil from it any more than she did, the three of them looking back and forth at each other.

The vibration reminded Daniela of the times when she was a kid and had hummed through a comb covered with tinfoil. Her nerve-endings were prickled alert right down to her fillings.

She snatched her hand away from both of them, hoping to get a little distance. What she got was a sudden sense of abandonment weighing upon her like a dark, iron cloak.

Forcing herself not to replace her hands on the two men took a power of will she'd never had to dredge up before. "What the heck was that?" Stepping back, she managed an arm's length of personal space before her feet just…stopped.

Darken took a breath, lifted his hand toward her then let it drop.

"Chosen." The giant's growling bass matched the size of him.

Trivia, Shamu. She was stalling, and she knew it. She'd heard that term before, knew it applied to her. Now she had an inkling what the frig Darken had been telling her.

The other truth sliding home was in the pudding, just like she'd ordered.

Nothing of the sort she'd just encountered with these two men happened among…

"Shit." Gripping the cowl neck of her sweater dress, she tucked her fists under her chin. "You really are a…" Oh, shit, she was going to say it, take that step off the cliff.

"Gargoyle?"

Guess the leap into the abyss came without having to say a word.

Nodding, she blinked the sting out of her eyes as she gazed up at Darken.

His giant of a brother lost the starch in his knees, and folded back onto the icy road. The keening oozed out of him like the air hissing out of the stretched neck of a balloon.

Corkscrewing itself straight back into her guts.

She forgot all about maintaining distance. Darken snagged her progress forward just as his brother grunted, "*No.*"

Next thing she knew, her legs were level with her shoulders as her body lost touch with gravity. Without effort, Darken lifted her like a bride to be carried over the threshold.

He set her down by her car, blocking her tighter than white on rice. "Stay, amica mea."

Like she could go somewhere.

Not with two arms, thickly muscled as pythons, walling her off.

"But, what about your brother? He needs—"

"Nothing you're going to give him." He cupped her face in his rough hands. "Please." Those silvery eyes caught the shine of the moon and glinted, reminding her of who, and what, she was actually dealing with here.

But as she placed her hands over his, her fingers did the walking all the way to the tips of his. Because she needed another reminder. Yep. Sure.

She nodded as she gulped, and the relief on Darken's face had her wondering what was so wrong with his brother. Beside the fact he was curled back up on the frozen road.

"Promise me." As he asked, his hands clasped a smidge tighter on her face. Yet for all the latent strength she knew him to possess, he held her gently, as though her cheeks were crystal stemware.

"I…" Could she? The corkscrew in her gut didn't think so. Then again, she'd called herself an idiot enough times tonight. For good reason. "I…promise."

Safer this way. She could hop back into her car if things went bad.

Oh, wait. Things already had gone south. Her car was stuck in a snowbank, there was a huge man who had or hadn't been hit by her lover's truck. With the cherry on this disaster sundae being that the man was Darken's brother.

A non-human creature just like him.

From afar, it was hard to see details. The brother was quite a bit bigger. And he seemed different somehow. But she couldn't tell how exactly with the long shadows created by the truck's headlights reflecting off the snowbank.

Niggling at her was the suspicion that the differences weren't hair color and size. Guess she'd find out. Darken had gotten the man into the cab of his truck and was coming back for her.

He was upset.

She remembered the way he'd walked toward her on their first date. Those long, strong legs eating up property like he could walk the earth in a matter of days.

While he tore out chunks of it in passing.

Her bulbous butt hit her car as she backed up.

Which was dumb. Darken wouldn't hurt her.

She shoved off from the vehicle and stepped toward him, not only to erase the distance she'd put between them, but also the doubt.

Darken had halted, the moon on his shoulders illuminating the world-weary sag of defeat. "I knew I shouldn't have brought you here."

"Don't be ridiculous. I'm still curious." Not that she knew it until she'd opened her mouth. "Take me to your home."

Chapter Fourteen

As he opened his mouth to say *No,* a curious thing happened.

The refusal stuck in his throat.

He shook his head, trying to dislodge it while giving her the negative physically. It didn't take much to solve the equation. What his Chosen One wanted, his Chosen One received.

He didn't possess the capacity to deny her.

Yet, there were other ways to skin a dead cat, as the gruesome expression implied. "Uri isn't well." He'd play to her sense of justice and fair turn.

"He's your brother? The man in your truck?"

"Yes." He glanced over his shoulder to make sure he stayed in that truck and didn't come near his Daniela. Not while hunger rode the poor fuck like dried egg on a fork.

The bear had receded, but in its stead stood the vampire. Uri hadn't been able to sheathe those two fangs any more than he'd been able to get his gray eyes back.

A testament to just how out of control his strong brotherkynd was.

He placed a hand on his Chosen's stomach as she stepped forward, halting her.

"Daniela, he is in pain."

"All the more reason I should go to him." For a brief second, there was a flash of confusion in her lovely, brown eyes. Or perhaps it was just the shine of the moon.

Why she would desire to come near any of them was a mystery for the ages.

She stayed where she was, her soft belly warm against the flat of his fingers.

So lush! As his body tuned to what he touched, his knees went loose, forcing him to engage his thigh muscles so he didn't pile his body on top of hers.

"It is a pain you can do nothing for. I'll get your car free of the snowbank, follow you home, then take care of my brother. Myself." Huh. It would seem he'd discovered a way to navigate around the denial snare.

Words, he knew, wielded their own kind of power.

Satisfied with his clever maneuvering, he dared brush a kiss to the velvet plush of her lips before striding over to the back of her car.

And discovered that God and His universe had other, more perverse, ideas.

Daniela walked up behind him to peer around his side. "They're both flat."

"Aye, so it would seem." Yet how could he be upset when his Chosen curled her arms around his midriff.

A glance back to his truck reminded him how. He wasn't going to let this woman within twenty feet of a starving vampire. Brotherkynd or no.

"I've only got one spare."

Need she sound so…smug? "Figures."

He felt her tug on his sleeve. "Come on. I can call a wrecker when I get to your house."

"Actually, that's not such a good idea." They lived down a two-mile track of dirt in the forest for a reason. "We're a little…*effed in the a-hole*…private."

"Ah." He felt her head lift from his back, as if she nodded.

"Aye, *ah.* If you choose to come to my house, I can't promise you'll get home tonight." But he'd do everything short of launching her from a catapult before he'd let her see what he became when the sun came up.

Hell, one look at him as Grotesque, and she'd run screaming for the hills all on her own. Her fear being the only launching pad she'd need.

His skin shrank tight as his stomach made a sickening roll. *God, don't let her see.* He refrained from lifting his eyes to the heavens, but the plea went out just the same.

"Then leave me with my car while you take your brother home, and I'll wait for you to come back. We can get a new tire in the morning and fix it then."

So independent. And forgetful. But then, she didn't think in terms of turning to stone every time that cursed fireball crawled up the sky.

"Daniela."

"Hmm." She snuggled up to his back again.

"I won't be able to help you in the morning."

"Why not? All we'd—oh."

Could the universe squeeze his balls while it was at it, please? Maybe just pinch them right off. Because not being able to aid her emasculated him. It was, in truth, a foreign sting.

Which didn't make it any less soul destroying.

"Neither will I leave you alone in your car." On that, he couldn't budge. The idea of her in these woods by herself gave him the willies. He'd rather she catch him shrieking with fangs bared at his bedroom ceiling, frozen that way for the next nine hours, than spend one minute in these woods without protection.

He knew what was out here, even if she did not.

"Then there's only one thing to do." Her arms slipped from his waist. "We go to your house."

He sighed as if he carried the worries of the world. Taking her hand, he led her to the tailgate of his truck. "You wait right here. Don't move. Please."

What in fuck was he thinking? He yanked open the driver's door, expecting to see eyes black as pits in a face he dearly loved. "Uri. You okay?"

"Get me home." Gray eyes met his as his brother curled in on himself, the scent of his Chosen drifting to fill the cab of his truck as Uri shifted under the cover of her coat.

"Aye, brother, I will." Darken swallowed the lump growing in his throat as his visit with Kristov wriggled into his thoughts. Perhaps it wasn't such a bad idea to take the Vampyre up on his offer to help Uri.

Obviously, none of his brotherkynd were doing a bang-up job of it. On that thought, he hated the words he was about to say to the man.

Here goes the knee to the balls. "Would you mind riding in the back. Daniela's coming with us."

When Urick's face went all *What in hell?*, Darken nodded. "Yeah,

141

there's not much to do for it. I'm sorry. Maybe you could teleport out the way you came in?"

A bowed shake of the head was his answer.

"Didn't think so." So, he dug deep. Mined for the cheekiness that had kept him in his skin for more than two thousand years when all he'd wanted to do was go raging ape-shit.

He folded his seat down, easing the access to his back seat. "Up and at 'em, Bear Man." He patted the center console. "She rides shotgun, and you get to ride the pine."

He flashed a smile he'd pulled out of his ass.

"You're crazy, you know that."

"Aye, I do." He winked. "But I've got company. Get your butt in the back, Fozzie. We have precious cargo."

As Uri wedged his enormous bulk into the back, Darken waved Daniela forward. And couldn't take his eyes off her.

Arms drawn up tight to herself, she shivered in her red, sweater dress as she hopped toward him on what he could only imagine were cold, dainty piggies.

Without a thought, his arms spread wide to welcome her to his warmth.

She squirmed right in like he was some kind of safe harbor.

Lord, he hoped he was. "Come on, amica mea, let's get you warm," he said, all light and jaunty. As though there wasn't a creature sitting behind them whose hungers would drive him mad by the time they made the last mile to the house.

"So. All snug as bugs in a rug?" He grinned wide and toothsome, like Dad during the first ten minutes of a family vacation. In the rearview, he saw Uri stretch across the back seat, presenting his bare ass and shoulder blades.

Daniela folded her coat in her lap, preoccupying herself so she didn't have to look at the naked man crammed in behind her. Her cheeks were a gorgeous shade of pink. "You could say that."

Her shy grin was a city block this side of awesome.

That she was sitting beside him, in his truck…

Filled him with nervous dread, kicking that sunshine-y feeling's ass.

A quick glance into the rearview again and he let out his breath.

Uri had dragged his torn leather jacket over his hips. Which meant the bear wasn't going to visit anytime soon.

If only he had some guarantee about the vampire.

"So," Daniela's hand crept to the console, her fingers moving like little spiders toward Uri. Unconsciously. As if she was drawn to touch him. "How many brothers are there anyway?"

He gathered those roaming fingers in his. "Hundreds."

"Six."

A smile creeping out, Darken scraped his palm over his lips. "Uri's counting the Kynd at the safe house. There are six of us there. Not including Angelia, Merrick's Chosen One."

If God hadn't decided Merrick's sacrifice had been worth it, there'd only be the five of them. The angel chimera would still be suffering in Hell, his wings torn off as payment for Angelia's freedom and the return of the Scriptum.

Man, that book. The stealing of that tome and the ensuing quest to retrieve it was what had jumpstarted the Kynd's rebellion from God's eternal punishment.

Darken hoped it would lead them to hundreds more.

"I'm the nice one."

Daniela's laugh sparkled through the truck like sunshine. Uri sat up, careful to keep the jacket balled up at the top of his thighs.

"Hey, I'm not kidding."

"I believe you," she said with a teasing lift of her eyebrow. Darken felt her twinkling gaze settle on him and glanced over.

"Come on, now. Just because you're the teddy bear, doesn't mean you're likable."

"Sure it does."

"No, it doesn't." Man, bantering with Uri lifted the weight off his chest. Thank God he held the steering wheel, or he'd be floating off his seat.

"Dani—I can call her Dani, can't I—you tell me. If I was furry right now, you'd have the urge to pet me. Right?"

"Probably, and don't ask him. Ask me if it's all right to call me Dani."

Both men sucked the air in between their teeth and settled back.

"Ookay. Got yourself a live one, brother. Glad she's yours."

Their smiles weren't as big as they were before. Because, yeah, Darken was practically flying to the moon that he'd found his Chosen One, but Uri and the others hadn't.

Suddenly, he felt like he was rubbing their noses in it.

They rode in heavy silence until the lights of the safe house rose into the view the closer they got.

"Holy cow." Daniela leaned forward as he nosed the Ram toward the garage. "Is this a castle?"

"Close."

"No moat," Uri announced from the back.

"That's the only thing missing." She craned farther forward, peering up toward the roof, her dark hair cascading across her shoulders and back. "Are those…"

"Gargoyles? Yeah. But not real ones."

Her gaze turned on him, her eyes narrowing as though thoughts were piling up in her cranium. As though she regarded him closely for the first time.

She tilted her head back up to take in the roofline once again. "Huh."

He had his hand on the door handle when she asked, "Do you look anything like that when you…you know…"

Uri clapped him on the shoulder just before he exited from the back door on the driver's side. "Like I said, I'm glad she's yours."

With a thunk of the door closing and a blast of frigid air, they were left alone with an expectant silence and the ugly truth.

Darken reached for her hand then thought better of it. A split second later, he said, "Fuck it," and grasped it.

"So?" She wore the twinge of a teasing grin, but her eyes sought his. She wanted his honesty.

"I'm worse."

She kept watching, like she didn't believe him.

"Really. This face you're looking at? Just the candy coating for what lies beneath. At dawn, the ugly peanut comes out."

"Fool," she giggled, slapping at him half-heartedly. "I'm serious."

"Me too."

"Candy coating, huh?" She leaned toward him, her gaze suggestive. "So, if I lick…" Daniela's fingers walked across the center console again.

144

He watched them, his brain misfiring. "Wait. I'm hideous and you don't know…"

She leaned closer, the scent of her warm and a little flowery. Her tongue traced her bottom lip. "I know I'm still curious."

Holy. Shit. And what do you know. His dick was curious, too. "I have to show…" Breathing would be good. If he could remember how his lungs worked.

He swallowed. "You need to see…to learn and make the right choice…"

Oh, who was he kidding. He'd keep her no matter what she thought. Now that he had her at the compound, he could indulge his inner cave man and lock her away if she wanted to bolt.

Cause that was such a way to win the love of your girl.

Actually, what he really wanted was to take things slow and gentle, savor the softness of her skin, give her time and space enough to back out if she still wanted to.

Except she wasn't backing up. Not even when he torqued himself to reach her with the steering wheel in the way. Which was when he found his mouth saying, "We should go inside."

Daniela nodded as she leaned back into her seat. "Okay." Her lips, moist from her licking them, held the shimmer of the moon. He bit down on his tongue to keep from lapping it off.

As Daniela exited the truck, he followed suit, walking around the hood to meet her on the other side. He practically levitated off the frigging driveway as his Chosen One burrowed into his chest. Arms wrapping tight around her, he lowered his chin to the top of her head.

"Your home is beautiful."

Darken lifted his head to play tourist, seeing the vast yard as Daniela would see it. Trimmed hedges, the more fragile shrubbery wrapped in burlap. Snow mounded and softening the contours of the various birdbaths and quaint garden fences.

He remembered Anton saying something about French gardens and Monet, but hadn't been paying much attention then. Back when they'd first moved in, they were without Merrick.

And freshly vomited from their Godforsaken punishments.

Purple flowers and pea gravel walkways were as far from his vengeful mind as the stars in a daytime sky.

Besides, it had been autumn when they'd accepted this refuge, the burlap already wound tight and the flower stalks shorn to the dirt. If he'd been paying attention, yeah, he would have still seen the fine bones of this supermodel garden, the artistic placement of the ponds and arching bridges, even without the flower embroidery.

But then, he'd been more concerned with the inner landscape. Worried that this haven would turn out to be the home of his eternal stay— where he'd be perched for all time beside the ornamental gargoyles lining the various roofs of this stone-hewn fortress.

It had been and still was a close call for them all.

As it was, even though he parked his stone carcass next to a window when dawn arrived, he was still only able to see the portion of the garden his eyes were locked onto.

No casting his gaze to purview the sprawling landscape. For any of them, except Merrick, who'd been freed from the Grotesque curse by his Chosen One.

Now, though, seeing it through his Chosen's eyes, he couldn't help but admire the beauty spread before them. A vast yard well taken care of.

Much like the inside—before they'd moved in.

Now, the interior was the ravaged opposite to its external counterpart.

The thought landed his shit-kickers back to earth.

Her eyes shining expectantly as she twisted in his embrace to look up at him, Daniela said, "I bet the inside of this place is as gorgeous as out here."

"You'd think."

She frowned. "It's not?"

"It's ah…yeah. You probably should see for yourself."

* * * *

Urick entered the kitchen through the door leading from the garage.

Not that he needed anything in this room with its nearly empty cupboards, and its black countertops sleek enough to reflect one's image.

He did not need to see himself. Bad enough he had to live in his skin.

Not only did he not require a reminder of the shape he was in, the sustenance his body craved wouldn't be found in the kitchen anyway. Not

146

unless there was a human blood donor hanging out in the commercial size Sub-Zero.

Ignoring the stainless steel monstrosity, he navigated across the tiled floor, double-timing it. The last thing he needed was to run into someone who'd witnessed him teleporting from the library as he and Kallen had faced off.

Playing mouse despite his size, he stepped from the kitchen into the dining room, and didn't have to veer to miss the long slab of table. It had been pushed against the wall months ago with the hope it wouldn't get smashed by a thrown body or a swinging dragon's tail.

Or a bear with a penchant for demolishing shit within his reach.

He only just noticed that someone had thrown a couple of bedsheets over it.

Probably Angelia.

But then again, she never seemed to mind that the house her father had provided for them was getting torn down from the inside out.

Glancing upward to the coffered ceiling, his eyes focused on the octagonal recess in the center of the room. Where a chandelier now hung free-style without the table to ground it.

Somehow the beauty had avoided the beasts and their rampages.

Kind of like how Darken's Chosen had had her own near miss.

Uri shivered though he rarely felt the cold. Not even buck-ass naked, as he currently was. Somehow when his molecules had reformed, he'd been put back together as grizzly.

Not gargoyle.

Or vampire. Thank fuck. For some reason, he really detested that part of himself.

Well, he knew the reason. Which was why he was hell bent on starving that third of himself. Which was cutting his nose off to spite his face.

But whatever.

Sure, the Vampyres of the ruling Triumvirate, especially Angelia's father Anton, had shown him and his brothers nothing but goodwill.

For the most part.

Goody for them.

But he couldn't forget the tortures of the past two thousand years so easily. It had left him unsteady as all fuck. And now he was teleporting uncontrollably.

If he didn't know the difference, he'd swear there was no God.

For the love of those things holy, he'd come within a bear's hair of drinking the Chosen One dry. Then turning his hunger on his brotherkynd.

If Darken didn't possess that humor…

"Where'd you go?"

Urick halted, like some guilty thief pegged by the cops. Resisting the urge to put his hands up, he turned toward that hollow voice. "Kronos."

The gargoyle sat on the floor, back to the silk-papered wall, elbows resting on bent knees. The lighting in the foyer should have lit him up like a work of art at the Guggenheim, but leave it to Kronos to wait in the shadows.

As though illumination flayed the poor bastard like a laser.

Which he supposed it did. Or used to, at any rate. As the witness to the world's nightmares, the gargoyle's domain for the past two thousand years had been darkness and the terrors lurking in that gloom.

The fact that his body was now only half in the shadows was actually an improvement. Still, though, that voice…

"Where'd you go?"

Not just hollow, but eerily cavernous. As though the man speaking had been carved out from the inside like a Halloween pumpkin.

Hard to be pissed off when in the presence of such…barrenness.

Again, it was an improvement of sorts for the gargoyle. The bouts of panicked shrieking were happening less and with lesser intensity.

Succumbing to the Kynd's urge to touch, Uri folded his huge bulk to sit with his brother, lowering his shoulders to rest his head in Kronos' lap.

The gargoyle straightened his legs, his big hand palming Uri's head.

It was the stroking of the fingers in his hair Uri had sought. Both as comfort to Kronos and reassurance for himself.

Two over-sized men curled up like puppies. Cute.

Except it felt too right. Too much like it had before they'd been cast from Heaven. Back when they'd been whole.

"I landed in Darken's truck."

When the only response was another pass of fingers through the hair at his temple, his mouth and his fears came undone. "While he was driving it."

Kind of funny, now that he was safe for the moment in Kronos' arms. But he didn't smile any more than the gargoyle did.

The quiet in the house lulled him, the shadows soothing his bloodshot eyes.

"Where is everyone?"

He felt Kronos inhale, and waited for the man to speak. Always hesitant, it was as if he had to make sure what was going to come from his mouth were words, not screaming.

"Merrick and Angelia went to see Anton."

Fuck a duck. He could well imagine why.

"Kallen's…upset."

Code for unglued. His instant disappearance probably flung the gargoyle into guilt city. So much for hiding. He'd have to see Kallen before dawn made sure he couldn't.

"And Drakus? He okay?"

Kronos grunted.

Drakus was never going to be okay.

"I'm sorry."

He felt the gargoyle shrug. "I think everyone understands you didn't mean to."

Didn't he? He hadn't wanted to fight Kallen, so vanishing before blood was shed was his way of…copping out. The last thing he wanted to do was face the real reasons he refused to feed on anything requiring a host.

Losing his Kyndness was an excuse and he knew it. They'd all lost pieces of that when God had exiled them to their various punishments.

Sitting up, he let himself lean against Kronos, still reluctant to lose the contact. "Darken's outside. With his Chosen One."

Kronos stiffened, the shadows etching the crags on his face ever deeper. "You're sure?"

"About her being his Chosen? Definitely. She accidently touched Darken and me at the same time, and we weren't trying to share the vibe, if you know what I mean."

Daniela had connected through her own…input. Exactly the way Angelia linked into the Kynd bond. Without either him or Darken consciously pushing the fused energy outward.

"It gives one hope." The deep channels cutting into that beautiful face didn't soften.

But he wasn't expecting them to. Kronos didn't exactly cover the motherboard of emotions. He couldn't. Not yet, anyway. And probably not for a very long time.

Suddenly, Uri felt very, very tired. The suck of gravity too much on his great body. Not that he could give in to it. He had yet to visit Kallen.

And wasn't that just the spur in the flank.

All for one, and one for all.

Jesus, they were the Brady Bunch.

On that note… "I guess now everyone knows why I'm not the best candidate to liaise freed Shades unto the heavens."

He waited for the answer, even though he hadn't asked a question.

"We hadn't been holding our breaths. None of us are good candidates."

But they needed one.

"I guess it's back to square one."

"Those same words were spoken earlier, my brother."

Shit. "What about Merrick or Darken?"

"Merrick can't get through. He and Angelia think it has something to do with his already being saved."

"Which cancels Darken out." Double shit.

Nor could they ignore this particular quest. The Scriptum hinted that there'd be a Chosen One in the Second Circle.

His muscles felt cooked on the bone, and he sat there on the floor with his brotherkynd for long moments in the shadows. Not a bad place to be, all in all.

Except he had someone else to comfort, and a new couple who'd seen enough of his bare ass for one night, thank you very much.

Heaving his carcass to the vertical, he held out his hand. "I'm heading upstairs. You coming?"

Kronos clasped the palm for the lift, but shook his head.

Urick waited as the gargoyle filled his lungs. "I think I might try…" The cragged face attempted a grin, but it came across more as the making of a crevasse—all monumental effort to crack the immovable.

"Want to meet the Chosen for yourself, eh? Can't blame you. She's a sight worth keeping your shit together for."

Kronos nodded, the failed smile sparking in his eyes before sputtering out.

Uri clapped the man's shoulder, then headed for the stairs.

* * * *

Outside on the crushed stone of the circular driveway, Daniela was finding it hard to peel her stare off the front of Darken's—insert air quotes for dramatical purposes—house.

The place was awe-inspiring.

And she'd had no idea such a megalithic, medieval structure stood in these rural Maine woods.

She bet she could come up with a shit ton more adjectives ending in–ic, too. Like gothic, artistic, and…gigantic.

"How many thousands of square feet is this place?" She'd stepped a bit closer, and Darken came up behind her to close the gap. Between him and his house, she felt positively puny.

Kind of her theme song since she'd met this…man.

And man, oh, man, did this place fit him. He'd looked out of place at Alfio's Pizzeria. But here? Wacky t-shirts aside, Darken and his brother would look…normal…sitting up on those ramparts.

She stifled her snort. *Ramparts.* She'd lived long enough to actually use the word in a sentence. And gee criminy, the three hundred—give or take—windows just at the front of the house looked like they were crafted with authentic leaded glass.

What do you know. Another –ic word.

"Big enough, most times."

"Most times?" She leaned back, a little incredulous. "What? You fly planes in the foyer?"

When he grinned, she saw the tips of his fangs. Because he no longer felt the need to hide them? *Holy Christ.*

It had taken the sight of the house to remind her she was way out of her depth here.

At least there wasn't a huge crack running up the center of the manse.

House, thy name is Usher. Or was it Brontë.

151

Meanwhile, Darken's smile pulled a disappearing act, replaced by what she'd have to call a frown.

"What?" It made her nervous seeing it, like maybe she should have listened to that whispering voice of reason back before her car had skidded into a snowbank.

"I shouldn't take you in."

"W-why." Now she understood how people could stutter when they were trying to appear brave. Trepidation stiffened the lips.

Darken squeezed his eyes shut, like the sound of that stammer hurt.

And instantly her fear fell away. What she felt in its stead was an elixir of concern, worry, and self-reproach. Since she'd met him, he'd shown her nothing but the utmost care for her well-being, anxiety that she'd think him a monster.

When in fact…he wasn't.

Despite the fangs and claws.

Two things he'd used to pleasure her. Remembering, her body heated and her core executed a little twist and roll, wetting her panties.

As if he sensed the sudden turn in her thoughts, or—*God! Can he smell me?*—he pushed that big body right up her back, his thick arms curling around her middle as he nuzzled her neck.

His breath was warm, his lips soft. As his fangs gently scraped skin, she couldn't stop the moan oozing up her throat.

She arched her back, grinding her ass against his hips and thrusting her boobs upward for some squeezing. Her hand reached for a hold on his hair so his mouth would stay…right…where…it…was.

"You like that." His voice vibrated through her entire body.

She answered by rubbing her butt back and forth across the front of his jeans.

The arms holding her coiled tight just as his hands skimmed…*so close*…the lapels of her coat. "Keep it up, and I'll have to take you right here."

"You like, hmm?"

He pushed his face under her hair. Cold air brushed her nape as he dragged in her scent. "Very much." It was as if he chose words that would shiver across her skin.

Sex on the snow seemed…like an awesome idea.

What, wait. She'd come here seeking proof about Darken before her car…and her needy little clit…veered her off track.

As though sensing her hesitation, Darken stilled for a long moment. Seeming to come to his own conclusions on the matter, he nodded, quick and sharp. "Let's go inside." When he took her hand, he didn't look at her.

Neither did he take her to the front door. Or doors, as was the case. Two huge planks of hardwood, their tops cut into an arch. Both had bulky cast iron knobs. Probably so you could open them at the same time and drive the airplane through you were going to fly around in the foyer.

Instead, he led her around the corner of the house toward the garage, to a Dutch door sitting to the right of five bays. Each bay had been designed to make the modern attachment look like an antique carriage house.

Going in, the echo of their footfalls told her what she'd see when Darken snapped on the lights.

Nada.

Not a single car. Just a long, empty room of absence.

"Are your brothers not here?" Seven of them lived in this house, so where were all the vehicles?

"Just Angelia by the looks of it. And Merrick, too." He looked like he'd swallowed a bad tuna fish sandwich.

When she didn't state the obvious, his jaw went tight, like maybe that sandwich rebelled.

"There aren't any other vehicles because my brothers don't drive."

Huh. A houseful of men and they didn't have cars. Kind of like having a house full of kids without the toys. Weren't men supposed to have automobiles, even if it was just to pet them and polish the chrome?

With a gentle hand on her elbow, Darken led her through the garage to another door.

Up three concrete and cobblestone steps, and he leaned over her to open the way into…

A hallway. Floored in slate, and lined with doors with little, square panes of glass, and drawers. The kind where you knew behind them would be spare chaffing dishes and ceramic platters, along with every cut of real silverware a well-placed table would require.

Behind the tiny windows of some of those doors, there was row upon

153

row of crystal. And not just the clear stuff.

Dear God, Darken and his brothers had to be loaded.

Daniela made sure she kept her mouth shut so it didn't hang open. For Pete's sake, they weren't even past the pantry yet.

"The kitchen."

She was not going to whistle, dang it. Instead, she stepped away from her escort while her head went on swivel mode. Talk about something being artfully done. The wealth was in the details, right down to the gold faucets.

In the three sinks.

Cupboards went from counter level to sky high. "It's gorgeous."

Darken watched her without looking around the room. "Aye, she is."

Hiding her blush, she tilted her head toward one of the two archways leading to the rest of the house. "May I?"

Darken's lids dropped slow over his slate eyes before he nodded. Yet his feet didn't take him anywhere. He leaned against one of those black as ink countertops as if immobilized.

"Hey, if this—"

"No, I'm good. It's good." He pushed himself off the counter. "I can't put off the inevitable." He forced a grin.

"Darken, this doesn't have to be—"

"Aye, it does, and it is. When I called you Chosen, I meant it. Poor you, but I meant it. I'm not going to force it on you, and if you stick around after—ah, hell." He ground the heel of his hand to the bridge of his nose. "If you still think it's worth it, think…I'm…worth it, I won't push. We'll take things as slow as you need to."

While Darken caught a case of the shits of the mouth, Daniela bumped up to him, hooking her finger in the belt loop of his jeans. Her body zinging to life as though there weren't inches between hers and his.

He smelled…masculine, and like clean sweat.

"But if you never want to have another thing to do with me…us…" Holding up his hand, he made a little circle. Encompassing more than just the two of them. "I'll let you go, I swear it. No pressure. No…pressure."

God, the man looked utterly defeated.

"Hey, hey, hey." Because she could wax poetic when faced with someone stressed as bad as this man in front of her. "What is this?" She tugged his belt loop again.

He didn't answer, just took her hand in his and walked deeper into the house.

Chapter Fifteen

Sometimes being scared helps you accomplish amazing things. Or can let you know you're onto something significant. Being scared can also be the greatest step toward being courageous.

But no one ever said being scared didn't suck ass.

He wasn't even sure why he was shaking in his shit kickers. He had his Chosen One in his sights, for Christ's sake.

He could touch her, smell her, recall the taste of her.

Which was the problem, wasn't it?

He knew now what he stood to lose. And it had nothing to do with avoiding the Grotesque curse, or even with the fact that she was the one person on this planet created solely for him.

Well, that part seared the skin right off his heart if he thought about it too hard.

His fear had more to do with losing the feeling of glowing from the inside out whenever she turned that beautiful brown-eyed gaze on him.

Him.

Who was nothing but a displaced, doomed, and damaged gargoyle. A beast who wasn't even human like she was. Yet still she touched him with tenderness, let him put his hands on her precious body, to give her pleasure.

As if the enjoyment was all hers.

He'd argue that one 'til the last cow stood in the barn with a bucket under her udder.

Pleasing her...knocked his fucking socks off.

As if his new purpose in this new life was to give her everything of himself he could. And didn't that make him the luckiest male on the planet.

Unless he lost her.

And how was he not going to?

He knew what she did for a living. Daniela helped victims of violence. Helped them escape homes where holes in walls were made with heads and glass was broken during dinners interrupted with fists.

Much in the way nightmares too torturous to be borne shattered the peace in this house.

The one he shared with this brethren.

The one he wanted to share with his Chosen One.

Feeling like he'd lost the calcium in his bones, Darken went a little loose, his joints slipping like they were too well-oiled as he walked with Daniela into the foyer. The chandelier above had the night off, the broken crystal droplets hidden by the shadows thrown by the sconces lit in the lower corridor.

So, his Chosen wouldn't see that part of the destruction, but it wasn't going to be long before she saw the rest of the wreckage.

Perversely, the thought occurred to him to light the house up like a bonfire so she'd see into every crevice, get a gander at every crack. She'd see how they'd desecrated this beautiful home with their fits of violence. Most importantly, though, she'd see she didn't belong with him.

With them.

That the life she'd been called to lead was one which fought to eradicate the destroyers. A life given in service to free the helpless and the frightened souls with too few options.

For all that she sat quiet and firm amongst the battered and bloody, she led a life of beauty and majesty.

What had he to offer her?

He released her hand and bit the bullet, so to speak.

With a flick of his wrist, the chandelier flared to flawed brilliance, banishing the shadows to the edges, where they demarcated details rather than obscured.

Kronos, sitting upon the bottom stair, raised his arm to his face to block the glare. "Bloody Jesus, Darken, you could kill the lights."

He didn't.

Startled, Daniela spun to face the newcomer.

Kronos preferred the shadows, and neither of them needed the extra illumination, but she did. Darken wouldn't extinguish his Chosen's advantage if the lighting burnt holes in their stony skins.

"Oh, hi!" She smiled like the house tour was just a big adventure full of fun and made safe with hand rails. "You must be another brother." She stepped forward, hand extended.

Kronos looked as if he'd suddenly found himself on the wrong end of a gun.

Eyes darting for an emergency exit, he ignored the handshake she offered, his big body getting bigger as tension took over.

Looking for any excuse to touch his Chosen, Darken stepped in behind her, his big hands curling on her upper arms.

The soft pliancy almost launched a groan, but he kept the indulgence to himself. Somehow, he managed to sound half-way normal when he said, "This is Kronos. A gargoyle, like me."

For a second, he caught Daniela's hesitation, as though a thought came to her, but she filed it away for later.

"It's very nice to meet you." Her hand dropped to her side and she fidgeted slightly, like she wasn't sure what else to do with it.

Letting his slide down her arm, he clasped the little bird of it in his fingers.

"Kronos isn't used to…many people. You'll have to forgive him for being rude. Truly, if he could, he'd greet you properly."

"No. No, I want to." Looking unsteady as hell, he took a step forward. "Uri said she's Chosen, and I…I wanted to see for myself."

Ah. So they hadn't disturbed him after all. Kronos had been waiting. Well, chalk that up as a first. It even looked like the scarred gargoyle was attempting a smile.

When Kronos raised a clawed hand, and reached out, as if he'd changed his mind about the physical meet and greet, Darken crammed and locked the lid on the hope surging into his chest.

His heart felt like it was expanding like a fricking flower at dawn.

Leaving the blanket of his hovering body, Daniela stepped toward Kronos, reaching out once again for the other gargoyle.

Kronos' eyes flicked from the woman to him, and back again. "Touch her, too."

Ah, so this was why. Kronos wanted to feel the connection of a

Chosen One himself. Hard to blame the guy. Daniela would be like pure heroin to a junky. "Kron, she doesn't know."

"Tell her then."

"She's seen and heard enough for now."

"She's right here, by the way."

As if her voice took on magnetic properties, two sets of slate gray eyes pinned themselves to her. Neither he nor Kronos could ignore her. She was like a magnificent, resplendent elephant in the room.

Who the hell didn't want to acknowledge her with touching, with feasting their senses on her.

"Touch her."

Darken resisted the urge to clap his hand over the other gargoyle's insistent mouth. If it wasn't for the fact the man was standing in front of them, looking about as put together as he'd ever seen him, Darken would tell Kronos to shut it.

The woman had enough on her plate without a repeat performance of the Conduit Theater she'd experienced with Uri. She could only absorb so much before she'd run screaming into the night.

Oh, wait. She was going to do that anyway when she wrapped up her House Beautiful sightseeing tour.

"It's like that with all of you?"

Didn't require a segue into what she was referring to.

"Yeah. When Kynd connect, we create a…circle of energy. It would seem our Chosen Ones can plug into it."

"Huh. Cool."

Cool?

Without warning, she clasped her fingers around Kronos' hand then grabbed his. The flare of electricity was instantaneous, and guess whose craggy face went all light bulb.

"It's…true." Came out as more hiss than a statement of fact, but Kronos actually appeared to be keeping his shit together. Like Uri, he seemed…comforted.

As if there was a little somethin'-somethin' going on with the other gender's contribution to the Kynd circle.

"Huh." Except he didn't add *cool.*

But he had to wonder if she realized the full extent of her effect.

159

His worry for the situation took a bus out of town as he stood in the foyer, linked to the other two. Until Kronos got a little too cozy with the groove-on.

Like a leaf drifting along the currents of a river, Darken's growl floated through the tentacles of energy, adding an ominous dimension to the subtle vibrations.

It took them all a few seconds to realize the intrusion.

Himself included. Though once he did, he also noticed he couldn't pull the warning back. Surprise, surprise—he didn't want to.

Possession claimed him like he was just the clothes it was wearing. Next thing he knew, he stepped in front of his Chosen One and stiff-armed his brother.

Then dropped the attitude like someone put a cat turd in his hand. "Sorry." He didn't know who to look at the most. "Sorry. I didn't mean that. I swear it, Kronos. Daniela."

She lost her enthusiasm for the adventure, and stood looking at him like he was a stranger who'd slapped a lollipop from a kid's grubby fist.

Which wasn't a stretch.

Kronos went back to his standard mien. All terrified glare. The juxtaposition proving just how screwed up the man was. Daniela's touch had given him relief, and Darken had not only rained on the parade, he'd blown in like a sudden storm.

Or a car bomb.

Because that was the vibe hovering in the foyer. The aftermath of something unforeseen and devastating.

He opened his mouth to say sorry again, then shut his yap. The damage had been done. No amount of groveling was going to fix it.

So he backed off. All the way to the far wall. As soon as his back smacked the pretty silk wallpaper, his ass fell in love with gravity and he slid to the floor, elbows on knees.

Kronos retreated to the bottom stair, where they'd found him when he'd snapped on the lights. Surprisingly, he hadn't latched onto Darken's caveman-esque challenge, or lost his chain.

The residual of Daniela's influence?

Most likely.

The woman herself stood in the middle of them, the damaged

chandelier beaming down upon her like the sun.

How apropos. She was of sunlight and beauty, while he was...

On the receiving end of a jabbing finger. "You stay right there." As soon as the words left her mouth, she bee-lined it for his brother, kneeling down in front of him, careful not to touch him again.

Darken strained to hear her whisper.

Good thing he didn't hold his breath. Daniela didn't say anything.

She just knelt there in front of Kronos. Quiet, unassuming, as if she knew her presence alone could bring comfort, relief. Security, even.

Which turned his thoughts back to her chosen occupation. He bet this was exactly how she sat with the female victims at the hospital. Waiting in the moment while the women clawed their way through the fog, the fear, to find their voices.

As black as the jealousy burning inside him was, Darken stayed on his ass and waited, too. Not that he couldn't find some positives in the view. Kneeling as she was, Daniela's long coat fanned out behind her, the burnished highlights of her hair resplendent as it hung like a living thing down her back.

Kronos remained on the bottom step, his elbows driven down between his knees, his legs clamped tight to his arms. The crags running down either side of his mouth appearing deeper under the light of the chandelier.

Yet his mouth wasn't opened in a tormented shriek.

There wasn't anything coming from his brotherkynd, except haunted curiosity. For all that his body was hunched in a fetal position of agony, he leaned toward the woman kneeling in front of him.

Then hesitantly he reached forward, a slow motion unwinding of his heavily muscled arm.

Darken curled his claws into his palm, forcing himself to stay put for the sake of his brother. For someone who didn't know, Kronos wouldn't seem on the verge of insanity. He looked like a man well acquainted with it.

Yet, Daniela remained close to him as the shaking, clawed, and so very inhuman hand neared her. Accepting it with the touch of her own, she said two words, "So beautiful."

* * * *

161

She would look back at this time and know it as a pivotal point in her life, the fork in the road where she took the proverbial path least traveled.

Practically shitting her pants as she veered off the safe lane, she told Jiminy Cricket riding her shoulder to shut it, and took her new and very uncertain future in her hands. Literally.

The one she now held wasn't Darken's, but it was similar.

In that it was clawed.

Dearest God in heaven, what am I doing?

Except she knew precisely what she was up to. She felt the certainty in that tranquil center of her gut, the serene place she drew upon when standing in the midst of misery.

She stepped onto the unknown path with the surety of someone who knows herself bone deep and isn't surprised by the surprises.

"So beautiful." Speaking of more than just the gesture of a broken man who dared to reach forth. She meant, too, this moment, the chrysalis of who she was and what she did with it.

The gray eyes looking at her from under lowered lids were nothing like Darken's, though. These were quake in your boots haunted. Troubled. As if the mind behind them had one hell of a time separating the here and now from the—

God, she didn't know what could put such a disturbed aspect into those mercurial eyes.

Yet the why didn't matter, did it.

Besides, unlike the women she touched in this manner, Kronos didn't seem inclined to divulge. Despite the massive physical strength of him, he merely sat there, as though touching another was about all he could stand.

Fine by her. She wasn't sure she wanted to bear witness to the horrors Kronos must have been privy to.

The gargoyle lifted his gaze just as she felt a familiar weight touch upon her back, the bulk looming behind her familiar.

Darken. He'd approached so quietly and still remained so. The expression on his face kept her mouth shut about the visit with the green-eyed monster. The warmth and understanding radiating from him proved he'd shoved his jealousy aside for the sake of his brother.

How...endearing, damn it.

She'd promised herself she wasn't going to let this kind of thing get under her skin. She'd sworn to stand tough against any macho bullshit, against any signs of domineering behavior.

And here she was, somehow standing betwixt two realities, where victims of violence weren't just weakened and manipulated women.

They were men who would be seen as monsters in the world she came from. They were men with fangs and claws, with sheer brawn that would turn a linebacker into a covetous nancy.

Proving that persecution didn't discriminate.

Reaching past her, Darken placed his big hand on Kronos' knobbish knee.

"You are stronger than I, brother, I am sorry." Head hanging, he remained bowed as Kronos inched a little closer, the knot of his body coming loose.

That Darken didn't say sorry to her...grew her heart to about twice its size.

Damn it, again. How could she remain objective when he wormed under her defenses like that? Apologizing to a brother so wounded his preferred position was ball-like proved Darken understood a little something about the abused.

Acknowledgement went miles toward building another's confidence. That he might know firsthand about it turned her growing heart cold.

With fear.

For him.

And if she was being honest with herself, this fear for Darken scared her. Because, really, what monsters out there had scarred the monsters in here.

Beside her, Darken maintained his contrite posture, his heat enveloping her, wrapping around her as if she were warmed by a space heater.

"I used to sever souls." Well, there you go. His words turned her cold again despite the surface heat. "The scythe I carried to do it is in my room." He didn't look at her.

Which was fine. She was used to confessions without eye contact. Plus, she needed the space to compose herself, even though she felt it on her skin that though Darken kept his eyes averted, he was deeply attuned to her just then.

She fought to remain impassive.

"They screamed even when the dying shells of their hosts did not." He took a jagged breath, as though he was now carrying that scythe. "And the horror of it is nothing compared to what you have endured, my brother."

Kronos' grip crunched her fingers like a vise.

"If my Chosen One sees it in her heart to give you comfort, I have no right to interfere with that."

Cue the double-take. Daniela lost her composure, her hard won serenity going all *duh, what.* On the heels of it was another flush of heat as her heart resumed its swelling.

Blinking at the sting in her eyes, she leaned into the man kneeling beside her, her shoulder bumping his upper arm, not coming anywhere near his shoulder. He was just too damned huge, and rock solid.

Yet, she felt him soften, his body welcoming her touch.

With his hand still clutched to hers, Kronos inched close enough to Darken so the other man could put his arms around him. When they came together, they didn't smack each other's backs, or brace off awkwardly inside those hugs.

They were comfortable in the holding.

Needed it, actually, by the way they maintained the embrace.

They'd be seen as queerer than three dollar bills anywhere else. And Daniela had to admit to herself, it was...odd.

The men she knew just didn't share emotion the way these two were doing. Or the way Uri had done. Was this some Kynd secret? Monstrous sized men in body and mien, yet tender beyond measure with each other?

It would seem so, but it was such a strange sight, she wasn't sure she could trust it. For all her suspicion, though, it seemed she had a part in it. Oh, and that vibration was probably telling her something, too.

Like, this was the most effed-up and wondrous thing she'd ever been a part of.

Talk about one's world getting turned on its head. Since meeting Darken a few nights ago, Daniela had been feeling like a damned gymnast.

As her head reeled with the possibilities open to her, Kronos extricated himself from their knot and stood up, increasing the distance between them as he backed up the stairs.

His height increased twofold with every step upward.

Daniela kept her jaw closed as her head tilted back, lest it seem as though she gawked. Kronos looked raw enough as it was, she didn't need to scrape him any thinner.

Victims of abuse did not need pity. They needed self-confidence. Kronos was barely managing his.

He left without a word.

"That's the tightest wrapped I've seen him in a long time."

"You have got to be kidding me." *Tightly wrapped?* The man who had just backed up a flight of stairs? The trembling one?

Darken nodded, but on the downward dip he kept his head low. She could barely tell if he was breathing. Which meant...

"That shames you."

Without warning, he snagged her close, his tension holding her tight to his chest, the heat of him enveloping her. "No, it enrages me, and that's what I'm ashamed of. Seeing my brothers like this makes it hard not to lash out." They stood at the foot of the stairs, embracing, not talking for a few moments. "I'm not always successful. Come here."

Where? She was already as close as she could get without intercourse. Like she needed the visual. She'd pasted her body to the front of his, pushing her hips so water wouldn't have been able to leak between them.

"You're getting the idea of things around here. You might as well get a gander at the rest." Holding her hand, he led her up that grand staircase. And wouldn't you know, she could use the word *grand* to describe it. Carpeted with something wool and expensive, the thing flared out at each end and tapered in at the center. It curved against the wall holding it, the back of a cat arching into a caressing hand.

It made her want to run up it, all Julie Andrews and the *Sound of Music.*

Or, since she couldn't sing, more like Carol Burnett in the episode where the set designers had fashioned a Southern belle's gown out of the draperies. Curtain rod included.

Comedy, yes. Singing, not so much.

At the top, they could have gone in two directions. A balcony left and another to the right. Forget remembering north or south. She'd need the sun to orient herself in a house this big.

Speaking of which…

"Didn't you tell me you turn to stone or something come dawn?" Man, she almost panted, there'd been so many stairs. If she'd known she was going to be doing a *Buns of Steel* workout, she'd have worn her yoga pants. Pfft. Like she actually owned a pair. Her ass and stretch pants? Can we say *Snausages*?

"We've got a couple of hours yet. Enough for me to show you something." The look he gave her suggested he meant to say more, but dropped it.

"You seem nervous."

He nodded. "You'll see."

They walked for what seemed a country mile, passing doors that lined the length of the balcony. Across the way, the set up mirrored the hallway they were walking down. Both corridors were lined with columns like she'd seen in the foyer.

Peering up a bit, she got a gander at that magnificent chandelier. The one with cracked and broken crystals, one of the pendulous arms stripped naked of its decorations.

Had it fallen?

And, uh, were those *claw* marks on the railing?

No time for closer investigation, Watson.

Darken stopped at one of the middle doors. "Ready?"

"Depends what I'm supposed to be ready for. If it's a torture chamber…yeah, no. If there's a new car behind door number three? Then open her up, Bob Barker."

He smiled, and suddenly he didn't seem so huge and scary. He became the man she'd fallen for, the one who wore funny t-shirts and dragged chairs around a room so they could sit closer.

The one who'd been scared stiff about revealing himself to her, hiding his clawed hands under the table.

Which he now used to twist the doorknob so they could enter.

With a flip of a switch, lights flared golden and soft, illuminating the interior, yet brushing the edges with shadows. *So…inviting.* Daniela stepped inside, feeling for all the world as if she should be dragging a silk gown, or a fur coat as she floated in on stilettos.

Heavy damask drapes stood like sentries on either side of the floor to ceiling windows. Like the lighting, they too were golden, so even though it was the middle of the night, it seemed like the sun shined. Dusk on a summer's day. Or an autumn dawn.

Against one of the walls was the king-size bed with its duvet and...

"You punched the wall." She felt punched in the gut, too, as she stared at the starburst above the headboard.

Swallowing, he nodded.

As she stepped deeper into the room, he didn't stop her. It was as if he wanted her to see, his confession silent because words wouldn't do.

The bed itself canted on one corner, a pile of books sitting on the floor as if waiting to be of use. Not to transport the reader to another time, but to buttress the tilted bed.

"You don't sleep in that." She didn't wait for Darken to shake his head.

Of course he didn't use the bed, even though the room looked well used. Actually, being honest, Darken's bedroom looked worn out.

He'd spent a shit ton of time in here.

Seeing the demolition made her a little sick. Her hand on her belly, she made a circle of the room.

"Right here is where I usually wind up." His head bowed again, Darken stood off-center, the wall of windows rising before him.

"Wind up?"

Silver eyes shined at her.

"Wind up, yes. Sunrise. I'm in the habit of looking out, and up."

"Up?" God, she was a flipping Chatty Cathy with a broken string.

Darken pointed at the ceiling. "Heaven."

When all she did was give him a vacant stare, he elaborated. "Come dawn, I'm screaming heavenward. Pissed off. Feeling betrayed." The pain in his nickel eyes belied his dismissive shrug.

"That's always how I am when the stone...when my body becomes stone."

Okay, yeah. The rephrasing went a long way toward reminding her not who, but what, he was. The culmination of the night pressed down on her, so she felt popped out of her skin. A voyeur watching the surreal unravel, one horrible scenario at a time.

"Darken, I've got to be honest." Hard to lie through the teeth when they were picking up a chatter. "This is all a bit much. I mean, it's been one hell of a day. And night."

Too much. She felt as if she was at a carnival and had eaten the cotton candy, the candied apples, the fried dough, and a sausage roll. Then went on every ride on the fairway.

He tried a grin, but lost it. Took a step toward her, but stopped. "Can I come to you?"

Just as he'd done the first time he'd been in her house, he hesitated, unsure of his footing. Unsure of her reaction.

She quieted, tuning her ear to what her instincts were telling her. Despite the shock trembling through her body, she felt the trust she had for this gigantic man.

In spite of what she'd seen of his house, had learned of him.

"Yes," she practically whispered. Although big, the room didn't echo. Instead, the air seemed hushed and sensual, as if all that luxury smoothed out the harsh edges of everything.

Herself included.

Darken knelt in front of her. A knight before his queen. Which was ridiculous. She was just a woman. Nothing special, especially here amongst…storybook creatures.

His look of anxious adoration annihilated her lowly self-opinion. As did the caressing of his thumb along her calf. "You are my Chosen One. An improbable dream come true." He flicked his silver gaze upward.

She couldn't muster a snort. She stood as if spellbound.

"A pity for you, really."

"No," she denied.

"Hmm. We'll see." His thumb continued to caress, the stroke of it seeming to ride up her thigh, to her mons, then deep into her core. "I want you." A breathless contradiction to what he'd just said.

"Yeah." With one step outward, she spread her legs. An invitation. His shoulders seemed impossibly wide, the muscles of his back flexing with every caress along her leg.

How she'd love to see those shoulders inserted between her thighs.

Her hand reached out, her fingers curling into his blonde hair.

The tension in him shot through her, his growl rubbing like a purr along her skin. "Amica mea," he said, pressing his head into her hand.

In a flash, he was upright, his arms lifting her as if she weighed nothing. With his foot, he kicked the stack of books under the corner of the bed before easing her down to the mattress.

So gentle, despite…a boatload of evidence to the contrary.

She hadn't walked through his home blind. This room wasn't the only one suffering under men with little or no control.

And those men.

Brutes.

Broken brutes who strove to be gentle.

Just like the man leaning over her now. His jaw locked, his fingers trembling. His eyes dragging the length of her prostrate body. "I won't hurt you." As if he read her thoughts.

"No." Huh, guess she believed him.

He trailed his fingers up her inner thigh, his claws snagging her tights in places.

She saw his bicep bulge, as if he made a fist.

Lowering her hand, she found his wrist, and returned it to her flesh. "They're replaceable."

"You aren't."

"A born romantic."

He shrugged, those mercurial eyes of his burning. She felt a tug at the epicenter of her thighs, then a tearing sound. He'd sliced a hole for access. The tip of his claw skimming her moistened folds sent her back arching.

"Oh, God."

He trembled more. Lowered. Those shoulders wedging where she'd wanted them in a time that now seemed far away. Heck, everything seemed so far away. Except Darken.

Lifting her knees, she gave him full access.

His mouth took her. No foreplay, no lead-in. He suckled as he darted his tongue in and out, a fiery brand fucking her.

Fisting his hair, she pulled herself toward that fire, her thighs falling ever wider. Her boots planting upon his shoulders.

Jesus, she still wore her boots. They were both still dressed, her dress hiked up around her hips.

With his hands gripping her thighs, she could feel him tense up, could tell his boots dug into the carpet as though to get a better purchase. In order to push his tongue deeper. The breaths coming out of him fanned hot, licking at her as surely as his tongue.

She was going to come. Oh, God, she was…coming.

He was growling.

And it tipped her over the edge. She screamed as he growled.

They both panted.

But he wouldn't stop. He kept lapping, and lapping, as if storing up the taste of her.

Chapter Sixteen

Stopping wasn't an option. High on the taste, he could feel her scent go through him, as though it swam over his cells, coating them. Consuming him, until all he could sense was her with him.

Their essences conjoined.

Upon his tongue, she…throbbed. Even as her body stiffened as she moaned.

With her fingers gripped in his hair, he thought he'd go mad with the gratification of it. So right, to have her cleave to him.

The pounding on his door may as well have been a death knell, so truly did it kill this moment of peace.

His Chosen sighed one for the ages, her arms flinging wide upon his bed. "Well, there goes my denial."

Unable to let go of her yet, he sat back on his heels, keeping his hands on her knees. "Yeah, you got that right."

Lifting her head to peer down the length of herself, she said, "What."

"What?"

"What, we're Laurel and Hardy? What did you mean *I've got that right?* I was kidding about the denial."

Oh. Shit. "I think this is one of those man-woman things where she asks if her jeans make her ass look big."

Daniela flopped her head back down. "Fine. Avoid the issue, ostrich man."

Oh, the sass. Chalk up another thing that had him falling for this woman—this feisty side, her irreverent lip.

He didn't get a chance to mouth back. The door was going to buckle with another round of pounding.

"For the love of all that's holy…" Darken strode to the door without opening it, his erection squashed in his jeans. "What!"

"Oh, hey, brother." *Kallen.* Who sounded for all this world like he was fucking with him. "Meeting downstairs. Bring your lovey."

If ever there was a time to bash his head against something.

"Now? I'm busy here."

"Yeah, now. What'd you think, I'd disturb you if it wasn't important?"

"You're not wounded, so cut the act."

"Fine. Angelia and Merrick are back."

"Hurray for them." He rested his gaze on the bed. Daniela sat on the edge, adjusting her hose, her leg stretched before her so she looked sexy as hell.

"Just get your ass down to the library." The clomp of boots faded.

Daniela sat up, pushed her hair back. "So."

"Up for more of…" He held a finger up, spun it around his ear.

Brown eyes with thick, long lashes narrowed. Lush lips puckered. A beauty in contemplation if ever he'd seen one. "Yeah, actually. I am."

So courageous. And brave. Unlike him. He knew what she was in for.

"Okay, but first." For some reason, walking across his room to her filled his body with butterflies. He felt fluttery and nervous.

Maybe because they were in his home instead of hers?

Probably. This case of the nervous-nellies had most likely hit him because she could still slip through his hands like water.

He lowered himself between her feet and reached out with shaking hands to adjust her dress. Little tweaks at her shoulder, a tug at the sleeve. Any place where he had an excuse to touch her, to fuss.

He held her gaze. "The meeting's in the library. It's…hell…the room's a frigging mess. For good reason. Well, it's not a good reason, but there's a reason—Damn. What I'm trying to say is, think of this room and multiply the destruction by six."

There. A little diarrhea of the mouth, but he got his point across.

"Ah."

He scraped up enough courage to maintain the eye contact. "Yeah. Ah. The library is our meeting place, where we…"

God damn it. Now he canned the courageous act to study the floor between his Chosen One's feet. He couldn't take her down there. Okay, he could maybe handle her reaction to the state of that once beautiful room, but that wasn't what had him taking the Lord's name in vain.

The library was where they discussed stuff.

Not normal, human shit, either. And what if Drakus and Uri, or even Merrick for that matter, couldn't hold their seams together. That's all he needed. Like, *oh hey, Daniela, I forgot to tell you. Those lions, dragons, and bears I mentioned? Ta-da! Here they are!*

Christ on a candlestick.

"Look. I know you don't mind going downstairs, but dawn isn't far off. If I'm going to get you home safely, along with your car, we should probably leave now."

Such. A. Coward.

"I didn't realize. I guess I lost track of the time." She stood up quick, pushing him back so he had to do the soft-shoe-shuffle just to keep from falling on his ass.

He'd offended her. She'd given him everything of herself, had lain bared and vulnerable, and he couldn't be truthful with her.

He swore he would be, just not tonight. She'd taken in a lot and by some miracle still wanted him. Her acceptance kept his throat from closing shut with fear.

So far.

But she needed time to digest. He needed to be certain he didn't lose her.

"Daniela, wait."

Stopped at the door, she kept her back straight as a yardstick. Without turning to face him.

Coming up behind her, he meant to lay his hands on her shoulders, buss warm breaths on her neck.

But she tensed, and his palms never learned the feel of her shoulders under that cashmere sweater. He stood at her back struck scared, her upset launching a thousand ships filled with burning arrows. Aimed at his heart.

Resigned, he touched her, lowered his head to breathe her in. "What we just shared was the most maddeningly glorious thing I've ever done."

"I'm listening."

He squeezed her shoulders as he drew her against his chest. Okay, he had her attention. But now what? He couldn't let her go to that library, so ceding to her wishes couldn't be an option.

He couldn't let her talk him into it.

And she could. All she'd have to do was insist, and he wouldn't be able to deny her. The power of the Chosen One over the beastly Kynd. All in all, a clever checks and balances, and he'd be ecstatic to be ruled by his Daniela.

God, the idea *thrilled* him. To serve her? To please her and make her happy? If he had a tail, he'd wag the thing hard enough to make his legs go floppy.

Just not yet.

There was only so much a mind could take before it shorted out. So, for her protection, he'd keep her from that library.

Liar. Oh, yes, he was. Nor would he forget to add coward to the running list of his faults.

"Nothing more to say? Yeah, that's what I thought." She twisted from his arms and ripped the door back so hard and fast, he thought it might finally surrender its grip on the jamb.

Not that she noticed. Her eyes were on the staircase.

"Daniela, wait." Fear crawled over his skin.

With feet still marching she turned, her finger pointed in his direction like a gun. "No. I gave you your chance, and you blew it. I'm so special, huh? Well, at least your brothers think so."

Red exploded behind his eyes. "You are mine!"

Daniela whirled to face him. "I belong to no one!" She thumbed her chest. "Only to me, you understand that? I am no one's property!"

Jolted to a halt, he thought, *Property?* "What in God's name do you mean by that."

"Oh, you obtuse bastard. The world doesn't revolve around you!" She resumed her charge for the stairs.

Rage like he felt every dawn exploded through him. Hands and face to the ceiling, he shouted, "What the fuck are you talking about!" Disgust washed through him. In his current pose, he was exactly as the sun found him every morning.

Way to win your Chosen, you doomed, selfish…monster.

To his horror, she turned at the top of the stairs. To accuse him of something else? Didn't matter. Her eyes became two mirrors reflecting his image back at him, revealing everything.

Grotesque.

Fuuuuuuck. Like a weed sprayed with poison, he curled in on himself. Was that wheezing…him? Oh, God. He had never known shame such as this. His Chosen One, the single being on the entire planet made for him, saw…

What he'd fought so hard to hide. *Himself.* What he'd become. What they'd all become.

The truth paralyzed him.

Even with his Chosen One at his side, Merrick still fought with the damage done to him.

There was no magic key to open the door back to what the Kynd had been before the Schism. No return path to the Heavens, to a time and place where they had been what their name suggested—*kind.*

They were lost to the dark gullets of history, their former selves eclipsed by what they now were and would forever be—*Grotesque.*

Beasts of violence. Helpless against their rages.

There was no cure, only this…unending madness.

His knees lost their hydraulic fluid, his weight slumping over them. Only his skin and bones seemed to keep his pitiful carcass from pooling across the floor.

Inside of himself, he felt black, sick, toxic.

Good thing he didn't eat, really. He'd be retching his guts out. Desecrating the handwoven carpet.

Another stain. Another wound on this beautiful house.

Anton should have found them a cave to live in, not something so…fragile.

They were going to fix it up? When they couldn't even fix themselves?

Maddened laughter bubbled up his throat.

Oh, Daniela was so right. They were all obtuse. Refusing to believe they were ruined. Pretending like innocent lambs, making plans to restore the glory of the walls surrounding them.

As though fixing their home would fix them.

Ignorant. Self-delusional. Brutes.

Still folded in upon himself on the floor, he felt Daniela return, her steps tentative.

"Darken?"

He shook his head, then stilled the instant her fingertips touched his shoulder. "You should go."

She fell still, her nearness peeling the skin from his flesh. He burned to touch her, to pull close the soul who meant so much to his. But he could not.

She didn't know about monsters. If he left her alone, she'd talk herself into believing he'd been just a human man. That the fangs, the claws she'd seen hadn't been real.

If she wasn't with him, she could live a good life. A *safe* life. He hadn't been lying to himself, after all. She'd be as doomed as they all were if she aligned herself with him.

"You can drive my truck?" The growling of words scraping up his throat did not surprise him.

"Y-yes."

He thought his skin would slip off his bones when he heard that stammer.

Digging his claws into the floor—no point in hiding the damage he could do—he bit out, "Take it. You'll be safe in it. I'll make sure you get your car back tomorrow night."

"Darken." She pressed her whole hand to his back.

He shook his head. "No. Go now. I'll not bother you again. I promise."

"You're angry I fought back?" She seemed to be angry now. But how did he tell her it wasn't their fight at all, that eventually he'd lose it anyway.

Keep her safe from the world?

He wouldn't be able to keep her safe from himself.

Only one way to make sure it never happened...

"Aye, I am." Guts quaking, he looked her straight in the eye. "Who do you think you are to get uppity with me?" *Only the most precious thing in all the realms.* "You're lucky I don't throw you down those stairs." *Oh, God, he really was going to puke.*

Disbelief looked back at him. A world of hurt, too.

He was dying. Sure as his lungs withered in his shrinking chest. If she stood there much longer, he wouldn't be able to keep up this...lie. She was everything to him, and he was hurting her.

Better this than a broken arm, or worse. What if Uri had gotten to her out on that road. *Jesus, Jesus, Jesus.* Bad. So very bad for both of them.

He had to send her away. He had to make her... "Go! I don't want you around anymore!" Lunging for her, she startled backward.

Then fled down the staircase, and out the main door they never used, his heart stuck to her heel like a tattered strip of toilet paper.

Better this way.

Oh, aye, and as the saying went, he had a bridge he could sell himself, too.

* * * *

After everything she'd seen and heard, how had she wound up drinking the Kool-Aid? The return trip a safe one, if a blur, Daniela now lay in her bed, the blankets strewn and twisted as she wrestled with more than just her good judgment.

It wasn't even a case of *didn't see it coming.* Oh no. Red flags had been flying like sheets in the wind on laundry day. And she'd made excuses for every one of them.

If there were awards for Dangerously Stupid, she could hold her bouquet and her tiaraed head high as she paraded toward the guillotine.

Punching her pillow, she fell back onto the punctuated dent she'd made, just so she could rise again to answer her ringing cell phone. The digital clock on her nightstand said nine a.m. Her phone said it was the hospital.

She swiped her finger across the face of it and pushed it up to her ear. "Hello."

"Morning, Ms. Salvai. Sorry to trouble you at this early hour."

Blah, blah, blah. The hospital called her at any hour. Although this early wasn't the norm. Usually the bad shit went down later in the day.

"What have we got?"

"She was brought in about an hour ago. Seems hubby didn't like how his eggs were cooked. It's a bad one. Can you come, or should I call Eileen?"

Damn it. Although good at her job, Eileen had the personality of one of her recorders. It made her a good ear, but sometimes it took more than that to draw out the full story.

"Yeah, I can be there. Give me about an hour."

Ending the call, she slid her phone onto her nightstand, and flung back what was left of the covers. Rising to her feet like a grandmother, she got up and hit the shower.

Half a pot of coffee later, and the rest of it in her travel mug, she grabbed her coat and bag and headed for the driveway.

So effing bright, the way the sun glinted off the snow. While she rummaged for her sunglasses, she kept walking straight for…Darken's black Dodge Ram. Her sunglasses, of course, were in her car. Which was sitting on a very lonely tract of ice somewhere in the Maine woods.

She felt kind of sorry for it.

An inordinate sadness welled up inside her. "Oh, hell, no." She would not feel sorry for that man. Or his weird brothers. Yanking Megatron's door open, she hoisted herself up into the cab.

As she drove for the hospital, she kind of liked driving the big truck. From her spot on high, she could look down at everyone else. Huh. No wonder Darken liked it. He could look down his nose at everyone. Make himself feel big as he deigned to…

Hitting her exit, her ire descended along with the road in front of her, and she lost her steam just as the truck slowed to merge into downtown traffic.

Finding a parking spot big enough for the Dodge took longer than it would have if she'd had her little car, but she made it to the hospital inside the hour she promised.

Entering the building with her travel mug still handy, she hit the glide upward and promised her arteries she'd give them some exercise on the stairs later. She just didn't have the gumption this morning.

By the time she hit the hub in the emergency room, all the coffee she'd consumed made her feel normal. Which proved how worn out she really was. No pep in her step, but it cleared her head.

Good thing, since the place was hopping. Not the usual for a weekday morning, so something was up. She sidled up to the tall kiosk, the heart of operations for a place revolving around triage.

She recognized the blonde bun at the phones. "Hey, 'Cilla, what's up."

Priscilla stuck a single finger into the air. "Yup, uh-huh, right. 332 and stat. We'll send her right up. Hey, Dani." Putting the phone into its cradle, she pushed herself closer without getting up out of her chair. "You got this one?"

"I do." Daniela dropped her bag between her feet as she put her elbows up onto the counter. "Where is she?"

"You're going to miss her. Head trauma. She's got the clear for x-ray. They're taking her up now. Surgery's in that woman's future, so she ain't talking for a while."

Damn it. She'd rushed over for nothing. "Who brought her in?"

"Davis and Benoit. I think they headed for the caf when the vic went tits up."

"Priscilla!"

"Hey, I call it like I see it."

Which was why Daniela really liked this woman. She didn't see her as often as the night staff, but the blonde had done her time in the ER. She'd earned the day shift.

"Fine." Laughing, she hitched her bag over her shoulder. "I'll go find Davis and get some detes. See you later?"

"I'm not going anywhere for…" she checked her watch, "another nine hours." With a wave, they parted, and Daniela headed for the elevator she'd just exited.

Punching the B, she rode the car to street level.

As soon as the double doors slid open, she got hit with a whiff of waffles and Mr. Clean. Walking down the tiled corridor, the fluorescents buzzed overhead. With no windows or dime a dozen framed prints, she had nothing to distract her from celebrating the fact her shoes didn't squeak. Just her and the two-tone walls on either side—brown and browner.

Hipping one of the double doors at the end of the hall, she entered another world.

The cafeteria had clawed its way out of the institutional fifties and glinted like the modern beauty it had been turned into. This time of day, it was sunshiningly clear why the bank of windows had been built into the southeastern wall.

Sections of the cafeteria were partitioned off with waist high flower boxes. Plants teemed like transplants from the Amazon. Even in February, there were blooms of all colors.

A cheery place meant to lift the spirits of those embroiled with the blood, death, and disease of life. As if those who came to the medical center needed the reminder that beauty was still a part of the world.

Nice touch.

Benoit and Davis were parked in a corner booth, out of the sun.

"Hey, boys, rough day?" The two men who turned to look up as she approached weren't boys. They were both old enough to be her father.

They'd been partners since she could remember.

"Hey, Dani, have a seat." Leaving his coffee mug on the table, Benoit got up to let her slide into the booth beside him. She wouldn't bitch about the tight fit, between their guts and their holsters, neither man was going to enjoy the shoe horn routine, either.

"Beauty before age, is that it?"

An old joke between them, but they laughed anyway.

"I hear our victim went south."

Benoit was the father of three girls, all grown up and married, so domestics never sat easy with him. "Hits to the head, by the looks."

No *allegedly* for these veterans. Like Priscilla, they'd been around long enough to call a fish lingering company.

"She wasn't talking, but she didn't need to. Hubby ran off at the mouth, says she was no good anyway, sleeping around on him." Davis shrugged. "You know, the usual."

Benoit shook his head, the thinning of his hair obvious even with his salt and pepper crew cut. But he had kind eyes, and that's what Daniela really liked about him. Though they were blue, they weren't hard, much like the gray of Darken's.

Sea water should be cold, but Darken's never were. Even when they resembled storms, they were always full of emotion. Never empty or flat.

"Hard to stay conscious when you wear a cast iron fry pan upside the head."

"Jesus." Daniela's gut went somewhere south.

"The woman had scrambled eggs in her hair."

Like she needed the visual? But she kept her mouth shut. The men were just talking it out, releasing the helplessness that came with cases like these.

Again, her thoughts returned to Darken, to his brethren, he called them, and to their house.

She had joked, thinking it reminded her of the House of Usher in the Edgar Allen Poe story. But there'd been nothing sinister about it, nothing forlorn, despite the gargoyles perched around the eaves.

Despite the real gargoyles living inside it.

Darken had said there were six of them. She'd met only two, and they'd been—pardon her French—fucked up six ways from Sunday. Yet they'd been nothing but gentle with her.

Even though they'd literally trembled with the urge to do violence. The way Darken had shrieked unholy hell at the ceiling and then collapsed? Aside from the blast waves, it wasn't much different from when the women who were really going to come out on the other side bawled their eyes out.

The outpouring was a cleansing of sorts and a bereavement. As though they'd known they were finally safe and could actually let the festering poisons inside them out.

Wasn't pretty, but it was an important phase of recovery. Never failed to make her shiver, but she always stood rock strong with those women.

Back at that mansion, she'd heeded her inner voice, and had returned to Darken when he'd lost it. She hadn't fled in fear. She'd gone to him to offer solace in the little way she could.

Like the women whose façades had slipped, Darken's shame had been tantamount. He'd pushed her away...

"I am such an ignorant ass."

"What's that, Dani?"

"Oh, nothing. You guys mind? I've got another case to follow up on." It wasn't professional, but the two men hugged her before she left. It was stiff and awkward, given they wore bulletproof vests under their uniforms, and holsters with more things hanging off them than Schneider the janitor in that '70's sitcom *One Day at a Time*.

But they were being kind.

Not one to pass on puns, she got the whole Kynd thing, too.

181

Those muscled behemoths she'd met last night were...*kind.* Treating her like the Virgin Mary dropping by for dinner. All agog, but pulling out her chair just the same.

"Six years of college and I can't read the handwriting on the wall. Brilliant, Dan." Hindsight being twenty-twenty, she saw the signs of PTSD clear as if—oh, hey—they'd been written on the wall.

She'd been a coward last night, had shied away from what her instincts were telling her. Instead, she'd fled. Too afraid to become a statistic, too accustomed to the status quo of men dominating then destroying.

The house and Darken's room proved he could destroy, but the dominating part of an abuser? The manipulation? Were blatantly absent.

Wasting no time, she called up to the ER to ask Priscilla to hand the frying pan case over to Eileen as she booked it for the parking lot. In broad daylight, Darken's truck wasn't hard to find.

What she couldn't locate was the way back to his house. Odd. Yeah, it had been dark when she'd left, but you'd think she could feel it out.

Three quarters of a gas tank later, she wasn't anywhere closer. In the daylight, there were more details to confuse her memory, and now all those lefts and rights on backwoods roads had become a knot in her brain.

Giving up the puzzle, she returned home.

If he wanted his truck, the mouse would have to come looking for the cat.

Chapter Seventeen

Rest wasn't for the wicked, and Darken felt black from the inside out. He'd stared at the same section of wall for hours until the sun finally dropped from the cock-sucking sky. Unable to move, his thoughts had tormented him. More than usual.

Mainly, he couldn't believe he'd given up his Chosen One. For her own good, yes, but the fallout was the shits. Nothing like sitting in stone for endless hours to drive home what his future held.

Without his Chosen, he had an eternity of this ahead of him.

Even so, he'd set Daniela free again.

For all his self-pity, one star shined on his ruined parade—the fact that an innocent hadn't been brought into the dangerous mess of his life. He'd almost convinced himself it would be okay if she stayed.

But then reality decided to knock some sense into him. Or rather, Kallen had pounded on his door, reminding him of the harsh truths of their lives.

In that demolished library, they were planning a trip to Hell. A real one.

A rescue mission where the champions could very well wind up being the ones needing help.

All of them were about one trigger pull from blowing their wads. The problem was that the catalysts constantly changed. It was hard to predict what might set one of them off.

When that happened, their size became a deadly issue. Add the muscle, claws, and fangs, and you got a blender full of Holy Fuckers.

A fragile human body standing in the midst of that shit storm might as well be a blade of grass on a golf course.

Even as stone, the image of his Daniela getting battered in the fray made his stomach sick. You'd think being granite would preclude such a thing, but no, his guts churned and rolled until he thought his stone bones would quake and collapse.

Such a pleasant way to spend a day. An. Entire. Fucking. Day.

Of course, when the sun set, the bellow that had seized in his lungs at dawn blared forth as his body unlocked. He expelled it until it became a wail, the expulsion of air from his lungs sucking the oxygen out of his muscles.

A cocktail of shame, fury, and frustration had him thinking the floor wasn't such a bad place to linger. Maybe he'd never get up again, maybe he…

Needed to still take care of Daniela. Her car remained stranded on the side of the road, two tires shorn off their rims from the skid into a snowbank.

Just a pleasant reminder of how wise his decision to sever ties with his Chosen had been. If that packed pile of the white stuff hadn't stopped her slide, if she hadn't been wearing her seatbelt…

The accident had happened in a split second, Uri's arrival sending their two-vehicle convoy into a crash.

God…Uri. The male had teleported, and he'd been terrified.

Which wouldn't have happened if Darken hadn't sent that call out four months ago. The bear had answered, so the bear was his responsibility.

They were all his responsibility. And he wanted to wallow on the floor?

Darken shoved his self-defeated carcass upright. He might not have his Chosen anymore, but he still had his brethren to watch out for.

A regular Musketeer, he was.

Fifteen minutes later, he strode down the staircase where his Daniela had placed her precious feet. As he descended, he felt as if he picked up the essence of her sure as if she'd left sparkling dust upon the carpet he tread across.

So she clung to him like glitter.

A silly fabrication, but it made him feel better all the same.

When he entered the library, his skin felt snugger, more secure.

"The prodigal returns."

Darken didn't rise to Kallen's taunt, but strode to the leather sofa, shoe-horning himself between the gargoyle and Uri. Turned the couch into a pea pod, but whatever.

The touch of his brothers kept his skin tight. He dropped a reassuring grip onto Uri's knee for good measure. The bear wiggled his ass deeper into the cushions.

"All right, what've I missed." The attention turned on him. But didn't leave. The words *bug* and *microscope* took up residence in his head. "What?"

Kronos, sitting deep and tight in one of the three wingbacks, spoke for everyone. "How could you let her go?" When he lifted his gray gaze, Darken felt the accusation like a spear to the chest.

If his hand hadn't been anchored on Urick's knee, he'd have clasped it to his heart. As it was, his lungs leaked like they'd suddenly burst a hole. Surprisingly, his voice came out steady. "It was for the best."

"Yeah, for who?"

"You know, you haven't said four frigging words for four months, and now you're Dear Abby?"

Kronos inclined his head. If the shoe fit…

"Christ Almighty." His ass itched to get off the couch, but he kept himself planted. "How about we drop it and discuss something more important. Like Uri traveling without a passport."

Beside him, the bear tensed. He hadn't wanted to spit out the subject like that, but there it was.

"We've got a handle on it."

"Really, Merrick?"

Rising, the male pushed away from the desk. For missing his wings, the chimera could still rock intimidation. "Really, Dark Vader." The corner of his mouth twisted, like he enjoyed the joke even during a confrontation.

Kind of diffused things a little, actually.

"Angel and I talked with her father today. You want to elaborate on how the meeting with Kristov went the other night?"

Ah, bloody shit. With finding his Chosen, he'd forgotten all about the Vampyre. So, now all of the Triumvirate were well aware of Urick's potential need.

"He offered to help."

Drakus, perched on his windowsill with the sheet of plywood covering the broken window behind him, leaned forward. "And?"

"I thought he should keep his nose out of Kynd business."

"Way to hit that one out of the park. Not."

"Kallen, I swear if you don't shut it—"

"You'll what, knock my teeth out?" The gargoyle wiggled his eyebrows.

Darken twisted to get a better look at the man crammed in beside him. "What the...God damn it, no. I'm not going to fight with you. So, cut it out."

Kallen shrugged. "Your loss."

"I thought we were here to discuss our trip to Hell. You know, the Second Circle and those wrongly accused Shades we're supposed to liberate."

The faces around him shut down, like he'd used the wrong fork at the dinner table or something.

Angelia, ever the voice of reason, spoke up from her end of the desk. Where she gravitated any time she had her nose buried in the Scriptum. "We hit a snag. It's why Uri *traveled without a passport.*" She winked.

God damn it. He loved them all. He actually, really did. "What snag?"

"I asked him to be our liaison to Heaven after we got the Shades past Minos."

He twisted to his left this time. To Uri. "Yeah? And that freaked you out?"

The male squirmed deeper into the sofa. "Last night wasn't the first time I've relocated. I've been doing it—I didn't think I was a good candidate." He left it at that.

Fine. There'd be other times to grill the information out of him.

"Well, otherwise, Uri is a good choice."

"We all thought so, too. At the time."

Apparently, the apologies had already made their rounds because the air seemed clear on that score. What wasn't so clear was who the hell— pun intended—was the right Kynd for the job?

Certainly not him. Darken was the reason the souls in this room had severed their ties with the Creator. If he hadn't called for their help with Merrick, they wouldn't all be sitting here.

So, no, he and God weren't exactly on speaking terms. No pearly gates would open for him no matter how far the line of rescued Shades strung out behind him.

"Angelia?"

"Over my dead body," Merrick answered for her.

Couldn't say as he blamed the chimera for the kibosh. He wouldn't have let his Chosen near Heaven either. Bad enough, Merrick had to endure her connection to the Scriptum and the dangerous missions she decoded from it.

Or rather, that the book revealed to her. Like the thing lived and breathed with a mind all its own. Scary, really.

Especially since it had supposedly been written by the hand of God Himself.

"What does that bloody book say about it?"

"Nothing straightforward, of course."

Of course.

"It implies a kind soul is needed. Which we took to mean Kynd. Though we lost the string of things when it babbled on about ears and hearts. Not sure, yet, what that means exactly."

Far be it from him to hazard a guess.

Besides, talking about hearts reminded him he needed to take care of Daniela. Not that she'd ever left his mind to begin with.

Clapping his hands together, he wrenched his ass from between his brothers and stood up. "Okay then. Looks like the meetings sewn up. Uri, you let me know if and when you want to see Kristov. Angelia, I want to steal your spare tire to use on my Ch—on Daniela's car. Can you give me a lift down the road?"

His action set off a chain of moving bodies and general chat. Things to do, and in Uri's case, a woman to watch.

Man, he positively itched to get going. Had nothing to do with taking steps to get closer to Daniela. Absolutely nothing at all.

"I'll get my coat." Merrick left the library with Angelia, a given that the chimera would accompany her wherever she went. The male followed her like a shadow, and bless her Chosen heart, she seemed to bask in it.

Rather than get wigged out by her Kynd's constant need for proximity.

Proving matches were indeed made in Heaven.

On that note, he needed to get a move on before his thoughts chafed him a new asshole.

An hour and a half later, he was nosing the shoebox Daniela called a car into the empty slice of pavement behind his truck. Not trusting himself to cling to it as the last vestige of her he was ever going to touch, he scraped himself out through the steel jaws of the tiny door and got a move on toward his truck.

Which, he discovered the second he nestled his ass into the wide seat, didn't have its keys.

A search of the visor, the glove box, under the floor mat…yielded absolutely nothing.

Fear sat on his chest like a pallet of concrete blocks as he turned his gaze to his Chosen One's house. Where a lamp sat behind an open curtained window.

Beckoning.

Hands gripped to his scalp, he took five minutes to relearn how to breathe from under the weight crushing him.

She wants me to come inside.

Oh. Man. He should just leave his truck. Buy a new one. It wasn't as if he couldn't afford it. The logistics and legalities were a bitch to maneuver around, but obviously, it could be done.

Yet his feet, despite dragging along the walkway, unerringly moved him closer to that house. *Panic, thy name is Darken.*

Surely, he was going to shit a load in his pants. What did she want? What if she refused to leave him? Okay, that's just wishful thinking. Most likely she'd just forgotten to leave the keys in the ignition.

Buffered with that boatload of crap, he lifted his fist when the door opened before he could rap his knuckles on it. On the other side of the threshold stood…

His every loving cell, breath, and reason for living.

"Daniela." Her name rode the air wheezing out of his lungs before he could stop it.

"Darken. Would you please come in?" She stepped aside.

His body continued its gravitational suck toward his Chosen, his feet pulling him right into her house like they needed to get there.

"Would you sit and have a glass of wine with me?" She swung an arm toward her living room.

Like an animal wary of a trap, he balanced his ass on the edge of the cushioned chair. He steered clear of the sofa, where there was too much room for her to sit beside him.

While he pretended the legs of the coffee table in front of him were utterly fascinating works of craftsmanship, she went to the kitchen, returning with two tumblers of wine.

The heavy, cut crystal kind. She remembered how he'd shattered her goblets obviously. Which was…considerate.

It felt like the hands of God were wringing his lungs like a washcloth. Darken swallowed a sip of red despite the twist in his throat. Went down as hard as he figured it would.

When nothing was said for two centuries of ticking, ticking time, he glanced up.

Daniela sat on the end of the couch closest to him. Watching.

Him.

She smiled when their eyes made contact.

Fuck him, but if he opened his mouth to say something, it'd be over for him. The diarrhea of *I'm sorries* sat on his tongue like horses jammed in the starting gate. One clang of the bell and his mouth would be off to the races.

And hey, what do you know, the legs on that coffee table really were…

"Darken."

…*well-crafted. Yep. Probably made with a machine along with ten thousand other pieces…*

"Seeing you last night…"

…*lined up for the trip around the lathe…*

"…reminded me of something I had foolishly forgotten. You had every right to go off like you did—"

"I had no right to go off like I did." He rocketed off the edge of the chair like he'd been catapulted.

Daniela bobbed right up along with him. Except where he thought he might have a gazillion spiders scurrying across his skin and under it, she stood like the eye of a hurricane.

More than a stillness, a vacuum, where the spinning going on around him felt the pull of her calm. Give himself long enough, and he'd peter out.

"Yes, you did." She took a step closer and the room shrunk, everything in it reflecting her, smelling like her. "You told me you had spent…two thousand years severing souls from their dying bodies. How could that not destroy you on the inside."

Oh…fuck. Her voice stroked him, soothed…made sense. *Crumbling…*

He couldn't look at her, and she took that as a green light.

"I know you felt shame last night. That you revealed your true self to me when you'd tried so hard to hide it."

Bingo. She was a flipping savant.

"I found your outburst beautiful. The true you shining forth."

He rounded on her. "Bullshit, Chosen. It was hideous and you know it. My face contorted, the hatred burning off me…there's nothing beautiful about being Grotesque. You're deceiving yourself if you think for one second I'm salvageable. If I'd been touching you when that rage struck, you'd be—"

"Unharmed."

That snapped his head back. And shut his ranting mouth.

"Oh, yeah. I suspect that, too. For all that you looked,"—she finger quoted *hideous* as she said it—"what was most obvious was the pain."

She nailed that. Pain the likes of which he could barely carry. None of them could.

"Acknowledging it and trying to release it, no matter how awful it looks, is the right thing to do."

"Right. Being Grotesque is soooo the correct path. Forgive me if I don't see the logic."

She sighed and set her glass down. Straightening back up, she reached out, a tentative gesture before her fingers alighted on his arm. "It is in a sense. You're all haunted. I've never seen such misery as what I've been seeing in you and your brothers. Lashing out is normal. If you didn't that would worry me.

"Is it pretty? Not in the literal sense. But the beauty lies in the progression, of the reaching out, which is what you and your brothers are doing every time you have one of your outbursts."

Okay, he was chewing on this food for thought.

"Darken, there are phases the abused go through. Necessary stages on the way to healing."

His eyebrows pinching together, he spoke without thinking. "I wasn't abused."

His Chosen One squeezed his forearm, her touch gently adamant. "Of course you were. Every time you were forced to do things beyond your control, every time you were subjugated, you were victimized. How many times, Darken, over those…centuries…had you done that which hurt you every time you were forced to do it?"

She was a little stuck on how old he was, but that didn't make her any less wise. Scary, but her intuition about emotional pain was downright shake-you-in-your-boots freaky. It was as if she housed the wisdom of the ages.

Where Angelia had access to a book that sang in her head, Daniela had this uncanny talent for not only calling a spade a spade, but for actually seeing through the mess blurring its true form.

How unnervingly…comforting.

Oh, God, he was caving.

"Amica mea, I mean, Daniela—" She actually pinched his lips shut? Too stunned to move, she kept his excuses at bay until his jaw relaxed.

She nodded as she let go. "Amica mea. Now, you were saying…"

What the hell was he saying? All he could process was the smell of her hand, the petal softness of her fingertips touching his lips.

"You're wrong."

"Had you said that with conviction, I'd keep arguing with you. As it is…" She took his hand in hers, bent her head to kiss the callouses on his palms, callouses he'd gotten from carrying that scythe for eons.

His ass went south, his legs sweeping out from under him on the tide of her *everything*—her words, the feel of her so close to him, her scent.

He gazed up at her. "Is that what we were doing. Arguing?"

She shrugged, straddled his legs. "Only if we're going to have make-up sex."

Jaw falling open…

191

She laughed. A sultry dulcet tinkling that aweighed his anchor, unmoored him from his chain, washed him down the river. He wanted to grin and frown at the same time.

"Chosen..."

She shook her head as she lowered her bounteous ass onto his thighs. "Uh-uh. No more talking. Unless it's with your fingers."

* * * *

Holy jumped-up frig, it worked! Said the spider to herself.

Her plot to get Darken into her house and talk some sense into him actually worked. So high was she on her success, she embraced the part of her that he stroked to life without his even realizing it.

He turned her into a seasoned harlot, just by his sheer need for her. For the love of all that was sensual, he trembled with want whenever he touched her.

How much of a turn on was that?

It coaxed her inner woman to the surface like nothing doing. Whitney Houston could sing proud and strong about being Every Woman. Singing along in her head, Daniela knew every word.

As a matter of fact, she rolled her hips to the tune. Right across the tops of Darken's thighs. Toward his very obvious erection.

He groaned.

Tilting her head, she waited for him to open his eyes.

Silver. What. A. Turn. On.

And the tips of those fangs? She never thought she had some kind of vampire fetish, but she burned to feel those teeth scraping her skin. The claws were a little weird, but not a turn off.

Not when she thought back to the night before, to when he'd used them to gain access to her thumping clit. As a matter of fact...

Taking his hand into hers, she isolated one of those clawed fingers and wrapped her mouth around it, wetting it with a curl of her tongue.

Darken bucked and rolled his hips beneath her, settling deeper into the chair.

"Amica mea," he squelched out, his other hand cupping the back of her neck. He sounded a little tortured, he looked a lot aroused, those nickel eyes bright under heavy hoods.

His arms felt like tree limbs. The kind that held up tire swings. He drew her closer as she felt his legs tense beneath her. He was going to lift her.

She stiffened. He made her feel small and feminine, but come on. She wasn't. Preparing for the awkward lift and fail, she…yelped as he swooped her up into his arms like she weighed nothing.

At the same time, he crushed his mouth down on hers.

Lost. She was so lost to him.

Tongues dueling, he walked them unerringly through her house. Somehow, he got them to her bedroom without some part of her banging into a wall. See? Even in a lustful haze, the man thought of keeping her from harm.

He was no abuser. No one she should have run from. She'd left him in a time of need, but never again. If this concept of being a Chosen One was true, he needed her specifically.

What a. Frigging. Aphrodisiac.

As he lowered her to the bed, her arms reached for his retreating form, trying to haul the bulk and heat back onto her.

As he stepped away, he shook his head. "Stay there, Daniela. Let me look at you."

She eased back on her elbows, legs still stretched the length of the bed. As he stood at the foot of the bed gazing down at her, she felt a blush bloom on her cheeks. "What are you doing."

"Watching you." His eyes caressed her as he answered.

Her face grew hotter. "Watching me."

He nodded. "Back before we were cast from Heaven, Kynd were witnesses. We watched everything. Except this." He thrust his chin forward, to her.

"We weren't carnal minded, even though we knew of the urges that could drive a man."

His hand drifted down to his erection. It looked painfully crammed in his jeans as he rubbed the heel of his palm over it. As he cocked his hip, he popped the row of buttons and fully palmed himself.

Rocking into his hand, he never took his eyes off her.

Oh, God. As if inspired, her hand crept to the valley of her thighs. Bending one knee, she made room for her fingers.

His voice thick, he said, "We were never moved to experience it. Until—"

"You found your Chosen Ones."

He nodded, his hand now riding the length of himself, squeezing the head.

Daniela untied her skirt, pushed her panties aside.

Darken groaned, his hips pushing into his hand. "I have never known the pleasures of the flesh until you. You make me…mad for it." Breathless, he worked his hand along his shaft.

"I came here determined to let you go. But you draw me in, and your words…" His head fell back on an inhale before he again locked eyes with her. "Your words are ambrosia to my heart. I can't let you go. As selfish as that is, I can't let you go."

He strode toward her, his lower legs bumping the bed. A quick twist, and his t-shirt slid up his arms and over his head.

Good God. Calvin Klein is looking for you. Her hips circled as she played her fingers harder.

On a growl, he covered her, keeping his arms straight to keep his weight from crushing her. As he peered down with a hunger she'd call ravening, she gripped his ass so he wouldn't move off her again.

"I am cursed, amica mea. For all your bravery and wise words, I am cursed to doom you." With a flip of his wrist she hadn't seen coming, he ripped her panties clean off and flung them behind him.

His knees spread hers as he settled into the cradle of her thighs. "We do this, all of this, Daniela Salvai, and you leave your world for the horribleness of mine."

She panted harder with every promise he spat at her. Why were his threats such a turn on? Leave her life? Get swallowed up by his? She felt pressure, but it was a building within her, a need for him to fill her.

Her legs fell open as a river gushed between her thighs. She squirmed, seeking, as she dug her fingernails into the hard muscle of his bare ass.

Arching her tits for his talking mouth, she cried out as it crushed over her covered nipple. His growl was all about the loss of his control. His tongue, licking, was all about her pleasure.

"Oh, God. Oh, God." She writhed, trying to touch him everywhere at once. Begging him to touch her everywhere.

Releasing her breast, he said, "There is no God where we're going." As he nibbled her neck, his words came out on hot breaths. "We are banished from the heavens. Cursed. Shunned, even by the other monsters."

Walking his fingers up her chest, he curled a finger down the collar of her shirt. Then tore a slit down the center of it with his claw, just as he'd done with her panties. Her thin bra never stood a chance.

Nostrils flaring, he plucked the garments from each breast, his attention rapt.

His eyes glinted sharply silver. As he curled his hips to seat himself along her ample inner thigh, he said through those sexy fangs, "Uri, the brother you met on the road, is grizzly bear." He bent to flick her nipple with his tongue, cocked his head to the side.

As though the jiggling of her tit captivated him. Still eyeing her nipple, he said, "Uri is also vampire."

Huh? He must have sensed her confusion, because he said, "Chimera. A creature of three. Utterly doomed in this humans' world." A flash of pain crossed his enthralled visage. So quick, she wasn't sure she'd seen it.

"Merrick is lion." Darken dragged his sinful tongue around the whole of her areola. "And he is angel." Then cupped his mouth to suck her nipple to a taut bud. She understood, and of its own volition her head nodded. Merrick was chimera. Releasing her nipple with a pop that made her boob wobble, he seemed entranced. "Drakus is dragon."

He lowered himself to rub his cheeks along her bared breasts, as though he scent-marked her. Or was trying to bury his pain, because when he reluctantly lifted his head, there was retribution in his hard gaze. "He is also stained human."

A little breathless, she said, "Someone hurt him?"

"Aye, and I will never forgive that." Oh, yeah. Retribution, with a capital Revenge.

She could barely think through the intensity of him, his emotions flickering like a needle on a broken compass. He grinded his weeping cock on her inner thigh.

Why wouldn't he just fuck her, and put them both out of their misery? She'd never been wetter, her empty, inner walls milking for him. With her body, she could give him solace.

She understood. Better than he thought.

He wanted her scared. While at the same time daring her to be a coward again.

He was testing her. Proving to himself if she was safe to lose himself in. Everyone alive needed a person or place in which to let go, in which to spew the hurt and pain from themselves.

She was no punching bag, but she could be a sounding board.

"I want to meet them, Darken."

His gaze softened, belying his next words. "Oh, aye, and you shall. You will come, and you will see, Daniela. And you will wish you'd never met me."

She shook her head, denying, and felt a moist burning behind her eyes.

"Shush, my Chosen One." He caressed her temple. "So fragile in your new world. I'll strive to keep you safe, but you'll be careful, too, aye?"

"Aye," she repeated, using her feet to drag his jeans down his legs. "Take off your boots."

He stared at her for a long space of seconds, then did as she said. Just as she shed the rest of her clothes, he returned, laying back on top of her as he'd been, his bare body seeming even bigger. Naked, he seemed brawnier, his muscles and bones thick and too, too strong.

A gargoyle. Not a human man at all.

His skin against hers burned hot, even as she felt the tiny tremors beneath it.

She canted her hips, seeking the satin steel of his thick erection. Like him, it was big. She'd seen it, jutting from his body as he'd returned to her.

He tensed the instant her entrance found the head of his cock. Turning his face away, he hissed, "Like molten lava." Then he fell queerly still.

After some moments passed, she asked, "Ah, Darken?" She lifted her chin as much as she could. "You with me here?"

On a long exhale, he lifted his ass, then puuuushed that hot silk shaft into her so slowly she felt every inch inexorably fill her.

Head falling back, her moan lasted long after she felt the bump against her womb. Deep. He was so fucking deep and thick. She couldn't think past the fullness within her. She felt skewered—to something she wasn't walking away from.

And then he rolled his hips back, and his hot, wet cock slid through her sheathe.

Her back arched to prolong the drag. Just as she felt the lip of his mushroom head catch on her clit, he plunged back into her. Then rolled his hips back once more for that slow drag. And rammed himself back in.

In the deepest reaches of her belly, she felt a twinge of fear.

This felt raw. Like this coupling meant more to Darken than sex. It felt as if he were branding her, every thrust another tether, bonding her to him.

Irrevocably.

Even if he spoke truth, and the time came when she regretted ever having met him, there would be no leaving the brutality of his world.

Chimeras. Vampires. Men with fur.

What had she wrought with her insights?

Claimed. A Chosen One. Fated irreversibly for something…not human.

Fear grew larger under her skin, fed by her imagination. Nourished by the things she envisioned but did not know.

"Darken." A whispered cry left her lips as she buried her face into his neck.

He stilled as though she shrieked in his ear.

And then, just as slowly as he'd first entered her, he withdrew.

Without looking at her, he put his forehead to her sternum.

Without forethought, she played her fingers into his blond hair, rubbing the ends of it through her fingertips.

"You are still free, my Chosen. The deed not yet fully consummated."

Like a flame in the melted wax of her fear, knowledge guttered, struggling for life until its flickering light grew consuming. It filled her skin far more thoroughly than her anxieties had done.

A lesser man would not have stopped in the throes.

It reminded her of what she truly was to him—his Chosen. Which brought with it power, and not something he alone surrendered to her. She would be cherished in that wrecked manor in the woods, by all the brotherkynd.

Darken let his full weight lay down on her, their naked bodies melding under their warmth.

"Let's just lay here a bit. Talk."

His chuckle, one of bemused male and indulgent lover, intoxicated her, smoothing out her edges. "I heard it's how women make love. Could I hope?"

She stretched to kiss the top of his head. "I think so."

He turned his face to nuzzle his cheek along her splayed boobs. She wished they were pert like thinner women had, but alas. She consoled herself that Darken seemed to adore them.

He caught her by surprise when he rolled to his back, taking her with him. He slid his big body up so he could lean against her headboard, and nestled her at his chest, between his thick, long legs. He pulled the sheet up to cover her.

"I'll keep no secrets. Ask away."

His words were blithe, but the tension as he held her reminded her of his most painful confession—he turned to stone. Every day, all day, he was stone. Holy Christ, she hadn't really thought about what that meant until just then.

Until she could feel how hard his muscles were even though he held her gently.

"Okay. First off, what I have to know is what, exactly, is the function of a rubber duck."

* * * *

At first, he didn't think he heard right. So caught up in walking this tightrope, worried thoughts fuddled his hearing. Yeah, he was tuned into his female like a border collie with a herd of sheep, but he'd been expecting something…not that.

His laugh exploded out of him like a gunshot, dispersing his tension like a startled flock of pigeons.

Squeezing this extraordinary treasure in his arms, he felt as if he'd won…his freedom. He hadn't, but so what. If she couldn't accept him fully, she still lavished him with gifts.

He'd cherish the parts she could give him as the precious things they were.

He had to learn when her birthday was, just so he could buy her some more funny t-shirts.

A paltry gift in return for what she gave him, but he didn't really have anything better.

She rolled over in his arms, beaming up at him. His heart flopped up and down about twenty times, a fish on land. "You're handsome when you laugh. Fangs and all."

Automatically, his hand went to his mouth as his lips dropped over his teeth.

She pulled his hand away. "Don't. I meant what I said."

"Handsome and grotesque are mutually exclusive."

"Not from where I'm standing."

"If I said you were kind, would you be offended by the innuendo?"

Still gazing up at him, she shook her head. "No." She lost none of the shine in her brown eyes. Seductive eyes, heavily lashed with a slight lift at the corners. An Italian beauty. "Things just came falling down all at once. I freaked a little."

"Pretty understandable, considering."

"But not forgivable." She readjusted herself into his embrace once more, snuggling her back into his front. "Tell me more about the Kynd. Why would others shun you?"

Where to even start. Taking a deep breath, filled with the pungent scent of her naked sex, he forged ahead, despite the fact his dick was lined up perfectly with the crack of her abundant ass.

Sweet Jesus. He cleared his throat as he mentally kicked himself back on track. "We are cursed by God, and the Others fear if they help us, the same fate will befall them. It doesn't help at all that united, Kynd are a force unmatched." Risking the resurrection of things probably best put on the back burner, he reminded her, "You've felt our power."

"When I touched Urick and Kronos."

"That's only a fraction. There are hundreds of Kynd scattered across the realms. Imagine if we were reunited."

"But that vibration felt, I don't know, rapturous. Something shared, to be joined, not...manipulated."

He couldn't help but smile at her clever observation. "Just so." Yet his smile slipped. "Those who aren't Kynd don't think like that. All they see are brutish monsters, with strengths and senses beyond their own. They fear what they see, what they believe to be true."

"That is so…"

"Typical?"

"I was going to say stupid, nearsighted, and repugnantly ignorant. But *typical* works, too."

Such a treasure! He resisted squashing her to his chest as he sobered under the memories. "Even though it has been thousands of years since we've been together, the old Others remembered the lessons of their elders, and taught their young to fear us, and so on and so on. Timeless lore meant to sabotage us."

"Sabotage you. Seriously?"

"Aye. Drakus has been permanently stained, his human skin tattooed by the fae so he can never hide what he is. Even to keep himself safe. Merrick had his wings torn off by the angels in Hell to cripple him. And a vampire lost his head…because I took it." The last part he said with pride, and no regrets. Still, though, he didn't want his Chosen to think he murdered in cold blood.

"Our freedom from the Grotesque curse lies with the Scriptum. Angelia's book. In it is everything you'd ever want to know about us. Our names, our fates, our punishments. What makes us Kynd.

"The vampire, Aro, once esteemed and now headless Head of the Literati, plotted to put it into the hands of those who can actually do us irreparable harm."

"The Literati?"

"Collectors of Knowledge. Sort of like your Library of Congress or your Smithsonian. Anyway, Angelia was sent by Aro to retrieve the Scriptum from Hell where it had been taken, and Aro didn't expect her to return.

"Merrick was to be her guide. Which was basically a trifecta as far as the vampire was concerned. He'd be getting rid of the Guardian of Hell's Archway, and dooming a Kynd to his final fate. Third, he was sending the only daughter of the Triumvirate to her death, which had the potential to weaken the only thing Others recognize as a governing body."

"Sounds devious."

"Aye. The plan might have worked, but Angelia turned out to be Merrick's Chosen One."

"That is so romantic." She snuggled deeper into his embrace, and he could not resist placing a kiss upon the crown of her head.

"It is, now that Merrick's back. We don't care if he has his wings or not, we have our brother."

"And Angelia has her soulmate."

He could choke on his squeezing lungs. "Aye, amica mea, as do I." His happiness, whether she'd ever be fully his or not, beamed out of him so hard she had to feel it. He sure as hell did. He felt like someone who'd just donated a katrillion dollars to his favorite charity.

Daniela, though, still had her questions. "What about Urick, though, and Kronos, and this Drakus brother I haven't met yet? There's a Chosen One for them, right?"

"So says the Scriptum. That's our mission now, to find these rare females who will save our brothers. No more curse, no more Grotesques."

"Without these women, you'll turn to stone. God, that's awful."

"It is. Our brotherkynd have suffered horrors no being should have to endure. As you have seen firsthand, we still struggle with coming to terms with the ways we have all been…ruined."

"Touching helps, though, right?"

"It is our life's blood, so to speak."

"What about this whole *Kynd are a force unmatched?*" Quoting him, she jested with her deep announcer's voice, then got serious to the conversation again. "Which is why Others want you out of the picture. So to speak."

How he loved her irreverence and quick mind. "Aye. They assume we are like most, and if reunited, we'll conquer them for world domination or some such nonsense."

"Will you?"

"God, no! As the Creator's witnesses, we saw enough to cure us of such folly. All we want is to be left alone. We are damaged, amica mea, most of us beyond repair. And most likely, we won't find all of the Chosen fated for us. The clock ticks, every day dragging us closer to our Grotesque curses."

"So, why don't you just tell these Others that so they'll leave you alone? Or maybe even help."

"Distrust for our strength runs eons deep. It is not so easy to undo the damage done over the ages. We will have to prove ourselves, and that

201

won't happen any time soon. Especially since our violent outbursts only prove their fears."

"Hm. Then I guess we work on that." She snuggled deeper, as thunder roared through him. *We.* She said *we* as if she considered herself Kynd. Hope swelled like a tsunami inside him.

Before he consummated their joining and turned her trust against him, he grabbed her up, righting her on her feet. "No more talking, Daniela. Come home so you'll have time to adjust before dawn."

"Dawn?"

"I will turn to stone, and don't wish to be…vulnerable."

"What am I supposed to do?"

"Watch. Learn. Run for the hills while you can." He joked. Sort of. She'd had the guts to stay—until he'd told her to run. Would she still, now that she knew even more about him and his brethren?

"Way to inspire, gargoyle." But she snagged her clothes off the floor. He smacked her bare ass, his eyes glazing as it rippled before him.

"Dayyum, woman. I will never tire of your curves."

She hit him with a beaming smile that burned straight to his soul.

Chapter Eighteen

Cold as this night turned out to be, Uri expected his pathetic ass to freeze to the brick window ledge. The steam of his breath wafted over his shoulder like he was a kettle simmering on a wood stove.

If only he felt that warm.

The stars, a thick blanket above him, didn't offer any heat either. Misnamed little pricks. If Darken was with him, the gargoyle would have come up with some lame pun about stars being pricks in the canvas of the sky or some shit, but…

The lucky bastard wasn't here.

He'd headed out after getting Dani's car operational, saying he'd switch the vehicles and be back.

Well, three hours later and he hadn't returned, which meant only one thing. Dani had welcomed him back into her arms.

"Are you frigging sighing, because shit you not, if you are, I'm going to smack you."

"You'd smack me anyway. You're just looking for an excuse." He took his attention off the non-drama unfolding behind the glass he was looking through, to growl at Kallen.

"Oh, yeah, scary. Woooo…I'm shaking in my boots. Wait. I am. Because it's frigging freezing up here. Man, the things I do for you losers." After wiggling his fingers in Urick's face in a sorry imitation of a voodoo priest, Kallen curled those fingers back into his armpits, trying to keep them warm when the temp hovered at zero.

Uri slid a glance at the gargoyle beside him then hitched himself a few inches closer. The proximity afforded a little warmth and a smidge of windbreak, but he reaped far more from it than that.

Kallen got comfort, too. He grumbled, but didn't budge.

Behind the window he'd been staring through for the past two hours, he watched bald kids sleeping, their too thin bodies barely making lumps in their neat-as-pins hospital beds.

Well-placed and well-meaning lamps were strategically positioned around the big room. The graveyard shift of nurses needed to see when they made their rounds, but the kids needed a semblance of normal.

Like maybe they were actually home, and the soft lighting came from a cracked door, or a Dora the Explorer night lite.

All about the room were stations trying their hearts out to appear average. Like, oh hey, I'm just a dollhouse and beside me is a trunk of make-believe clothes. Another trunk of blocks and trucks sat like an ogre, legs of dolls sticking out of its grinning mouth.

Behind all the toy land fun, lurked the barely camouflaged reality of IV poles and beeping machines monitoring the line between sick and dead. Empty wheelchairs waited like saddled ponies at the hitching rail.

Chances were none of these tykes would ever get to ride a real pony.

Human lives were short, and these kids had barely stumbled out of the starting gate before sickness hobbled them.

Which made him want to hike up his pants and brave the public. To go in there and hug them up, maybe even let them cuddle into his fur.

Was never going to happen, but that was the beauty of fantasies. In them, anything could transpire. He could be happy. He could have what Darken had found, a woman made by the great Creator just for him, and they...

Kallen sat up straight at the same instant he did. "Hey, isn't that..."

As if his bottom jaw hadn't only dropped, but dropped off, Uri just stared. At the woman who had snuck into the shadowed room through a slivered opening of the door, tiptoeing so as not to awaken the sleeping dolls.

His Chosen One.

Maybe.

He couldn't be sure since his balls shriveled up every time he saw her. Figuratively speaking, anyway. With his hungers riding him, Uri didn't dare go near to find out for sure.

A catch-22 if ever there was one. He needed her because of what he was becoming, but he couldn't go near her…because of what he was becoming.

If she wasn't his Chosen One, he might eat her. And that wasn't figurative, not at all.

Made a grizzly want to bellow in frustration.

And a vampire lust for…things too horrible to contemplate. Drink a woman dead. Woo-hoo! Arm pump and yessss!

But if she was his Chosen, he'd still lust for…things too horrible to contemplate. Which would be an utter desecration of who she was as a God honored Chosen One, and what he was, a God damned Kynd.

Who were vegetarian, or they had been before they'd been hurtled from Heaven.

What, pray tell, had the Creator been thinking with his grand design? Add a little meat-eater here in this Kynd, and a little blood-sucker into that one.

For some inexplicable reason, some were singly gargoyle. Like his comrade sharing the window ledge and a case of the looky-lookies.

At the woman inside, who went from bed to bed, staying longer with some, while others only got a quick check.

As he leaned forward to watch her, he practically became the glass. Or fell through it. Inside his body, he felt the shivering that always arrived with her. The funny vibration he associated with getting a gander at his soul mate.

His eyes drank in every detail of her. From her shoulder length blonde hair to her lean body. She reminded him of a dancer, all lithe grace.

Especially when she bent to place her face upon the crook of a child's arm…

"What the hell?"

Uri didn't look at Kallen as the gargoyle spit out exactly what he'd been thinking. Because, really, *what in the hell was his Chosen One doing to that child?*

* * * *

As Daniela peered out the passenger side window into the dark, she tried to memorize landmarks as the headlights washed along the sides of the road. She'd been doing good for a while, until the city stretched out into suburbs, and the 'burbs petered out into stretches of no man's land. With nary a sign post in-between.

But then that was the point, wasn't it?

The Kynd were hidden. Not by magic, but by some clever arboreal strategizing.

Say that ten times fast.

No wonder she'd gotten lost trying to find where Darken lived.

He, on the other hand, drove with his eyes plastered to the road in front of him, and his hands at ten and two, as if the truck was going to start bashing its Ram head into the snowbanks if he lost his focus.

"Hey, you do know how to get home, right?"

"Huh? Aye. Why do you ask?"

"Aside from ditching the one hundred and one attempts to touch me, you're driving with a lot of concentration. So I just wondered."

He peeled his gaze sideways. "I am concentrating. Just not on the road necessarily."

"Oh? Mind if I ask what you're necessarily concentrating on?"

She caught the lift at the corner of his mouth. A begrudging smile. "You."

Calm down titties! "Me, huh? Me, as in how?"

He white-knuckled the steering wheel. "I…have concerns. Like how you're going to take meeting a lion and so forth."

Oh. Well that was disappointing. "Best to know now, rather than later, right?"

He didn't respond to that. Like maybe no time would work for him. Because he was already bonded to her, had been since their first encounter when he'd looked lambasted just from being in her presence.

He still got that look.

Which made her a lucky woman. If all turned out well. If it didn't, can we get an S for stalker.

For the thousandth time since meeting Darken, she felt out of her depth. And no wonder! Hello, Narnia. Talking lions and all.

Now that the woods had swallowed them, Daniela fell back in her seat, concentrating, too. The cab of the truck was silent, unless you counted the wheels turning, inside and out.

An eon later, the truck's headlights fanned across the front of the house and then glared at a garage door doing the slow reveal. As it trundled up, she got a better gander at the five bays.

All were empty but one, soon to be two, reminding her what Darken had said about his brothers not driving. Because they couldn't keep it together long enough to use their blinkers.

If Kronos represented the status quo, she could see why. Which meant Darken's level of function was miraculous.

As they got out of the truck, she had to ask. "How do you do it? Keep your shit together, I mean."

For a few seconds, he stood there like she'd pole-axed him. Then he took her hand, and instead of leading her into the house, he made sure she looked him in the eye.

Those nickel eyes that were now gray as a storming sea. "I don't. I'm just as responsible for the state of this house as the rest of them."

If she gulped, she might as well turn around right here. "Not one hundred percent true," she challenged, if only to appear brave.

He squeezed her fingers. The witness seeing through her bluff. "Humor. Laughing is good medicine."

A coping skill.

"And I have to, even if I'm faking it. I'm why my brethren are here. I called them, and asked that they challenge God and his decree. I'm responsible for their well-being, and I can't very well be looking out for them if I'm punching walls."

"Lead by example."

"Right. But sometimes the control slips. As you very well know."

His own challenge? Probably. He wanted her eyes open, which meant he wasn't blowing smoke rings out of his ass when he warned her about becoming part of this.

Irrevocably.

Right now, he thought he could let her go. Or at least, be able to function without her at his side.

A control freak? She spied the splintered door frame leading into the main house. Obviously not.

He kissed her hand. A tender gesture conveying so many things. The butterflies kicked up a ruckus in her belly, she felt the prickle of cold sweat.

Fear.

She now knew what she was in for. Pretty much.

Just open the door to the wardrobe…

Darken led her through the kitchen and the half-empty dining room, where the table was still pushed to the outside wall, out of the way. Wooden chairs lined the walls, making the room look as if it were staged for an upcoming junior high dance.

As they left the pre-teen dance floor for the foyer, Daniela caught sight of two men sitting at the bottom of the staircase. She saw them this time because the lights were blazing, that chandelier above them beaming like the sun…with a mild case of an eclipse.

Marble inlay spread out beneath her feet for what seemed like acres.

She wanted to gawk at the grand interior because it warranted it, but the man getting to his feet grabbed her attention instead.

He was just as tall as she remembered. His features handsome, but the affect had been marred by the deep gouges running down his cheeks. His gray eyes looked positively ancient.

But they were warm. And welcoming.

Daniela found herself walking from Darken to greet Kronos.

He went down on bended knee, as if addressing his queen. She joined him. "Kronos, it's good to see you. May I?" She extended her hand.

With as much trembling as before, he took it, and closed his eyes when the contact had been made. "Drakus, come."

The name yanked her attention sure as if she were a fish on the end of a line.

Darken sidled in close, protectively. She felt him there, since she didn't peel her eyes from the newcomer.

The dragon. The stained man.

Sure enough, Darken hadn't exaggerated. She couldn't see all of him because he wore clothing, but there was no hiding the rest.

The representation of a dragon's fiery head covered three quarters of the man's face. So life-like she stared. As a shiver rippled through her, she wasn't sure if there were four eyes watching back, or two.

Both faces sported fangs, too. One set real, the other…imagined? She couldn't frigging tell. Whoever had tattooed this man had been a master of the masters.

She only barely kept herself from breathing, "Holy shit."

Because according to Darken, there wasn't anything divine about the man's appearance. The stain was fae wrought.

Whatever the hell that meant. She suspected, but her plate spilleth over for the time being. She'd ask after she'd compartmentalized the info of her current reality.

The dragon-man didn't move, except to wrap a ham sized fist around a baluster. As it curled around the ornate wood, the Kynd curled his shoulders along with it.

As if to hide.

Jesus. This guy took wounded to a whole new level.

The hairs on her arms prickled to attention just as Darken stepped in front of her. Putting his body between hers and the giant mooring himself to the stairs.

Now she couldn't see all of him, but she saw plenty.

Somehow, the tattooed Kynd seemed divided. A cowering man full of menace she felt on her skin.

"Let him touch." *Kronos.* Darken had managed to plant himself between her and the other gargoyle, too. But her man was only so big. He couldn't handle them both if they...

Oh, shit. Was this why he'd lost it the other night? He'd feared this meeting?

"Let him touch her, Darken." A guttural demand. More growl than a normal voice would carry. Like a dog trying to talk. Eerie. So effing eerie.

Darken seemed divided, too. As if he couldn't decide whether to let Drakus touch her as Kronos had that first night?

"If I let you..." There was a world of torment in that unfinished sentence as he looked down at this brother. Daniela's stomach got too light, like maybe it wanted to springboard the contents.

This was Darken frightened, and it scared the bejesus out of her. Fear spreading like a contagion, feeding and feeding until panic reigned. She realized she was panting, her chest heaving up and down.

"Drakus, touch."

"Would you shut. The. Fuck. Up." Darken turned his chin just enough to warn Kronos without taking his attention off the other threat. And what do you know. There was that talking dog again, only now those growled words came from her protector. What was that he'd said about losing his shit, too?

"Repeat that." The growling dare came from her right again, so her head bobbed back and forth from Darken to Kronos like she was at Wimbledon. The whole time, she kept part of her attention trained on Drakus.

Kind of like you would do when backing away from a snake when your whole family was at risk of getting bit.

"W-wait a minute, guys."

As Darken ground down on his molars so hard his jaw bone grew wider and his cheeks hollowed out, four eyes riveted onto her. Or was that six, what with that dragon tattoo looking as if it watched her, too.

"J-just hold up." The foyer they'd entered, the one where the marble went on forever, suddenly shrunk to the size of a dog carrier. She'd thought these men huge and intimidating before? Now they looked as if they could take on an entire team of Navy Seals and yawn while doing it.

Gargoyles. Not human men at all. How many times had this reality crossed her mind since meeting Darken. Jesus, what, pray tell, was she taking on here exactly.

Something that gave the Paul Bunyon sized guy who wanted her desperately, a case of the vapors.

Still, though. She hated violence, so how was that for irony. "I'm sure we can figure something out." Because she was sooo excited about having these...males...touch her.

"Daniela, go back out to the truck."

"Say what."

"Hey brother, looks like your Chosen One listens as well as I do. You want to repeat that, too?"

Darken lased Kronos with a silvery glare.

"Kronos, cram it," she said, and owned it. She'd shit her pants later when things calmed down. As it was, she reached for the gargoyle as she told him to quiet his yap.

Looking as if he'd swallowed a mouthful of galvanized nails, he grabbed ahold of her hand, the contact felling his anger like a tree. Kronos dropped to his knees again. And still he was almost as tall as she was.

She held her empty hand out for Drakus. "Take it." She wiggled her fingers. Dearest lord, what was she commanding him to do? This freaky Kynd who had a tattoo that turned 3-dimensional?

Oh. Oh, man. It wasn't the tattoo, it was the man himself. His skin. Getting shiny with burnished scales.

Eyes wide, she froze. Her hand staying where she'd offered it, as if her brain had short-circuited.

Darken looked as if he didn't know whether to puke or go ape shit.

She couldn't pull her eyes off the sight…breaking open before her. She thought the way his skin stretched and his clothes tore, that the dragon would burst from the man in the way a chick hatches from an egg.

Instead, the dragon began to swallow the man…or gargoyle…or whatever. Everything happened at once. Teeth like blades slid from an ever-expanding jaw as the body fell forward, landing on…four toed feet with claws twice as thick and long as a man's fingers.

While all that drama unfolded, a frigging ten-foot tail whipped out, three spikes sliding out of the end of it.

A fucking dragon emerged before her, as she lived and breathed.

It opened its mouth to roar at the same time she opened hers to scream. Although if she'd screamed, she never heard it. Her eardrums got sandblasted by the agony shrieking out of that thing.

And the eyes were not the same eyes that had watched her from behind the barrier of a man's skin. They shared the same color, but the anguish in these split her wide open.

As though she'd been snuffed like the flame on a candle, everything about her just…went out. As in stopped. Uncannily still inside, yet, beyond a stillness. There wasn't anything but this vast…quiet.

Not even fear.

The dragon blinked. Then blinked again.

Darken found his pie-hole, because he started murmuring, "Easy. Easy Drakus. Go slow." The last part he said with that dog's talking voice as the dragon stepped closer to her, its lethal claws scratching on the marble.

Its tail cut a swathe behind it—or him, actually—skittering an upholstered bench to a new location, minus a leg.

"Soooo…this explains the state of the house. Hard to house break a

211

dragon, I suppose." Did that suave declaration come from her? "Keeping the fridge stocked must be a challenge."

Beside her, Kronos coughed something up. Or maybe that was a laugh.

Darken still looked like the puke fest or the Hulk show could go either way.

She held out her hand. The dragon stopped mere inches from it, his breath warm and moist on her fingers. "No fire?"

Drakus tilted his head. Then pushed it into her outstretched hand, the smooth scales sliding like silk across her palm.

She felt the connection instantly.

The vibration singing through her body, as if she were a conduit for an electrical current passing between the two Kynd.

The sensation felt magnificent. As though the earth had found its true axis and was now spinning perfectly in its orbit.

Or maybe that was just her. Because she could have described it as curling up on a rainy day with a good book and a bottle of wine.

Consensus—she just felt...right.

"Darken, come." Kronos stretched out his free arm, beckoning. He wore the same expression as Drakus. Not that they shared features just then, except for the eyes.

Which were beautiful shale. Shining like beach stones.

She looked up from them to watch Darken. There was a question in his eyes, as though he asked for her opinion before he dared come near.

She dipped her chin. And would hold a hand out for him, but she didn't have a free one.

Turns out he didn't need it. He placed his on the dragon's shoulder. The second the contact was made, she felt it. Another spark, then the constant increase, an amping up of the vibration.

She mouthed the word *Wow.*

Chapter Nineteen

Darken wanted to remain knotted with his brethren and his Chosen One for the rest of his existence, it felt so good. He honestly couldn't say how long they stood together in the foyer.

All he knew was that Daniela grew pale, and the sight of that made him snatch his hands away.

His Chosen blinked, as if surprised by the way the vibration blipped whenever a Kynd unplugged. Would she get used to it?

He honest to God didn't know.

She obviously liked the contact, but she'd been terrified only moments before. She hadn't needed to scream for him to feel it in his gut, a big fist ripping out his innards. Leaving him hollow and shaken. And furious.

To think straight, he'd joined in the love-fest. If he was going to be able to speak in complete sentences and not just grunt when Daniela came to him with her questions, he needed to chill out.

So he'd latched on.

And lost track of time.

Now, though, it was time to tend to this precious being in his care. "Party's over boys." He physically pried their fingers from Daniela's.

Tucking them so she held her own hands, he resisted the urge to kiss her bruised fingers.

And resisted the urge to beat his brothers to within an inch of their doomed lives.

"Kronos, stay with Drakus. I'm taking Daniela upstairs."

The gargoyle cleared his throat as he got to his feet. One hand on his head as he looked around, he seemed as if he'd come to not knowing what the hell had happened.

"Kronos, you okay?"

Misty eyes looked up. "Ah, yeah. Yeah, never better."

Sure.

But the gargoyle went to their brother, putting both of his big hands on the dragon's back. Drakus arched into Kronos' touch, emitting a purr.

Jesus. He hadn't heard the poor bastard do that since…never. Not even up in Heaven when he still had a full marble bag. He'd love to gaze at the transformation, but he had a more pressing concern.

The well-being of his Chosen One.

He itched to get her upstairs and alone. To somewhere…safe.

"Amica mea, come with me." Tenderly he gathered her to him. As if in shock, she let him sweep her up in his arms. When she rested her head on his chest, he thought he'd crow, he was so fucking bursting with pride.

His Chosen One, in his arms. The miracle of it!

As she held onto the front of his t-shirt with a bruised hand, though, that sick feeling he'd felt earlier wallowed a hole in the bottom of his stomach.

He took the stairs slow so as not to jar her.

After walking through the house for what seemed like a frigging year, his room, for once, was a welcome sight. A quick twist of the knob, and a kick behind him took care of the door, and then he was laying her ever so carefully down upon his bed, drawing the duvet up over her.

"Darken?" She held onto the front of his shirt. As if afraid.

Dear God in Heaven. If Drakus had harmed her more, he honestly didn't think he could've stopped himself from damaging his brother tenfold. How did Merrick endure this?

First chance he got, he was going to have to separate the chimera from his Chosen One long enough to find out.

"I'm right here, amica mea." He kissed her bruised hand once he'd gently removed her grip. He tucked it under the duvet then drew the blanket up over her shoulders.

"Don't go."

"I wasn't. I won't. Wild horses, and all that." He gave her a smile he barely felt.

"I'm tired."

"You should be."

"Hm-mmm." When she closed her eyes, he thought he'd collapse to the floor right there. Where was his great strength now? If the Others saw this, they'd remap their strategies on how to sabotage the Kynd.

They'd be tripping over themselves to help find the Chosen Ones, rather than thwarting the search.

When she rubbed her cheek into the pillow and murmured, "Snuggle with me," he thought he'd jump out of his clothes, he leapt so fast. "Of course." *Redundant idiot. Talk about tripping over yourself.*

All was forgotten once he was beneath the duvet with her and she squirmed into his embrace. Kissing the top of her hair, he all but roared at the ceiling in triumph.

Until he remembered this was but a small victory.

He most likely would lose the war. And for all that he thought he might lose her yet, she couldn't have been more precious to him in that moment.

She'd been so brave and fierce with Drakus and Kronos.

If he wasn't such a selfish prick, he'd let her go. Make it so she didn't have to make the decision whether to stay or not. If he had even one ounce of honor in him, he'd leave her life.

Well, he'd tried that and look where it got him. She nailed him with some psycho-crap about victims of abuse and he'd gone all yep, that's me, and taken her to bed.

Playing on her sympathies. And her hope.

After tonight, she probably wouldn't have much of either.

He let his fingers play with the ends of her hair, stroking the softness of it, watching how the lighting played with the highlights. As the tresses slid over his callouses, he thought the curls seemed like living things.

The petting made him sleepy. The ring of awesome he'd shared in downstairs had gone a long way toward smoothing him out, too. Now he felt his lids get heavy, a sensation as foreign to him as…holding peace in his arms.

He hadn't slept in…a piss poor long time.

Hadn't needed to. The closer he got to becoming Grotesque, the less he needed to sleep. Or eat.

He should stay alert. The sun would rise in a little while and this beautiful woman didn't need to see him in all his stone glory. Her shopping cart overflowed as it was. It wasn't every day a human got the chance to see a real dragon, let alone touch one.

A piddle-shiver ran up his spine as he thought of how close his Chosen had been to that dragon. Drakus, fucked up ten feet from center, had managed to keep himself together long enough to experience a golden moment in his otherwise dismal life.

Darken closed his eyes, and sent a silent salute to his brotherkynd.

With a half-smile gracing his lips and his heart, he slipped into darkness.

Then woke suddenly, his body flinching. Heart rapping so fast his breaths chugged out like a locomotive, he stole a look out the window.

Still dark, thank fuck.

He hadn't dreamed, so why did he wake as if—

As a door slammed downstairs, he knew why he'd jolted awake.

Sounds like that meant someone in the house was upset. And because misery loved company, he eased himself out from beneath his Chosen to go check on the noisemaker.

Clothing separated them, but he still felt his heart cinch up tight as their bodies slid along each other. Daniela made a little mew before sighing, and he thought his skin might rupture with the bliss of hearing such a thing.

He almost couldn't leave her.

Hand shaking, he drew his fingers along her temple as she settled deeper into his bed.

Where she belongs, instinct roared. Even though he'd never slept there before this night, now an awakening part of him understood the rightness of his female laying with him.

In all ways.

Against his inner thigh, his dick squirmed to life, as if it agreed and was raising its…

Silently, he pushed away from the bed before his arousal made it too hard to leave. Har, har. Thinking his little pun wasn't funny in the least, he slipped out of his room, keeping the door as closed as possible lest any more banging from downstairs disturb his Daniela.

His sleeping female…the miracle of it. With the doorknob still in his fist, he rested his forehead against the door he'd just closed. *Please, God…*

A prayer. To the One who'd set him on this path those thousands of years ago.

Let her stay. As if the Almighty had any say in the matter. Darken knew all about free will, but it didn't keep his thoughts from flying heavenward.

She had every right to leave him. He had little to offer her. Just this strange and compelling urge to treat her as sacred. Which wasn't love, he knew that. Not in the way humans understood it.

But what more could there be? If there was more than believing your other half to be sacrosanct, he sure as hell didn't know what it was. All he knew was that the woman lying in his bed was the most blessed being he'd ever known.

His heart hurt thinking about that, and he rubbed his pec, pushing the heel of his hand into his flesh to ease the ache.

Ah, God, how hard it was going to hurt if she left him. Wait, not if…but when.

"Fuck." Dropping his arm, he lifted his forehead off the door, effectively dragging his head out of his ass. There was still banging going on downstairs. Skipping stairs, he leapt downward to the foyer, following the rising voices to the library. Where they always seemed to gather when…

The door flung open, throwing him across the hallway. Feet braced under him, he pressed his spine to the wainscoting as the dragon's tail whammed the wall a few feet away, the barbs puncturing the paneling. As a leathered wing scored the ceiling, plaster fell like powder into Darken's hair.

Kronos followed tight, keeping clear of that thrashing tail as he stayed as close as he could without touching. Because sometimes putting your hands on Drakus launched his memories, making the situation worse.

What the fuck?

Last time he'd seen these two, they'd been cozy as kittens in a basket.

Angelia came out on their heels, stopping long enough to peg him with a frustrated glare. "I'll go with Kronos and Drakus, you go in there." She jacked her thumb over her shoulder then ran after the dynamic duo.

He watched them disappear into another room and left them to it. Obviously, they'd ditched the drama, hopefully to recoup a little of Daniela's quietude, and bask in Angelia's humming mojo.

Stomach churning, he thought of his Chosen upstairs, in the same house...

So much for praying. Eyes heavenward, he snarled, "You son of a bitch, can we have one fucking day. Is it too much to ask!" Darken shoved himself into the library, scanning quick to get his bearings.

Merrick looked like he'd had his guts ripped out and held his drooping intestines in his hands. Probably wasn't far off the mark with that guess. Merrick's Chosen One had just exited with a dragon, and a gargoyle so fucked he bore the scars on the *outside*.

Not that the male had any final say in her going. Angelia wasn't one to get bossed.

Kallen stood with his back to the door, ramming his fist into the dark paneling, over and over again.

Uri was glaringly absent.

For the umpteenth time today, Darken felt his stomach drop south. "Where the fuck is the bear."

He probably shouldn't demand that while striding over to grab Kallen from his downward spiral, but what the hell. Last he knew, the two of them had been pulling sentry duty at the hospital, so Mohammed Ali here would have the right answer.

As his hand clapped onto the gargoyle's shoulder, Kallen twisted, his fist connecting with Darken's jaw, spinning stars behind his eyes that made him think of the Looney-Tunes.

The instant his head quit spinning like that girl in the *Exorcist*, Darken brought back his own fist, the haymaker halfway to its target, his face contorted with fury and fear for Uri, when...

The sun oozed its first pink rays over the snow, its beams weak but unrelenting. Both gargoyles went immobile, their bodies ceding to the inexorable stone emerging forth.

Unable to turn his head because he was now a fricking statue, Darken heard Merrick voice his thoughts to the letter: "Well, fuck," the chimera spat.

Amen to that, brotherkynd. Amen to that.

Chapter Twenty

Falling asleep is a vulnerable time. For no matter how many locks are put on doors and windows, they don't prevent the disorientation that comes from waking in a strange place.

Heart kicking to life as if she'd had ten cups of coffee, Daniela bolted upright in the bed, and took a few blinks to recognize where she was.

Darken's bedroom.

Morning sunlight streamed through the cracks in the drapes, bathing the room in buttery yellow, lending a softness to the otherwise hard edges of the objects within.

Even the hole in the wall beside the bathroom door took on an artistic quality. A starburst, rather than busted plaster. The man who made it…

She knew he wasn't with her, yet she still twisted upon the bed, searching.

Sadness befell her as she realized he'd be somewhere in this rambling house. Hidden. So she wouldn't see him as a statue.

Oh, God. All of this, the strange room, how she got here, the men living in torment. All of it was real. And somewhere, they were all…

For a moment, she refused to believe it, but it passed as the reality of where she was settled over her. Somewhere, all those men were stone.

And didn't that just make her feel sad all over again.

The thought took away her gumption to get her ass in gear. Instead, she gathered the blankets around her and propped herself up on a mountain of pillows. Previously unused, if her first impression of this room had been spot-on.

Darken didn't sleep in this bed.

He said he stood at those windows…

Probably looking as he did the night she'd fled. His face twisted with fury, lending truth to the Grotesque myth. They straddled ledges and rooftops, grimacing, sneering…

And bellowing?

Yeah, she could believe that. Roaring at the heavens for the pain they carried.

Because God had kicked them out for not choosing sides when He'd battled Lucifer.

A ridiculous myth. Surely. Except she'd seen something she couldn't pass off as fantasy—a dragon.

A real, living dragon. Wings and all. Bursting from the skin of a man…who was also a gargoyle.

"Jesus." Thinking on it flipped her from sadness to disbelief then toward fear. A cocktail of What the Fuck proportions. And got her off her ass. Pulling herself with her legs as she pushed with her hands, she left the bed so she could leave this house.

If dragons were real, then guess what. So were that frigging bear and lion Darken had mentioned.

Damn it. *Darken.*

When he found her gone, he'd be…hurt. She'd talked him into opening his heart to her, into trusting her, and now she was going to essentially kick him in the nuts.

But come on. When she'd gone all Dr. Phil, she thought she'd be dealing with a man with textbook issues. And yeah, she could swing with the fact that maybe he really was a gargoyle or something.

Something like…oh, maybe a really strong man prone to losing his shit and smashing the furniture.

Same with Urick and Kronos. She'd seen the state of this beautiful home. Now she understood how the chandelier in the foyer had taken a hit.

From the wings of a dragon. Jesus, a real, live frigging dragon.

Which meant Darken really was what he kept telling her—a gargoyle. Right along with Kronos. And Urick really was a bear, and Merrick a lion, and thrown into that there was a vampire, and an angel…

"Jesus jumped-up Christ." Yeah, she kept dropping the J-bombs, but she was freaking out a little here.

She needed space to think.

These men were victims. Hard core. As in the farthest end of the spectrum when it came to issues. They'd been suffering for…more than *two thousand* years. And she thought she could help them with her mumbo-jumbo?

Oh, hey, look, it's Oprah time. Let's all cry and hold each other's hands, blah, blah, wah.

Yeah, wasn't going to work. These men…males…whatever…carried scars. Upon scars. Upon scars. Some seriously deep damage.

She thought she could help them face *God*, for criminy's sake? No wonder those Others Darken mentioned never came near. These guys *were* seriously screwed.

They were super nice in their own messed up way, yeah, but let's get real. Holding their hands…

Daniela stopped in the middle of slipping on her boots and let her butt fall back down onto the edge of the bed. Just to sit for a second, quiet-like while she digested the latest swerve of her thoughts.

Holding their hands…

Taking a deep breath, she ran hers up and down her thighs. *Exhale slowly, and repeat. Then once more with feeling…*

There was a key to the hand-holding thing. Before she ran off hysterical, and reneged on her show of courage with Darken, she owed him a few minutes of quiet contemplation.

Nothing less than what she'd give the battered women in their hospital beds. Okay. Yeah, she could do that.

Inhaling air like the stuff carried secrets to healthier living, Daniela finished putting on her boots then got up. Her coat was…there, thrown over a chair that still had four legs.

God, she shouldn't think that way. As if it was only a matter of time before it, too, suffered the wrath of a male trying his damnedest to be better than his brothers.

For their sake, not his own.

So complicated! With her fists clenched and her face aimed skyward, she had a lightbulb moment. Because what do you know. This was Darken's exact response to the frustration with his life.

Okay, point in his favor. But she still needed to leave. Because honestly, serious violence happened here, beyond even what she had fathomed. How could she stand up to bears and lions and vampires?

She couldn't.

Unless she touched them, like she had with Drakus. Somehow, her touch effected these Kynd men, but she didn't know how, or even if such a thing could be repeated.

"Gah!" Tucking her coat over her arm, she left Darken's room. Before she shut the door, though, she took one last gander at it. Where she'd lain safe and warm in the broken bed, had fallen asleep in his strong arms.

As her gaze swept the sun-bathed room, she felt a dropping from her belly, as though her great weight fell down through the trunks of her legs and roots grew out from the soles of her feet into the wood floor.

Centering her.

Drawing her into that placid part of herself where she remained still while the rest of the world spun in chaos around her. In that place, she could reach out her hand to hold the women getting battered in the storm and ground them to her.

A gift, her adopted *nonna* had told her. Even now, Daniela could picture that craggy face, the rheumy eyes brimming with warmth. And love. So much love in her family it had spilled over to flood through a little girl who wasn't of their blood.

That she wasn't born unto them had never mattered. They had all adored her. Spoiled her. A big Italian family full of cousins, aunts, and uncles, none of whom had ever made her feel anything but a part of them.

To this day, she had to remind herself she was adopted because she never felt as though she'd been.

Such generosity of heart…

"Shit, *Nonna*." For the first time ever, she wondered if her gift had been meant for something less pedestrian.

What if it really was God-given? Because right then, standing with her hand on the doorknob looking into Darken's forsaken room, it sure as hell felt like it.

Why else would she be thrown into a parallel world of gargoyles and chimeras, creatures long-associated with those ancient, gothic churches of Europe?

Need she add how she felt in Darken's arms? How he made her feel every time he looked at her, or couldn't resist touching her in some small way.

Full-circle to the touching thing again.

Just like her brain. Circling, circling…

Shutting the door turned into something more symbolic as far as all this was concerned—she closed her mind off from the way Darken made her feel.

Feminine, seductive, beautiful.

Yeah, thinking on it was really closing her mind…

Making her way down that dramatic staircase, she followed her nose to the kitchen, the aroma of fresh brewed coffee pulling her along.

But she kept her blinders off, and gawked at all the damage, letting that sink in as well.

"Oh, hey, you're up!" The greeting came from a blonde with girl-next-door beauty, the kind that made teenage boys spend too much time in the shower. Like she needed the apron to enhance the whole ooh-la-la effect?

Or those heels with well-worn jeans.

Daniela felt like the gum stuck to someone's shoe.

"I'm Angelia. You must be Daniela." Her arm extended, girl-next-door swung her hip out to come around the counter, confident as you please, the blonde braid swinging down her back all heavy and wispy, like it had been played with. A lot.

Daniela stuck her hand out for the greet, more reflex than manners. "Ah, yeah." This close to such beauty, she felt all the grime of sleep, and the residuals of an encounter that left her feeling like she'd been ridden hard and put away wet.

"This," blondie said with a chuck of her chin toward her right shoulder, "is my broody guy, Merrick. A.k.a. Duncan Hines."

Daniela's mouth fell open. Reaching past Angelia was a man straight off a GQ cover. Black hair, thick muscles on long bones, gray eyes so much like the others, and an…apron.

How effing sexy was that. Men doing housework was the stuff of calendars.

"Uh, hi," she said, like the professional, grown up woman she was. She gawked at the hand reaching toward her.

S. C. Dane

"It is truly a pleasure to meet you." Gawd, he had a growly voice like Darken's. Thick and rich. When she looked up, she saw how warm those eyes were, too. After their shake, Merrick pulled his hand from hers before placing his other to the small of Angelia's back.

Because he didn't want to experience the circle thingy?

"Nope, I don't. You look as if you've had enough for one day." His smile could charm the pants off Mother Theresa. What a beaut. And this was the lion, right?

Huh. Thought he'd be more prowling, or something. Bad enough he read minds, so now she flushed for other reasons. "Ah, yeah. I'm ah…"

Angelia smacked her moody guy's arm. "Stop it." To her, she said, "He's just observant, typical Kynd thing actually. Don't worry, he can't read minds."

But she could?

Must…get…off…the…ride…

"Good to know," she managed to say. "Listen, I ah…"

"Need some breakfast?" Merrick spun back toward the stove, waving a spatula like the Swedish Chef on the Muppets.

Angelia leaned in, whispering conspiratorially, "He doesn't cook much, so he gets a little excited."

"Heard that."

"We don't usually leave him unattended with an open flame, either." When she winked, Daniela felt a smile creep its way out.

"Heard that, too. Oh, shit!" Merrick started slapping at the ring of flames with a dishtowel as he shoved the pan of scrambled eggs to another burner.

"See." Laughing, Angelia rolled her eyes as she went to help.

Daniela found her feet planting to watch the Desi and Lucy show, surprised by just how ordinary this was. When smoke began to roll out of the toaster, she smirked, then sobered as she remembered her first date with Darken.

He'd said Angelia had taught them how to make toast.

If Merrick was their shining example, Darken hadn't been kidding.

There was murmuring between the couple, and then Angelia threw her head back to laugh. An unselfconscious eruption, an explosion of happy.

224

Merrick ogled the woman like the sight of her struck him sappy stupid, completely oblivious that their breakfast billowed black smoke.

With a deft lean and flick, Angelia popped the burning bread, a smile as big as Kansas on her face.

"Want coffee until we can get things restarted here?" As she ambled over to the coffeemaker on her high heels, with the bow tie of the apron sashaying across her ass, Merrick stared after her, shaking his head as if the sight was just too fricking unbelievable.

With a sheepish grin, he tore his eyes off his woman's ass. "Breakfast can be ready in about five minutes, tops. I swear."

Daniela shook her head. "Naw, I'm good. But I'll take the coffee." To be polite. Especially since she wasn't a hundred percent sure how she was getting home.

If she took Darken's truck, there was a high probability she'd repeat last night's performance—keeping his keys so he'd have to come into her house to talk to her.

Right now, she needed some space to think things through, and she didn't need Darken's sexy influence. Not with all the red flags waving in her face.

She had made a vow to herself not to become one of her own cases.

She would not be a statistic.

Darken needed to touch her constantly. He had a jealous streak. He had a violent streak. He turned to stone every frigging day…

Okay, so that last one wasn't on the Ten Warning Signs You're in an Abusive Relationship poster.

"Here you go." Angelia slid a steaming mug across the island counter. "Cream and sugar?"

"Yes, please." As Daniela doctored her brew, she could feel the other two watching her. Sure enough, when she looked up, they were both leaning on their elbows, faces rapt. "What."

They stood up together, like they were trying out for the Synchronized Swim Team. "Nothing, sorry."

Daniela tried the coffee. As soon as the rim touched her lips, Angelia said, "It's just neat, I guess. To see another Chosen One."

Daniela lowered her mug.

"I mean, we figured it would happen eventually, but so soon? We thought we'd have to go through Hell, literally, to find one."

"Hell. Literally?"

"Second Circle. Guarded by Minos the Beast. This time he's not going to be so nice."

This time? Nice? Like this sort of thing was normal?

As Daniela looked from Angelia to Merrick and back again, her body went all weird and still as it had in Darken's room. Another reason she needed to take about two hundred steps back from the people and goings on in this house. "Okay, listen. This all might seem like run of the mill for you guys, but this whole thing's wigging me out."

As she stood up off the stool, Angelia's hand slid into Merrick's. To keep the man in place? Or was this more of that Kynd-touching thing?

Angelia nodded. "Sorry. You're right. We're so embroiled in all of this, it's easy to forget no one else is."

Pretty and nice. The blonde had the whole package. No wonder her gargoyle-chimera guy panted after her. "No, no worries," she said, like they'd bumped shopping carts, or something just as trivial. "I get it."

Angelia opened her mouth to say something, but Merrick spoke over her. "It's a lot to take in."

"You got that right," she murmured while she scanned for the door to the garage.

"Merrick, do us a favor? Check on the boys?"

There was a pause where Merrick the big, bad chimera didn't budge, he just stood there watching Daniela like she was an ant under a kid's microscope—fascinating, the intensity of the sun burning through the glass making her squirm.

"Ah, sure. Okay." He left without saying anything though.

Angelia went to one of the tall cupboards, the skinnier one next to the fridge, and pulled down a couple of travel mugs. Sauntering over to the coffee machine, she said, "Listen, Dani—can I call you Dani?

Daniela nodded.

"Good." She placed the lids next to the cups. "So, anyway, I hope we don't scare you off. This is a lot to take in, I know that. Even more so for you, so we want to give you time."

Angelia stood back, her hand resting on the handle of the coffee pot. "It's just that we're so dang thrilled for Darken. He's found his Chosen

One, and we love seeing him happy."

Well, there was a relative term. She highly doubted she could make him happy, what with his history and all. He'd probably need two thousand years of therapy to undo the damage.

Same with his brothers. Although Merrick seemed like he had both oars in the water. Because of Angelia?

"Can I ask you something?"

"Anything. Any time." Angelia started pouring coffee into a mug. "What do you want to know?"

"This is going to sound so...I don't know...weird." Wrapping her hands around her mug, she settled back onto the stool.

"Try me."

Skipping the toe in the pond routine, Daniela dove right in. "This Chosen business. Besides the whole Circle-thing, how do you know? How can Darken be so sure I'm who he thinks I am?"

As soon as she asked, she realized how important the answer was. As if she could overlook all those warning signs if she could have some guarantees. "I mean, he says he would never hurt me, and I believe him. But..."

"He says you work with battered women." Angelia brought a freshly filled and steaming travel mug over to the island and copped a squat on one of the other stools.

"I do. I get called in to help the women who arrive at the hospital on stretchers. The police need their stories for a conviction, and a lot of times it's easier for the victims to talk with a woman. One without a uniform."

"Ah. So, you listen. Bear witness to their pain. But most important, see the carnage, first hand."

Yeah, that was it in twenty words or less.

"And you don't want to wind up in one of those beds."

Daniela didn't bother to answer the rhetorical.

"Well, I don't have promises for you, Dani. I can only tell you that I've lived with them for four months now, and not once, during all their rages and fights, did I ever worry about my safety."

"Merrick?"

"Gets in the thick of half of them, once he knows I'm out of harm's way."

"But see, that's just it. It doesn't seem like it would take much to put you in harm's way. I've seen the damage here, and it doesn't look like a wall would stop these…males once they got into it."

"No, probably not. But then, I'm in danger every time I get behind the wheel of my car. I can wear my seatbelt, drive a vehicle with airbags over every window, on every panel, but there aren't any guarantees I won't still get into an accident.

"Which is what it would be if one of them ever did hurt me. An accident."

"You sound so sure."

"Because I am." Angelia glided over to the walk-through pantry, her heels clacking on the polished tile.

Disappearing for a few moments, she clackity-clacked her way back, a pair of tennis shoes dangling from her pinched fingers. A hint of a blush colored her cheeks. "I need my sneakers if we're going to see Darken. Merrick loves the heels, but they're impractical as all get-out."

So, she wore outfits to please her man. Which, if that earlier blast of happiness coming out of her meant anything, the other Chosen One reaped the rewards.

How functional and healthy.

Amidst the chaos of hulk-sized males grappling with sanity.

"Darken knew I'd bolt, didn't he…"

With a sadness Daniela felt, Angelia nodded as she took her arm in her hands and pressed in close. Such compassion…

She didn't mind the other woman's closeness at all. They stood tucked together, even though Daniela was a couple of inches taller than the blonde. And much bigger.

To her credit, Angelia didn't seem to notice, or care. She snuggled up to her like it was the most natural thing in the world to do. "He worried you would, yes." Her sigh expressed the futility Darken most likely had felt. "And now that you've seen?"

Well, there was the million-dollar question, and she had the ready answer. "I want to bolt."

"Just so." Angelia gave a squeeze before letting go. With a couple of quick toe to heels, she shed the stilettos then slipped on her Reeboks. "Ready? You're going to take off anyway, so you might as well go fully informed."

Preparing to bristle at the accusation, she found she couldn't. Not when there hadn't been any anger behind the other Chosen's words. Only resignation. And a sense of fairness.

Damn it. The blonde was the whole package, wasn't she?

The woman's honesty made her feel…secure. Like her feet were still firmly planted in the world, even though the scenery had changed drastically.

And what do you know. Being grounded like this gave her the courage to proceed. To see Darken as he had never wanted her to see him.

Because it would be the final nail in the coffin.

The straw and the camel's broken back.

And still she wanted to see him.

"Am I being cruel?" She found her feet didn't want to move.

With a sad smile, Angelia shook her head. "You are Darken's Chosen. You are entitled to want to know, to have to know. You are his deliverance, his peace, but you can't be that if there are secrets between you."

Smart woman. "You learned this through experience?"

"Pretty much. But I had an advantage. I was already a part of this world. To me, vampires and shape-shifters are normal. It's the human world I struggle with. Not the other way around."

Lucky her. Daniela thought she might have an aneurysm if she learned too much more. Didn't matter, though. Instead of leading them out of the kitchen, Angelia padded over in her practical sneakers to yet another counter in this colossal room.

When she turned back around, she was holding a leather bound tome.

Eyes growing wide, Daniela blurted, "That's the Scriptum Darken mentioned."

"Yep." Angelia winked as she pointed at her temple. "It's all in here, too. Crazy, right? Even for me." She dropped the book onto the island with a thud, then cracked it in half. Rolling a few pages to find her place, she leaned back to give Daniela a good peek.

"See, this is Urick." She pointed at the most gorgeous and well-preserved illuminated script Daniela had ever seen. Not that she'd seen much, but you couldn't miss the golden gleam.

Or the creature. Who looked like…Daniela leaned in for a closer look. "A bear man with black eyes. Not gray like the other Kynd."

"Very astute of you." Angelia bumped her shoulder with her own, then went back to looking over the page. "That's the vampire in him."

"He's gorgeous." Apparently, since meeting Darken, her vocabulary had dwindled to words like beautiful and gorgeous. As if the things she saw stunned her to stupidity.

"Yes, as they all are. Too bad the Others don't see them that way…" Voice trailing off, Angelia bent her head closer to the open pages, but Daniela caught the sorrow in the woman's dark blue eyes.

Darken's surprise that she'd find him drool-worthy really had been a genuine reaction on his part. Huh. "So, why are you showing me Urick when I'm itching to see what this book shows about…my…Grotesque."

Two could play at this honesty thing. And wasn't that fun, actually.

"Okay, here's the thing."

"Why'd you shut the book?"

"Because everything there is to know about Darken, you already know."

"No, I don't."

"You do." Angelia pressed her finger right on top of Daniela's hefty cleavage. Right where her heart beat a little fast from all the caffeine. Truly.

"The final answer to all your questions, all your uncertainty, is here." She pushed a little harder on ye olde skin-covered thumping box.

Daniela leaned back from the pressure. Which suddenly seemed to be coming at her from all sides, not just the stab to her heart.

Angelia offered her a sympathetic smile, her eyes so blue they were almost black. But very warm, all the same. She gave her arm a squeeze, then suddenly all business, turned for the coffee maker.

After slopping cream, sugar, and coffee into their travel mugs, she handed Daniela hers. Like the house was so effing big, you needed to carry supplies to voyage from one end to the other?

You probably did, if how it looked on the outside ran true to the interior.

As they headed back through the dining room, she found her mouth had a case of diarrhea, now that someone was around to answer her questions. "And what about the constant touching thing? I notice Darken fighting that almost non-stop. My heart tells me to let him, because it gives him comfort as much as it does me, but my head? It's screaming controlling abuser every chance it gets."

"You think he touches to control you."

"No! Yes. God, I don't know." They headed down a wide corridor, her boots making no sound on the thick pile of the runner. On either side, the oak floor stretched to kiss some gorgeously scrolled baseboards.

Details. So many artistic elements throughout the house. Higher up, antique wall sconces bathed the corridor with just enough light to guide them along. Nothing harsh, except for the far end, where a window the size of an eighteen wheeler rose up before them.

With the morning sun blazing in, it made a person feel like they were walking into the light. Any minute now, St. Peter's hand would be reaching out.

"Okay, here's the thing." Angelia stopped, and Daniela, playing tourist, almost plowed her the frick over.

"Ooh, sorry." She stepped back, but not before Angelia placed her hand on her forearm. Like blondie touched automatically, just like the men here. She waved her other hand as if Daniela's apology was nothing but some nagging gnats, and kept up with her *here's the thing* intro without a hitch.

"Uri didn't come home last night. Which, I'm sure I don't have to tell you, isn't good."

Daniela shook her head then her eye caught the flash of something white on the carpet runner. Plaster? As her head started playing *Clue,* she raised her gaze upward.

"Are those…"

"Claw marks? Sort of. Drakus caught his wing."

Ookay. The look on Angelia's face told her they were about to walk in on Colonel Mustard in the library with a candlestick up his English ass.

And what do you know. Blondie opened the door they'd stopped at and there was the library, with book cases rising up to the coffered ceiling, the wood of the beams overhead matching that of the book shelves.

Stepping in, she couldn't help but think—another beautiful room…ransacked. As she pivoted to get a gander at the demolition, the

231

sadness she'd felt earlier rolled in like a fog bank.

Despite the heavy medieval style furniture, the room had fared as badly as the rest of the house. And there were deep grooves gashed across the walls, the book cases, the windowsills.

One of which had apparently been smashed, because it had been boarded up. All along that sill were more gashes, and punctures in the silk wallpaper. Looking for all this world as if a dragon perched there.

As Daniela's mouth fell open, Angelia stepped up beside her. "I know, and we're all really sorry about this. We'd hoped to have the house fixed up before Darken brought you here."

But they hadn't had time. Because she'd insisted he show her his home, even though she'd seen how bad he wanted to tell her no. And yet, he had brought her. As though he could deny her nothing. Even if it cost him...her.

He'd known what she would think, how she'd react. That she'd draw conclusions and they wouldn't be in his favor. Which wasn't how a control freak acted, was it.

The sadness chilled her like the fog it was, and as she peered deeper into the cavernous room, she noticed that Colonel Mustard wasn't there with his candlestick.

But Darken was.

Or who she thought was Darken. It was hard to tell, what with the monochromatic theme going on. He was gray from the tips of his hair down to his bare...clawed feet.

"Holy Christ." The words plopped out, and she didn't try to shovel them back in. Instead, she tread deeper into the room, putting one foot in front of the other like someone relearning how to walk.

The...statue...was indeed Darken. She could see that as she stepped around him, getting a lids-stretched-wide eyeful.

"He's stone." In the back of her mind, a little voice chimed *No shit, Sherlock,* but it barely registered. The rest of her mind was too busy reaping details.

Like how fucking big and hard he was. Because he was a statue.

Heartbeat getting a little thready, she said, "Is he alive?"

"Yup. And he can hear you."

Daniela flinched, not expecting Angelia to be right over her shoulder.

232

A woman's arm stretched out past her, finger pointing. "You can touch if you want. He feels that, too."

Her hand trembling like she had Parkinson's, Daniela reached out, barely brushing her fingers over the stone of Darken's hip. "He's..."

Magnificent.

Trailing her fingers as she rounded to the front of him, she said instead, "...upset."

Because it was the first word that came to mind when she looked up to see his face. The beautiful lines were there, the hard cut of his jaw. Which now seemed like a razor blade the way it was stretched open, fangs and sharp teeth prominent in a wide-open mouth.

It was the eyes, though, that drew her. Stretching up onto her tiptoes, she tried getting a closer look. "Can he see me?"

"Only once you get in his line of sight. Here." Angelia dragged a chair over for her to stand on.

Dropping her heels back to the floor, she shook her head. She didn't want to get in Darken's line of sight. What would she do, wave? Be all, Yoo-hoo, you in there?

Of its own volition, her hand reached back out to touch, and her fingers glided over the tendons in his forearm. Encased in stone, they were as defined as piano wires.

Abstractedly, she noticed he wore the same clothes he'd had on when she'd seen him last. They, too, were stone. Which struck her as strange, that everything concerning him would be cemented, but he could still hear and see.

As though the inside of him were still...living.

She felt the tingling pinch of her nose as her vision went blurry. "He...his heart beats?" She didn't really care if she got an answer, really, as she pressed her hand to his bulging bicep.

This was so...fucking sad.

Only hours before, he'd been a living, breathing, very sensual and responsive...person. Now, he was like one of those statues you saw in a cemetery. Life size, and life-like, but forlorn in some forgotten way.

"He can feel me? Touching him like this?"

Angelia came up behind her, placing her hands on her shoulders to offer comfort. "He can."

Daniela found herself leaning into the touch of the other woman. God, there was something to it, wasn't there. Having the solidness of someone with you, standing strong while you...didn't.

Tipping her chin up, she felt a tear tickle its way down her cheek, but she didn't rub it off. "Are you always like this?" Darken couldn't answer, but she felt a strength course through her as she spoke to him directly.

It was like when she sat with the battered women. Like the last victim whose jaw had been wired shut. She couldn't talk well, but that wasn't the point. Not at first, anyway. What mattered was the connection.

What mattered was that there was someone to sit with you and just be...there.

Touching, whether it was through actual contact, or simply a held gaze between two souls in commiseration.

It was the communion that mattered.

Granted, the pose of the two Kynd suggested they were doing anything but holding hands like skirted girls gamboling through a sun-kissed meadow. And she was sure that if she stood in that chair, she'd be able to follow the lines of where those two males were looking—at each other.

Not in a kindly way, either.

But in a Kyndly way, she supposed. As two men would who shared the same battle scars would look upon each other. Even if those two men had fought on opposite sides of the battlefield, there would be a fellowship in the wounds received.

She didn't recognize the other gargoyle, but figured him to be Kallen, the sixth Kynd she had yet to meet. Studying his chiseled countenance, she could see the comparisons.

Not so much in the lines that made a face unique, but in the expression. Kallen seemed as outraged and upset as Darken. So they'd fought, she supposed. Two sides warring for the same purpose.

"Uri." She merely mumbled the name, but Angelia remained close. Merrick, she noticed, stepped up to be near Kallen, placing a big hand on the other's granite back.

Offering comfort. Because the...man...could feel it.

"Yes," the other Chosen agreed. "He'd been watching a woman at the Medical Center. A woman who could be his, and from what we gathered from Kallen's…broken story, was that Uri teleported through the window when he saw her doing something vile to the patients.

"He'd roared *vampire!* And then snatched her. Kallen doesn't know if he meant to teleport with her or not. But he did, and no one's seen him since."

Which meant Urick was out there in the world somewhere, frozen solid like his brothers here, and helpless. Well, as helpless as one could be when they were solid stone.

"And they fought over it."

Angelia released her embrace to run her palm along Kallen's cheek. "They worry."

Excuses. Daniela had pretty much heard them all. *You got me upset. You know what sets me off. It won't happen again…* The list ran long for the reasons men abused the women in their lives.

Women they could love, yet still blame for the blackened eyes, the bruises, and broken bones. Placing the fault on the poor soul who bore the violence.

And yet.

Darken and his brothers did not sit upon both sides of the same coin.

Not at all. For what she saw in these stone visages was fear. For someone they loved dearly. Did it matter that it manifested in violent outbursts?

Of course it did.

Violence in any form shouldn't be tolerated.

But it should be understood. If only to pare down to the root of it.

The Kynd lashed out because they didn't know how to channel their pain.

Two thousand years of it…

The concept filled her with wonder, shoving aside her sadness and replacing it with resolve.

"Merrick." With her hand clasping over Darken's fist, she turned to the only other Kynd who could answer her questions. "Why are you not stone? Is it Angelia?"

His chest bowing, he pulled the blonde woman to him and nodded. "She is my life, Daniela. The reason I breathe, and I mean that in so many ways. She is the light to my darkness, and I would not be who I am without

235

her."

He tugged her closer as Angelia's face went all gooey for her guy. She ogled up at him, planting a kiss under his chin.

Merrick's gray eyes flashed then softened. "Granted, she scares me to death when she won't listen to reason, but most of the time, she and that damned book are right."

"And the make-up sex is awesome," Angelia admitted. Without a hint of modesty.

Daniela fought to suppress her smile. After coming into this library, she'd wondered how they could have been so cheery back in the kitchen, but now she got it.

They were in love. Like newlywed in love. Only, if Merrick's enraptured gaze meant anything, the honeymoon was going to last for fricking eons.

"When you fight, do you…"

"Ah…" Narrowing her eyes, insight struck the doe-eyed look from Angelia's face. "You wonder if he ever loses control and hits me."

It might have crossed her mind.

"Absolutely not," Merrick growled. *Did his hair just get longer?* "And if anyone ever laid so much as a finger on her, I'd not only take their whole hand off, I'd eat it while they watched." As he said this, he glared at the two stone gargoyles.

Angelia snuggled up his arm. "He would, too. Isn't he great!"

Huh. In some freaky way, that just made…sense. Convincing sense. Like not only would the chimera do it, but maybe he already had.

Daniela found her eyes drifting to Darken's hands.

Two. *Not guilty!*

Jesus Christ, she was getting giddy. Like you do when you're getting by on too little sleep. Or when you've seen too much already, and the gears in your brain are slipping.

Ah, yeah, definitely the latter. Plunking her butt into the chair Angelia had brought over for her to stand on, Daniela didn't know whether to heave a dramatic sigh, or put her head in her hands.

And wouldn't it figure that sitting so close to Darken and him not reaching out for her would make her feel even sadder. She wanted his comfort. Counted on it, she realized. She missed his touch terribly, and it was then she conquered her own indecision.

If she gained comfort and strength from this man's touch, then it obviously wasn't one of the signs of being in a relationship with an abusive partner.

On the contrary. It meant what she felt with this huge hunk of stone was the cornerstone of a healthy relationship. Pun intended. Still a little punch drunk, she grinned as she looked up at her gargoyle.

"My cornerstone, get it."

Merrick and Angelia slipped away, as though to give her privacy. Except she and Darken wouldn't be alone, would they. And it wasn't as if the other stone gargoyle could go anywhere.

Well, neither could they, so there you were. One more detail for how it must be like to live with Kynd.

Wait. Why was she thinking about that? Moving in furniture already? Daniela shook her head. Anyway…

"This is a lot, Darken. A lot to take in. You. This house. Your brothers."

Inside, her heart went all thpthpthpthp like a sewing machine, her belly going butterflies. Because she was seriously contemplating this.

Coward that she was, though, she needed Darken's strong arms around her to do it. To bolster her courage as she committed to…this.

So, what she said instead was, "I'm going back to my house. I'm sure I can hitch a ride with Angelia." She had to pack, decide what she should take, and what she shouldn't. Contact the hospital to let them know she needed some vacation time. So much to do. And think about. "So, good-bye then?"

Fingers dragging down his thick arm as she walked away, Daniela left the library.

Chapter Twenty-One

She's leaving? Holy shit, no. No. Just no. She couldn't. Not while he was helpless to...stop her?

Yes, God damn it. Stop her from leaving him, from destroying him. Said his heart, which was flinging itself around inside him like a caged rabbit. He couldn't breathe to ease the building pressure.

And that fucking rabbit just kept jumping, jumping, jumping until he thought he'd scream.

Daniela! Don't go. Fuck, don't go. Please. *You said we could talk this out.* She'd said the violence was a normal reaction, so please, oh please, fuck, the house doesn't matter.

Right? *The shape of the house doesn't matter!*

Jesus loving Christ, sure as shit he was going to have a heart attack.

In front of him, Kallen stood impassive, while Darken thought he'd lose his ever-living mind. The other gargoyle just faced him, haunches bent for an attack.

That wouldn't come for another five fucking hours!

Oh, Kallen looked as if he could tear the nuts off a sundae with his teeth. But he was just as impotent to do it as Darken was to stop his Chosen from leaving him. Damn, but he could still feel the trailing of her fingers down his arm.

As she'd backed away!

From him, while he could do...*nothing!* Frozen in form like the poor fucking bastard in front of him. If he needed a reflection of what he himself looked like, well, take a God damned gander across the way.

Sure as shit, Kallen was screaming inside his stone suit, too. No fucking doubt.

Yet, there they stood in the wrecked library. Like a matched set of fucking end tables, gathering the fucking dust motes swirling in the sunbeams…

Fuck! Come back to me, Daniela!

Silent. He could roar inside his stone prison, splinter, and shriek, and outwardly he would ever be the same—nothing. Just a carved stone creature.

While inside…*I'm going fucking insane! My Chosen, she leaves…*

She'd seen him at his worst. At his absolute worst. How could this not be too much for her? A woman of peace and order.

When the beast who loved her offered nothing but violence and chaos?

Uri gone and the nascent tendrils of control they'd so carefully nurtured over the past four months…gone. Like, nuclear bomb, gone. The discharge leveling what little composure they'd managed to scrape together.

It had been Darken's responsibility to keep the bear safe, and he'd failed.

He couldn't even protect his brother. Why, pray tell, had he really thought he could do so for his Chosen One.

Guilt choked the life from his fear, and although outwardly nothing changed, inside he withered, collapsing in on himself to weep at the futility of all of this.

Living? No. He and his brothers struggled. Those rare moments of true happiness, like when they'd gathered in the kitchen to learn how to cook. The seven of them laughing and grousing at each other, even when they'd failed to the point they'd abandoned the stove, and had turned their bumbling attentions to the toaster instead.

Safer. Heartening in the way it had built up their confidence.

And all it took to destroy it was to have one of them falter. As though without that one beam of support, the whole building collapsed. Without Uri, the battered unit of Kynd could not stand on its own.

Like crutches. Jesus, they enabled themselves, didn't they? Kristov had offered to help Urick, and what did Darken do? Turned him down flat. Told the Vampyre to keep his nose out of Kynd business.

Well, look how great that turned out.

Uri was MIA. Teleporting like the vampire he was and Kristov had known what would come. Might have prevented this.

I am. Such. A. Selfish bastard.

Thinking he alone could repair the damage done to his brotherkynd.

Well, not alone. He'd found his Chosen One. A woman designed by God to help them.

And she'd been right—Darken and his brethren were victims of abuse; wounded males unable to stand alone against the damage done to their souls.

So where did she think she was going, damn it?

Like Uri, she was an essential girder in this fragile Kynd structure. As was Kristov, if he was still willing to help. Angelia, too. And Merrick, now, in his own way, leading by example. Anton, Angelia's father, and fuck...but, Godrick, too. For the Triumvirate was just that—a triad of strength.

Godrick might be the one to doubt the Kynd's deliverance, but it was his skepticism that kept them balanced. He represented the Others who did not trust the Kynd and their newfound freedom.

Their trust was the goal to which to aspire.

And they so needed something to look forward to.

To get better so their forays toward finding their Chosen Ones weren't so wrought with destruction and pain.

Ah, God, the truth of that humbled him. He'd fall to his knees if he could, and...*fuuuck.*

He would give thanks to God to have all of these people in his life.

He would give thanks to God for the suffering, without which he would not have learned of...the grace in forgiveness.

Yes, forgiveness. He felt his heart grow quiet and then light as his thoughts became so. A weightlessness in his chest as he accepted the many hands reaching out to help him and his brethren.

Not a thousand hands by any means, nor a thousand hearts opening to them, but he'd be grateful for the few they had.

As his thoughts calmed, the running rabbit in his ribcage did too. And with all things being connected, his body quieted as well. So relieved was he, that he felt as if his knees gave way and he reached to touch Kallen.

Not only to support his sagging weight, but to connect with a fellow being, as humans did in fellowship when they knelt in prayer.

For the first time in centuries, he wanted to raise his eyes to God. Not in anger for once, but with gratitude for this unfamiliar lack of burden.

And found that he...could.

What the?

Muscles in an instant shiver, he lowered his gaze. To look not at Kallen's face as he'd been doing for hours, but at his brotherkynd's ripcord waist.

"Holy..." Tongue truly tied, he shot a look up to Kallen's immobile face, then straight back down at his own bent knees. Pulling his trembling hands out to stare at them, Darken's throat squeezed tight as his skin.

His skin that wasn't...stone. It was day, and he wasn't stone.

As if his brain kept skipping like a needle on a broken record, he couldn't jar his thoughts out of the rutted groove. The sun was streaming in through the library windows, and he wasn't...stone.

Finally, he thought maybe he should jump up and shout to the rafters, like a victorious knight at the end of a hard won battle.

Except, he didn't feel triumphant.

He felt weightless, as though a great truth had been revealed to him, and the knowledge had rendered him humble.

Remaining upon his knees, he let his head drop between his shoulders. "Kallen, my brother, I thank you. I thank you," he repeated, reaching once again for that fellowship. Wrapping a hand tight around his brotherkynd's calf, he pressed his forehead to the male's granite knee.

"Thank you, Kallen. For being with us, for being...everything you are." As he spoke, his voice took on a watery raspiness he didn't recognize.

Was he...crying?

When his finger came back wet after wiping it under his eye, he began to laugh. At first, it chugged like an old beater car, coughing in fits and false starts. But then it gained momentum and the quality of his laughter became that of a man whose neck had been saved from a last minute pardon by the governor.

Or God, as the case turned out to be.

Tears streaming as though the laughter wrung his gladdened heart, he pressed his face to Kallen's stomach, and hugged himself to the stone male who was bearing witness to his liberation.

"Thank you, thank you, Kallen. My brotherkynd." Fawning all over him, Darken suddenly realized he was probably torturing the poor guy. "Oh, God, I'm sorry."

He began to smooth the stone clothes draping the great male's chest and bubbled another relieved laugh. "I'm sorry." Clasping both sides of Kallen's jaw in his hands, which still hadn't stopped their palsy, he pressed his lips to the cold stone.

"I love you, brother," he said, brushing his thumbs over cheeks so sharp they seemed carved. Like so many of their brethren who were now perched on ledges and rooftops, a thin channel of water streamed down Kallen's cheeks, as if he were outside in a summer shower.

"Shush, brother, I will not leave you," he murmured, wiping the tears as he pressed himself close.

As he spoke the words, he realized he gained a measure of comfort in remaining, even as his thoughts rayed out through the house and beyond. To where his Daniela and Uri would be.

As he settled himself at Kallen's feet, making himself comfortable for the long stay, he mulled the miracle of his particular Chosen One.

She had freed him, only not in the way he had expected her to.

Like she was the iron object herself, she had been the key to unlocking him from his resentment. And like a key on a map, a quiet inset in the fabric of his world, she had shown him that he didn't travel alone.

That there were others around him and his brethren with their hands extended and their hearts open. He and his brethren did not walk this path by themselves.

Reminded him about some poem he'd read on a wall during one of his soul-reapings. *Footprints*, he thought it was titled. So. He'd had to travel for millennia in the desert sands before realizing the truth.

He had never been alone.

And the beautiful thing was that when shit exploded, there were people around to help him pick up the pieces.

"Jesus Chri—" With a glance skyward, he corrected himself. "I mean Jeezum Crow." Now that he'd made his peace with God, he probably ought to quit using His name in vain. Show more respect, or something.

Nestling his back against one of Kallen's stone legs, he rambled aloud. "I guess it was a good thing Aro got greedy and tried to get the

Scriptum into Hell. If he hadn't, Merrick and Angelia would have never gotten together."

And they never would have learned about the existence of Chosen Ones.

Which meant Darken wouldn't have found Daniela, nor the forgiveness toward his Creator, which had freed him from his Grotesque curse.

He pushed his back harder into Kallen to ground himself as the urge to leap to his feet and chase his Chosen home swelled inside him.

He wouldn't leave the other gargoyle by himself. Yeah, they usually spent their days alone, but never after one of them had been freed of their curse right before their very eyes.

He'd been selfish long enough. If he was truly going to help his brethren, then he had to start making sacrifices. Letting Daniela go was one of them.

Hold up. Shit, wait a sec. He didn't mean let her go permanently. Especially since his skin got furiously itchy for a second there.

Live without his Chosen One? Panic shrunk his balls. Great Chr— *damn it, this is going to be hard.* Holy cow, he couldn't let her go.

But he should.

It would be the honorable thing to do. Just because he'd had his breakthrough, didn't mean the violence would suddenly come to an end. The others still needed to find their Chosen Ones to help them find their own kind of peace.

Which meant plucking his selfish thoughts off Daniela and onto the best ways to help his brothers.

Maybe he would invite her to come and visit them, if she thought she could handle it.

He'd be so fucked, but he could live in her shadow. Tailing her, keeping Others from harming her as best he could. Oh, and hey, he'd even go so far as to beg a Mage for a protection spell. Without haste.

Before all that, though, he needed to call for a library meeting. "Kallen, what do you say we ask Drakus to take me into Hell and I lead those Shades to Heaven? You know, ask the Big Guy for entrance."

"Yeah? I think it's a great idea, too." As he spoke, his thoughts kept curling back to Daniela. To the way her body moved under her clothes.

How her curves were sensual, broadcasting an appetite for sexual pleasures. And promises.

At the mere hint of them, his cock quivered to life.

Cramming the heel of his hand against the bulge behind his zipper, he tried peeling his imagination off the seductive, dark chocolate gaze of his Daniela and onto the present.

Because he was sitting on the floor at the legs of a brotherkynd, and practically masturbating with the heel of his hand.

I'm just adjusting for the growth. Pushing over and over…

"Shit." He sprung up, keeping his back to Kallen before moving completely out of the stone gargoyle's line of sight. His shaft had swollen so much his jeans felt uncomfortably tight.

He had to cock a leg to make room, work his pelvis until the damned thing found a home that didn't hurt.

"Ants in your pants, Darken, or are you just glad to see me."

"Jesu—*fuck,* Merrick!" For the second time in like, five seconds, Darken turned his back to a brotherkynd while he figured out what to do with this…complication.

"I'd tease the ever-loving hell out of you right now, but I'm so frigging flabbergasted all I want to do is hug you, cock-stand and all. You're not stone."

Arranging his t-shirt so it covered the mushroom cap sticking out of his waistband, he turned just as Merrick engulfed him in a hard hug.

Three slugs of a hand clapping to his shoulder blades, and Merrick stepped back. His smile so grand the points of every tooth showed. "Awesome, brother, so damned awesome. Wait till I tell Angel! She's going to flip out. Oh, and hey, we only just took Dani home, so you can still catch her before she…goes…any…where. What?"

Merrick's enthusiasm dwindled like his erection.

"I'm not going after her."

"Not going after her? Are you frigging insane! She's your Chosen."

"I know! But she said good-bye, Merrick, and I have to honor that." Saying it out loud felt like a kick to his guts, and he found a chair to park his ass before his knees gave out.

"What? You're sure?" He glanced up at Kallen, too, like the guy could confirm. "Angel said she'd been thinking about bolting, and she was quiet on the ride back to her house, but I figured she just had a lot to think about."

"Yeah, well. She thought about it." If he leaned back into the chair he sat in, would it swallow him whole? Please?

"Shit." Merrick deflated into his own seat. See, that was the problem with bad news. It sucked everybody down.

Darken had no idea how long they pouted, but the sun dropped far enough to cast Kallen's long shadow across Merrick.

Seriously, he had to get up out of his chair. He wasn't stone anymore—halle-fricking-lujah!—so he shouldn't be acting like he was. Dragging his hands down his face, he at least hitched himself forward, elbows on knees.

"Right. So, I need to keep myself busy, or I'm going to go postal. What say we figure out what the hell to do with Uri, while we make plans for Hell. I'm sure Kallen wouldn't mind the outlet."

"I thought you weren't going."

"I changed my mind. Me and the Big Guy have made our peace."

"Ah. Explains the whole moving about in daylight bit."

So it did, thank God.

* * * *

Sometimes all it takes to set your day back on its wheels is a long, hot shower. The kind that turns your bathroom into a sauna and your skin lobster red.

Wrapped in a towel with her damp ass sitting on the end of her bed, Daniela pulled the comb through her wet hair. God, those teeth dragging across her scalp were ranked right up there with a foot massage.

Eyes shut to the sensation, she lost herself to the raking while her thoughts took leisurely strolls along the things she needed to get done today. Nothing pressing, really, which was why she gave in to the luxury of pampering herself.

Leave-in conditioner. Check.

Full body lotion rubdown. Check.

Muscles liquefied by steam. Roger that.

Two weeks of vacation with non-stop Darken—glitch. The days would be interrupted by his turning to stone. Never had she been so glad of winter and Daylight Savings Time.

The nights would be long. And she had every intention of indulging them both in…exploration. Houston, we're clear for take-off.

Stretching herself out on her bed, she didn't care if her body's impression left a damp spot.

Not when there was something dampening as she imagined Darken's big body on hers. The bulk of his weight held up on his strong arms. His long, thick legs stretched out between hers.

Closing her eyes to the image, she let the sensations run all over her, stretching her body as if to accommodate her dream lover.

A loud rattling bang shot her upright. When you lived alone, sounds like that meant you weren't…alone. A noise that big didn't happen by itself.

Heart thumping, she reached for her bathrobe, swirling it over her shoulders and punching her arms into the silk holes as she rushed from the bedroom.

Since her home was a single story cottage, she didn't have to be Sherlock to deduce her way to the cellar door. The bang she'd heard had sounded like a box dropping. A box with stuff she had packed away with her own hands.

Like the carton of mismatched saucers and cups that had belonged to her *nonna*.

"Son of a bitch." Fear that there was someone in her house took her anger by the hand, so she stepped back into the kitchen. To slide open her tool drawer. Eyes still trained on the cellar door, she rummaged until her fingers curled around her prize.

A hammer. Easier to wield than a baseball bat, and far more devastating than a knife. Bolstered by the heft of her weapon, she eased open the sole barrier between herself and safety.

"Get a grip, woman." It was broad daylight. The chances of having an intruder were…fine, not nil, but pretty darned close. It was probably her neighbor's cat again.

The cat had found its way inside in the summer, when Daniela kept her windows open to cool her house with the salty breezes off the ocean. Right now, being February, every window wasn't just closed, but locked, to keep those cold ocean winds out.

Still, if it was the cat, she didn't need the South Portland Police Department wasting their resources when there were actual crimes going on. Like assault and battery on women who didn't cook their husbands' eggs right.

She thought about the woman in the hospital, the one she'd pawned off onto Eileen. If she'd needed head surgery, the poor soul was probably still unconscious. Proving there were far more dangerous things than the unknown right in front of you.

Resolved, she gripped the rubber coated handle of the hammer, and flicked up the light switch at the top of the staircase.

Light bloomed beneath her feet. Her cellar wasn't big, because her house wasn't. Descending slowly, she peered around the lit space, noting the shadows while letting her gaze pass over the shelving.

Searching for where the box had fallen, her quick inspection stopped at dead center of her cellar. Where, directly under one of the overhead bulbs, but just out of the slash of sunshine coming in from the rectangular window high up on the wall, was...

"Urick?" Now her heart thudded for other reasons. "Urick, what are you doing here?" What little stealth she'd been using fled as she tripped down the stairs to get to him.

Small as her cellar was, it didn't take long. And she slowed the nearer she got. With his back to her, she got a really damned good gander at the size of him.

He was massive. Given how he was poised, though, he should have seemed smaller than the gargoyles. Urick's shoulders, unlike Darken's and Kallen's, were hunched, his shoulders rounded.

As though he curled in on himself. Rounding his huge, stone mass, she saw instantly that he wasn't curled in on himself at all. Urick held a woman.

A woman she recognized. "Violet!" Kicking the box of her *nonna's* broken treasures aside, she rushed to the other woman, falling to her knees as she did so.

The whole time her head started spinning with the whos, whats, and whys.

Oddly, too, she wanted to ask them both, as if Urick could answer her.

But he couldn't. Any more than he could release the woman he held in his stone hands. Her friend Violet, the woman she shared late night coffee klatches with in the hospital caf, was locked in Urick's embrace.

Where she'd obviously been since dawn.

"My God, Violet! How is this possible?" Hands butterflying all over the bodies in front of her, they never lit. Hell, she didn't know where to touch. She couldn't pry Urick's fingers loose, and she couldn't pull Violet from his grasp.

Violet turned her face what little bit she could, her blonde hair riding up the stone wall of Uri's chest. The male himself didn't move, his head bowed, proving he'd been looking down at the woman in his arms as the sun had come up.

"Daniela?" With the crease etched between her eyebrows, the woman was obviously as confused to see Daniela as she was at seeing Violet. Then the other woman closed her eyes, a curse escaping on a whispered breath.

Like she was put out for being found in this state.

Like, come sunset, she was going to color herself gone. Promises, promises.

The hardness she glimpsed in those averted eyes said Violet had every intention of ridding herself of the bear chimera.

Yeah, good luck with that. "Are you hurt?" Aside from being stuck for the next...Daniela glanced at her bare wrist...*four hours?* Violet seemed okay.

As though begrudging her answer, Violet bit out, "No."

Huh, still not one for many words, even in this strange situation.

Still though, Daniela felt compelled to reassure the woman. "He won't hurt you." She didn't think. Urick was Kynd, and so far, she believed her gut on them. Violent and physical with themselves, yes. But never with a woman.

Daniela believed what she'd seen with Merrick and Angelia right down to her painted toenails.

Which meant...she was in for the same if she fully committed to Darken. Shivers tickled her inside and out. Four more hours and her own Kynd would be here.

"Maybe he won't hurt me, but I'm not going to be so considerate."

Such fire, and why did she suddenly feel defensive. For Urick.

"I'm sure once the sun sets, this can all get worked out." Couldn't it?

But what if Violet reported this to the police? What would happen to the Kynd?

Out of her depth, Daniela got up off her knees. "Listen, I'm going to run upstairs to make a call." *Sit tight* almost left her mouth, but she bit down on it.

Hitting the stairs like they were to be mastered, she went for her phone, tapping the screen as soon as the number Angelia had given her came up.

One ringie-dingie, two ringie-dingies. Then a third ringie-dingie. "Come on, Angelia, pick up. Don't go to voicemail."

The phone clicked, and nothing but vast emptiness filled her ears, like the Universe picked up, instead of the woman she'd been calling.

"Hey, chica, what's up? I didn't expect you to call so—"

The suddenness of Angelia's voice startled her, so she blurted, "Urick's here. In my basement. And he's got my friend locked in his arms."

"Get out. Shit. You're sure? Of course you're sure." Rambling, Angelia? Where was that sophisticated poise she'd worn earlier? "Hold on. I'm getting Merrick."

Daniela heard heavy breathing and rapid footsteps. "Are you running with me on the phone?" She must not have put those high heels back on.

"Yes. This dang house. Merrick's still in the library with…ooph…hey, guys! Uri's at Daniela's house!"

Daniela had to yank the phone from her ear as Angelia shouted into it.

More heavy breathing, muffled movement in the background…

"We're on our way." *Merrick.* He must have commandeered the phone. Then hung up.

Well, ookay. Standing in her kitchen, with the sunlight spilling over her knees on its way to the floor, she stared at her disconnected cell phone like it had turned into a beer bottle all of a sudden.

At least she couldn't fault their responses. As much as Merrick and Angelia had laughed and pretended all was well in the kitchen this morning, their relief now told her how much Urick's disappearance had scared them.

Oh, God. Violet is scared, too. How could she not be? Kidnapped by a huge man, brought to a strange house, and then locked in the embrace of her kidnapper—who had turned to stone right before her eyes.

"Shit." She needed to do some serious damage control. Violet couldn't call the cops. Maybe if Urick let her go, she wouldn't press charges.

Fantasize much, Dan.

She needed to get her head on straight, corral her thoughts as they jumped in all directions at once. First, get dressed. Somehow, clothes were important for the job she had ahead of her.

As if not wearing her housecoat would make her feel ready, at least.

Second, get her ass back downstairs. There was a frightened woman trapped down…okay, so Violet didn't exactly come across as scared. A little odd, but maybe she was in shock.

Third, no effing clue. How did she convince someone to stick around to hear the whole story? How could she nurture understanding toward a kidnapper?

Fourth, when did she fall off the turnip truck and decide that collusion with beings who weren't human was A-okay?

Well there. If she'd harbored any lingering doubts about joining the dark side before, Urick's arrival annihilated those. Because make no mistake, her heart was clearly on Team Kynd.

Taking a deep breath, she straightened the hem of her shirt around her ample hips, and headed for the cellar door.

Chapter Twenty-Two

As Darken pulled his truck in behind Angelia's Audi, he tried not to notice how different the place looked during the day. At night, which was the only time he'd ever been here, the beach wasn't visible.

Not that there was an awesome view now, what with the houses across from Daniela's hugging the shore. But in the spaces between the homes, rectangles of blue were visible, along with the brightness only stretches of sand and sun could achieve.

And it might be winter, but seagulls still floated aloft on the air currents, their screeching cries grating, but buffered somehow by the scent of brine, and the whoosh and roaring thump of curling waves.

The rhythm of tides was a soothing place to reside. No wonder his Chosen lived here. The sea could render someone calm much in the same way his Daniela could.

And yes, damn it, she was his. It didn't matter that she didn't want him.

She had been selected for him by God Himself, as evidenced by the fact his boots were making tracks in the sun-softened snow as he walked up to the house with his brother and sisterkynd.

"Should we knock or just go in?" Angelia was the first one up the steps, but she hesitated at the front door, letting him and Merrick fall in at her back.

Protecting her, even on this Norman Rockwell stretch of normal.

"Rap a little to alert her and then go in. She might be in the cellar with Uri."

As Angelia lifted her knuckles to the wood, the muscles of Darken's chest grew tight around his skipping heart. Yeah, it was all well and good to accept that his Chosen One didn't want him, but in the face to face?

His body reacted. Made demands that logically he knew he couldn't heed.

The second he stepped through the threshold, he doubted his wisdom in coming at all. Could he help Uri while he was up here, fallen upon his knees as he sucked in Daniela's scent like a coke addict?

A quick shake of his head got him back in the game.

Merrick couldn't handle Uri on his own. Not with his suspected Chosen One in the mix. A woman who had been taken forcibly.

Man, what a cauldron of shit. *Good one, bear.*

Because of Uri, Darken was back here a lot sooner than he was ready to be. Hell, he was still reeling from Daniela's good-bye, and the subsequent fall-out. So, having his shit together in order to pretend he could live without his Chosen was, well, a little too frigging soon.

But in the words of the late, great Francis of Assisi, *Start by doing what's necessary; then do what's possible; and suddenly you are doing the impossible.*

Yeah, noogie the bald head of that wise little monk. He had to start somewhere, didn't he?

Locking his fricking knees so he didn't go all Jim Bakker and blat his eyes out, Darken cracked his neck a couple of times then headed for the kitchen. "The door to the cellar is here."

Not that he'd ever been down there, but sure as his hardening dick was a divining rod, he knew where his Chosen was.

Plus, the scent of her wafting out of the open door may as well have been a neon sign. As his boot hit the first step down, his hands fisted so hard he felt the bite of his claws.

Start with what's necessary.

Which was acting strong on the outside, when inside he was fighting the urge to close the distance between him and Daniela by jumping the entire distance of those stairs.

And then some.

But come on. She'd said good-bye. She'd seen him in his perfectly grotesque rage and couldn't stomach it. Who could blame her.

Not him. Never. Anything Daniela needed to do to be all right, he would honor. Whether it killed him to do it or not.

"Hey, brother." The hand clapping onto his shoulder pulled his head out of his ass. "You okay?"

"Ah, yeah. Yeah."

"Come on. I'll go first." Merrick shouldered by him with Angelia stuck on his heels. 'Cause really, when Merrick said *I,* what he actually meant was *we.* Merrick couldn't separate himself from his Angel any more than he could cleave the lion or gargoyle making him chimera.

Raising his eyes heavenward in a silent prayer for strength, Darken followed.

The first thing he saw, naturally, wasn't Uri. The sloped muscle and curved bone of his brother's broad back was merely the background for his central focus—his Chosen One.

Standing on that concrete floor, he almost croaked *Daniela* before locking his jaw tight.

Then do what's possible.

As Merrick let out a curse that would redden the ears of God, the chimera faded into the periphery. Along with Angelia and the woman trapped in Uri's stone arms.

Front and center as if a floodlight beamed down upon her, Daniela stared at him, too, as if the others had never arrived.

For a flash of a second, he thought he'd seen excitement and anticipation on her face. But he must have read it wrong, because she lowered her eyes, and turned away, her fingers twining and twisting in a nervous knot.

Of course, she felt their connection. She just didn't want to act on it.

He nearly howled as pain bloomed in his chest, his heart flopping slow and irregular, like a fish dying on a sun scorched riverbank.

Not knowing what to do, he turned to his brotherkynd and Angelia, and the other woman. The vampire.

Who took that moment to hiss, baring her fangs at them. "Get away, scum!" Trapped in Uri's embrace, she looked full of righteous anger.

Daniela gasped. And Darken just stopped himself from roaring at that vampire, scaring her so she'd shut her fucking mouth. Daniela was not to be upset. Ever.

And they were not scum. To be called such gouged like a hot poker, instinct screaming at him to strike back. To deliver pain, just as much and even more than the insult had hurt him.

Merrick bristled beside him, giving his brain a chance to stretch outward, to widen his myopic focus, so logic could get a foothold.

This scenario just dropped more shit at his beautiful mate's feet.

"What the heck?"

See? More shit. Not only had she just gotten a front row seat in how the Others viewed the Kynd, she just saw her first vampire. Who also just happened to be a friend.

So much…*shit*. A frigging cauldron the size of an oil tanker of it.

Before he realized what he was doing, he stepped up behind his Chosen, curling his big hands around her fragile fingers. "Come on. Let's go upstairs and give the…your friend, some space."

Yeah, because he was all about being considerate to someone who thought being around Kynd was worse than stepping in dog shit.

At least Fido's foul smell could be washed off.

The curse of the Kynd? Treated like it was leprosy—stay far away lest it rot you, too.

Aaand didn't that just put him in a rosy mood.

Selfish ass that he was, he kept hold of his Chosen's hand, siphoning off some decency to level himself out as he led her upstairs.

Their steps out of sync as they ascended, he thought it apropos of how things were now between them. Always he would be different from her. And yet, in tandem with that sad thought was the realization that, despite his volatile reaction to the vampire's insult, he had not cursed his Creator.

A tiny step, for certain.

But like the stairs he now ascended, it was a step in the right direction. *And suddenly you are doing the impossible.*

* * * *

A little dazed by what just happened with Violet, Daniela let herself get led upstairs. Easy to do when the one leading her encompassed so much breadth of shoulder, muscle…vulnerability. Nobility, even.

To not strike back at her friend's insult proved Darken's strength wasn't merely on the outside.

The second they were out of the shoebox of her cellar and in her kitchen, she recovered, and stopped abruptly enough to swing him around by their joined hands. "What are you doing here? I thought you were stone."

"I told you, you are my Chosen One." He shrugged, like he stated the obvious.

He also released her hand and stepped back a few paces. Putting distance between them?

Wait. Why was he wearing the same expression as when he'd first come down into the cellar—determined and...resolved.

The obvious answer dropped the bottom out of her stomach, no matter how hard she tried dragging the feet of her thoughts away from such a horrific idea.

Now that Darken isn't stone anymore, he doesn't need me.

And now she wasn't going to experience his love-making. She wouldn't get to feel him pump into her, gliding back and forth across her sensitive skin until his big body locked in orgasm. Jetting his hot seed into her womb, while she...

Gaze sliding from his wide shoulders, down the length of his considerable chest, she stopped to feast on the bulge growing in his jeans.

Darken growled.

Attention flicking upward, she didn't look away from his mercurial eyes as they shimmered from gray to silver.

"What?" Why was he fighting his emotions? Why wouldn't he just close this distance between them and hold her. Curl his hips against her so that bulging shaft...

"Daniela." Another warning growl.

"What?" Though she knew. He didn't need her anymore, and he didn't need to want her, either.

Or her wanting him.

Darken didn't want her in his life.

His voice clipped and strangled rough, he said, "Would you help Uri and my brothers. I know how all of this looks to you, but if you could find it in your heart—"

"Find it in my heart?" Her skin grew cold.

Darken at least had the decency to look bothered by the insult he'd hit her with.

"You want me to help your brothers."

"I do. I'll do anything you ask, give you anything, if you would."

The nerve! Well, at least she wasn't cold anymore. Oh, no. Her blood was speeding up, flushing her skin. "You think I would—" Ah, the fucking gall of this guy! She couldn't even finish the sentence. He thought she would take payment for helping his brothers?

Wow. Just wow. Blood boiling, she felt strangely calm.

Which put Darken on alert. He straightened, pulling his head back as his nostrils flared. Like he could smell *pissed-off* when he gave it a try.

As he turned all Sherlock Holmes on steroids, Daniela let that familiar calm drape itself around her. Man, she loved how responsive it had become. The dang thing had become like a super power, a steadying strength she could call at will.

Voice composed as she now felt, she walked over to her front door and pulled it open. "Go home, Darken."

He took three steps before grinding his boots into the carpet. "Merrick will need help with Uri."

Ah, so that was why he stopped. His refusing to leave had nothing to do with changing his mind, to wanting to stay with her.

What a fool she'd been, believing his lies. *Oh, my Chosen, I love your big ass.* And other words to that effect. The pathetic part? She'd believed him. He had made her feel beautiful. He'd made her feel like a worthy treasure.

And it had all been a lie to free himself from his curse.

She'd been used.

Well, then screw him. She'd take these feelings of sensuality he'd stirred in her and nourish them. She wasn't Hugh Hefner's monthly flavor by a long shot, but that didn't mean she couldn't be sexy.

It didn't mean there weren't other men out there who would truly— *and honestly!*—enjoy her curves.

If Darken didn't want her, then it was his loss.

Heading back down to the cellar, she made sure to shake her ass and work her hips, just to show the jerk what he'd be missing.

She didn't have to look back to know he followed her. Any closer, and she'd have to turn the thermostat down. The man radiated heat like a fricking furnace, making her think of the times she'd backed her butt up to campfires.

Once one side was cooked, it was time to rotisser-ate and heat the other.

Except she kept her eyes forward, hooking a right at the bottom of the stairs to head for the others.

While she and Darken had been gone, Merrick had positioned himself so he could touch and hold the other chimera and still keep out of biting range—oh, jeez.

This was her friend Violet, for goodness sake! And her first thoughts were *biting range*? Angelia turned her gaze from the woman trapped in Uri's arms to greet her. "Hey, you all right?"

"Yeah. Of course." *Don't gulp, damn it.* "Hi, Violet. Are you all right?" So she deflected Angelia's concern from herself onto the...vampire. They were friends—in spite of the recent developments, and she honestly cared if Violet was okay.

Violet glared at her.

But what did she expect. Clearly, she was on the wrong team, siding with the...*scum.* An inflexible protectiveness rose inside her like a feral thing. These males—including Darken, damn it—weren't filth, and didn't deserve the prejudice or the hatred.

With the slur still chafing her, she reminded herself that Violet was a friend, too. Taking a deep breath, she touched base with her inner calm again, stroking it until her pulse quietened.

Sincere concern for the other woman swirled to the surface. Her smile genuine, she reached out to place her hand on her arm when her own got pulled back.

"Don't touch. Please." *Darken.* His tone gentle, yet commanding. And was that fear flashing in his eyes for a second there? For her? "Uri won't like it."

Aaah, no. Attempting to hide her disappointment...and her hurt...she pulled against his hold, snatching her hand back. "It's you who needs to step back. I'm female. Ergo," lancing him with her best *Duh!* expression, she finished, "not a threat."

Glowering, he stepped back.

Good. Better. Though her soul cried for the distance now wedged between them.

A detachment Darken would cultivate because he didn't need her anymore.

But Urick did. And it wouldn't hurt if she tried to help Violet, too. Just so long as the woman didn't try to sink those fangs into—

The bear chimera came to life so fast, readjusting his hold on his reluctant prize, Daniela fell backward from the force of it. In an instant, Darken straddled her like a tiger guarding his kill from other predators.

Muscles drawn taut, he eased back as his challenge faded to a warning snarl. "Easy, bear," he growled through tight lips drawn back over sharp teeth. "We can figure this out."

With his treasure held tight in his thick, long arms, Urick shook his head. "No, brother." The despair and anguish in his black eyes swamped Daniela in sorrow.

Before she could gather her wits to realize she was looking at Urick the vampire, he disappeared. Vanished.

Taking her friend Violet with him.

"Well," Angelia said, "at least he's found his Chosen."

* * * *

"How in bloody hell do you know that?" Darken snapped. Beyond infuriated with Uri popping hither and yon—and worse, threatening his Daniela—he didn't mean to be so sharp with Angelia, but there you have it.

Naturally, Merrick stepped up to the plate, his black mane already sprouted around his neck and jaw because of Uri's sudden aggression. The lion had sprung forth to protect his own Chosen.

What. A. Freak. Show. They were. They really were. Could they bring Drakus over, too, so there'd also be a dragon to wreck Daniela's house. She'd said good-bye, had washed her hands of them, and now look.

A My Pretty Pony show. And his snarling puss hadn't even been the main attraction.

Just...great.

Holding tight to Merrick, Angelia went to Darken, rubbing her palm up and down his arm. "Vampires have blood mates. Uri's Chosen One needs to be a vampire."

"Oh, well, that's just brilliant." Acerbic sarcasm aside, Darken started to settle down, his muscles no longer yanking at his bones. "The bear hates vampires. Hates himself. What's he going to do when he finds out he needs that female vampire he obviously detests?"

"I don't know." Angelia's confession tweaked him like a double shot of cheap tequila, and he pierced his claws into his palms to keep from reaching for his lifeline.

Daniela. Who stood off to the side, as if unsure of her part in all this.

Chr...*man*, it killed him not to wrap himself around her. It really did. But he could do something about making her more comfortable without touching, like wrangling this mess out of her house. Giving her the safe, neat life she wanted.

And probably needed.

Suppressing a growl, he forced the soles of his boots to uproot themselves and move from her resonance. Even from a few feet away, he could feel her. As if her aura vibrated for him alone.

"All right. So maybe Uri flashed home. Let's head there and see." Lame. So lame. He wondered if anyone saw through the ruse. Probably, but at least they didn't call him on it. Everyone followed him upstairs, since there wasn't anything left in the cellar to remark upon.

Unable to look back, he dragged his reluctant carcass out the front door, every atom shaking frantically, desperate to stick themselves to their Chosen One, to the being created exclusively for...*me*.

She's mine, damn it. Not some human male's who couldn't appreciate her the way only he could.

Okay, time to man up and do what was right. Minus the whole *see ya later* routine. No matter how physically strong he was, facing his Chosen and saying good-bye just wasn't something he had the cajones for.

Present breakthrough in mind, he figured God would forgive him this particular weakness. Muscles back to yanking on his bones as they'd done when he'd faced Uri to protect his Daniela, he got in his truck and drove off.

Without waiting for Merrick and Angelia to bid their adieux.

Chapter Twenty-Three

Three weeks. Twenty-one days, and still Daniela pined for a man who wanted nothing to do with her.

Can we all say pa-thet-ic?

After Darken left her house without a look back, she'd raked up her dignity from the floor where it had fallen during her crying jag and pasted it on.

For a date. With a human. Who was everything the gargoyle wasn't— boring, measured, soft from years of desk duty, brown eyed…

Aaand the list went on. Unfortunately, she'd checked it twice. During their dinner date. It was nice of Ericka to set her up with one of her teacher friends from school, but…

The guy just hadn't done it for her.

Oh, he'd been polite enough. Didn't touch her except to help remove her coat, didn't drag her chair around so she could sit under his arm and lean into his hard, thick chest…

Ah, wait. Mr. Nice somehow morphed into a certain sexy gargoyle.

Who wanted nothing to do with her…

Gah!

She needed off the merry-go-round. Maybe she should quit going to the safe house to hang out with Kallen, Kronos, and Drakus.

But, hell, she'd miss them. Angelia, too. "Speak of the devil…" Daniela fished in her purse for her cell phone while AC/DC screamed *Highway to Hell.* "What's up, blondie."

"Hey, glad I caught you." There was a slap in the background, then Angelia's laughter. "Merrick, would you stop…"

Daniela pulled the phone away from her ear as she hooked a left onto

Congress, careful not to run over people in the crosswalks.

Sure, driving and talking on her cell was illegal, but screw it. Maybe she'd get pulled over by a hunky cop, who would sign the ticket with his phone number.

Like that was ever going to happen in real life.

"Hey, you still there?"

"Yeah," tapping the screen for speaker, Daniela set her phone on the dash. "Ready to talk now?" Maybe she was a little jealous that Merrick adored his Chosen One and wanted her around like…all the time…but she had to smile, just the same.

The two were cute together. Especially when Merrick wanted to fix lunch for them. He still hadn't mastered the stove…but he made killer tuna sandwiches.

On wheat bread. Not toasted.

Darken made himself scarce, so she never saw him while she visited.

The rat bastard.

"Where are you?"

"Congress Street. Just pulling into a parking space. What's up?"

"I was just wondering if you were still planning to meet up with your college friends tonight."

"Yep. First Friday of every month." Craning her neck, she crept the ass end of her car toward the bumper of the Jetta behind her.

"Cool. Olive Garden?"

"Nope. Alfio's this time." Which was why she was wedging her car parallel to the sidewalk. Snagging a sweet spot right in front of the store she planned to visit before meeting Ericka and Amber.

"Ah. Okay. I'll see you tomorrow, though, right?"

"Sure. If the hospital doesn't call, I'll be there around ten." At least now she knew how to get to the safe house. After Darken had been all Speed Racer out of her life, Angelia and Merrick had stuck around to make plans.

As in, beg her to keep visiting the others. Her caving came with directions at least. In the form of some mumbo jumbo hex Angelia took the time to mutter over the hood of her Honda.

Scary shit, that. But she filed it with the vampires and lion-men, her new reality.

"See you then."

"Right." As she slid the phone back into her purse, she thought the call a little odd, but the sight of the boots she'd been coveting snagged her attention.

Showcased front and center in the shop window, like Lady Gaga wannabes, was a pair of black leather, hugging all the way to the knee, high-heeled Chase me-Fuck me boots.

Per. Fect. She'd ripped a page out of the Merrick and Angelia play book and decided a couple of weeks ago that her ample ass needed some lift. And some noticing.

Time to don the heels.

These boots would go perfectly with her new coat. The one with real honest-to God princess seams and ballerina-esque merino wool darted, pleated, and flaring out from her hips.

A month ago, she wouldn't have been caught dead in it. But Darken had breathed his warm, sexy breath onto her inner flame and now she liked the idea of wearing something that accentuated her hips.

Because it made her waist look—not small—but curvy. Like something a man might want to run his hands down.

So there, gargoyle. Miss that.

God, she so wasn't over him. Not when she was dressing to make him jealous.

The bell over the shop door jingled as she stepped inside, the hardwood floor creaking under her every step. Which is what she liked about these shops around the Old Port.

Their bones still wore the costumes of crowned molding and intricately sketched tin ceilings from the turn of the century. Attention to detail, just like Darken's home…

Shit. She was doing it again. Like the serpent eating its tail. Round and round, every thought circling back to the gargoyle.

As the clerk headed into the back to find her size, Daniela browsed the pedestals of shoes on display. Such pretty things. She wondered why she never bothered with them before, when they were the epitome of femininity.

Well, duh. She'd never felt particularly feminine. At least, not in the way Darken had made her feel.

Agh! There she went again!

Fifteen minutes later, she had her old boots in the shop's bag, and the new one's wrapped around her legs and feet like a lover's naked body.

Exactly what she'd been craving. Sad that she had to find it in a new pair of shoes, but there you go. Masturbation took many forms.

The second she entered Alfio's, the three hundred smackaroos she'd lain down for the boots had been worth every cent. Ericka's jaw dropped open, and Amber performed a literal double-take, completely turning around in her chair when she realized who had walked through the door.

"Daniela!"

"Don't get up, don't get up," she said, relishing the attention as she glided over to their table. "I hope you ordered for me already." Such chutzpah!

But, what the hell. It beat mooning over someone who didn't give three shits about her. Though the accusation felt hollow, the proof, so to speak, was in the pudding.

And Darken's persistent absence in her life.

* * * *

As Darken stood outside on the sidewalk freezing his balls off, he thought back to the night just over a month ago when he and the bear had sat on a hospital window ledge looking in on a world they didn't belong to.

Much had changed since then.

For one, Darken had become part of the world. Okay, so he hadn't exactly joined a bowling team or book club, but he was going into grocery stores.

He'd even ventured into the cavernous monstrosity of the Home Depot to buy supplies for his new Home Improvement hobby. Trying to keep his thoughts off Daniela, he'd thrown himself into fixing the house.

Not that it had worked.

She came to visit his brethren, so her scent was everywhere. As big as their home was, he'd thought he could escape it. But no, it was as if her scent permeated the woodwork, the rugs, his blood...

Okay, so that last one wasn't true, but damn it, he wished it was. He wished with a rabid madness that her smell was all over his skin, on his clothes, in his hair.

And now that he was eating, he'd learned to cook. Just like before, Angelia had been a patient and very kind teacher. A little competition with Merrick didn't hurt, either, but it hadn't lasted.

Merrick couldn't reheat his way out of a Chef Boyardee can.

Poor bastard.

As he laughed to himself, steam billowed around his head, and passersby gave him a wide berth.

'Course, why wouldn't they. Most likely, they'd think he was one of those idiots who fried their brain cells one huff of gold spray paint at a time. Which was the cool thing about one of Portland's main drags.

It carried the imprint of all sorts of folk. Kind of like the Yellow Brick Road.

Kind of like his breed of crazy. Staring in through a window at a woman who didn't want him made him a stalker, didn't it.

Except as the days had turned into weeks, things weren't adding up. Mainly, why was she coming to see his brothers when he thought she'd washed her hands of them and their volatile, Other world.

He figured when Uri landed in her home with a damned vampire that had put the icing on her fuck-this cake.

Only it hadn't. She'd been immersing herself deeper into their lives, one visit at a time. And he'd had to twist his left nut to stay away from her. Because, man, having her so close was chewing him a new asshole.

Yeah, he was learning new things, like how to eat and sleep like a normal creature, but come on. Dreaming of her put a serious kink in his z-time.

Plagued him, actually, so he'd come awake with his fist wrapped around his cock…coming, the damned thing kicking as his hips rocked his ass into his bed sheets.

He'd almost rather be stone again. Almost.

But if he was granite, he couldn't follow her everywhere, all times of the day like he could now.

Like he was doing now.

Angelia had called to get a bead on her, and the second she'd let him know his Chosen was down here at the restaurant they'd gone to together, he'd one-eightied his truck so hard he almost tipped it over.

Pitiful. Really.

If she knew how he tailed her, she'd call the cops on his stalker ass. And would have every right to.

Three weeks in, and he was…fraying.

He needed her. Neeeeeded her. Need-ed. Her.

Not for allaying his curse, he'd come to realize. But to make him whole. Make him feel like he was actually living. He may as well be stone twenty-four seven for all the suffering he endured from not being able to touch her.

As a couple neared, walking arm in arm, his stomach knotted so hard he thought he heard the membrane squeak. Like a frigging balloon getting twisted into one of those little animal shapes.

When the gentleman held the door to the pizzeria open for his lady, he slipped inside behind them, unware his feet had moved until he was breathing in the warm scents of oregano and baking cheese.

Peering over the heads of the couple…to Daniela's table, it was all he could do not to bowl the pair over as they fiddled and farted with their coats. All, oh, let me, why thank you, tee-hee as he quelled the urge to mow them over on his way to his Chosen One.

Because…fuck it. He missed her. And probably it was personal, given that she kept coming to the safe house anyway, but hell…she was coming to the safe house anyway.

So, she didn't mind his world, just…him.

Fine. He'd be whoever, whatever, wherever she wanted him to be.

He'd wear glasses like that pansy human she'd dated that one time. Thank fuck she'd ended their night early and had gone home alone. Talk about torture, having to lurk in the shadows while that…male…yammered on about himself.

Not admiring her. Or drooling all over himself. Or bowing at her feet. Dumb shit. The man needed clubbing just for his lack of reverence alone.

Approaching her table turned into a horror flick, the span stretching farther and farther as he struggled to near. In some dim recess of his mind, he realized he was sweating. And that balloon animal that was his stomach squeaked itself into another shape.

God, give me strength.

"Hi," he said. And like a girl, he almost did one of those cute waves.

Get a grip! he thought, at the same instant Daniela turned in her seat and looked up at him. "Darken!"

With that surprised look on her face, it was hard to tell if she was glad to see him. Didn't matter. Like the Blob in that movie with Steve McQueen, he was rolling forward with nothing stopping him.

"What are you doing here?" The way her cheeks flushed? Roses from heaven.

"I ah…was just in the neighborhood…*lame, lame, lame!*…and thought I saw you, you know, sitting here, so I thought I'd, ah…you know, come in." *Cause I ah, can't frigging talk, what with my brain damage and all.*

"Oh. Well. Yeah. Of course." She scooted over like he'd asked to sit down.

Awesome. He took the chance before her friends could protest.

Although, once he dragged his stupefied gaze off his Chosen, he noticed they didn't seem to mind the intrusion. In fact, the one with the short, spikey hair wore one of those Cheshire Cat grins.

As if she knew some great mystery none of them were privy to.

Good friend to have. Just one more reason he thought Daniela was superior in all things. She had fantastic judgment.

Even in the other friend, the one he'd seen her with the first night he'd met her. The blonde. Pretty for now, but it would fade. Unlike his Daniela's beauty. Hers was the classic kind, where she would just keep growing more beautiful as her features matured.

Not that it was going to happen. One of the bennies to being a Chosen One, as Angelia had discovered, was they took on the immortality of the Kynd they freed from his stone curse.

He would have his Daniela forever.

If she wanted him.

Feeling a little cut off at the knees, he cleared his throat and took off his coat. As he turned around from hanging it on the back of his chair, Daniela's two friends burst out laughing.

"What?" Daniela grinned, even though it was obvious she didn't really know why her friends had busted out like that. But then, neither did he, and he had on one of those dumb ass smiles, too.

He kept his lips together to hide his teeth, though, which he was sure just enhanced his doofus expression.

"Your shirts!" The spikey haired one, Ericka, cackled.

He looked down at where she was pointing, then braved looking at Daniela's chest.

Well, when he could look beyond the swells...

They were both wearing the same t-shirts. On the front of them was a picture of a hedgehog, and below it were the words—*why don't they just share the hedge?*

When he lifted his eyes to hers, those chocolate browns were glittering impishly.

So, she didn't mind that they shared this? What other things might she not mind? Immediately, he pictured her in his arms. His hands sliding over every inch of her curves, exploring, tasting. Yeah, tasting her as he'd done in her hallway.

Without thinking, he rolled his hips in a bid to make room for his filling cock.

As the rosiness of her cheeks blossomed farther, her pupils blew open, nearly swallowing the rich brown of her irises.

"Whew, is it hot in here, Ericka, or is it me." In his periphery, he saw the blonde fan herself as she bumped shoulders with the other woman.

Daniela's blush deepened more.

Suppressing a needy growl, Darken leaned back, careful to keep his hands under the table. Which meant they itched to slide across the tops of his thighs for Daniela.

"If you guys would excuse me?" Pushing her chair back, she bolted upright, revealing an irregular cut skirt fashioned from some red, silk-like cotton.

May as well have been a bull's eye for the way it grabbed his attention.

Then, as she sashayed away to the back of the pizzeria, he lost all ability to think, or breathe. Black boots *hugged* her lower legs, as if the leather loved her skin.

Bussing all that gorgeous flesh upward was a pair of spikes under her heels he'd want to have pierced through his chest wall. If Daniela would stand over him to do it.

So he could look up that tantalizing skirt. The pointy end of which swayed in concert with her ass.

"Fuck me…" he groaned.

"You should let her."

Huh? He blinked rapidly, trying to shift his focus to the woman who'd spoken, not the one who'd just paraded in front of him, walking away…

Once he finally looked at her, spikey haired Ericka hit him with another stunner. "I've heard about you. Enough to know she'd go all the way with you."

So direct. He kind of liked that, and her forthright demeanor held his attention span. Otherwise, it was going to drift…hope blasting out of his every pore…

"Although, she should ream you one for ignoring her these past weeks. What did she ever do to you to make you think you could shit on her?"

…then shriveling at its zenith. "Say what?" Baffled, he didn't understand why the woman's tone had gone from Ask Jeeves to Battle Axe. "What are you talking about?"

Eyes narrowing, Ericka leaned back in her chair. The other friend leaned back, too, but stroked the stem of her wine glass. Coupled with the fierce glint in her eye, there wasn't anything inviting about it.

"You seduced her, got what you wanted, then threw her to the curb. How's that for short and sweet?"

"No I didn't." He must have looked as honestly stunned and mortified as he felt because Nurse Ratched relaxed a little.

"No? Well, that's how she saw it." The woman might have eased her body's position, but her inquisition hadn't lost the sharp edge. A damned good friend to have, indeed.

This woman had his Daniela's back, and he couldn't get offended by that.

When he said as much, she sat up straighter. Only this time, it was her turn to look a little stunned. Then she smiled. It came out slow and knowing. The Cheshire Cat again.

"Well, Darken, it seems you have some 'splaining to do."

He did indeed. And if he could keep his heart from skipping through his ribs, he'd do plenty of *'splaining*. He rushed to his feet the second Daniela emerged from the restroom to do just that. "Ladies, it has truly been a pleasure." The *you have no idea* went unsaid, but his eagerness to get to Daniela pretty much said it for him.

Grabbing her coat before she could sit down, he took her hands in his. "We've gotta talk."

"What? Wait." As he ushered her with his hand at the small of her back, his knees almost gave out with the sheer delight of touching her. The glitch in his step gave her time to glance over her shoulder.

To see her two friends waving at them. With cute girlie wiggling of their fingers, and kisses blown across their palms. They giggled like hyenas the entire time.

An endorsement if he'd ever seen one.

This time when Darken didn't look back, he had his Chosen One in his grasp.

* * * *

She didn't get the chance to wobble in her high-heeled boots as they navigated the cobblestone sidewalk. Darken had her tucked up tight. "You can leave your car here, yes?"

"Ah, yeah. For a while, I guess." Hedging? Like the hog on her shirt?

Outwardly, she smiled at her own joke. Inwardly, she was doing freaking back flips and cartwheels. Which was wrong, so wrong.

She needed to be mad.

How dare Darken just show up and charm the pants off her friends. She didn't know what had been said while she'd escaped to the bathroom, but when she'd returned, her friends had turned traitors.

Waving her along like Darken was her knight in shining armor. Without them at her back, her feet went all slippery. Sliding her right under Darken's big, manly protective wing.

As if he hadn't been a total, non-existent jerk for the past few weeks.

Just as he'd done on their very first date, he guided her up into the cab of his truck, reluctant to let go of her hand, then speeding around the hood to hurry up and get inside with her.

Of course, now she knew why he didn't want to break the contact. She just didn't understand it.

What had changed?

Not that she got an answer right off. Darken remained silent.

As he drove them down country roads she now knew very well. "Hey, we can't go to the house. My car!" She sat up, twisting around to look out the back window. As if the city wasn't way behind them at this point.

"Merrick will get it."

She opened her mouth to squawk something, couldn't come up with anything scathing, so she shut her pie hole. Inside, she went all frenzied cheerleader again, her heart pumping a woo-hoo! Go team!

Fighting to not fidget, she concentrated on staring back at herself because her side window was black as pitch. *Way to be suave, Dan.*

Finally, with the tension ramping up so thick she could give it a karate chop, they pulled into the garage. As the door trundled shut behind them, they both hopped out fast. Eager to breathe, she guessed.

Darken was on her in a flash, his hard body covering hers. His gaze intense and silver. Which meant he was emotional as shit.

"What," she croaked, her breath barely seeping out through her closing throat.

"I thought you said good-bye," he growled, obviously needing air as badly as she did. Although he didn't step back to catch a lung full. He pressed tighter, pushing his hips against her stomach. Proving he was hard and very aroused.

"What? When?" Darken's sexual aggression was eating her gray matter like candy. Could she at least buy a vowel, for the love of God? Solve the puzzle that way, since she couldn't speak in complete sentences.

"Before, when I was stone and you came to the library. You said good-bye." His voice grew raspier as those mercurial eyes searched her face. "I thought you meant forever."

The truth dawning was just that. As if rays of light beamed outward from inside her. She felt their warmth fan through her, paradoxically consuming and filling her at the same time. "Oh, Darken, why didn't you just say so."

For some reason, he went blurry, until she felt his thumbs caress the thin skin under her eyes. She was crying?

As she watched him, though, his eyes grew shimmery too, the stark lights of the garage swimming in the silver pools. "I thought you didn't want me. Us. I wanted to respect your decision, your need to live a normal life." His grin was shaky, cock-eyed.

As if he was scared and nervous about the words—the truth—he spouted.

"No. No, Darken. I was leaving to go home and pack. I was coming back here, for us. To try…to see if we could make a home together. You, and your brothers, and Angelia. I didn't care. I wanted to try—"

His hold on her grew hard, his gaze piercing. His inhalations ragged. "When Uri didn't come back," he rasped, "I grew afraid, and I realized I wanted…" He shook his head, so when he looked up again, a lock of his blonde hair fanned across one eye so he seemed to peer out at her, wild as a wolf.

Hands shaking as he held her face, he forged on, eyes riveted on hers. "I realize I need you, Daniela. In my life. Not to break some curse, but because you make my life better. You make everything so much better. You're like sunshine brightening everything around me, and I love that. I love…*you,* my Chosen. I love you."

Weepy as shit, she blubbered, "I love you, t—"

His mouth crashed down on hers as a fierce growl rumbled up his throat. Their teeth scraping as their tongues slid off and around each other, she felt the guttural vibration, felt his need wash over them as if to drown them both.

He gripped her tighter, as though afraid she'd get lost in the surge. "*Amica mea!*" he roared, drawing his head back as he sent his exultation heavenward. "I am yours, yes? Tell me I'm yours."

As he gazed back down at her with all that love shining forth, her heart knew instantly he'd said the right thing.

"Yes, Kynd. You are mine. Now, let's go upstairs and consummate this thing, and make sure we put this curse to bed the proper wa—aay!"

Darken scooped her off her feet so fast the ends of her hair swung away like a banner, his hold pressing her tight against him, his expression fierce and raptured.

As if he couldn't believe he held her, but was afraid she'd slip away.

The two-person parade slowed down once they were inside, then stopped entirely in the grand foyer. Made even more striking now that the crystal chandelier had been repaired to its former glory.

With all of the prisms in place, rays of golden light bathed everything beneath it with a summery gentleness.

Warm and inviting.

That's how the great foyer seemed now. And how appropriate was that. Since Darken had shed his curse, he'd been busy. Not just with repairing the damage to this resplendent house, but with reaching out to the Others.

Merrick had snarled when he'd admitted his brother wasn't having much luck, but the grumbling didn't hide the hope. Especially when it shined from Angelia's eyes whenever the subject came up.

Oh, God. Finally! Squeezing her arms around her Kynd's neck, she buried her face into Darken's thick chest so he wouldn't see her relief, her joy, the exhilaration that finally...*finally*...she would have what Merrick and Angelia shared.

"Amica mea, you cry again?" By looking down upon her, his chest pulled away from her cheek, revealing what she tried to hide. "Shush. Shush now." Beneath her, he tensed, his voice gone to gravel.

Without letting her go, he gently lowered her to the warm marble beneath his feet, his big body covering hers as she'd dreamed, and had mourned the loss of. But now he was here, his calloused hands caressing her face.

His regret stark upon his features.

"No, no, none of that," she consoled, her own hands cupping his hard jaw. "We both made mistakes."

Shaking his head, he pressed a kiss to her palm. His lips soft, warm, melting her, so when he unfolded across her, she opened to welcome him.

"We will make up for that."

Oh, God, his heat. The smell of him wetting her panties. Squirming her hips to ease the ache, she moaned, "Wait, they'll see."

He pressed a hand to her chest, easing her back down as he rolled atop her, the bulk of his weight suspended upon his thick arms. Trapping her within, her body spread upon the marble so she felt like a virgin sacrifice.

The hunger in his gaze made her tremble, an all-over body shiver. "No," he rasped, "they'll leave us alone."

Breathless, she said, "How can you be sure."

Grinding the bulge in his jeans into the valley of her thighs, he growled, his jaw locking tight. "Tonight has been..." The thick muscles of his shoulders knotted as he twisted and ground his hips again. "...a conspiracy. To bring you home." He grew as breathless as she. "We will have our privacy."

Chin dipping, he took her mouth, plundering with his tongue.

Arching for him, she dug her nails into his neck, forcing him to be harder, to take more.

They'd planned this. Angelia's call earlier...Darken's arrival at Alfio's.

A trick to snare her, and it was...wonderful.

Widening her legs, she reached between them, popped the buttons of his jeans. His erection dropped out like a great tree cut down and toppling. As her fingers caressed his tight ball sac, his hand squashed down on hers so they cupped him hard.

"Yes," he hissed. As he worked himself on their joined hands, his hooded gaze lowered to lock onto her. Then his hand left hers, and without pulling his fevered gaze, he snagged a claw at her neckline, and tore it down the center of her shirt.

Oh...God...that was hot. She arched more, pushed her palm harder...

Growling and unable to keep his eyes on hers, he let them drift...to what he'd revealed between the two halves of her torn shirt, and the cups of her bra. His attention once again went rigid as he homed in on her exposed nipples.

"So...ready," he wheezed, as though the revelation shocked and pleased him in equal measure. Before she could beam from the compliment, his mouth latched onto her left nipple.

He sucked on it as if pulling from a bottle of Jack Daniels.

"Ah, God!" She wanted to tear her panties off.

Observant Kynd that he was, he fisted her skirt without releasing his mouth from his latch-hold. Panting now, his breath left coats of steam on her bared boob.

Surely, she was going to die from over-stimulation.

With a yank, her skirt slid the length of her legs, and never even caught on the heels of her new boots as he slid the fabric all the way down. Before tossing the skirt, he balled it up under his nose, breathing in her scent.

A quick flick of another claw, and her panties were history.

Such. A. Turn. On.

Now Darken sat on his haunches at her feet, as she lay utterly bare before him, stretched out on the warm marble of the foyer floor with nothing on but her boots.

And he looked positively struck stupid.

* * * *

"Thank you, my dearest Savior." Never had he meant his prayers as he did in this moment. Gazing down on his Chosen One, in nothing but the rosy skin she'd been born in…excepting those boots.

God had lifted him on high.

Delivered him unto Heaven.

He started stripping off his clothes before he realized he had to stand to do it. Snarling, he peeled himself free, never once removing his hungry gaze from the woman at his feet.

His balls were sucked up so tight, he felt the pull through the crack of his ass.

His cock kept bouncing, too, like it was trying to kick free because the dipshit it was attached to was taking too fricking long.

Yet for all his yearning, he wanted to take this slow. Wanted to savor every revving beat of his Chosen's heart as he explored the ways she liked him to touch her.

Oh, yes, he would learn her body. Inside and out.

Lowering himself, he first went to her feet and slowly drew her boots off.

"Oh, shit. Wait." A bit of a mood breaker, but his Chosen shouldn't be laying upon a bare floor, no matter how polished it was.

Dashing for the closet under the stairs, he returned with his prize.

"Furs? Darken, where did you get all these!" From where he'd get a thousand more now that he knew she loved them so much. There were plenty to make a pallet, and more to throw over them.

"They're synthetic. Not real, but it's hard to tell."

"No kidding," she mumbled, slinking her naked body all over them.

It was several moments before he realized his hips were pumping, that he was fucking air. Damn, but he couldn't believe this beauty was all his.

At long last.

Lowering for try number two, he crawled up her body.

So much bounty! Her curves luscious, her skin soft against his tongue. When he pressed his naked body to hers, she felt to him as he'd dreamed. Her woman's flesh molding to his hollows and hard angles.

She was fire where she spread her thighs, inviting him. Sweat prickling his skin, he coiled his calloused fingers through her locks as he lifted his ass, sliding his shaft through her plush lips.

Then plunged.

And was instantly consumed. Her core gripped him, milked him, and her arms and legs wrapped around him.

Her scent swallowed him, maddened him. But it was her breath in his ear, her words given with her body, which urged him to madness. *Love me, Darken.*

Impossibly, she grew hotter, tighter as she writhed beneath him. Her breasts slapping the wall of his chest, and he'd never felt anything so erotic.

So intimate.

Her abandon released him, and he thought he would burst into flames. Her sheathe soaking as her cries drove him wild and wilder still. Then the universe blew apart behind his eyes, and as they clung to one another, his iron cock kicked and kicked until they both collapsed.

He onto her, and she beneath him, her languid body accepting his.

Too many breathless moments later, he remembered himself, and raised his weight to his elbows as he cupped his female's precious, flushed face.

As she looked up at him, he saw himself in the sheen of her doe eyes.

And what he saw humbled him.

He was but a man in the reflection. Not hideous, or grotesque, but loved.

By his Daniela Salvai.

God's judgment to save, and He had in His way. By condemning the Kynd, he had freed them. His judgment saving them. For it was Daniela, Darken's Chosen One, who had soothed him and whispered into his soul the seeds of his persecution.

Where they grew into the realization that he and his brothers were not doomed, but held their fates in their own hands. If they hadn't been cast from Heaven, they would never have the chance to learn what love truly means.

Thanks to God, he now knew.

And he would hold his woman's love close to his heart forever as the sacred thing it was. Still seeing himself in the deep brown of her eyes, he said, "Thank you, my Daniela, amica mea. You are my salvation."

His declaration to his Chosen One both a prayer and a benediction.

THE END

About the author

S.C. Dane currently lives in Wyoming on a working cattle ranch. When she's not riding horses on the range, she's immersed in her second passion: writing. She loves traveling, too, and isn't sure what adventures her next move will find for her. You can get to know a little more about the author on her website *scdane.com*.

Other Works by the Author at Melange Books, LLC
Luna Chronicles, Book 1, Luna
Luna Chronicles, Book 2, Grane
Luna Chronicles, Book 3, Kenrickey

Lover in Stone, Book 1, The Darkest Kynd Series